BRIGHT WEB IN THE DARKNESS

by the same author

GRAND CROSSING

THE GREAT MIDLAND

THE INDISPENSABLE ENEMY:
Labor and the Anti-Chinese Movement

THE RISE AND FALL OF THE WHITE REPUBLIC:
Class Politics and Mass Culture in
Nineteenth Century America

BRIGHT WEB IN THE DARKNESS

ALEXANDER SAXTON

AFTERWORD BY TILLIE OLSEN

UNIVERSITY OF CALIFORNIA PRESS
BERKELEY · LOS ANGELES · LONDON

University of California Press
Berkeley and Los Angeles, California

University of California Press, Ltd.
London, England

First Paperback Printing 1997

Published in hardcover in 1958
by St. Martin's Press, New York.

Library of Congress Cataloging-in-Publication Data
Saxton, Alexander.
    Bright web in the darkness / Alexander Saxton.
        p.   cm. — (California Fiction)
    ISBN 0-520-20931-1 (alk. paper)
    1. World War, 1939–1945—California—San Francisco—Fiction.
    2. Afro-American women—California—San Francisco—Fiction.
    I. Title.
    PS3537.A976B74   1997
    813'.54—dc21   96-38104
                                                            CIP

Manufactured in the United States of America
1 2 3 4 5 6 7 8 9

The paper used in this publication meets the minimum requirements of American
National Standard for Information Sciences—Permanence of Paper for Printed
Library Materials, ANSI Z39.48-1984. ∞

To my Wife
Without whom this book could not have been written

FOREWORD

The time of this book: 1944, early 1945—the World War II years, so rich in drama, complexity, immense changes for and in millions of human beings.

The place: the San Francisco Bay Area, swollen with the great migrations, people of every human hue streaming in from the South, the East, the Midwest.

The focal point of action: the shipyards. And the weaving of a bright inspiring web of hope, of presage, for us today.

ℰ

More than one such web glistens in the vast heaped underground where Time, and History (always selective), relegate most human events to the darkness of the forgotten. Year after year relentlessly add their heavy weight of succeeding events to the seemingly ever more impermeable cover. So vanishes the sense of the living, moving, changing human beings; what transpired within, and between, them; and how they were shaped by—and shaped—that time, that place.

Occasionally in literary history, it happens that a gifted writer, with passionate caring (Blake's "for a tear is an intellectual thing"), fiery conviction of the importance of retrieval—with the help of imagination (that "magic of art") and stubborn hard work, penetrates the seemingly impermeable—livingly recreates into visibility, passes into the future, that time, that place, those human beings.

Alexander Saxton is one of those writers. This is one of those books.

Tillie Olsen

PART 1

PART 1

1

Even the smell of chalk dust and old blackboards was welcome to her. All schools smelled alike, all had the same creaky stairs and echoing corridors. So the sounds and odors of the building brought to mind her own graduation when she sat on the platform with the class officers, and after they finished their speeches, she played the minuet and an étude by Chopin. Played both very badly, she remembered; not so much because she had stage fright—she hit the right notes— but the music sounded as if she were copying letters on a typewriter. Still, most of them would never have known the difference if she had been playing with mittens on. Except her mother.

Room 201, she read, *second floor.* Elderly men at the doorway were squeezing the last puffs from their cigarettes as Joyce Allen slipped past them into a hall grimly illuminated by bluish globes that hung chained from the ceiling. Blackout curtains covered the windows. The instructor at his desk stood leafing through the pages of a book, the students were scattered sparsely among the chairs. Night classes must be very different, Joyce saw, no longer entirely glad that she had agreed to come. But she was accustomed to sitting alone, and busied herself taking her fountain pen from her handbag and opening her notebook. In the row directly ahead, which had been empty, a colored woman was preparing herself to sit down, and as she turned, caught Joyce's eye. They exchanged nods and smiles.

The instructor had approached the blackboard. WELD-ING EQUIPMENT, he spelled in sprawly capitals. With book in hand, he proceeded to trace out the lines of diagrams, pressing the chalk till it squealed on the down strokes. No, he had made a mistake, he rubbed out his work and began again. If it were only the copying and learning, Joyce told herself, which always had come so easy for her, she would have nothing to fear. But she had seen the welders swinging from their ropes alongside the hulls and their torches sparkling like blue stars. That was something she had not taken into account at the time—the Sergeant had been so insistent. She had remembered only that she had been a good student in high school, thinking all the while of the graduation and her mother waiting by the door of the auditorium like a thin, beady-eyed bird, perched there amid that out-rushing throng of white faces. At least she could write that she was going to school again.

But of course her mother who had been a teacher herself long since in New Orleans, would not be at all pleased to hear that she was taking a night class in welding. Joyce laughed silently as she copied the diagrams. The instructor had circled the room, filling one board after another with his charts and lists of names; and the students shifted un-easily in their creaky chairs, sneezed, blew their noses, writing furiously till the buzzer sounded for the end of the first hour.

"Go take a smoke," said the instructor, and this was the only word he had spoken all evening.

In the corridor, Joyce found the other colored woman at her side. They were presently joined there by a tall, dark-

4

skinned man dressed in a black suit, who, unlike most of the other men students, was wearing a shirt with a necktie. Shaking their hands, he at once introduced himself as a minister, Reverend Beezely. The woman had brought out a cigarette and the Reverend gallantly struck a light but declined to smoke himself. So they stood rather close together in the crowded corridor, the woman telling them she had come all the way from Memphis, Tennessee to work in the shipyards. They discussed which of the various yards were best to try to get into; and when Joyce mentioned that she was working on the cleanup gang in the new San Martin yard, Reverend Beezely inquired if it were not the Sergeant there who had sent her.

"The Sergeant?" she repeated, thinking, how does he come to know the Sergeant? "Yes he did," she told him. "Do you work at San Martin yourself?"

"No, not yet, but I hope to," he said. She noticed that he spoke with a precise, slightly foreign-sounding voice. "Oh, we've heard of the Sergeant even over here," he explained. "His fame has traveled before him. Are you the only one he sent?"

"I don't know." But she must be, she thought. There were no others. Though of course he might have talked to others who had been unable to come. Or afraid to.

"And where are you from, Miss?"

"From Signal Springs," she said. "In Nevada."

"I don't believe I ever even heard of that."

"Oh, nobody much has. It's a railroad town not far from Reno."

"Why, I'm learning something new every day," cried the Reverend, and he stepped aside to let her walk in front of him as the buzzer summoned them for the second half of the period. But when the class came to an end at nine o'clock, Joyce hastily avoided these new acquaintances. She hurried from the building, ran to the corner and caught the trolley back to Fillmore. Through the long clattering blocks and shadowy intersections, she sat with her notebook open on her knees, staring at the diagrams she had copied. *Generator. Clamp. Welding Rod.* Now she ought to return to the Hendersons' right away, she was arguing with herself, they might likely be waiting up for her. She would be tired in the morning in any case. *After the hard day you've put in, dear,* she said, mimicking Mrs. Henderson who had been a childhood friend of her mother's in New Orleans.

And that was true enough, she was tired; but not in any way that going to bed at nine o'clock could cure. It was not really the work that tired her. A day in the shipyard seemed easier than the café of the Signal Springs Hotel had ever been. More than anything else, it was the confusion, she thought, the noise, the sense of never knowing what to expect from one instant to the next; and wondered suddenly if the Sergeant felt the same way at a day's end. Then she wondered, too, why she had not waited at least long enough to say good night to those two in the welding class. She did not know. Her mind seemed to be spinning like a top. The nerves in her legs and back were stretched tight as piano wires. When she got down at Fillmore, instead of turning toward the Hendersons' apartment, she walked in the opposite direction.

On many evenings after the dishes were finished, she had told the Hendersons she thought she might run out to a movie, she wasn't quite sleepy yet—inviting them to go along though she knew they would refuse. And it was pleasant enough to sit in the dark theater carried out of herself by the story on the screen. But more often, instead, she would simply walk out along Fillmore Street which always was crowded at this time of the evening. Here she could almost lose herself, and as she moved with the moving crowd, past Fillmore and Geary, past Fillmore and California, she could even imagine that she was going somewhere, that someone was waiting for her, man or woman, young or old, it scarcely mattered; but someone who *knew* her, and whom she knew, waiting on some corner, in some tavern, in some apartment. As she walked, she carried on a conversation with these imaginary friends. She had been in San Francisco almost a year, she told them. What had she come looking for? she asked. How much longer must she wait? Was it not time at last to give up and return home to Signal Springs? Or *was* that her home any longer? The lights and shadows, the stream of passing faces, remained as indecipherable as always, till Joyce unwillingly retraced her steps toward the Hendersons', where she had her room and board.

2

From behind the jagged mountains, the sun raised a dazzling eyelid. Sunlight swept over the desert, leaped the hollows, turned the salt flats to silver and sparkled from the metal roofs of the warehouses down by the railroad. Even the old broken bottles and tin cans in the hard clay beyond the fence suddenly flashed like diamonds. Waking, Joyce Allen wakened as she often did with the odd sensation that some other figure of herself was reliving some other and perhaps more genuine moment of her existence; while she herself (whatever *she herself* might be, she wondered) watched from her vantage point, listened almost casually as Mrs. Henderson called, "Time to get up, Joyce. Mr. Henderson's out of the bathroom now." But the gray fog was at the window. Who would ever guess, here, that it was morning?

Sunlight used to make rainbows in the steam from the teakettle, she remembered, extinguishing the flame of the kerosene burner so that one might almost think the stove had run dry of oil. By squinting her eyes hard, she had always been able to find that dim little wisp which was all the sunlight left of the flame. And there would be her own shadow upon the wall over the stove as she began furiously scrubbing her teeth at the kitchen sink, laughing to see the antics of the shadow.

Once her father had said, "Quiet down, little Joyce, you'll wake your Mom first thing you know, all that giggling." When we used to eat breakfast together, Joyce thought; and remembered that she had made corn-meal mush for her father for breakfast, remembering the first time she ever had tried to make it. He had sprinkled on sugar, poured canned milk, cautiously taking a taste. Then clasping his hands in front of him, he raised his eyes to the ceiling, let a smile blossom over his face as if he were drifting away to heaven.

"Oh, man, you're sure getting to be a fine cook, little Joyce."

"Do you think I'm as good a cook as you now, Dad?"

"Well, I don't know about *that*."

"I bet I can cook mush better'n you."

"Why, I think most likely you can. But what about Salisbury steak now? Can you cook that?"

"Salisbury steak? How do you cook that, Dad?"

"Oh, that's a mighty fancy dish."

"Did you used to cook Salisbury steak when you were working on the trains?"

"Certainly I did. Almost every night."

"Tell me how you cook it."

"Well, the first thing, you get some *beef*, and you have the butcher grind it up in his grinder. And then you take the meat with your hands and make little patties of it like this and sprinkle salt and pepper and dry mustard all over—"

"Oh, Dad," she had shouted. "That's just hamburger!"

Outside, the trolley cars came banging past the corner of Fillmore. She counted three one after another—already gathering their loads of men and women for the shipyards; and counted back and it was ten years since she had last eaten breakfast with her father. Though sometimes it seemed much longer, or sometimes as if only a week or two had gone by. She had had an argument with him once, after breakfast, about the new shoes, and she recalled now the place outside the kitchen door, exactly where they had both stood. Getting up from the table, he had put on his black suit coat over his work shirt and jeans. She followed him down the path between the yellow-green aspen trees, and there he had stopped and turned around looking very severe. "Your Mommy says you haven't been taking the bus to school," he had said. "Can't you mind what your Mom tells you?"

"I like to walk, Dad. What difference it make?"

"Difference you scuff your new shoes all up. Let me see 'em," he commanded.

Clinging to him with one hand, she had balanced first on the right foot, then on the left, holding her shoes up for inspection. "All scuffed. You ought to be ashamed, you're ten years old already, Joyce. Mind you ride that bus today, you hear?" She had nodded gravely. "You don't like the kids on the bus?" She stood staring at her shoes while her father had studied her from above. Then he pulled out his gold railroad watch from the pocket of his work shirt. "Come on, come on now," he said. "We'll be late."

Hand in hand they hurried along the road where it slanted down from the bluff and meandered across the slope of the desert, the wheel tracks picking their way among the scattered clumps of sage and greasewood. At the railroad crossing, her father had consulted his watch again. "We're four minutes ahead of time," he announced, and they stood waiting, she peering down the lines of the rails where they marched off and away to the point of their disappearance behind an outthrust finger of the mountains. And suddenly there was the train in the distance, its headlight flashing like a silver dollar, the smoke pouring back from its stack like a roll of dirty cotton across the flats. The wail of the whistle, the thunder of wheels, the earth shaking under their feet; and now the engine itself wrapped in clouds of its own steam came blotting out the sky above them.

She caught a glimpse of the engineer in his goggles leaning out the window of the cab. The baggage cars hammered past, and when the coaches came she already could feel the slowing of the train for the depot. Beyond the coaches, but in front of the Pullmans, in the same place as always, came the diner, and she saw the faces of dressed-up white people in the windows. At the open door of the kitchen, there was the cook, a huge man whose arms and face appeared startlingly black against the starched white of his apron. He was laughing and waving and she saw that he was shouting to them, too, but she could hear nothing over the noise of the wheels. The Pullman cars rolled past more slowly and over the rear platform leaned the brakeman in his brass-buttoned uniform. Joyce and her father still stood with their hands raised waving, but the brakeman paid them no heed. He was peering out squint-eyed toward the faraway engine.

Dust and cinders tinkled like hail after the train had passed. "Where will it go when it goes from the station?" Joyce asked.

"Salt Lake City, Omaha, Chicago. Same as yesterday and the day before," her father said with a laugh. "Comes from San Francisco. Same train, same time, goin' the same places. 'By, little Joyce. You go on back to the house now till time for school." He kissed her on the forehead and struck out along the tracks following the train to the depot. There, Joyce knew, since he had no longer been going on the trains himself, he mopped the floor of the station restaurant and scrubbed the table tops, and hauled out buckets of slop and ashes; and for a moment yet she remained hugging the blankets over her ears to hide the clatter of streetcars on Fillmore and the voice of Mrs. Henderson, her mother's old friend, who was calling anxiously, "Joyce, you got to get up now. Mr. Henderson's all dressed. I'm putting the eggs in."

Her mother, working nights in the kitchen of the rancho, would still be in bed this time of the morning. Thin, white-haired, sitting in the double bed; laying aside the newspaper that came in the mail from New Orleans; removing her rimless glasses as she peered like a beady-eyed bird. "You got a clean blouse on?" Oh, of course she had. "Your Daddy feel all right this morning?" Had he? Had he felt all right, ever, on any of those mornings? "Come round here where I can see your shoes." So she squeezed between the bureau and the foot of the bed and stood in the patch of bare floor where her mother could look down at her feet.

Her mother shook her head disapprovingly. "You take some polish and polish them good, Joyce."

"All right, Mom. Only, can I go practice now?"

"You can practice. But you clean your new shoes first. And you ride on that bus today like all the other children, you hear me, Joyce?"

Fetching the can of shoe polish from under the sink, she had smeared over the scuffed places and rubbed till she could feel the heat right through the leather into her toes. The shoes began to shine like the sides of an automobile. Pleased, she thrust them into the square of sunlight, wiggling them this way and that to see the flashing highlights. Then she pulled a chair over to the old stand-up piano and began to play carefully through the various exercises. Each time she struck a wrong note, she would pause, waiting for her mother to call, as she always did.

"That's wrong, Joyce, go back to the beginning now."

When she had finished the exercises, she ran through the scales. By this time she could play the scales without looking or thinking about them and while her fingers moved over the keys, she began thinking instead of the train with its

12

headlight flashing like a silver dollar and how it went roaring away from the depot through the mountains and the desert to all the places her father had used to go. Her fingers moved across the keyboard, making the wheels roar over the mountains on the dark bass keys and the whistle wail and shrill on the trebles.

"Joyce. Joyce! That's not practicing."

"All right, Mom."

She shut down the cover over the keyboard. It was time to leave for school anyway and she could practice again in the evening while her mother was at work and only her father was home. Picking up her school bag, she ran outside where the sun sailed high in the cloudless sky and the shadows of the aspen trees lay in round circles almost directly beneath each tree. There was no wind. As Joyce followed the road from the house, the air shimmered like quicksilver above the sage and greasewood bushes. In the distance the salt flats had become a lake of blue sky where she knew there was no lake at all and beyond the flats, where she knew the jagged mountains were standing, the mountains had withdrawn into their midday haze.

But when she reached the railway, Joyce paused, shielding her eyes with her open hand. The road, crossing the tracks, led between storage tanks and rows of sheds covered with shiny-colored metal, up to the highway. There on the corner, two of the half-dozen white children who boarded the school bus at that point, stood waiting.

Joyce glanced down at her newly polished shoes.

She hopped carefully on one foot and then on the other. She swung her school bag in a circle like an airplane propeller. She twisted her face into a sudden grimace and giggle, thumbed her nose at the children on the corner, and then set off along the tracks, taking the short cut by way of the freight houses. But she had been careful to hop on the ties or to walk tightrope along the rails, she remembered, for fear of scuffing the shoes again in the gravel. Though it was not really the shoes her father had cared about at all, Joyce thought, as she gobbled her breakfast and raced down the stairway after Mr. Henderson.

3

The mass of ships loomed vaguely in the fog. Sometimes when a pale wash of sunlight came filtering through, Joyce could make out the shapes of masts and funnels; but in a moment the fog thickened, a slight breath of wind wrapped it about them, again everything vanished except the two sawhorses and the straw-headed little carpenter working over his pile of planks. The fog was cold and at the same time stifling. It seemed to contain no air but only dampness, only the bitter fumes of the welding torches which she saw sparkling along the decks of the ships;—and a salty smell too, and a rotten muddy smell, and now and again, scarcely noticeable through the stronger odors, a flavor of burning pine wood. That was the only good smell among them all; she kept sniffing for it through the others.

"Pull her over!"

The carpenter's voice sounded angry and she realized he must already have called to her and she had not heard him. He seized one of the planks, she taking the other end, and they slid it on to the sawhorses. Then she helped him place his pattern over the next plank, and he set to marking that. She had no idea what he was doing. It seemed to her she had no idea what anybody was doing. The fog was full of an immense clanging and hammering, roaring and hooting. Huge objects which she could not see rumbled past high overhead. People scurried through the fog, some carrying tools, some munching sandwiches, some pushing carts, rushing or sauntering, an endless stream.

She tried to appear busy picking up scraps, having nothing else to do, and it came as a relief when a truck-load of lumber rolled up alongside the carpenter's sawhorses. She joined the other women sliding boards down over the tail of the truck. And as the women stacked the lumber, the carpenter looked it over piece by piece, complaining about the low-grade materials a man was supposed to work with these days; while the gang foreman and the truck driver chatted beside the cab. Joyce, nudging her end of a plank into place on the pile, glanced up and saw the Sergeant coming towards them.

Through the fog, she recognized his odd, stiff gait, which was the first thing she had noticed about him. His name actually was Mr. Brooks—no one seemed to know why he was called the Sergeant, except that he was said to have been in the army once. The other women told her he had been blown up on some island out in the Pacific, and had his back fastened together with pieces of silver wire. Joyce stepped quickly to the truck, hoping he would pass by.

But he called out, "That you, Miss Allen?"

She nodded and smiled, casting an uneasy glance toward the foreman.

"You get signed up in that class all right?" he asked.

"Yes I did, Mr. Brooks."

"How long it going to take you?"

"Six weeks, they say." She felt herself half angered by his questioning, as she had been the first time he had spoken to her. *What's your name? How old are you?* he had demanded. *Where you from?* Yet there was something about the way he carried himself and the tone in which the other women had talked of him that made her unable to turn away. She heard the straw-headed carpenter howl out,

"Hey, sister, we goin' to get those boards off the truck to-day or tomorrow?"

"Oh, yes, I'm sorry." And to Mr. Brooks, she said, "Excuse me, I—" But he detained her with his hand on her arm and stared across at the carpenter.

"Whyn't you talk to her some other time, Brooks?" the carpenter asked. "I got a job I need them boards for." The others on the gang, and the foreman and the truck driver, had all paused now and were standing listening.

"Anybody stoppin' you from pullin' some of those boards off the truck yourself?" Brooks said. The carpenter shrugged his shoulders several times rapidly and went back to fussing over the lumber pile. The foreman and truck driver resumed their conversation.

"How's the class goin'? You like it all right?" He was studying her closely, his eyes fixed on hers. She knew what he meant, and she told him,

"Yes, it's all right."

"How many colored up there?"

"Only two others."

He shook his head, then demanded, "You goin' to stick with it now, Miss Allen?"

"Well, I will if I can. I . . . I never did anything like that before." And she tried to explain to him, "I can learn all those notes they give you easy enough on the blackboard, but I . . . I don't know—"

"You ever figure how much a welder earns? Dollar-twenty cents an hour. Ought to see some of those welders I see workin' up there—drawin' their pay too and they don't know enough to blow their own noses. Woman with a high school education like you got nothing to worry about." And giving her arm a slight squeeze, he turned and walked off toward the shipways.

Joyce, as she moved back and forth between the truck and the lumber pile, glanced up now and again at the ships with their sparkling torches, and shivered in apprehension. Yet the Sergeant's visit had left her a feeling of pride too. She found both oddly mingled—the fear and the wishing overturned each other in her thoughts so that she was frightened one instant, and in the next began anxiously planning ahead. Her anticipation of the class that evening carried her through the afternoon's long hours of sweeping sawdust and gathering scraps. As she kept mulling over what the Sergeant had told her, she realized that beyond this night class opened a prospect of possibilities she had never thought of before. If a welder earned as much as he said—and he must know, he was a shipfitter himself—she would have money to send home to her mother and some left over for herself too. She could begin looking for a room of her own—why not?— where she could make her own meals and have her own things.

And the city must be full of schools, she thought.

When she finished this class, she could take another and another. There was no limit to the subjects she could study, the new things she might learn. Why, she could go right through college in evening classes. Or take up her piano lessons again. It seemed so wonderfully much better to look forward to going to school, to spending her evenings studying and learning than sitting alone in the movies, or walking alone through the dark streets. Into her mind sprang pictures of the months ahead: she imagined herself meeting a *friend* in the welding class; and wished there had been somebody colored that was close to her own age. For being in the same class, trying to learn the same things, must make it that much easier to get to know one another. But if not in this class, she thought, then in one of those she would take later on. Oh, there were bound to be young people in some of them; and for the first time during the whole year she had stayed in San Francisco, she felt glad that she had come.

The four-thirty whistle sounded, releasing from the buildings and sheds and shipways an avalanche of men and women that rolled ten abreast toward the gate. Joyce found Mr. Henderson outside the fence. The car in which they shared rides pulled up for them and they climbed into the back seat over the knees of the other passengers who were crammed together with their metal hats on their laps and their clothes smelling of smoke and oil and sweat.

Through heavy traffic, stop light and intersection, the line of cars moved over the railroad tracks, over the ramp that curved up and up till they were rolling across the high arch of the bridge. Now at last the fog was breaking. There was blue sky above, sunlight dazzling out of the west. Streamers of mist floated over the water which in all directions was dotted with ships. The opposite shore swept towards them— the jumbled buildings, signs, chimneys, the hills stepping away into the distance wreathed in mist, and over it all pouring the liquid sunlight of late afternoon. Even the sunlight seemed different here, not clear and sharp like the desert, but half light, half mist, flowing and dissolving as you watched.

She wished tonight she could play the piano—she had scarcely thought of playing again since she had left home. But to play once just for herself! as she used to do at the old stand-up piano in the kitchen. Oh, it was still there, she thought, standing silent, waiting. Her fingers itched so hungrily for the keyboard that she even wondered if one of the taverns along Fillmore might not have a piano; maybe they would let her come in after hours sometime when no one was there except the scrubman. And as she and Mr. Henderson walked toward the apartment from the corner where the driver had let them off, she listened to the blare of the many juke boxes. Maybe they did have some old unused piano and no one to play it. But she knew she would be too timid to push open the doors and look inside.

4

Tom O'Regan, braking his pickup truck to a halt, caught a glimpse of Sally Kallela on the steps of the school building side by side with a tall colored man. He honked and beckoned to her. The man looked his way—a thin one, he observed, black as the ace of spades; while Sally only waved and went on with her conversation. However, he could see that she actually was speaking to another girl, a colored girl who apparently was with the man. Does she think I got all night to be sitting here, for God's sake? he demanded, pushing again at the horn. She came running then; but as he opened the door, she turned, laughing, to the people on the steps behind her and pressed one finger to her forehead as if to blow her brains out with exasperation.

"Can't you even wait half a second, Tom," she cried, "till I finish what I'm saying to somebody? Are we in that big of a hurry?"

He glanced both directions, and finding no squad car in sight, swung the pickup in a U-turn across Van Ness Avenue and headed back for the bridge. "So who's the smoked Irishman?" he asked.

She switched around in her seat and stared at him.

"Is he your latest?"

"I don't like that," she said.

"What don't you like? The U-turn?" But he thought, always quit when you're ahead, kid; and he told her, "Oh, it's only a joke, Sally, don't act so huffy. After all, I'm an Irishman too, like you're all the time telling me, aren't you? Have they made a welder of you yet?"

She shrugged her shoulders; and Tom drove the length of Mission Street, catching the green lights one after another, before she spoke to him.

"Oh, come off it," he said.

"We were welding tonight, if you're interested."

"There's progress, kid!"

"They have a shop downstairs," she informed him, "with workbenches and everything. I did a butt weld. I bet you don't know what that is."

"Bet I could make a good guess."

"Mr. Know-it-all."

He laughed; and as they swung up the bridge approach, he set his course by the towers ahead. Steady as she goes. Lower your altitude a couple points for the tunnel. Traffic had thinned to almost nothing: check rear-view mirror for cops coming up behind. All clear, he announced, bearing down on the accelerator, and the old Dodge truck roared through its course like a heavy bomber.

"I was reading in the paper where they'd given up the idea of using women welders. Too risky."

"Ha ha ha," she replied.

"They haven't hired any at San Martin."

"Of course they haven't yet. But they've got plenty at Marinship. Soon as they lay down the keel on Number Two ways they're going to start hiring here too."

"How do *you* know?"

"Because I went and asked, that's how."

Beyond the toll plaza, as they rolled down on the East

Bay side, Tom spotted a cop pulling away from the curb. Nice work, kid, that's keeping the old eye on the ball. The cop tailed him through Oakland to the San Martin city line, while Tom drove just under the speed limit. But once on the highway heading for the shipyard, he opened up again. "Your old man said he's quitting the business agent job," he told her, "going back to Saw Creek this spring. Do you think he really will?"

"I guess he will. He and Mom never liked it down here much."

"Are you going too?"

"No."

"Bet you haven't told him that yet. Bet you do go back with him."

"Bet I won't. Bet I'll stay right here and work in the shipyard."

She probably would too, he thought. She always knew how to tell the old man where to head in, even if nobody else did. And where will *you* be keeping yourself all that time? he wondered. Parked on some tin can in the middle of the Pacific Ocean, most likely. "You'll have to be riding the bus home tomorrow," he said. "I got a date."

"You have, ducky? At eight in the morning?"

"With my draft board," he added.

"Oh." And after a moment, she asked, "How come, Tom?"

He was pleased by the seriousness of her tone. "Nothing special, I guess. Only I'm supposed to check in once a month while I'm on the construction here. I forgot last month. They probably want to chew my ears off." He wheeled across the highway into the parking strip outside the wire fence of the yard. Below them, the half-completed buildings stood like ruins along the waterside. Steam from the pile drivers and the smoke from the burning mounds of rubbish and the red glow of the fires and the smoky blue glare of floodlights made it seem like the relics of some catastrophe. Some city after the bombers had gone over, he thought. But in the distance, up by Number One ways, he could see the line of new ships at the outfitting dock. "I'd just as leave they drafted me anyhow," he told her. "I'm tired of hanging around."

She made no reply.

"Damn if I see how your old man can stand to be going back to Saw Creek. I had enough lumber mills to last me a lifetime."

"He's crazy as a woodtick," she agreed.

"Well, carpentering's just as bad." He offered her a cigarette, and taking a match from his shirt pocket, cracked the head with his thumbnail. "I get bored, God damn it. I'm out there on a job swinging a hammer or pushing a saw, I think I'm going to burn up inside. I want to throw my tools down and walk off sometimes. I've done it too, sometimes, not because there was anything wrong with the job . . ." He stopped, and she said,

"I know what you mean, Tom."

Only she probably didn't. He supposed she must get fed up with being a waitress in the lunch counter and the mobs that were in there every night. Or she'd get sick of welding quick enough too, if she ever really got into it. But she was too gay and sociable all the time to know what he was trying to talk about. It was all a big game to her, he thought, like a checker game; being around with her always was; and he wondered whether she acted the same way with other people. If you said anything without thinking out the next move, she was right there to take a double jump off you. That got tiresome too.

"Mom sent a piece of cake for your lunch," she told him, opening her handbag. "It's a little bit squashed."

"Thanks."

"Said to tell you she's expecting you for supper tomorrow."

"All right." Staring straight out through the windshield, he said, "I been knocking around quite a stretch, Sally. Just about everybody I knew in Saw Creek—my Dad, my sister's husband, your old man too, I guess, everybody I can think of—they all knocked around the same way when they were young, and what have they got now? They took what was left over. Trucking, sawmilling, railroading, not because they wanted to, but they had to. I sure don't aim to do it that way—"

She passed him the cake wrapped in wax paper.

She had done that on purpose: as if she had to cut him off every time he tried to say something that meant anything to either one of them. She and her damn cake! He ought to throw it out the window. But at once she startled him by saying, "I think it's good to want a lot, Tom. I do too." And then said, "I hope you get everything you wish for, Tom."

He fetched up to a full stop. Well, what did she mean by that? Yet he saw that it was he himself who drew back. Changing the meaning with his tone, he repeated, *"Every-thing?"*

"Almost everything."

"That's not enough." He did not really intend that; he knew he was only playing with the words. They were playing checkers again and it was he who had renewed the game. Sullenly he unwrapped the cake and they shared it between them.

"We still got time for a cup of coffee," he suggested. "Want to go in to the lunch counter?"

"If you want."

But instead, he leaned quickly forward and kissed her. She traced his lips with the tip of her tongue, leaving the flavor of chocolate icing from the cake. Tom banged his elbow against the steering wheel. Full and solid in his arms, he held her against him till the parking spaces began to fill up on both sides. Then shaking herself free, she opened the door, laughing, and jumped out. It was almost time for the change of shift, and hand in hand they walked along the mesh-wire fence towards the gate.

The nights of union meetings, Tom had a standing invitation to eat dinner with the Kallelas (which he was always ready enough to do in any case) and ride over with the old man to the hall afterwards. But by the time he had mended his fences with the draft board in the morning, he did not get to bed till noon, then overslept, and it was almost dark when he pulled into the alley behind Kallela's house. He ran up the back stairs to the apartment on the second floor.

"Thought you never *were* going to get here," said Kallela's wife, Liz. "You ready for supper?"

"I'm starved. Sally up yet? Where's Kallela?"

"In the bathroom. Tom's here," she called; and to Tom, said, "You better bang on Sally's door or she'll sleep right through till midnight."

Tom stepped down the narrow hallway and rapped on the bedroom door. There was no sound from inside at first, and rattling on the knob, he shouted, "Hey, wake up, will you, Sally."

He heard a moan in answer. "Your Mom says she's going to pour a bucket of water on you if you don't come out for supper."

"All right, all right, all right . . ."

"You really awake? Want me to come in roll you out?"

"You keep out," she cried. "I'm getting up."

Tom returned to the kitchen where Liz was dishing up dinner and Kallela himself had settled down at the table. He was a square, red-faced Finnish logger, Kallela, with a stubble of colorless hair over his skull. "Get her while she's hot, Tom," he bawled, filling the coffee cups from the enormous enameled pot. "How about we take your pickup tonight? Got gas enough? My fuel pump's on the fritz again."

"Sure," Tom said.

"Come on, come on, we'll sit down and eat even if nobody else around here wants to, God damn right we will." Kallela's wife set a plate of meat loaf and potatoes in front of him and he plowed in, while she served Tom and then took her place on the side of the table nearest the stove. A bony-faced, graying woman, queen of trumps to the noisy jack, Tom thought, with her silverish hair pulled straight back into a crown. She seemed to be most of the time a trick or two ahead of anyone else and her eyes met his with the silent flash of amusement that was always between them.

"Nominations tonight, Tommy," Kallela said.

Tom nodded with his mouth full, then asked, "Haven't changed your mind yet?"

"Course not, kiddo. I'll let somebody else take over for business agent. Me and the old lady got our noggins pretty well made up to head for the home town."

"You're like a God damned elephant," Tom said. "You never forget."

"Never learn nothin' new and never forget, that's me!" Kallela banged his hand on the table and let out a howl of laughter. "You're the one should have stepped in as business agent down here, Tom. You'd make a good one, kiddo." The hard blue eyes in the bristly red face fixed on his. "How long you been on that stewards' committee now?"

"Oh, five months I guess."

"If only you'd showed up around here about a year sooner, I'd had you all set to win the business-agent election hands down."

"My draft board would get a kick out of that."

"They chasin' you? *Hey, Sally!*" he bellowed. "Want to eat with us tonight or not?"

"Called me down to bawl me out this morning. But they

know when construction's due to wind up out at the yard as good as anybody. Whenever you drive that last nail, boy, they say, just make sure you get your ass into the army or navy." Then feeling himself flush, he added, "Excuse the language."

"Never learned what the word meant," Liz Kallela assured him; and her husband suggested,

"You could hire out over at Richmond, couldn't you, and get another deferment?"

"I don't want another one. I'll leave you to finish up the shipyards around here, Kallela. Wouldn't be a bad idea for you to practice up with your tools a little bit. I bet you can't even drive a nail any more."

The other grinned and nodded. "Ready for a refill?" he asked. "Hey, what's for dessert, Liz?" And he shouted again, "*Sally!* You goin' to be spendin' your life in the bed?"

"Oh, stop yelling!"

Sally at last, in dressing gown and slippers, padded into the kitchen, knotting a scarf over her head to cover the pin curlers. "You'll have the neighbors complaining."

"What a way to come out when we got company!"

"Company? Is Tom company?" She favored Tom with a smile then. "Hi there," she said.

"Hi."

"Want to go bowling tonight?"

"Union meeting night."

"Oh, it is." And turning to her father, Sally asked, "Well, did you talk Tom into running for office yet?"

Kallela shook his head.

"Pop thinks you ought to be boning up on your brogue a little better," she suggested to Tom. "Then you'd be a dead cinch over there at the hall. *Shure, brothers,*" she proclaimed, "*we best be thakin' a good look at the situashun.* Only I don't do it right, it's the hardest thing for a

Swede-Finn. But all the time I have to listen to those crabby old carpenters at the lunch counter, I might run for office myself one of these days. . . . Do you know, Mom," she said, looking up at her mother and speaking rapidly between bites, "Tom was having coffee the other night, some fellow sat down beside him, some brother member of the stewards' committee, I expect—" She choked on a piece of meat loaf while Tom stabbed at the squares of carrot scattered about his plate. "And I said—I was passing by with a tray of cups, see Mom—I said, *An' could I be br-ringin' you another spot o' coffee, sir-r . . . or a cup of tay? Oh, Tom!*" she cried. "Oh, you should have seen his face when I said that! I thought . . . I thought he was going to climb right over the counter." Throwing herself back in her chair, she pressed her hands to her face, shrieking with laughter. The scarf slipped aside, exposing the pin curlers, allowing a few strands of red hair to straggle across her forehead.

Tom sat silent—and then began to laugh. Kallela and Liz were laughing too, and Tom laughed with them, while Sally, whirling up from the table, made him a slight curtsy. When Kallela demanded, "Can't you sit still long enough to finish your supper?" she called back from the hallway,

"Please, sir-r. An' I got a date to be goin' out bowl-lin'."

This set Liz laughing all over again. But Tom could see from the look she gave him that she knew how angry he was inside, which made him only the angrier. She cleared away the plates, set the cake on the table. Sally returned, dressed now in jacket and slacks; and her red hair, freed from its pin curlers, was rolled into a knot at the back of her head. She reached for a piece of cake which she began to munch without sitting down.

"You better get home early," Liz told her, "and take a nap before you go to work. That's why we couldn't get you up tonight."

"All right, Mom."

"Maybe Tom could drive you over. He'll have to bring Pop back here anyway."

Tom said nothing to this. A horn heehawed from the street below. "Oh, there they are!" Sally cried; and with her mouth full, tried to say good night, but choked and giggled at the same time. Her freckled face turned red, she waved and ran out, the half-eaten piece of cake still in her hand.

With Andermas, Tom thought. Out bowling with Andermas who had a nice safe spot in the naval net depot, a cozy berth for the rest of the war. He should have gone along too. Maybe he wasn't much of a bowler, but he could straighten Andermas out on some other things. So instead he was driving the old man to the union meeting. He pushed himself up from the table. "You want to go?" he asked.

"That time already, kiddo?" Kallela peered at the alarm clock on the stove. "Haven't quite finished my coffee yet."

"You haven't emptied the pot, you mean," his wife suggested, and Tom told him, "Well, pour it down or you'll miss the reading of the minutes. Maybe they'll fire you."

As Kallela was struggling into the shiny, double-breasted blue serge coat he wore for union meetings, Tom called good night to Liz and thanked her for the dinner. She followed him out on the back landing. "Girls that age can be real bitches, Tom," she said to him. "After a while they get over it mostly."

He shrugged his shoulders as if this made no difference to him; yet as he went down the stairs he knew he had not fooled her at all.

5

As Walter Stone was leaving his conference with the executive board of the San Martin Shipbuilders' Local, he saw that the woodworkers on the first floor had just ended a meeting. From the stairway, he caught sight of their business agent, Kallela, in the crowd scattered across the lobby between the meeting hall and the club room. He recalled having heard that Kallela was planning to return to Saw Creek, and it occurred to him he ought at least to stop and wish him well; but the man by this time would be in the middle of a noisy circle at the bar, and Walter Stone, who had been in court most of the day and in conference with the shipbuilders since dinner time, wished for nothing so much now as a few moments of silence and solitude. He hesitated at the foot of the stairs.

"Hello there, Mr. Stone," said a voice beside him.

He saw an unfamiliar face, a young man in a leather jacket and open-collar shirt.

"Remember me, Mr. Stone?"

Walter smiled and shook his head. And then he did remember: one of the kids who had been working in the Saw Creek mill. Why, his star witness, of course! "Tom O'Regan!" he exclaimed, and said as they shook hands, "I've often wondered about you. Even if I didn't quite recognize you. You've changed a good deal in three years."

"You haven't, Mr. Stone."

"One doesn't at my age. So what are you doing? Are you working here in San Martin?"

"I'm on the construction over at the shipyard."

"I take it you're a carpenter now, Tom? You've given up sawmilling?"

"You're damn right I have."

Walter laughed and asked, "What happened to you afterwards? Were you able to get back in the mill?"

"I never even tried. Some of the guys got back on, I guess. But I took off."

"And where did you go then?"

"Seattle, Chicago. I been all over the place. What they call a boomer in the trade."

"Seeing the world. I remember now, you were talking about that."

"Oh, I've seen some of it all right. I guess I'll see plenty more in the next few years too."

"You're not married, are you?"

"Oh, hell, no. I'll sign up in a few months, I guess. In the navy, I guess."

"My son has just gone into the navy," Walter told him; and recalled that he had thought of his son the first time he had ever seen Tom O'Regan. They were approximately the same age. "Your family?" he asked. "Are they still up there?"

"They're down San Diego."

"Well, Tom," Walter said, hefting his brief case, but wondering suddenly why he so often felt insincere in saying things he sincerely intended, "It really is a great pleasure to see you again. I noticed Kallela heading into the clubroom a moment ago, I thought I ought to say hello to him. I don't see him very often."

"Why sure, sure," the other agreed, so readily that Walter realized he must have been casting about for some means of disengaging himself. "Come on in, Mr. Stone. I got to shake Kallela loose anyhow; I'm supposed to drive him home before I go to work. I'm on the midnight shift," he said, as he led the way into the clubroom, past the crowd at the pool table, and elbowed a path to the bar. There Kallela was holding forth, gesticulating with a half-empty beer bottle. "Come off it now, Kallela," O'Regan broke in. "You better be buying this man a drink before he has you locked up again."

Kallela swung around.

Then his face lighted, he grasped Walter by the hand and pulled him up alongside him. "Here's the smartest springer in the league," he announced. "The man that got me out of the Saw Creek pokey. God damn right, he'd have to be smart for that, wouldn't he?"

"Were you guilty, Kallela?" someone asked.

"Guilty as hell," he shouted; and when the laughter subsided, Walter said,

"I can assure you, gentlemen, he was innocent as a shorn lamb, as anyone could tell by looking at him. All he did was organize a union."

"Tried to, anyhow," Kallela amended. "Let me buy you a beer, Stone? That's the best they got here. Maybe you could fix us up with a regular liquor license some day when you're up to Sacramento. Well, here's to better times," he proposed. "You keeping busy?"

Before Walter could answer, however, the other plowed on in his great booming voice, "I see your picture in the paper every once in a while, Stone. I guess you must have every labor faker on the West Coast for one of your clients by this time." There came a chorus of appreciative laughter; and Walter, after taking a drink from his beer bottle, acknowledged the laugh with what he knew must be a rather thin-looking grin of his own. He understood that Kallela could not resist playing the grandstand a little at his expense—and in a way he had asked for it, stepping in here with his tweed overcoat and his pigskin brief case. Yet a lawyer was a lawyer and every calling has its traditional attire. Upstairs there, they would have begun to doubt his qualifications if he had appeared in a coat, say, like the one Kallela had on. And Kallela would be the first to grow suspicious of a carpenter who reported for work in the wrong kind of overalls. But then it struck him that Kallela perhaps had been genuinely touched at his stopping and was playing the horselaughs to cover his own uncertainty as to how to respond. Walter liked him better at once.

"I heard rumors you're going back to Saw Creek," he said.

Kallela nodded. "Had enough city life, Stone. Me and the old lady want to be back where we can shoot our dinner out the kitchen window."

"Man has to carry his rifle when he goes to the outhouse up there, don't he, Kallela?" someone asked; and another called,

"They don't go to the outhouse all winter, it's across the river."

"All right, all right," Kallela shouted, pretending to have taken offense. "You fellows can laugh, but when you're lined up with your ration books trying to get ahold of a pound of hamburger, just think of me packing away the bear steak and venison. God damn right, go ahead, split your sides open!" And to Walter, he said in a lower voice, "That's kind of our home up there, we always intended to go back. We'll leave things in the big city to lads like Tommy, now." Walter saw the boy's face redden with embarrassment.

"He'll be business agent down here one of these days," Kallela said. "Or maybe runnin' around with a lawyer's brief case, hey, kiddo? Sky's the limit for young fellows that age, Stone, if Uncle Whiskers will ever leave loose of 'em again . . ."

But Tom O'Regan was prodding Kallela from the other side and Walter heard him saying, "For Christ's sakes, I got to get to work at twelve o'clock. Do you want to ride with me, or walk?"

"Gettin' late already, Tommy? Why damn right it is! Say, you better take off. I'll catch a ride with somebody else. You drivin' your car tonight, Stone? I'm on your way over to Bayshore anyhow. You can drop me off at the corner of Poplar."

"I'd be delighted," Walter said.

Under Kallela's elbow, he shook hands with O'Regan, amused at the mixture of respect and irritation with which he had addressed Kallela; and as the boy moved away, Kallela said into his ear, "He's a good kid, all right. Smart as a tack. The old lady's tryin' to get her hooks into him, but our girl don't seem to take to the idea very good. Skittish as a young horse." He laughed so loudly that Walter jerked his head back. "*Well*. Guess I better not hold you up too long, either, Stone, you got quite a ways to go yet." Kallela threw down a dollar bill on the bar, picked up his change. "Still live over in the city, hey?" Gripping Walter by the arm, he began pushing along towards the door. But Walter, who glanced up now and again at the clock over the cigar counter, observed that it took them almost thirty minutes to make their way out of the clubroom. Kallela had something to impart to each person they passed. "Just lay off the old bottle now, Hank," he counseled one; and nudging the next with his elbow, ordered, "Keep a sharp eye on that foreman, Calahan. Maybe ought to bring him up on charges one of these days, straighten him out

a little. . . . How's things down to city hall, Gus? . . .
Old lady on her feet yet, Giorgio?"

So they reached the entrance at last and crossed the street
to Walter's car. As they drove through the intersection of
San Martin Avenue and turned west toward the bay,
Walter asked, "Will you be able to find work up there,
Kallela?"

"There's a bunch of new mills goin' in with the war. I
figure it won't be long till they might be glad to have me
back."

"But before," he said. "You weren't able to work at all?"

"Hell, no. When there's only two outfits in a town, they
can put on a black list that sticks like ticks to a dog."

"Couldn't the union help," Walter asked, "after they
reached the settlement?"

"The union help?" Kallela repeated. "Why, the International representative come in there and dissolved the local.
Then he set it up again with a couple of his stooges for the
officers. They were the ones decided who was to be on the
black list, I guess. They pulled the rug out from under us,
all right. Maybe I shouldn't say this to you, Stone? The
International must be one of your best customers."

"I won't tell on you, Kallela."

"Wouldn't make any difference. They know I'm an old
Wobbly from away back. They'll try to keep me out of
holding office up there. But they may not come out so good
this time."

"Is that why you're going back?" Walter asked curiously.

"There's a couple things I'd like to catch up with." Then
he laughed and shook his head. "Oh, that's mostly talk,
Stone. I'm not as young as I used to be. I don't go out of my
way lookin' for trouble any more. If they leave me alone,
I expect I'll leave them alone." After a moment of silence,
he added, "Been around that territory since 1920. I hate

to let anybody chase me out. . . . Here we are. Just drop me off at the next corner."

"Can't I take you to your house?"

"No, no, I'm only a couple blocks away."

Walter eased out of the boulevard traffic and pulled to a stop. "You know, yours was the first labor case I ever took on," he said to Kallela. "In a way I suppose it was you and the others up there made a labor lawyer out of me."

"Maybe that's not much to thank us for."

"On the contrary. I was very much impressed by the Saw Creek affair. Largely as a result, I suppose, I parted company with a man I had been with in partnership a good many years, and since then I've entered a new firm that tries to specialize in labor law. My son just married the daughter of my former partner," he added, laughing. "Nothing is ever simple, you see. But I was glad to get into a new field. Very glad indeed. I've always been grateful to you for that."

"I always been grateful to *you* for gettin' me out of the pokey," Kallela replied.

"I was certainly a greenhorn. Later on, I realized how little I knew of what I had stepped into."

"I guess if you had, you wouldn't have come up there in the first place."

Walter opened his mouth to answer, but it appeared there was more in this comment than quite met the eye. He said simply, "I had accepted the case, I would have come," and thrust his hand out. "I'm glad you're going back," he said. "Good luck to you." They shook hands, and as Kallela stepped down to the sidewalk, Walter called after him, "Tell young O'Regan to come see me sometime if he's interested in law after the war. I'd like very much to see a few young fellows out of the trades pick up a legal training."

He saw Kallela turn to stare almost suspiciously before

he nodded and waved an acknowledgment. "All right. I'll tell him, Stone, I'll tell him."

The bayshore highway swung in curves of wet black asphalt, the headlamps swept over the darkness of mudflats beyond, picking up a row of salt-crusted pilings, the carcass of an automobile half buried in mud, a tire left on edge by the receding tide. Far in the distance, the lights of San Francisco glowed like a huge heap of moldering coals.

Walter, as he drove, took time to digest the remark with which Kallela had left him. *I guess if you had, you wouldn't have come up there in the first place.* A suspicious man, Kallela. Well, he had described himself accurately enough when he said they all knew him for an old Wobbly. One of the ancient radicals, and as so many of those did, he hated the international office of his union like poison. With reason, perhaps, he admitted. Yet men of Kallela's stamp, left to themselves, would tear the union into a thousand pieces, any union. They were anarchistic, intolerant of any restraint; whereas the very nature of an organization as large and complex as a modern union required that certain restraints be imposed on the various parts. Kallela nevertheless was an honest man in his way—but what he had said was not true. To that charge, Walter thought, he could properly plead not guilty. Nothing he learned afterwards, he thought, had ever caused him to regret the Saw Creek case, or to reconsider his break with his former partner Richards; harsh blow though this certainly had been to his wife and his son. He had not realized the boy was already engaged to Richards' daughter at the time. Well, they had all survived, more or less; and the boy had his own decisions to make. So we've been successful enough, he pronounced half aloud (choosing his words, as he often did, as if for an imaginary jury), not in the sense of making a great deal of money, though we've not done badly in that respect either—oh, yes, he still could wear his Scotch tweed overcoat like any Montgomery Street attorney; but in the sense of engaging in activities which seemed useful and decent to us.

Is not that sufficient? What more can a man ask? Yet why should this accidental glimpse of Kallela suddenly force him into defending his patterns of life? He realized, in examining the question, that Kallela—Kallela and the boy, young O'Regan, who had charmed the county courthouse with his slightly Gaelic speech and his ingenuous, offended manner (even if he added nothing particularly new to the testimony)—that both these were fixed deep in his own mind, at the apex of one of the turning points of his life. Indeed it was a turning point, he thought; and as he drove on over the empty roadway of the bridge, there came to him with shattering vividness the recollection of the moment when the hung jury had at last been dismissed: the men on trial had come streaming out of the courtroom, their wives clinging weeping to their arms; surrounded him there on the courthouse steps in the late afternoon, in that twilight heavy with fragrance of burning sawdust from the mills at the outskirts of town; surrounded him, patting him on the back, one after another shaking his hand as they moved past. As if it were he who had saved them, he thought; a moment not easily forgotten.

6

Tom, after he left the union hall, drove back to the Kallelas' to take Sally to the shipyard. Sally however had not yet come in. Liz sat mending socks at the kitchen table.

"Sit down now, have a cup of coffee," she urged him.

"I can't, I'm late already."

"Oh, wait a minute, Tom. She'll be along right away, you got a minute or two." And she explained, "There was a whole bunch of the kids went out together—"

"I got no time at all," Tom said. "Let them drive her out, they got nothing else to do." He slammed the door behind him, and as he banged down the stairs, thought he heard Liz laughing inside the kitchen. The treads creaked rapidly beneath his feet. She was out! Almost midnight already and she was out! Below him, the vacant lot back of the Kallelas' house lay silver-green in the moonlight, crisscrossed by the black lines of paths tramped in the tall grass. He stumbled over a child's scooter lying in the shadow on the landing under the garbage pails, and kicked it down the last flight; followed it in two jumps; swung round the end of the building bright with moonlight into the blackness of the alley beyond.

Here he stopped. She could no longer see him from above, even if she were to step out on the landing to look. So let her laugh, he thought; it was funny! Leaning against the fender of his pickup, he reached for a cigarette, fumbled in his pocket for matches. But instead of striking a light, he suddenly broke the cigarette between his fingers and let the pieces drop to the ground. God damn her, he said to himself. *Out with a bunch of the kids!* Out bowling with the girls and boys. Like hell she was. All right. The hell with *her* then.

Stalks of weeds at the side of the alley grew waist high and he caught one in his hand and yanked to pull it up by the roots. But the stem cut across his palm driving its sharp spines into the flesh. The pain laid open the darkness of Tom's anger like a flare of light and, in the same moment, lights swung across the opposite end of the alley. He straightened up, stiff and tight. He heard the sound of a car stopping, voices and laughter, and his heart hammered up into his throat. Flattening himself against the building, he inched forward to the mouth of the alley and looked out. They were there.

A model-A Ford was pulled up by the door of the apartment house. In the rumble seat were a couple with their arms around each other, and in front—the top was down and the car had stopped under a street lamp—in front, he could see Sally's red hair and the blond close-cropped head of George Andermas from the naval net depot. Been parked over by Bayshore necking hell out of each other, he thought. Andermas was lighting her cigarette. She leaned towards him, telling him something, laughing. Go ahead, kiss her —what the hell am I getting mad for, he's probably had it more times than he can count already. Kiss her good night, you son of a bitch, I'll kick your ass from here to San Martin Boulevard. He waited, feeling suddenly calm and quiet inside, rocking forward and back on his feet and clenching and unclenching his fists.

But the two in the front seat exchanged no kiss. Sally got out, ran into the house while the car remained where it was. Waiting to drive her out to the yard, he thought. And remembering then that he was late himself, he jumped back to the pickup, gunned it out of the alley along the wheel tracks that crossed the vacant lot to the next street. At the shipyard, the only openings left in the parking strip were at the further end. By the time Tom had hurried back to the entrance gate, Andermas' Ford was there and Sally just climbing out.

She saw him, waved, motioned him over. But Tom shoved through the turnstile. The familiar crowd swept him between the buildings, past the mountains of lumber and the lines of boxcars, toward the skeleton framework of the shipways. He walked fast and he was halfway across the yard before Sally caught up with him. From her quick breathing, he knew she must have been running. They walked along in silence side by side.

"Mom said you stopped at the house," she said when she had caught her breath.

"That's right. I stopped. How'd you make out tonight?"

"I shot a hundred and eighty," she told him. "That's pretty good for me."

"You made out all right, hunh?"

"What's eating *you?*" she demanded.

Tom shrugged his shoulders. He could feel her staring at him but neither spoke again till they reached the rear of the lunch counter. As he started on toward the shipway, she caught his wrist and pulled him back.

"What's the matter with you, Tom?"

"Nothing's the matter with me. I'm all right."

"You're mad because I went bowling with George Ander-mas?"

"I'm not mad."

"You are too."

"Go out with anybody you want. I don't give a damn."

"Don't think you *own* me," she cried, "just because I went out on a date with you."

"I don't think I own you," Tom said. "And I won't be standing in line waiting my turn like the last dog in the pack."

She stared at him as if she had not quite understood what he said. Then without a word, she threw herself at him, not scratching or biting as he had always expected a girl would fight, but swinging her fists. The attack took him by surprise. He warded off the first blow with his elbow but the second caught him flush on the mouth, knocked him half off his pins and he felt his mouth fill with blood. He stumbled sideways, regained his balance and lunged back, ready to kill her. But she had slipped through the rear door of the lunch counter and slammed the door in his face.

As he stood wrenching at the knob, the whistle blew for twelve o'clock. He was late. He turned, raced alongside the wall of the plate shop to the shipway. His gang was already crawling up the ladders with their tool boxes slung over their shoulders; and Tom struggled into his overalls, dragged his box out of the locker and followed them.

When he returned at four o'clock in the morning, there was a crowd of men around the cash register loading up cartons of night lunch and the waitresses were scurrying back and forth from the icebox to the coffee urn. But the counter itself was almost empty. Tom sat down and Sally trotted past, showing him her hand with a cut on the knuckle approximately the size and shape of his front tooth.

"The other girls think I ought to get a dog-bite shot," she told him.

He said nothing and she paused, watching him. "Cup of coffee, champ?"

"You're darn lucky you got through that door in a hurry, I'll just tell you that."

"*You're* lucky I didn't have a milk bottle or a carving knife handy. I'd of killed you."

She set a mug of coffee in front of him and hurried back toward the cash register, singing out, "Three pies for you, Jack. Four doughnuts, three coffees, cream and sugar in two—"

"Sugar in all three," the customer interrupted.

"Oh no, Jack. Howie never takes sugar in his coffee."

"Howie ain't workin' tonight, Strawberry. And throw in a slice of cocoanut cake if you don't mind."

"Who's the cake for, Jack?"

"Never mind who it's for."

"You better take something that's not so fattening, you're growin' kind of plump, Jack."

"Me? Growin' plump?"

The customer was a stringy-muscled, knobby-jointed man of fifty or fifty-five. "I don't think you're getting enough exercise," the girl told him. "When are you goin' to take me out roller-skating?" This brought a guffaw of laughter from the other buyers at the counter, and Jack, leaning back, patted his gaunt belly.

"Gettin' fat, she says! You hear that? Don't get enough exercise! You hear that?"

"You better not let your wife hear that," one of the others warned.

"Your wife catch you out roller-skatin' with any young strawberries, Jack, she'll give you what for."

"All right, quit kidding me now. Get your money out and pay for this stuff or I'll put it back on the shelf."

44

Jack was still cackling to himself like a hen over a couple of new-laid eggs, as Sally came down the counter to bang a dish of apple pie in front of Tom. "What right you got to talk to me like that?" she whispered. "Who do you think you are, anyhow?"

"I was mad," he said.

"Were you mad at me? Did I do anything to make you mad?"

"Did you kiss him the way you kissed me the other night?" he asked.

"What if I did? Is that any your business?"

He glanced up, startled, and found her greenish-gray eyes fixed on his, steady and serious. "But I'll tell you if you want to know. No, I didn't, I never kissed anybody just like that. Did you?"

"No," he said.

She was gone at once. He saw her at the cash register, ringing up Jack's bill, and his eye followed the curve of her neck, the freckled arm, the line of the green waitress dress and the apron. She was not very tall, stocky and rather thick-set—built too much like her old man, he thought; he never had considered she was anything much to look at, back in Saw Creek. But that was three years ago. She had changed. What would keep a girl like that from going crazy, he wondered, just lying down in the same bed with herself? His half-hour was almost at an end before she found her way back in his direction. Leaning her elbows on the counter, she told him, "I can hardly wait till I go to work as a welder. I'm getting awful sick of smiling at customers." And she fixed him with a glassy deadpan while he scowled back.

"You want a ride home," he asked, "or you already got one?"

"I'll ride with you if you're going my direction."

"Listen, Sally, I'm getting sick of smiling too. Why don't you quit kidding around?"

"What do you mean by that?"

"Do you want me, or do you want Andermas? Or do you want me to come over and break his neck for him?"

"Why, Tommy! What makes you think I want either one of you?"

He opened his mouth but could say nothing. Then he got up from the stool. "I won't be around much longer anyhow," he said; and turned and went out.

In the morning, however, when he had stowed his carrybox and his overalls into the tool room, Tom stopped at the lunch counter and found her waiting outside the door. Silently they walked toward the gate together, past the throngs of incoming day-shift workers. Only after they had checked by the guards at the turnstile, she said,

"I been thinking I might go down to visit my girl friend Nell in San Jose next weekend."

Tom said nothing, and she explained, "Nell was in high school with me, Tom. Would you like to come?"

"What do I care about your girl friend?"

"Oh?"

He spun around to face her and she was staring intently at something across the highway. But her eyes came back almost hesitantly to his. He caught her hand and she laughed.

"You'll just adore my girl friend Nell," she cried, dancing alongside him.

7

All her life Joyce Allen had dreamed so much while so few of her dreams had come true, that now as one seemed to be taking form in front of her eyes, she almost feared to believe it was real. Instead, the hard corners of the day assumed a dreamlike quality, everything became strange and disconnected. The clanging, pushing, shouting of the shipyard scarcely touched her all day long. She floated through as if she were no part of it. Afterwards, in the Hendersons' apartment, she bathed, fixed her hair, put on the gown which she had not worn since her high school graduation. Raising the blind at the window, she saw the fog, low over the street-lamps, dripping and dripping down on the black pavements. She took her raincoat from the closet, a scarf to put over her head, laid them ready on the bed and then stood examining herself in the mirror. The watcher and the watched; the one so often lonely and frightened, the other cool and smiling, untouched and untouchable.

Wearing the same dress, she thought, the gown her mother had made for her to wear on the platform of the auditorium —it was as if she had been looking down from some high gallery—but of course not to wear to the senior ball in the evening. Who would have danced with her?

"What an accomplished musician you are, Joyce," Mr. Mallory, the algebra teacher, told her; and Miss Benwood, the English teacher, agreed. "Oh, it *was* simply beautiful. Don't you look lovely in your new dress, Joyce!" Smiling, watching the figure in the mirror, she said, *I'm glad you enjoyed it.* And after the ceremony, she had walked home under the trees along the streets of town, till the streets turned into the highway, and she crossed the railroad through the blaze of sunlight that vibrated over the greasewood flats. Her mother, having taken that half day off, had gone back to work at the rancho; and so with evening, when she knew the dancing must have started in the auditorium, she had sat alone in the kitchen, silently staring at the old piano.

But it was only a few minutes after six yet. Why had she gotten ready so early, he wouldn't be coming before half-past six in any case? Was that what he had said? Or six? No, it was half-past. But he might be late; people often were.

Turning from side to side, she fluffed her skirt below the knees. She wished her father could have attended the graduation. He would have been glad to know she had finished high school. Certainly it would have pleased him that she had sat there on the stage with the principal and the class president. And about San Francisco, she added, he would have been glad to know about that too. If only she could have told him. If only somehow she could have known beforehand that she really was coming here, and told him on one of those afternoons when she found him waiting for her as she returned from school, lying out on his blanket in the winter sunlight. "I'm sorry we ever had to get stuck into a place like this Signal Springs," he had said to her. "Would have been better if we could have lived somewhere you could grow up with your own people. I guess that'll make things hard for you."

"Aw, we'll get along all right, Dad." She remembered she had used the word *we* purposely.

And he had smiled at her for a moment before he said, "*I*'ll get along all right. I always have. And you will too. But it'll be hard. I suppose it's hard enough already."

She had shaken her head vehemently, and he had laughed and wiggled sideways with his blanket to keep up with the patch of sunlight that was moving away from him. "I wish we could have lived someplace with lots of young folks, and you were out dancing every night and having fun and going to parties. Well, we didn't, that's all. But you got a good schooling, that's one thing. You got a better schooling than your Mom, I guess, and your Mom was a schoolteacher." Then he was silent and he had taken out his watch and was studying it back and front as if he hadn't been quite sure how it looked. "Schooling ain't so much," he told her finally. "Schooling's something but it ain't everything. Soon as you finish school it's time for you to move out of this town."

She had wanted to cry out, "Where will *you* be? Won't we all be going together?" But she had only stared at him, frightened, silent, and he said again,

"Soon as you finish school, honey, then it's time you figure you're grown up, time for you to kick up your heels and move on down the road."

"Where to, Dad?" she whispered. "Where should I go?"

"Any place. San Francisco, Denver, Chicago. Any place the train go, honey."

She remembered. Not a day passed that she had not remembered. And hoping he would have been glad to know, she arranged her face again into a smile, sat down on the bed and folded her hands across her knees.

At half-past six the bell rang.

Mrs. Henderson pressed the buzzer to release the street door, footsteps came creaking up the stairs, knuckles tapped on the door. Mrs. Henderson opened the door and he came in. Joyce could scarcely remember his name though she had had it on her tongue a moment earlier. "Mister . . . Mister . . ."

"Gammon," he sang out, shaking hands with the Hendersons. "Charlie Gammon." And then turning and looking her up and down, "My heavens, you look beautiful! I'm ashamed of myself."

"Oh, girls do like to dress up," Mr. Henderson told him.

"Well, I do too," Charlie Gammon said. "I got my best suit on but it's no match for that! You most ready to go?"

Joyce ran into the bedroom to fetch her coat, and through the open door she could hear Mr. Henderson beginning to put Charlie Gammon through a cross-examination, just as if she, Joyce, had been his own daughter instead of a boarder.

"You work in the shipyard, Mr. Gammon?"

"No. No, sir, I don't. I'm a seaman. You make the ships and I ride on 'em." Only he was not really a seaman at all, she thought, but only for the war. The Reverend Beezely in the welding class had told her he was an artist and her heart faltered in astonishment at the word. Still it was best he had said seaman to Mr. Henderson.

"A seaman. Well now, a seaman. And you and Joyce met in this night-school class?"

"Oh no, I don't take the night class. They'd ship me out before I had a chance to finish my homework." Charlie Gammon broke into his laugh that had made her laugh too the first time she had heard it. "No, I got a friend of mine taking the class, Reverend Beezely. Reverend introduced me to Miss Allen. Miss Allen, I said, are you *occupied* next Saturday night? That's how it happened, Mr. Henderson. Here she is! All set?" He waved and made a little bow and called, "Good night. It's a pleasure to have made your acquaintance, ma'am."

Down the staircase, she went first and he a step behind because the stairs were too narrow for them to walk side by side. At the curb a car was standing, its dimmed headlights making pale circles in the fog. "I borrowed us a Rolls Royce for the evening," he explained, and they drove several blocks along Fillmore, then turned and stopped in a side street. He was pressing one of the bells on the ladder of push buttons in the entryway. The door clicked open and with his hand under her arm, he guided her up the stairs till they saw the Reverend Beezely in his black suit leaning over the banister. The Reverend's wife helped Joyce out of her raincoat, exclaiming over the dress,

"Oh, what a lovely dress that is, and that wasn't bought in any store!" Joyce said no, her mother had made it for her graduation. Mrs. Beezely told her she had two girls herself, one going into high school in the fall. At that, they both glanced up together, neither one knowing what to say next, and both laughed. Mrs. Beezely led her to the living room where they sat down on the day bed.

The Reverend was pouring glasses of wine.

"How are you feeling now, Charles?" he asked.

"Better than ever."

"Honestly?"

"Cross my heart. I won't say the rest of it, though."

A gas heater with an orange face like a neon sign glared at Joyce from the fireplace, ticking over its bank of tiny flames. Charlie, glass in hand, was wandering about the room.

"How long do you expect to be ashore?"

"Another two or three weeks, I guess, Rev, before they give me the all clear."

"By that time," said Reverend Beezely, "Miss Allen and I ought to be expert builders, capable of putting together a ship to your specifications."

"My only specifications is one that don't break apart at the seams. Do you think you can do that?"

51

"I haven't the slightest doubt. Do you, Miss Allen?"

Joyce shook her head. Charlie had dropped down beside her, throwing one arm across the back of the day bed. She felt his hand touch her hair and moved slightly sideways.

"See that picture over the fireplace?" he asked.

She raised her eyes to a painting of a ship at dock, with oil tanks and low hills behind it. "There you have the SS *Petrolea*," Charlie told her, "the latter-day ark on which I first made the acquaintance of the Reverend here. I came aboard, went down to the galley, behold, there he was cooking up doughnuts for Sunday morning breakfast—"

"Yes. An original and early Gammon," said the Reverend, tapping the wall beneath the painting. "We're tremendously proud to own it."

"Oh, a collector's item," Charlie agreed. "You'll all be millionaires someday. But as I was saying. There stood the Rev himself frying doughnuts in the grease they'd been cooking Friday-night fish in for the past six or seven years. Oh, man! What's for chow tonight, Rev?"

"I couldn't say. The young ladies are making dinner."

"Thank heaven then, we're saved! You know what they used to call him aboard the *Petrolea?* Hard-times Beezely, the West Indian Belly Robber."

At this Reverend Beezely broke into a laugh for the first time and covered his face with his hands. "Now let me declare in self-defense, Miss Allen, that every sea cook is called a belly robber. That's an occupational title. I prepared the food the steward gave me and did the best I could with it. My conscience is clear."

"The crew has rickets but the Rev's conscience is clear. And just why are you giving up this soft berth, Rev, may I ask, going out to do hard labor in the shipyard?"

Reverend Beezely filled Charlie's glass and his own from the wine bottle, pulled over a chair and sat down. "First, old friend, allow me to correct you. This has not been a soft berth. I deliver half a dozen sermons a week. I call on members of the congregation during the day. I raise money for people to bring their families out from Texas and Louisiana. I find jobs for people. I find houses, I find hospitals, doctors, dentists, lawyers for people." He waved his hand as if dismissing what he had just said, and then added, "But still I'm only the assistant pastor, Charles. My wife Janet presses pants in a cleaning and dyeing establishment."

"I know she does. I stand corrected."

"Why do *you* go to sea, Charles? You've been ashore with pneumonia. Why are you hurrying so fast to go on the ships again?"

"Oh, that's not my idea. I might wind up in the infantry if I stick around shore too long."

"Well, it's a matter of personal preference," said the Reverend. "After all, you're a seaman and seamen are badly needed. But the point is, our people are going into the army and navy as fast as the army and navy will take them. Why? Why does Miss Allen come down from Nevada to work in the shipyards? Why do people come from all over the country? Because of better wages, because they want to get out of the South? Of course, of course. But more than that. There is a common mind, a common heart that moves people when they move in unison. The common heart says, these battles, these ships, are for freedom. Freedom in Germany, France, China, Japan. We're for freedom, aren't we?"

"I'm for freedom in Texas," Charlie said.

"Yes, exactly. And the frontiers of Texas may be on the Rhine, as they say. God sends us a test for his own reasons. There's no need for me sitting all day in the church when our people are in the shipyards."

After a moment of silence, Charlie said, "I wouldn't disagree with that, Rev. I bet you'll weld a seam that won't break open very quick, too."

"I hope we will. With a certain assistance. Don't you, Miss Allen?"

She felt uncertain as to whether or not he was joking; but Charlie nudged her, saying, "God bless our welded joints!"

The Reverend asked, "You're working in San Martin, aren't you? Yes, you told me the other night. And how's my friend Mr. Brooks? How's the Sergeant?"

"He's all right, I think. I haven't seen him in several days."

"And have you joined the union?"

"We went to some union office," she told him. "Over in San Martin, Mr. Henderson and I. We each had to give three dollars."

"Yes, that would be the Laborers'. But we still have another one to join before we can become welders—the Shipbuilders' Union. I expect Mr. Brooks will tell you about that, he seems to be closely acquainted over there. . . . Well, who knows," he cried. "Maybe we'll all be neighbors one of these days. Janet and I, and our young ladies, are intending to move to San Martin after I finish the welding course, if I can be employed in the yard. I hope to open a church in San Martin," he said. "There is no church for our people there, not yet—"

He was interrupted by a shout from Charlie. "Hey!" Charlie called. "Hey, here's my girl friends, here they are!" The Beezelys' two daughters had come into the living room to announce that dinner was ready. Charlie seized them both and kissed them, which set them shrieking in delight. Then with the two clinging to his arms, he led the way to the kitchen.

"Rev sounds phony as a nine-dollar bill sometimes," Charlie told her after dinner, after they had said good-by to the Beezelys and were on their way down the stairs to the car again. "I've known him a long time. Oh, man, a long time. Why, we were on the *Petrolea*, that must have been eight years ago, and they sold her for scrap right here in San Francisco. I went on WPA, and the Rev— Are you warm enough?" he asked.

"Oh, yes."

He tucked her coat around her as they sat down in the car. "Man, that was a hungry winter. Couldn't get near a job on a ship, there were fifteen or twenty men for every spot. I was prying up rails from an old streetcar line for the WPA and that's when the Rev got the call. Some foundation gave him a scholarship, I guess. Oh, I don't mean he got the call because he was hungry, he always did pack a Bible around in his sea bag. But anyhow, that winter, off he went to divinity school in South Carolina or someplace."

The car moved across Fillmore Street, past the crowded and brightly lighted intersections. "Always have thought a lot of the Rev," he was saying. "What a ride they used to hand him on the ship! The West Indian Belly Robber! But he could come back all right. The Rev has a kind of dry British wit about him. And guts. He believes what he believes and he'd just as soon tell anybody— These damn stop lights! . . . Well, you all set for a humdinger of a party, Joyce?"

It was the first time he had used her name.

"Where . . . where are we going now," she asked, "Charlie?"

"Where are we going? Didn't I tell you? Why, I must be up high as a kite—on that glass of wine the Rev gave us! Asking a girl out and never let her know where we're going! You ought to tell me to mind my manners . . . Well, we're going to call on a fellow named Joe Baratia. He was an old schoolteacher of mine. Met him back on WPA too. Oh, the best people around here used to be on WPA—some of them don't like to admit it. But Joe's all right. And he throws a sharp party. . . ."

Beside him in the front seat, Joyce felt the movement of his knee as he pressed the gas and brake pedals. He talked; and she, listening, saying nothing, knew that the very thing she most feared was happening to her. She felt herself growing stiff and cold, detached, watching from a distance. What a fool he must take her for to be sitting so long without a word! If only they could have stayed at the Beezelys', she thought, where the other two did the talking. She was all right there, beside the Reverend's wife, sitting on the day bed. But in the car, alone with him, she was miserable. The whole evening would be miserable. Oh, she had hoped too much, she had done nothing ever but dream; and now sat frozen, unable even to turn and look at him. An artist! And if they danced, she did not really know how to dance, she never had danced before except with her father and his dancing had been twenty years old, and even that five years ago. She would have to tell him she didn't know how. *You might have told me that before we came,* he'd say to her. Only he wouldn't say it, but he'd be thinking it all evening long.

She looked out at the fronts of the houses sliding past, the strange sad-looking San Francisco houses with their high steps and their bay windows and little corner towers. In the fog that was half rain, it seemed as if the whole city were weeping. It seemed as if everybody who lived in those houses must be old and sad. She wished that she had never come.

The car bumped over the cobblestones along the water front where the masts of ships appeared beyond the docks; and turned again, grinding uphill and down through narrow streets, while Charlie, letting out cries of mock fright, joked about the brakes of his borrowed limousine—he certainly hoped it had some. When he stopped, the car slanted so steeply sideways she thought it must surely topple over. But it did not. They crawled out, groped through a kind of tunnel to a flight of stairs; and as they climbed, she heard the noises at the top growing louder. Music, laughter, many voices. Oh, take me home, she wanted to beg him.

"You're kind of shy, aren't you, Joyce?"

She shook her head, but he was not waiting for an answer. "I'm shy, too," he told her.

This struck her as so ridiculous that she began to laugh; yet it was true, there was a shy, almost bashful quality about him, that was why she had liked him from the first.

"I've known most of these people for years," he explained. "So I don't have to be shy any more. And you're an old friend of mine now, so you don't have to be shy with them now either. Do you?"

"No," she agreed.

And he said, "Good then," taking her by the hand, and they went on up the stairs to the door which stood open at the top.

8

Tom visited the men's toilet three times in quick succession, wondering whether something had gone wrong with his kidneys. At each visit he looked himself over in the mirror, smoothed his hair and straightened his tie. When he came out after the third trip, the clock said nine-nineteen; the bus from San Martin had just pulled in. He rushed for the gates in a panic that she might already have grown tired of waiting and disappeared. The first passengers were stepping down and she was not among them. The line lengthened, the bus was half empty—she must have changed her mind. All right, he thought, I'll wait one more bus and that will be the end of it, she needn't expect me to be coming around the lunch counter either. Maybe pick up some chick here in San José; and glancing up, he discovered Sally Kallela ten feet in front of him in the line of the disembarking passengers.

She was wearing a light green suit with a fluff of white at the neck and she carried a suitcase in her hand. As their eyes met, her freckled face reddened under the dark red of her hair, and Tom felt his own face flush from his collar to the tips of his ears. He fell into step beside her, reaching out to take the suitcase, and she with a quick movement, slipped her hand under his arm.

"Hi, Tom," she said.

"I was afraid you wouldn't come," he told her.

"Why?"

"I don't know. I was scared you'd change your mind."

She tightened her fingers on his arm. They went out to the pickup and he drove across town and over the hills beyond San José toward the ocean. "Where are we going, Tom?"

"I don't know. Where are *you?*"

"I'm going with you, ducky."

"No, I mean . . ."

"Where am I supposed to be? Well, I have Nell's address but I don't know exactly where it is."

"What if they call her up or something?"

"They won't. Mom knows better."

"Your Mom knows? Did you tell her?"

"No, I didn't tell her. But I guess she knows."

"How about your old man?" Tom asked.

"He doesn't know."

"I'd sure hate to have *him* out lookin' for me."

"You aren't scared of him, are you?"

"Damn right I am. He could take a couple of guys my size and knock our heads together."

"Well I'm not," Sally said. "I'll protect you."

They both began to laugh, and he looked sideways at her till the truck veered across the center line, and his eyes jumped back to the highway. But he wanted to keep saying something, as soon as they stopped talking the silence disturbed him. He kept remembering the first time he had gone to a dance, how he had been unable to find a word to speak to the girls all evening. This was like a dance too, he thought: may I have the pleasure of this dance with you? —and at a time like this even worse to have nothing to say.

So what had he talked to the last one about? But the last one he had picked up in a bar on San Pablo Avenue, she was pushing thirty and it hadn't mattered much what he said.

He was relieved when Sally began talking again.

She told him she had stolen one of her mother's frying pans and packed it in her suitcase wrapped in newspaper so it wouldn't blacken her underwear.

"What for?" Tom asked.

"Why so we can cook supper on the beach, of course." Taking a piece of paper from her handbag, she set to making a list of the things they would need: a loaf of bread, quarter pound of butter—"Shall we get steaks, Tom?" she asked. "I sneaked out some meat stamps."—an onion, salt, tomatoes, half a dozen bottles of beer. She looked up at him for a moment with a thoughtful expression. "Did you bring your pajamas?"

This caught him flat-footed. "No," he answered as seriously as she had asked the question. "I haven't got any." Then he felt himself blush furiously and Sally went off into a gale of laughter.

The pickup puffed over the spine of the ridge, and there, halfway into the distance lay the ocean, blue and still, sunlit and hazy at the same time. They rolled down the long slopes into the gulches of the lower mountains, and emerging, joined the coastal road where it twisted over the cliff tops. A country store stood at the junction. They filled Sally's shopping list, and went on, coming to a break in the cliffs which opened down into a hollow of pasture and cabbage fields against the sand dunes. Along the margin between the dunes and the fields rose a structure of gray shingle with sagging porches and pointed towers. The name *Bodensee Hotel* was painted across its face.

"Want to stop?" Tom asked. "Looks like there must be a beach over there."

"All right," she agreed.

On the porch of the hotel, a row of elderly ladies in rocking chairs bobbed at different speeds, and as he stepped down from the truck, the ladies peered over the tops of their magazines and their knitting, some putting on glasses the better to see with, others snatching their glasses off. "You go in," Sally suggested in a small voice. "I'll wait out here."

Tom pushed across the porch into the lobby which seemed dark as a cellar after the glare of sunlight. Advancing to confront the woman at the desk, blinking, he demanded, "You got any rooms?"

"Single or double?"

"Double." His voice sounded much too loud. She must know or she wouldn't have asked that so quick. "Me and my wife," he said. But what if she did know? People must be coming in like this all the time. All the time.

The woman was turning the pages of her register. "With bath?"

"Sure. That's okay."

"Do you want twin beds or double?"

"How's that?"

"Do you prefer a room with twin beds or double?"

"Oh. Either one you got. Sure. Double if you got it," he added. She pushed a card and pen across the desk and he signed, *Mr. and Mrs. T. O'Regan, Los Angeles.*

"Shall I show you your room now, Mr. O'Regan?"

"All right. Sure. That's fine. I'll get—my wife. She's right outside . . ." One step beyond the door to the porch, Tom halted, fixed from both sides by the eyes of the ladies, the flashing points of their glasses. Sally was not in the truck. She was nowhere to be seen. He stared about in consternation, then spotted her some distance away sitting at the base of one of the sand dunes, and hurried over to her.

"I couldn't stand all those biddies staring at me," she whispered. "Did we get a room?"

"Sure. We're supposed to go see it."

Side by side they ran the gantlet of the porch again. The woman led them upstairs, through a long corridor into a room large and barren with sunlight—the gray carpeting, the bed under its patchwork quilt transfigured and consumed in this radiance, while the sand dunes brushed against the window outside and great glittering triangles of ocean reared up beyond.

"Oh, it's beautiful," Sally cried. "It's a beautiful room." The woman, who had set the key on the bureau, now departed, closing the door behind her. But Sally remained at the window, her lips parted in an expression almost of pain, and Tom after a second glance at the shore line, looked only at *her,* feeling as he had felt many times already that day, a sense of bewilderment. She turned and threw her arms around him. "Tom, this is a wonderful place," she said into his ear. "We can have such a lot of fun!" Then switching over to his other ear, whispered, "I love you, Tom!" and kissed him hard on the lips. But as soon as he responded, she kicked up her heels, swinging her full weight on his neck, and Tom, pulled off balance, clutched the bedpost to save himself. She broke away, bouncing on her toes.

"It's time to go swimming now," she announced. "I'm going to change my clothes."

Opening the suitcase, she took out the black iron skillet wrapped in newspaper, and next her bathing suit which still retained something of her shape, empty though it was. Holding the garment up by the shoulder straps, she made Tom a demure little curtsy, then two-stepped over to the bathroom, closing the door and leaving him to dress by himself. She reappeared, inside the bathing suit, over the outside of which she pulled on slacks and a blouse. They dumped the contents of Tom's canvas grip into one of the bureau drawers, stuffed into the grip the food they had bought and the skillet. As they went out through the lobby, Tom called "Good afternoon" to the woman at the desk as if he were an old resident; and he noticed that Sally's shyness too seemed to have slackened, for she gave back a haughty stare to the ladies on the porch in return for the cold eye they gave her.

A path between the dunes led down to the beach. Here a few people were scattered along the sand and a few swimmers splashed in and out of the low surf. Tom and Sally plodded past the last group of sun-bathers, set down their things, and ran out into the water. Diving through the breakers, they raced and splashed each other; but the ocean was too cold to stay in for long. They marked off squares on the beach and played hopscotch. They practiced broad jumps and hand stands. They spoke little to each other, and then only of small things—how to number the hopscotch squares, or whether it would be best to fry the onion with the beefsteak or slice it up raw. Tom no longer felt any need to fill in the silences. Since they had come to the hotel, something had changed between them; he found her eyes constantly fixed on his, serious and intent. Yet through the afternoon he scarcely touched her, or she him, though his fingers begged to; and only once as they floated in the deep water beyond the surf, he laid his hand against her, feeling under her breast the hammer of his own heart. The sun hung huge and orange over the western horizon.

What was she thinking, he kept wondering. Why had she agreed to come? Was she expecting that he would ask her to get married? Was that what she was waiting for? But she had set no conditions. Had she come for the fun of it then, simply because she wanted to? Could that be true? And if it were, she might as easily have come last month with Andermas, he thought, and be coming again next month with somebody whose name he had never even heard. So why not? He was amazed how little he knew of her.

The beach was almost empty, a few bathers only remaining at the water's edge like figures of string with thin shadows drawn across the sand behind them. Ocean and sky turned to gray and silver. Carrying their satchel of food, Tom and Sally hunted along the base of the dunes, gathering driftwood. They chose a hollow in which to build a fire, and he coaxed the flame through the polished sticks, watching the tiny green tongues chasing each other inside the larger orange flame. Still, he was glad to let the details of preparing the meal take charge of his thoughts. Sally fetched out the iron skillet, the beefsteak and the onion. Tom buttered the rolls. He noticed that he was hungry only when the smell of meat and frying onions reminded him he had not eaten since breakfast, and little enough then.

From behind the dunes, the moon, round as a dinner plate, sailed into the sky. The air had now turned cool, but the sand in the hollow retained something of the afternoon's warmth. He let the fire simmer down to a circle of sparks and they sat silent. In a few moments they would go back to the hotel, he thought, to the double bed belonging to the couple from Los Angeles. And here on the beach in the moonlight, the restraints they had imposed on themselves through the long day became meaningless. He leaned towards her until their lips met, till their arms went around each other. She was ready. No, she would not stop him even here, he thought.

A piping voice shattered the silence.

They jerked apart, Sally's hands springing down to the disarray of her slacks and blouse.

"*Mister Andrews,*" the voice wailed. "*Mister . . . Mister Andrews . . .*"

At the crest of the dune in the moonlight, Tom saw a figure, hunch-backed, like a dwarf wearing an enormous hat. "*Mister Andrews!*" The figure plunged abruptly in an avalanche of sand, and coming to rest only a few yards distant, revealed itself as a small Boy Scout, hatless and howling. Sally brushed him off, found his hat which she replaced on his head. She dried his tears, wiped his nose with a handkerchief he had produced from one of the many pockets of his uniform. The howls gradually subsided, and as Sally felt him over to make sure he had broken no bones, Tom could see her face twitching with the effort to smother her laughter. But she asked in a serious tone,

"How did you happen to come down this way?"

"I . . . I'm . . . looking . . . for Mister Andrews . . ."

"Is that your father?"

"He's . . . the . . . scout . . . master."

"Does he know you're here on the beach?" Sally asked.

"I . . . I . . . got lost."

A whistle sounded from above. They heard feet crashing through the brush that grew over the dunes, voices falsetto and bass from many directions.

"He ain't on the beach, Mr. Andrews."

"You found him yet?"

"Hey, Mr. Andrews, think he got drowned in the water?"

The little boy's face blossomed. He pulled away from Sally and scrambled out of the hollow. They heard his feet plopping in the sand, then a new series of shouts:

"Hey, guys, here he is."

"Hey, Stupe, whyn't you watch what you were doin'?"

"What kind of Scout are you, gettin' lost, hey, Stupe?"

An adult voice remonstrated, "All right, Rogers, let's not ride Lufkin. That could happen to anyone on a night like this. On the double, fellows, let's count off to make sure we haven't lost anybody else."

Tom and Sally kicked sand over the remaining sparks of their fire, gathered their things and headed back to the hotel. As they passed along the beach, they could see a swarm of small figures in a scramble of activity, digging, spreading blankets, jumping up and down; while a taller figure hurried this way and that swinging his arms. "Smooth out the sand under your blanket, Roxbury. . . . No, no, not here,

Lufkin, we're going to be sleeping here. . . . I'd put your feet down the slope, Cherney, not your head. . . ."

The face of the Bodensee Hotel rose from the sand hills in front of them. A few windows were lighted and a festoon of electric bulbs glowed rustily along the cornices of the porch. They had thought it was quite late, but as they came up the steps, there were the ladies still in their rocking chairs, reading and knitting under the blizzard of moths that whirled across the light bulbs. As if by signal, all the ladies halted what they had been doing and turned at once to fix their eyes on Tom and Sally.

"The Boy Scouts and the old ladies," she whispered. Inside the hotel door, she burst out laughing and clung to Tom's arm all the way up the stairs, laughing uncontrollably. But as soon as they entered their room, she turned businesslike. As methodically as if they had been living together for ten years, they set about preparing for bed. This, to Tom, seemed the most extraordinary aspect of the entire day. He stood at the basin in the bathroom brushing his teeth, just as he had brushed them nightly in his own boarding house, imagining night after night that he was about to share his bed with Sally Kallela; yet never once had he imagined that he would be brushing his teeth when that night came, or that she herself would be waiting her turn.

He opened the door into the bedroom, and she was there, cross-legged on the bed reading a book. The pang of pride made his eyes fill with tears. He turned quickly to hide his face, pretending to be looking for something on the bureau, and heard her get up and then the door of the bathroom close behind her.

Snapping off the light, he watched the darkness of the room fill slowly with moonlight. He raised himself on his elbow, saw through the window the patterns of shadow on the dunes, the silver triangles of the ocean. He listened for the sounds enmeshed in the night's silence—the wind, the hush and fall of surf, even the distant dwindling cries of the Boy Scout troop encamped on the sand. She had picked the little boy up like an older sister, trying to be kind, yet bursting with laughter. She had sat here on the bed, reading, not like the pictures he had made of her, but like any young girl anywhere, sitting on a bed reading. When they were back in San Francisco, he thought, he might buy a ring and ask her to wear it. For an engagement? All right, so they could be engaged if that was what she wanted—he could buy it on time, even with a sliver of a diamond. He tried then to remember what her fingers looked like, but could not.

Sally . . . Sally in the moonlight pulled off her clothes, having quite a tussle to peel her still damp bathing suit down over her buttocks. Having waited so long, they could wait no longer, and the making of love, quickly finished, was inevitably less than they had hoped. They fell asleep in each other's arms.

Tom waked in a panic. He had dreamed he was in the mill the day the old Swede was going to be killed on the conveyor, even hearing the whistle of the morning freight as it bucked out of the Saw Creek yards, southbound at daybreak. He struggled to the surface. Sitting straight up in bed, he heard the soft rolling of surf, noticed the gray light at the window. Then, remembering, he searched for her wildly, discovered her lying beside him again, a shoulder pearly and freckled at the edge of the blanket, her hair strewn over the pillow.

When he touched her, she woke with a little cry. But completely herself at once, she smiled up at him while he groped towards her as if from a distance; yet knowing there was nothing, nothing he could do to bring her close enough, to make certain even for once of himself, and of her. "Will you get married to me?" he whispered. "Now, I mean, Sally, now? As soon as we go back—before I leave?"

Her eyes, still smiling, remained puzzled, uncertain. "This is so sudden, Mr. O'Regan," she said. Then nodded her head violently, and reaching out, pulled him down against her.

PART 2

9

Leaving his partner still at work in the office, Walter Stone walked out with Garnet to the corner of California Street. Here the newsboys surrounded them yelling their extras.

"Yanks blast Jap fleet!"

"Big Pacific Battle!"

Garnet swept them aside with a gesture of his arm. To Walter he said, "We'll grind the little bastards up like hamburger. They don't stand a chance against American production."

"I hope I'm not taking you out of your way?" Walter asked.

"No, no. I kept you overtime. I'll drive you to your plane if you want."

He thought the other was going to insist on driving to the airport and braced himself to refuse. This was the kind of man who would insist, he thought, simply for the satisfaction of forcing his way over someone else. It occurred to him that he was on the edge of being afraid of the man, as if he were feeling an echo of the kind of fears roused in a small boy by a slightly larger boy. He glanced at the other as they stood waiting on the corner—at the expanse of shoulder and chest and paunch clothed in the flashily cut double-breasted suit, at the square face with its blue shaven cheeks. The idea of physical fear repelled Walter and angered him, and the man himself he found less and less to his liking; while at the same time he could not conceal from himself a sense of respect—even envy.

The man took out a cigar, offered one to Walter which Walter declined, then bit the end off his own, struck a match, puffed a cloud of smoke over his head. He carried himself with the air of a champion prize fighter.

Walter knew that he himself presented an appearance which often intimidated other people, and that he used this deliberately despite the fact that he always felt contemptuous of the persons upon whom it proved most effective. For it was a trick that should be easy enough to see through, a manner inherited from the medium he had been born into. It served for a suit of armor, insulating the wearer from direct contact with other human animals. Definitely a professional asset.

Even this man Garnet, he noted, circled him at a respectful distance, and he was glad of that. He had no desire to draw closer.

Garnet, he thought, was like a bull on the open range—a stupid, powerful animal. Yet that was not true, he was far from stupid. The speed with which he had picked up the central points of the analysis this afternoon indicated a shrewd, disciplined mind. It was not that he was stupid, but rather that he was single and undivided; and this to a person as departmentalized as himself might easily seem the equivalent of stupidity. Could one imagine a bull pausing to question his impulses? Faltering in mid-course to investigate the relation between his own roaring and some abstract principle of goodness or truth? Here was a man whose only apparent principles were his will and his impulse. Was that a symptom of stupidity? He remembered a portrait of one of his own great-grandfathers, a stocky, bald-headed figure in Daniel Webster collar who had come down from New Hampshire to set up a leather tanning business outside Boston. That must have been a man like Garnet. There, the car was coming.

A black Chrysler pulled to the curb. The garage attendant unhitched his three-wheel motor bike from the rear bumper and sputtered off down California Street. Garnet moved under the steering wheel and Walter sat beside him.

"So you think I'm primed?" Garnet asked.

"I would say you were well prepared for them."

"I appreciate your help, Stone. I've paid some lawyers some fancy fees and gotten damn little for it. Where does your bus take off from—the St. Francis?"

"Right across from it." So they were not going to have to argue over driving to the airport. He relaxed slightly.

"What do you think of the buggy?" Garnet asked.

"Beautiful. Brand-new, isn't it?"

"One month old, and you got to know your way around to get ahold of a new car right now. I traded in my '41 Packard. Believe me, this has got Packard beat." Walter had wondered if a labor official might not feel slightly sensitive driving a car like this one, patent-leather black and polished chrome, conspicuous consumption with white-wall tires; but Garnet apparently did not. He sounded like a boy talking about his new bicycle. They rolled uptown on California, turned left and left again toward Union Square. "I put thirty-five, forty thousand miles a year on a car," Garnet explained. "Before gas rationing come along, anyhow. It don't pay me to buy anything but the best. That goes for legal advice too, Stone."

Walter made no effort to acknowledge the compliment.

"There's hardly a month goes by, Stone, I don't have to go up there to Sacramento. Or Washington sometimes. Maybe it's a new law on accident insurance. Or an amendment to the State Labor Code. Or War Labor Board hearing or whatever the hell. And I tell you there're some smart cookies up there, trained lawyers almost all of 'em. But they don't get to tangle me up very often. And I never went beyond the sixth grade."

Walter could hear the man's pride challenging through the harsh earnestness of his voice.

"I never had no education at all, Stone. Went to work pushin' a broom in a boiler factory when I was thirteen years old. And I can take these lawyers, some of 'em that went to school for thirty years, and back 'em clean out the door. But I got to have the guts of the thing right in my hand. I got to have it clear!" He lifted his hand from the steering wheel with the fist clenched. "I could take those bills you went through, and if I had a day, or a day and a half, I'd go through 'em myself. I'd get it all out clear just the way I want it. Only I got no time for that. These hearings are a side line with me, Stone. I got to do it, but I haven't got time for it, that's about the size of it. You know, the Shipbuilders' Union tripled its membership out here on the Coast since this time last year, Stone, what do you think of that? Well, that's my baby. Los Angeles, San Francisco, Portland Oregon, Seattle. Then maybe I get a telegram sayin' get the hell back to Washington D.C. for a national conference. So how'm I goin' to take a day and a half to study up on amendments to the Labor Code, State of California, you tell me that?"

Walter shook his head.

"That's why it's worth my while payin' fancy prices for a lawyer. I don't mind the price if I get the service. You'd be surprised some of the fancy lawyers we've had on the pay roll, Stone, and damn few was worth their journeyman's pay. Maybe yes, maybe no, Mr. Garnet; a little bit of *if* and a little *maybe*. What am I goin' to do with that? I listen to 'em, I don't know as much as before I started. . . ."

"Many legal problems are too complex to summarize very simply," Walter said.

"You think I don't know that! All I want is for the man to get ahold of the guts of it and put it out where I can see it, without me havin' to take the time and do the diggin' for myself all over again. That's what I want with a lawyer. . . . All right, here you are, Stone. I appreciate your help. I like to do business with you and Chantry. Give my regards to the Missis."

Walter stepped down in front of the hotel and watched the automobile glide off around the corner. A remarkable individual, he thought; not at all what he would have believed a labor leader would be like—before he had come to know a few of them. He had thought of the labor movement as a Cause, and labor leaders as being, or assuming to be, crusaders for that Cause. He had thought of labor as being the Other Side. If one side were corrupt and petty, the other must hold opposite qualities.

Perhaps so. But Garnet was no crusader. Garnet was more like one of the characters out of the Renaissance, a Machiavelli or a Benvenuto Cellini. If Garnet were to write his autobiography—and he scarcely would have been surprised to learn that he was doing so—one would find the word "I" twenty times to the page as in Cellini's; and the book would be a mass of the most despicable bragging about his own courage, strength, and resourcefulness. Yet most of it true.

He was glad to be rid of the man. For the time being. Then, as he stood waiting for the limousine, he wondered how Garnet and Kallela might get along if they ever happened to be thrown together. Like two cats in a barrel, precisely because of their many points of resemblance. Both were domineering, self-confident, aggressive. But beyond that, they were opposite numbers. Who could imagine Kallela driving a brand-new Chrysler; or Garnet up in Saw Creek working the gang saw in a lumber mill? Obviously

Garnet, who had done plenty of manual labor in his younger days, took pains to let no one forget the fact—that was part of his stock in trade; but it was equally clear that he had no intention of returning to the conditions from which he had come. He had found his footing too easily, as it were naturally, on the upper slopes of Olympus.

Walter examined the contrast between these two—the one figure straight out of the Renaissance; the other straight out of Cromwell's Ironsides: utterly incompatible. And somewhere between these two poles, repelled almost equally by both, himself, who hailed neither from the Renaissance nor the Puritan Revolution; a slightly decrepit winter apple left over from the deflowering of New England. The limousine rounded the corner of the park and he took his place in line. As for Garnet, he thought, despite the flamboyant characteristics, he was a man who was doing a job. In Sacramento tomorrow, Garnet would throw his immense power and energy into the contest to which he applied himself day after day, year after year. And the issue? The issues were a few dollars, a few days' leisure, a few extra years of life perhaps, for a few thousand workingmen, their wives and children. This was simple and straight. Whatever Garnet might be, this was the reason of his going to Sacramento. And whatever Walter Stone might be, he was part of it. The limousine moved slowly through traffic, crossing Market and rolling out past the factories and warehouses toward the airport.

To this extent, uncontestably, he had advanced himself.

The terminal was crowded as it always was nowadays with mothers lugging babies and officers flashing top-priority travel orders, all in a desperate scramble to board the next mainliner for Chicago or Washington. One more installment in the continuous series of home-front farces: like the mayor's air raids, he thought, and the brand-new siren which no one had been able to hear. Or the lights suddenly thrown off in the streets leaving wretched pedestrians to sprain their ankles and crack their shins while overhead, whisky and cigarettes continued to illuminate the heavens for a hundred miles. And in the morning, army and navy both gravely assured the newspapers there really might have been unknown planes.

He stepped aside as the throng stampeded past him when the gates were thrown open for the nonstop to Chicago. Fortunately there was no great pressure of travel on the local Nevada flights. His Reno plane was called on time and it seemed to Walter they had barely risen from the twilight that lay over the bay before he saw the granite cliffs and forested shoulders of the Sierra rocking under the wing. Yet behind the farce, the liturgy was real enough. Ships had been torpedoed in sight of the coast. And on the islands— out on the islands, they must be pouring in men like the Argonne and Chateau Thierry and Belleau Wood. God help them. He thought of his son Wendel, suddenly glad that he *was* in Washington, safely ensconced for the time being at least with his briefcase and his lieutenant's commission. However, Kallela would be enjoying no such satisfaction over his new son-in-law—would he?—the boy must have spent his honeymoon in boot camp. Someday, Walter told himself, you should entertain Kallela with a brief description of your own military career. That certainly ought to bring out the anarchist in him. The bright young shavetail touring the cafés of Montmartre in uniform never once muddied by the trenches. A soldier of good fortune, he had come too late for Belleau Wood, and only remained in Paris to study for six months at the Sorbonne.

So it was here again, the wheel swung full turn. And what would this one bring, a beginning or an ending? For whom? Or was there any difference? I am alpha and omega, the beginning and the end. They coasted down towards the flats of the desert. A checkerboard of colored lights swept beneath. They plunged, dropped, bumped to a halt on the runway of the Reno airport.

His wife Sylvia was there with the car to meet him. She was perfect and poised as usual, and when he kissed her he caught the familiar smell of her perfume and powder— and the dry martinis. They drove through town, followed the westbound highway a few miles farther to the railroad division point of Signal Springs, then swung up over the line of hills to the guest ranch which overlooked the valley beyond. An ancient porter hobbled forward to carry Walter's brief case. They crossed the patio with its fountain and palm trees, circled the floodlighted swimming pool to their cottage.

"Are you hungry?" she asked. "Do you want to eat now or wait for the midnight smorgasbord?"

"I had a sandwich on the plane. I can wait."

She sat on the arm of the sofa watching him expectantly. As if to say what further does the master require of me, he thought; I'm interrupting her routine, taking her away from her game—and from the bar.

"I think I'll go for a swim," he said. "Do you want to come?"

"I don't believe I do, Walter."

He took his bathing trunks out of the closet and she suggested, "Why don't you swim and shower and join me over at the ranch house?"

"All right. Is John coming tomorrow?"

"Oh, yes indeed, John's coming. He phoned twice last week to make sure you'd be here. And then dropped over this morning and left a note. It's on the bureau. There's a letter from Wendel and Carol too." And as he turned toward the bureau, she said, "I'll see you in a few minutes?"

"Yes, I'll be right over."

John's letter was scrawled in pencil on the stationery of

the County Historical and Geological Museum. *I want to go up into Topaz Canyon in Creosote Range tomorrow,* the note said. *I'll stop for you at 6:30. I'll bring the food.*

Walter smiled and picked up the letter from his son, but laid it aside thinking he would read it afterwards. No one was swimming as he went out to the pool. No one was even in sight. The water, lighted from below, lay as still as if no swimmer had ever broken its surface. Walter could hear music and voices from the far side of the patio, from the bar and the gaming tables in the ranch house. He plunged in, swam the length and back, opening his eyes into the light-filled water which swirled in an effervescence of bubbles. Like swimming in a glass of warm champagne.

When he climbed out, the night had taken on a pleasantly cool tingle. He turned back to the cottage, stopping for a moment to look out through a break in the hedge of aspen trees at the desert beyond. There was no moon, but the night was not dark; the sand seemed to glow with a light of its own, silhouetting the mounds of the creosote bushes, and he could see the shape of the land itself, a fan with its fronds stretching down into the pale sea, the salt flats of the valley bottom. Close at hand, the clay hills came shouldering up alongside the lighted oasis of the rancho, while off to the east rose the jagged peaks of the desert mountains under the sky and the stars. That must be the direction of John's Creosote Range, he thought.

And John himself would roll around at six-thirty sharp, indignant if he were not ready and waiting. Then they would rumble off in John's truck, from the highway to some wheel track, till they reached a point where the truck could travel no farther. After that they went on afoot, old John scaling the canyon sides with his geologist's pick, searching for rock specimens, Indian relics, traces of ancient mining operations. This was one of the few persons he had ever known, Walter thought, who seemed to have struck a satisfactory bargain with life—even with old age. John knew his way about the desert as familiarly as Walter knew the labyrinth of his law books, and loved the desert as Walter never had loved the law; while something of its splendor entered into the man, just as something of the vicious pettiness of law entered into those who spent their lives pursuing it. Perhaps, after all, the earth was the only proper pursuit of man. How could a landscape, an agglomeration of rock in various stages of decomposition, contain such ecstasies of perception? What would Thoreau have made of this?

He himself had always fixed his vision of beauty by Thoreau's description of Walden Pond with its lush foliage, and only in the past few years had the desert taken a grip upon him; on Sylvia and himself both, he thought, in different ways. Very different. Yet essentially it must be the same thing that touched them both: an irony, a mocking voice. The flower blossoming for an hour after the rain in a cleft of some rock that measured time by the passage of ice ages. Or the oasis here, this artificial blossom with its palm trees, the emerald pool, the music, lights, laughter, planted—for how brief an instant?—on the unchanging slope of the desert. But beneath was a deeper mockery, a sequence of meanings within meanings, for the slope of the desert was itself a moving current, carrying the mountains down into the salt flat at the rate of a few inches a century. Mountains, flats, clay hills, all were the waves and troughs of an ocean as restless as the Pacific. When Thoreau was at Walden Pond, he thought, the first covered wagons had come crawling across the salt flats. The same flats. The gray lake he stood looking down upon.

Shivering slightly, he wrapped the towel about his shoulders and returned to the cottage. There he took a shower, shaved, dressed.

He went to the ranch house where a few couples were dancing on the terrace. But most of the guests were inside around the roulette and poker tables, and there he found Sylvia.

"I'm doing very well tonight," she told him. "I'm twelve dollars ahead."

"Time to quit."

She pointed to the small stack of chips in front of her. "When I lose this, I quit. But if I win, I cash half and put it away. That's my system. Want to join me?"

"Maybe so. I'll walk around a little first."

He bought himself a drink and strolled among the tables, watching the games and the gamblers. He could see that a considerable amount of money was changing hands across some of the tables, but everyone was quiet and well-behaved. Here at the rancho, unlike the raucous palaces of Reno, pretense was maintained that the gambling was merely a pastime, a social interlude. Yet many of these people would sit for twelve hours straight, scarcely stirring from their tables except to fetch a drink or a sandwich. He could see his wife, rapt in her concentration on the board: she spread her bets, waited for the ivory ball to choose its number; she had won again, she divided her chips, laid one pile aside, set out the others for the next spin.

He wondered how much she had drunk this evening. She remained perfectly controlled. He knew that she never allowed herself to come to the game room till after dinner. Her "system" set a limit to her losses; and these averaged over a two-week stay were expensive, but not terribly expensive. *What else could I do that would cost so little?* she had asked him. *If I even went to the theater in San Francisco, wouldn't it cost more?* Her gambling was like her drinking; she went so far but no further; she rationed it to squeeze out the last drop of satisfaction. She was like a person walking along the parapet of a high building merely for the excitement. But *why?* he burst out inside himself, for God's sake, *why?* Was it simply because he had insisted on their leaving New York those many years ago? Was it the failure of her pilgrimage to Hollywood where she had tried to continue her dancing and not succeeded? Was it the coming of the child she had never wanted? Or had all this been implicit in the first glance, the very first words exchanged between them? He returned to her across the room, drew a chair beside hers, bought a few dollars worth of chips which he lost on three spins.

"All right," she cried. "That's enough for the evening. Good night, Charles," she said to the croupier; and they went outside to the terrace where the waiters were setting up the smorgasbord.

Afterwards, when they returned to the cottage, Walter noticed on the bureau the letter from Wendel and Carol which he had forgotten to read earlier. He glanced through it. They had discovered a cute apartment in Arlington (Carol wrote) after a terrible amount of hunting, and now they would be able to move out of the downtown hotel, which would be a great relief for them both. Wendel found his work very interesting, she herself was researching for the Voice of America. They had just received a swell letter from Father (*her* father, obviously) with important news. Father wanted to discuss Wendel's joining the firm, after the war of course, and Wendel felt this was an outstanding opportunity. "Wendel," she wrote, "is very anxious to know what his father thinks . . ."

Was he? Then why didn't he write and ask?

He finished the letter, dropped it back on the bureau top. Sylvia, who was reading a book in bed, asked, "Well, so what *does* Father think?"

"He thinks it's an outstanding opportunity too."

"Oh, Walter," she cried, "you never change. You're like a signal that always flashes the same light. You've made it very hard for Wendel. You chose the exact moment he was announcing his engagement to Carol to break with Richards—"

"I didn't choose the moment," Walter said. "And if I'd waited longer it would have been worse."

"I'm *glad* he's going in with Richards."

Choosing his words carefully, Walter told her, "I expected Richards to make that offer. Yes, it *is* an opportunity for a young man. Because I never got along with Richards is no reason why Wendel shouldn't. I'm sure he'll do very well."

She was watching him with an oddly detached expression. "You're happier now, aren't you?" she asked. "I mean since you made the change. It's been a good change, for you?"

Immediately touched by her question, he said, "I think it was." Had he only made it sooner, he thought, it might have been better for all three of them. Sitting on the foot of his bed, he started to tell her what had been in the forefront of his thoughts: about the man Garnet and the legislation Garnet was going to Sacramento to oppose. But the slightly pained smile on her face as she shut her book and turned to listen told him how uninterested she was.

He snapped off the light and got into bed.

10

On the nights she went to the welding class, Joyce would find Charlie Gammon waiting for her on the steps and often they stopped for coffee with Reverend Beezely and the schoolteacher from Memphis. The white girl who shared their workbench sometimes joined them also. Being, as she said, recently married, she never could resist showing off her rings—a wedding band and an engagement ring with a tiny diamond. The engagement ring, however, was really cheating, she whispered to Joyce, because her husband had bought it after they were married, not before; and added, blushing, that he had not had time before. Now he had already left to go in the navy—though the girl seemed to take this cheerfully enough, and Joyce hesitated whether to feel sorry for her, or envious. But as they sat chatting at the cafeteria table, she easily understood why the other so often glanced down at her hand, as if to make certain the rings were still there.

Afterwards, having finished the coffee and doughnuts, they all departed in their various directions—Reverend Beezely to his shipyard, the schoolteacher to Oakland, the white girl to San Martin; while Joyce and Charlie boarded the streetcar for Fillmore.

On all other nights of the week, Charlie arrived at the Hendersons' at half-past five, scarcely allowing her time to be out of the bathtub and into a dress. With only a week or two remaining of his sick leave, he insisted, there was no sense in his wasting any of it. He had caught pneumonia on a voyage to Alaska, she learned, and after four weeks in the hospital, had been released to rest up before going to sea again. She worried whether it might not be too much for him to be out every night as they were. But a cheerful mind, he assured her, was the best way to keep healthy; and he had not felt so cheerful in years. As far as resting went, couldn't he sleep all day while she was at work in the shipyard?

She knew he was supposed to return to the hospital for a checkup at the end of the rest period—after that, he told her, it might take six or seven days for him to catch a ship. "So I'm putting in an official application for a date *every* night until I ship out. How about that?"

"I'll have to check my date book." She fetched out the little memorandum pad she carried in her handbag, and holding it so he couldn't see the blank pages, studied through it and then shook her head. "I'm afraid I'm booked up on all of those evenings."

"Couldn't you shift things around a little bit?"

"I could *try*," she said.

Sometimes they had dinner at restaurants in the Fillmore district, sometimes went to an Italian café in North Beach. Here Charlie seemed to know most of the people who stopped by; Joe Baratia, the art teacher, and his wife, often joined them, and they would wind up with a noisy party, everybody laughing and singing at once. The café had a piano—no juke box, but it actually did have a piano, an old upright like the one in Signal Springs, only worse. After the Baratias learned from Charlie that Joyce could play, they teased her into banging out accompaniments for ballads and spirituals and hymns, and for the folk songs from different languages which Joe Baratia collected and brought with him.

Joyce was delighted by these evenings. But her favorite of the places they went was still a Chinese restaurant near Stockton Street. The color and strangeness of the Chinese section fascinated her. She and Charlie would peer into the store windows, stopping sometimes to buy a fan or package of paper flowers to send off to her mother in Signal Springs. When it grew dark, they turned back to their restaurant which was down a steep flight of stairs from the sidewalk. The waiter greeted them with nods and smiles; he never bothered to ask what they wanted, and they could not have told him anyway, but he simply confirmed how much they wished to pay that evening—"One dol-*lar*? One dol-*lar* and half?"—and brought platters of food till their table was loaded. Inside the bamboo-curtained booth they would sit talking long after they had finished their meal, holding hands under the table and drinking tea. Now and then the waiter thrust his head through the curtain, hefting the teapot to see if it needed refilling.

Joyce had never talked much about herself to anyone before. She knew that Charlie understood she wanted to talk, but was too shy to do so without prodding; for he drew her on with questions until she had told him about Signal Springs, and the house she had lived in, and the school, and about her father and mother. He on the other hand needed no urging at all when it came to talking. He said he never would get to be much of an artist because he let it all run out his mouth. But Joyce did not take that too seriously, since he had already assured her he intended to become a famous painter after the war. This he had said as a joke, but she was certain he believed he really would; and she believed it too.

Having known him three weeks at most, she felt as if she had known him all her life. In the shipyard during the day or lying in bed at night, she imagined him in a hundred different pictures which sprang almost as if from her own memory. He was running barefoot through the dust of a Texas farmyard—crawling under the barbed-wire fence, racing across the weed patch with chickens squawking out of his path. She saw the drab, dusty, smoke-overcast cities where the Texas oil ships came in, and he was down in the galley scrubbing pots while the ship moved through the channel between the oil-storage tanks. When the ship began to roll, he stared out the porthole and saw the ocean, a blue circle of empty horizon, waves splattering against the glass.

So she followed him through the steps that had brought him from a forty-acre dust farm in Texas to the door of the School of Industrial Arts where she had first met him.

San Francisco she saw again not through her own eyes, but through his. She herself had seen it from the deck of the Oakland ferryboat on the day she had taken the train from Signal Springs. The city had risen before her in the sunlight, beautiful as a piece of music. But Charlie had first come into San Francisco one winter morning when there were bread lines two blocks long down the Embarcadero and rain lying so low the sea gulls vanished from sight when they roosted on the lampposts. He had wanted to leave as quick as he could, he told her. But there were no jobs on the ships. He worked on WPA, finally deciding to go to high school at night. There he became acquainted with several young fellows from the WPA Art Project and made up his mind he ought to become an artist himself.

"Just as easy as that!" he cried. "Struck me as a simple way to earn a living"—and they leaned together over the table, laughing till their foreheads bumped. It seemed to Joyce that everything he told her about himself was in pictures as if he thought and spoke not in words at all but in the bright colors of sunlight, or the heavy colors of the old houses in the rain; and listening to him was like hanging up a whole gallery of paintings. He saw things in pictures, just as she sometimes heard them—or felt them—in music.

"Why, that's wonderful to hear," he cried, when she told him of this discovery. "I must be a born artist after all!"

It was in the Art Project he had met Joe Baratia, and later followed along as student when Joe went to teach at the California College of Art. In the art classes, he told her, he had been quick to catch on, picked up scholarships and part-time jobs, stayed there studying and painting until the war came and he went back to sea.

And after the war? Well, who could guess what things would be like after the war? One thing was certain, there was not much chance a man would make a living just by painting. He had planned sometimes on going to school long enough to get a teacher's certificate; and other times thought the hell with school, an artist was better off without it, he'd hunt up some kind of a job, any job for a meal ticket.

She saw him grinning at her across the table. He filled the cups again, picked up one of the rice cookies with chopsticks, but halfway to his mouth lost the cookie which fell dead center into his teacup. "Bull's-eye!" he exclaimed, fishing out the soggy remains with his fingers. "Or maybe— maybe I could hunt up some young lady with a trade, shipfitter or welder, some line that pays enough for two. Think so?"

She shook her head, sparkling with pleasure inside.

Midway through the week, Charlie informed her he had bought tickets for the Friday night symphony; and Friday afternoon, home from work, Joyce dressed again in her graduation gown. They ate dinner with the Baratias in North Beach and went together to the opera house. The seats were at the top of the balcony, and they rode the elevator to its last stop, then climbed another flight of stairs beyond. Charlie and Joe Baratia were joking about the altitude—no place for anybody with a weak ticker—while Joyce, as she had known beforehand, was now unable to utter a word.

From this height she gazed downward into the brightly lighted chasm of the stage, at the rows of empty chairs where only the harp and round-bellied kettledrums were yet in position. The musicians at last came filing in. She watched them shuffle to their places, counted the number for each instrument, heard them fitfully tuning their violins, sounding out horns, plucking a startled squawk from a cello. As the audience coughed and hushed itself into silence, the conductor mounted his stand. Face to face with that glittering bank of bald heads, white shirt fronts, poised instruments, he slowly lifted his arms. How could he dare give the signal, she wondered, and the bows of the toy violins rose and fell together.

Into the web of their playing she followed, fitting her steps to theirs. Patterns shaped themselves, precise as lacework, the shadows of leaves in the moonlight, each note anticipated with indrawn breath and eyes now closing. Oh, God, she thought, oh, God to have made such a thing as this! The bright web in the darkness, the heart singing like a violin string. No, wait, wait, under the silver pattern the sound of wind and distance, the louder song rising; and she, breathing deep, as if breathing the sound itself, swept upward by the music, the speck of foam on the wave, the tatter of cloud across the desert sky.

Yet even as she was whirled up and even as she was carried helplessly beyond herself, she felt the music had become her own. She felt as if she were making it, not they, she with her own fingers, the music she had played for herself alone because only she could ever hear it, distant and magnificent beyond the twanging keyboard of the old piano. How could she have believed she had left that behind? No, no, nothing could be left behind, nothing was ever lost or forgotten. Each day remained always, she rejoiced, though she had called good-by from the station platform; though she had waved from the window and run to the vestibule at the end of the coach, waving as the train rolled clanging its bell slowly past the little houses and back yards of the town. The upper half of the vestibule door had stood open, she leaned out, feeling spray from the steam of the engine blow back against her face, while the lumberyards, the freight sheds with their shiny roofs she knew so well came rolling by. The flats of the desert stretched out beyond; and the mountains. And oh, it was springtime! Over the gray sand lay the haze of green, the honey-like fragrance of the desert drifting to her between the sharp whiffs of train smoke.

Nothing could be lost. She saw the clump of aspen trees on the opposite slope of the greasewood flat marking where their house stood. She saw the wheel tracks meandering down across the flat. Faster and faster, the telegraph poles rushing towards her, the *Look Out for Trains* sign jumping out from the line of poles, the way the little road turned as it swung up the embankment. For an instant, beneath her very eyes, the crossing itself, the ruts and gravel, the place they had stood so many mornings waiting for the express. He would never stand there again. Yet somehow must always be there, since he had been there once, standing looking anxiously at his gold railroad watch. Oh, good-by, good-by. A rampart of the hills swung across blocking her view. The wind whipped against her face. Laugh-

ing and crying at the same time, she drew back, the tears
streaming down her cheeks.

Finale. Up and up and the descent. Silence, leaving the
structure like some mountain in the distance, unchanging
and indestructible. The lights rose in the concert hall; the
pit, the galleries applauding, the conductor bowing from
the stage.

Charlie Gammon turned to look at Joyce. She was hunched
forward in her seat, breathing rapidly as if she had just
run a race, the tears had left tracks through the powder of
her cheeks. And she was laughing now, clapping, laughing,
trying to catch her breath. She never had been to a symphony
before, she whispered to him.

They returned with the Baratias to their studio where
Charlie had taken her to the party the first evening they
had gone out together. Tonight however there were only
Joe and his wife and one other couple who joined them
after the symphony. Charlie at once became involved in a
discussion about painting, while Joyce, beside him, traced
out the moving patterns of coals in the fireplace. Occasionally she glanced over her shoulder at the windows through
which the fog looked directly down at them. The room was
dim and quiet; a beautiful room, she thought; drifting
within reach of the near-by voices, she let the music she
had heard that night sing inside her again. Yet it must be
awfully late, she supposed. The Hendersons would certainly
be angry. She ought to go in the kitchen and look at the
clock, perhaps ought to begin telling Charlie it was time to
take her home. As she leaned toward him, anticipating his
protests and the quick pressure of his arm against her
shoulder, she wondered, why must I do that? Who says I
must? What do I care how late it is? she thought. She sat
straight up then, laughing, held her glass out to be refilled

from the gallon wine jug. Joe Baratia, red-faced and bristly mustached, had begun proffering snatches of song in his operatic baritone; and Joyce moved over at once to the piano.

Later, Joe Baratia fetched out a package of drawings Charlie had left with him from his last trip. These were pencil sketches, half finished, a few lines shadowed in— here a man swinging at the end of a rope, painting the smokestack of a ship; and other pictures showing men working over a cannon, and two young sailors playing checkers by the ship's rail, and a waiter stepping through a doorway carrying a great tray-load of dishes. As they handed the pages back and forth, Joe Baratia kept insisting,

"You ought to be painting again, Charlie."

"How can I paint on a ship, man?"

"You did these on the ship."

"I can make a drawing in a couple of minutes, all I need is a pad and pencil, the guys come around, get a big charge out of it." Joyce pictured this as he spoke, the very people out of his drawings crowding around him, catching themselves in those quick lines as they peered down over his shoulder. "But I got no time on shipboard for painting," Charlie said. "No place even to set up an easel, Joe, you know that."

"You been ashore at least a month. Why don't you work some of this stuff up?"

"I got different things to look after this trip."

As Charlie gathered his drawings together, Joyce saw the others smiling in her direction; but she did not care. She held up the package while Charlie tied the strings around it; and when Mrs. Baratia went to the kitchen to make coffee and scramble some eggs, Joyce, getting up to help her, saw through the windows that it was daybreak. Charlie noticed at the same time. He pretended to be staring at his wrist watch (where his wrist watch would have been, if he had been wearing one) in consternation. Together they stepped out on the roof behind the studio to watch the gray light touching the buildings below them along the water front; in such softness, she thought, and such silence, this magic city was engulfed in its glowing mist. How could I ever have found the place, she wondered, after waiting so long? Oh, anywhere, anywhere the train takes you, honey, anywhere. . . . He kissed her and Joyce returned the kiss passionately, declaring inside herself, no, this isn't a dream, not any longer, this is what it's really like, Charlie, Charlie, I'm in love! She clung to him, holding up her mouth to his.

They went down to catch the Columbus Avenue street-car, and long before they reached Fillmore, it was broad daylight. Joyce opened the downstairs door with her latch-key, Charlie following after her to the foot of the stairs.

"Think they'll be mad?" he asked.

"I don't care if they are."

"Want me to come up and soothe them?"

She shook her head. "They're probably still asleep."

"I'll wait here for a few minutes," he suggested. "If they throw you out you can come live at my house." She laughed, knowing he lived at the YMCA, and they kissed once more and she ran up the stairs. She tiptoed across the kitchen and across the parlor, but just as she reached for the knob of her own bedroom door, she heard Mrs. Henderson cry out in a frightened voice,

"Is that you, Joyce?"

"That's me, ma'am."

Silence.

"Just woke up thirsty and went to get a drink of water, Mrs. Henderson." Oh, she'll *never* believe that! Joyce quickly closed the bedroom door behind her. Dropping down on the bed, she pressed her face into the pillow to smother her laughter.

11

For the final session of the welding class, they went down to the shop in the basement as usual, but no one did much work that evening. The instructor, visiting from one bench to another, repeated the latest shipyard jokes, asked where each one expected to hire out, warned them not to fall for any sucker tricks when they went up for their tests. He never liked to see too many old students come back to take his course over again—that was hard on a teacher's reputation; and wishing them all good luck, he dismissed the class half an hour early. However, they used up the rest of the time packing their helmets and coveralls, goggles and gloves, saying good-by several times inside and once more on the steps of the school.

Charlie was waiting there for them.

With Reverend Beezely and the white girl, Sally O'Regan, they crossed the street to the cafeteria for their coffee.

"This will be my last night waiting on counter," Sally O'Regan announced. "For the rest of my life, I hope, believe me, if only I can pass that damn test tomorrow. I'm going right over when I get off work in the morning. Shall we go together?" she asked.

But Joyce said she had to report to her job and request time off from her foreman; and the Reverend explained that he was waiting on the application he had put in at the housing project because he wanted to move his family to San Martin Village before he switched to a job in the shipyard over there. Joyce noticed that he seemed to have no doubt of his ability to pass the welding test; however she was relieved that Sally O'Regan appeared less confident, because this kept company with her own uneasiness. Yet she had not wanted to make any arrangement for going to the test *with* Sally. She knew she would do better alone—and hoped no one else from the welding class would show up at the same time.

Sally O'Regan had just received her first letter from her husband, she told them, in which he wrote that he had been assigned to the armed guard pool, although she did not know exactly what that was. Charlie explained it meant he would be one of the navy gunners aboard the merchant ships. "Why, I'll probably run into him myself one of these days, Mrs. O'Regan," he cried. "What does he look like?"

Medium height with dark curly hair, Sally said; and whispered to Joyce, "I want to pass that test tomorrow so I can write him I'm really a welder. I bet that'll take him down a peg or two."

They parted, laughing, at the streetcar stop.

She and Charlie rode out to the Hendersons' where they sat with their arms around each other on the bottom step of the stairway. He left early, not to keep her up too late the night before her examination, he said. But in her room, when she turned off the light and lay down in bed, her anxiety overcame her at once and she knew it would have been better had she stayed longer with him. Trapped halfway between sleeping and waking, she labored the whole night long welding seams. Or trying to. But the rod refused to melt. The arc was never hot enough, the machine refused to operate properly. The metal peeled off in flakes like hard butter instead of flowing out as it should, and when finally the examiner came to her, the two pieces of steel she had been supposed to weld fell apart of their own weight. By daybreak she had repeated this process four or five thousand times. She was exhausted, and convinced that she was certain to fail the test.

But she passed it. Before noon that morning she was back with her cleanup gang, carrying the welder's certificate in her handbag. The other women were jubilant; and even the sour, straw-headed carpenter congratulated her. After work, Mr. Henderson drove her to the Welders' and Shipbuilders' Union Hall out on Folsom Street in San Francisco.

She joined the line near the front entrance where a sign announced: *Welders' Clearances Issued Here*. A man who had been standing at the doorway came over to her, tapped her on the shoulder and motioned her upstairs. On the second floor, she found another window and another line, but here the people waiting were all colored. The man at the window was white, and Joyce could see that those ahead of her in the line were passing him money, for their dues payments, she supposed. When her turn came, she held out her welder's certificate and opened her billfold.

"We got no call for women welders right now," the man told her. "Got a long waiting list. Put your name down if you want." He passed her a sheet of paper on a clipboard. "We'll send you a card if something comes up. Don't know when that'll be. If you go around to the laborers' union, they probably put you to work right away."

Joyce shook her head and went down the stairs, back to the car where Mr. Henderson was waiting.

"That don't sound right to me," Mr. Henderson said.

When Charlie came for her at six, he threw up his hands and shouted, "My God Almighty, what a dirty run-around!" Charlie took her out to the liquor store on the corner where there was a phone booth, and they found Sally O'Regan's telephone from information, and called, waking her. The union had given her a welder's clearance right away, she told them, and she was supposed to start work that night at midnight.

"We better get ahold of the Rev," Charlie said.

Reverend Beezely was asleep too when they came, but his wife waked him and he padded out of the bedroom in a pair of straw sandals and a dressing gown that struck him above the knees, while the sleeves ran out halfway between his elbows and his wrists. He sat rubbing his eyes with his knuckles as Charlie told him what had happened, and Joyce kept saying to his wife Janet, "Oh, we shouldn't have waked him up!"

"I expected this might happen," the Reverend Beezely said. "Yes. Don't worry about waking me, it's almost my supper time in any case." And turning to Charlie: "You asked the other evening why I was leaving my soft berth, as you like to put it, Charles, to go into the shipyard."

Charlie nodded and placed his hands with the fingers together in a gesture of repentance.

"Perhaps we'd all like some coffee?" the Reverend suggested. "This is happening every day, in every shipyard all over the West Coast," he told them. "Our people work as laborers, janitors, they work in the cleanup gangs; and nobody minds that. But as soon as we learn the higher skills, as soon as we seek admission to the skilled trade unions, then our difficulty begins. If you and I had been white, Miss Allen, the shipyard would have trained us on the job and paid us for learning. But we are not white, so we have to enroll in a class on our own time. Then the union tells us they have no need for welders. Yes. The shipyards place notices in the newspapers saying come one come all to the shipyards. Learn as you earn. They hire every man and woman to whom the union will issue a clearance. We know that.

Everybody knows it. *Learn as you earn,*" he repeated. "Perhaps we will. Yes. I hope we will learn."

His wife brought a tray of coffee cups and Reverend Beezely passed around the canned milk and sugar, then poured milk in his own cup, filling it to the brim. As he continued talking, he held the cup half raised to his mouth in the long fingers of his hand, while Joyce wondered how he could keep from spilling it.

". . . the National Negro Improvement League here, of which I am a member," he was saying, "has undertaken to draw together a committee, of shipyard workers, ministers, several lawyers perhaps, to seek ways of protecting our people. We intend to petition President Roosevelt's Fair Employment Practices Board to hold a hearing directly on shipyards. But all this is a slow process. It won't get you your job as welder, Miss Allen. Not today or tomorrow."

He paused and took a drink from his coffee cup, emptying it halfway down.

"Our friend Mr. Brooks?" he asked. "The *Sergeant.* Does he know about this yet?"

Joyce shook her head.

"He seems to be in a curious position, Mr. Brooks. Officers of the white union appointed him as president of the auxiliary—that's what they call the section of the union into which they take colored members: the auxiliaries. But there never yet has been any meeting of the auxiliary to confirm Brooks as president, or to elect the various other officers. Several months ago I had a long talk with Mr. Brooks. I went over to San Martin to see him. He's highly regarded by our people in San Martin. Mr. Brooks, I said to him, I wonder if it's really wise for our people to go into this auxiliary? And he said to me, they can't keep us out of the shipyards. They can't build ships without us. When we have enough of us, we'll run that auxiliary to suit ourselves. I said to him, Mr. Brooks, our people pay their dues to the white business agents, but we have no membership in the union. We have membership in an auxiliary which never has held a meeting. I wonder if they're not using you for a cat's paw? And he became very angry—"

"*A cat's paw!*" Charlie interrupted. "We used to call them Uncle Toms in Texas. You'll find he's getting a double pay check from the company. Or from the union. Or both."

Reverend Beezely shook his head dubiously. "I'm not sure of that, Charles. He's very well thought of by our people in San Martin. He does a great many things for them. I said to him, Mr. Brooks, I wonder if you ever will really be able to hold elections in that auxiliary? Then he yelled at me that I was a fool, that a minister had no business meddling in the shipyard where people had to work for a living . . ."

Charlie broke into a laugh at this.

"You see, he hit me in my most vulnerable spot," the Reverend agreed, and he smiled at Joyce and hunched his shoulders. "People seem to believe that ministers don't need to eat. Or that God provides them with manna in some mysterious fashion. Yes. Well, I'm afraid we are not yet in a very good position to help you. But I would say this: go back to your friend Mr. Brooks. Tell him what happened—though I wouldn't tell him of course that you talked to me. Then we'll see what kind of weight he can swing with those white union officers. If this does no good, we'll take it up through the Improvement League. But that would be a long haul, a very long haul. Our people come to the League every day— from San Martin, from Oakland, from Berkeley, Richmond, Alameda, Marinship—with the same story. The same story."

They sat for a time in silence as the Reverend Beezely finished his coffee and then set down his cup. In the morning, Charlie suggested, she ought to ask Mr. Henderson to hunt up the Sergeant as soon as they got to the shipyard. Joyce agreed that she would; and the Reverend, rising from his chair, excused himself to go and get dressed.

His wife pressed them to stay for supper, but Charlie declined the invitation, making her a bow and kissing the back of her hand. When they were outside on the street again, Joyce cried, "Oh, Charlie, I wish I never had gotten into this! It's going to make so much trouble for everybody. I don't care about it that much. I *don't*—"

Charlie hooked his hand under her arm. "But there's lots of other people care about it, Joyce." And then he told her, "Why, I care about it myself. It's like what I was saying, I been looking around for years for a young lady that knew some high-price skilled trade. Come on, let's go eat."

They rode the streetcar to Chinatown, to their favorite restaurant; and went to a movie afterwards, to take her mind off her troubles, he told her. As they walked home after the movie, over the hill between Van Ness Avenue and Fillmore, Charlie said to her, "You passed your welding test today, honey. But you got nothing on me. I passed a test too."

"The doctor, Charlie! You saw him?" And she asked, "What did he tell you? Are you all right?"

"I'm healthy as a horse. And that gives me about ten days to stick around." He turned abruptly to face her. "I know this isn't the right way to do it, Joyce. But I want to get married."

She had known what he was going to say. She had known for many nights, yet now looked at him in confusion and finally whispered, "I—I don't know, Charlie. I don't know what to say . . ."

His face changed. The eyes clouded over with disappointment and doubt.

Oh, I shouldn't have said that to him, she thought. Yet she could say nothing other. Her mind writhed in a net of timidity and indecision. There were so many obstacles in the way of getting married! Certainly she would need to have her mother meet him before she finally made up her mind—and what about the Hendersons, and what about her job? And she had known him so short a time. "We'll talk about it tomorrow, Charlie. Please . . . please give me till tomorrow to think . . ."

"All right," he agreed.

Even in the midst of her own anxiety, she kept imagining what his thoughts must be. *She's been kidding me all this time*—was he thinking that?—*she's been taking me for a ride and now she's stalling till I have to ship out again.*

Oh, tell him that's not true! But she could find no word to speak, and all the way back to the Hendersons' house they walked in silence. But in the hall, as they stood at the bottom of the staircase, he said,

"I guess I shouldn't have been in such a damn hurry. We don't have to decide everything tonight or tomorrow either. Well, I'll ask you again when I come back. And I'll just keep on asking."

"Oh, I hope you will, Charlie! I'll say yes, but I can't—I can't—I just can't say it so quick."

He kissed her good night, and she let the door swing shut behind him and remained there at the foot of the stairs in the faint glow that filtered through the glass panel from the street outside. She twisted her hands together. Then with a little cry she pressed her hands against the wall, pushed herself away, opened the door and ran up to the corner.

At the corner, in the liquor store with the public telephone, she called the YMCA. But he had not yet come in. What if he should not return all night long? Where had he gone? Where would she ever find him? She got a handful of nickels in change from the clerk at the counter, who was watching her with a broad smile, called again, but still he had not come. Then her heart failed her. How could she marry him, how could she, without knowing him longer? Without thinking it all through much deeper than she had? The decision she had half taken slipped from her and dissolved. She left the store, walked back to the house where the Hendersons lived.

In the morning, halfway through the morning, the Sergeant himself came to fetch her. He took her with him to the plate shop to see the business agent. The business agent wore a gray gabardine suit and a gray felt hat, and dark red polished shoes. His face made an oval shape, and as the Sergeant began angrily talking, the business agent listened with no change of expression at all. Then he said,

"Slow down, Brooks. You've bawled me out twice already this morning. The man made a mistake, that's all. We've got a lot more applications from women welders than we're getting any calls for." Glancing towards Joyce, he asked, "Did you tell the dispatcher you were working in the yard?"

"No—I don't remember if I did."

"That's the reason right there, Brooks. People working in the yard take priority. If he'd known she was working here he would have sent her up last night." Filling out a slip, he told Joyce to present it at the shipyard personnel office when she finished work, and that she would have twenty-one days to pay her initiation to the union, which was twenty-five dollars, and after that her dues would be three dollars a month.

It was not till they had left the plate shop and were walking back toward the shipways that Joyce remembered how she and Charlie had telephoned Sally O'Regan the night before, and she said she had been assigned right away to a welding job. Yet she was not working in the yard at all: she was a waitress in the lunch counter. Joyce wanted to tell the Sergeant, but he remained so silent and harsh-looking that she said nothing; only to thank him for his help as she rejoined her cleanup gang, which was sweeping off the runways between the lumber racks.

12

In the early morning Tom's ship was torpedoed some two hundred miles off the coast of Ireland. The ship, returning from England, had developed engine trouble during the night, and daylight found her limping along horizon-down behind the convoy. Some wandering U-boat found her there too, before the corvettes could reach her. The first torpedo chopped off her rudder and propeller; the second took her dead center in the engine room, blasting a skyrocket of steam and fire up through the smokestack. But she was almost half an hour sinking. They lowered the lifeboats like a fire and boat drill and got away, all except the engine gang that had been on watch. Afterwards the boats rocked gently in the green swell and trough with the sun warming through the mist, while the corvettes scurried in circles dropping depth charges; and returned finally to pick up the men from the lifeboats.

They landed in Liverpool which they had left only three days earlier. All this seemed as simple as changing trains at a railroad station, Tom thought; but for the first week after they were put ashore, he found he could not sleep through a whole night. He would start up thinking he had just heard the whistle signaling *abandon ship,* and hurl himself from his bed in one leap. Sleeping little at night, he was half asleep on his feet all day long. So he dozed during the train ride and saw nothing of the countryside except a few glimpses of green fields checkerboarded with hedgerows; and the smoky compartment crowded with other sailors sleeping or playing cards.

They were herded off the train in a town called Immingham, half in ruins, set in the greenest fields he had ever seen. A bus carried them down to the docks where they boarded a new C-ship to which they had been assigned for transportation home. They joked about how jumpy they felt setting foot on a ship again, though all of them were anxious for the trip back to the States and they kept guessing the days until she would be ready to sail. More or less passengers aboard, they had been given watches though there was nothing for them to do, and they leaned along the rail of the flying bridge counting the sling-loads of ammunition cases that came rising up out of the holds.

When they were off watch they rode the red tramcar into the village of Immingham.

Here they found not much to do either. The servicemen's center served tea and buns and there were pubs where you could drink warm beer; and sometimes girls in black uniforms with shiny tin buttons came in town from the anti-aircraft batteries out on the marshes. Watching the girls made Tom think about Sally, and he would count the months since he had seen her and wonder how long till he would see her again. He got out the last of her letters that had come just before they sailed (he had been carrying it in his wallet when the ship was torpedoed):

> . . . yes I DID pass the welding test and I'm hard at it now, on midnight shift just like always. Don't think I was sorry to kiss the old lunch counter good-by, either.

I'm pretty good TOO, Tom. Foreman says he may advance me to production welder in another couple weeks. But you can't imagine how crowded the yard is. Launched our fifteenth last week with a big celebration. Admirals from Washington, movic stars from Hollywood, of course they put on the bite for more war bonds. Our little apartment seemed so lonesome after you left I asked another girl I met in the welding class to move in with me (yes I said GIRL) and share the rent. Oh, Tom [she wrote], I miss you so bad I ache all over. . . .

He smiled at this, tingling inside. Yet he had been three days in Immingham before he could bring himself to write an answer.

When he felt finally that he wanted to write, he went to the servicemen's center, took his cup of tea to the desk in the dark little reading room. But after all, there was not much he could say. Where he was and what happened to the ship he could not tell her anyway. So he was all right. He was feeling fine. He was having a cup of tea, thinking about you. Everything okay hope you are the same. He had to make the writing large even to fill the page, and at the bottom put a double row of x's. Then he sealed the letter and slipped it in the back pocket of his tight blue trousers and sat still at the writing desk, not knowing what to do next.

What was *she* doing? He could not imagine her not knowing what to do with this minute or that. It was a little after six o'clock and she would be waking up, coming into the kitchen for supper, pouring her cup of coffee before she ate. But of course it wasn't six o'clock in San Francisco, and she wasn't living with her family any more—Kallela must be in Saw Creek by this time. It would be one o'clock in the morning in San Francisco, later than that. She had just started work. And what did she say to the guys that tried to joke and shine up to her as he once had done? Was she wearing the sliver of diamond and the gold wedding ring they had bought together? Maybe they had not been very smart to get married, he thought. He must have gone crazy that morning in the Bodensee Hotel. She never had insisted, had she? It was himself had convinced her and dragged her down to Monterey, taken her to the marriage license bureau that Monday morning and sent the telegram to Liz and Kallela, GETTING MARRIED HOME FRIDAY.

Why had he not just given her the engagement ring and let it go at that? Suppose they didn't feel the same way when he came back? Maybe in a few years, she wouldn't be any different from all the other women he had ever seen: nagging and fussing all the time the way his own mother had done—she wanted a house on the other side of town; she wanted the whole family to go to church with her every Sunday morning so she could make a showing with the rest of the ladies; she didn't want to associate except with people who wouldn't have anything to do with her, and she wanted a bank clerk for a husband instead of what she'd got, a truck driver. Or his sister the same way—lucky enough to catch any husband at all, but no sooner she had one than she went to chewing the life out of him, poor son of a bitch! So why would Sally be different from the others?

What was the use trying to cover it up then?— He had not really intended to get married. Did she know that? No, not yet, he thought. But Liz knew; Liz knew almost everything, you couldn't keep anything from her. She must have known they were going on the weekend together too, maybe she figured it was better they just do that, if that was the way it was, and not tie themselves down. Liz had plenty of sense, he thought. But Sally had some sense too. She was cool and collected as if she'd been out on a dozen weekends like that one. Maybe she had, yes probably she had. But the next day—

They both went crazy the next day. Why? He did **not**

know. The war, and his going away so soon and all the rest of it. Yet after the weekend things had quickly changed between them. It was as if they had traded places after the Bodensee Hotel and their trip to Monterey. Instead of himself being the asker of favors, he was the one who could give them or hold them back. She got a little love and right away could never have enough. What had he done, he wondered, to stir her up like that? But it was not himself so much as her imagining what love was supposed to be. Like the song, "Falling in love with love"—she had told him that herself. So they had to have the house in San Martin Village in the new housing project, they had to move in right away; she painted the kitchen, rushed off buying sheets and blankets, curtains, pots, dishes. She was not cool any more, she was hot as a mink. "I used to think a person could hold off until they were ready to fall in love," she told him, "only it isn't like that, it just happens and takes over everything. . . ." She must not have intended it then, any more than he had. There was no halfway with her. As soon as she got her feet wet, she stripped and dived in.

With himself he knew it had been very different. By the time the construction wound up at the shipyard, he was already anxious to be on his way. Whatever was coming, he wanted to be into it and have it over with. It seemed to him now that all his life he never once had been in any place but that he had been glad enough to leave. Always it had seemed good to leave places, he had always looked forward to that.

"Both of you are pretty young to get married," Liz had said. Oh, she must have known. Sitting there knitting him a pair of wool socks to wear on watch under his heavy weather boots. Where were they now? Bottom of the Atlantic with the rest of his gear. He'd have to write for another pair.

The tea was cold and the bun long since gone, and he sat at the desk in the reading room remembering the dinner Liz had put on the night before he left. She must have used up two months' worth of meat stamps for the roast beef. And Kallela with a full quart of hundred proof on the table —how had he managed to get his mitts on that? Just pass me a short shot right now if you don't mind. But there wasn't any left; they had killed the quart quick enough, the four of them. While Kallela, a little bit lit up, kept working on him about what he was going to do after the war. In a way, that was only a cover-up, he thought: you sounded off with a lot of high-power plans to keep from admitting that for some people at least, there might not be any after the war. But he could see that a man changed his outlook, too, even Kallela, when he got to be a father-in-law. So he had it lined up for Tom to be coming back to Saw Creek. "We'll clean things up around there and have the best little local in the state, kiddo."

"Oh, no. Don't believe I could sell my wife on going back up there," Tom had said, laughing. Sally sat silent with her glass in her hand, and Liz, knitting the socks, watched him across the table.

"You made a hit with that lawyer all right," Kallela told him, trying out some new bait. "He said for you to come around and see him if you're interested in law. He meant it too. Good lawyer can do a lot for the labor movement, Tom."

"So how long would that take? Five, six years?"

"A-nnh, you're a kid yet."

"I'll most likely be as bald as you are when I get out of this monkey suit." The old man had no answer to that one. But he was a tough nugget, Kallela, like a damn elephant, going back up there to Saw Creek to knock his head against that stone wall. And they'd be a long time finding another business agent as good as he was. "Don't be making too many plans for me," he had said. "I'll write my own ticket." And Kallela, scowling at him, filled the glasses with the hundred proof; while Liz passed him the socks and he took off his shoes to try them for size. It was getting late, Sally said. They shook hands around and he gave Liz a kiss, and out they went, down the back stairs like always to the old pickup in the alley. She'd probably smash it up, he thought, or run it around without any oil. Up and down those hills. From Kallela's, they drove back to their house in the San Martin Village. It was not really raining but the fog was over everything almost as heavy as rain. The street lamps in the fog; roofs of the little houses wet and black and shiny stepping away down the hill, the foghorns out toward the channel.

He lighted a cigarette and sat staring at the kitchen window. But Sally had to keep on being gay if it killed her. She turned on the radio, made him dance with her on the linoleum-covered floor. "Whenever they station you someplace, Tommy, I'll come and join you."

"They'll station me on a destroyer in the middle of the Pacific Ocean most likely."

"Maybe it won't last much longer. . . ."

Sure, maybe it won't. They went into the bedroom, pulled off their clothes and in the cold sheets, kissing her, he tried to make up to her on the last night for he did not know what exactly. He had seen her eyes quivering, knew how harsh the parting came to her, how she had tried to cover the grief. With him it was the other way: he had tried to appear sadder than he felt. He was sorry for her, half amused, and irritated at the demands she made for return; and inside himself a sense of shame as if he were dealing her his own game from a marked deck, and she so eager for the cards.

On that last night, when they came home from the Kallelas', he knew she was crying inside, biting her heart out to seem cheerful; while he himself was not really thinking about her at all, but about the new things that might be awaiting him. He said her name and she his as they strained closer to each other, and the alarm clock ticked toward morning and the fog drifted over the black tar-paper roofs of San Martin.

Oh, Christ, what if she were making love to somebody else like that! To Andermas? Andermas with his safe berth in the net depot, he wouldn't be torpedoed on any rustbucket! For an instant Tom pictured her in the moonlight, struggling out of the still damp bathing suit, and the bitterness of his own wishing blazed through him like a torch. This was a pain he had never imagined, a tearing apart of his lungs and kidneys, a whirlwind of cutting fragments inside his head.

He sat perfectly still at the writing table, grinding his knuckles against the table edge until the blood oozed out.

Some merchant sailors from the ship stepped up to the snack counter and Tom joined them. He went outside with them afterwards to the common across the street. The common was lush green with a row of trees on one side, and after walking under the trees they would emerge suddenly into an expanse of ruins. Here were empty staring windows and shattered sections of brick wall and front stoops that led halfway up and stepped out into nothing and charred rafters lying across heaps of rubble. This was where couples from the common came after dark, but it was a long time yet till dark, not till almost midnight here, the summer evenings were so long. They crossed the common again, back and forth, and three of the sailors, young fellows, struck up a conversation finally with some girls from the anti-aircraft batteries. But Tom did not stay with them. He and the bosun, middle-aged and bald-headed, went to one of the pubs and drank beer until time for the last tramcar.

It *was* dark now, Tom saw, yet not really dark even so, for the houses and trees appeared clear and distinct along the roadside, and overhead there was a glow in the sky and the stars soft and pale. On the car, crowded though it was, everyone was quiet, scarcely speaking as they trundled down through the quiet countryside to the dockhead.

"How soon we ready to shove off, Boats?" he asked.

"Couple days, maybe."

They watched the cases of ammunition creaking and clanking up from the cargo hold. Then Tom said good night, went off to the fo'c's'le and crawled into his bunk.

He fell asleep thinking about Sally; but no sooner slept than he started up to the wild mooing of the ship's whistle, the crash and lurch, the terrifying hiss of steam from broken pipes. Clawing out of the blankets, he crouched wide awake in the middle of the empty fo'c's'le. Everything was quiet except the muffled clank of the hoists. And birds chittering in the field alongside the docks. He was glad his fo'c's'le mates were all on watch.

13

Walter Stone found his partner Howard Chantry and Mackay, their luncheon host, waiting for him in the cocktail lounge. It was after one and the rush had subsided leaving a scattering of leisurely and apparently occupationless drinkers at the little tables and at the bar. Waiters moved softly over the carpeting; there was a hum of serious conversation, occasional laughter, the delicate clink of ice on glasses. Walter, who had long since given up hard liquor in the middle of the day, ordered sherry, while Chantry and Mackay took refills of their old-fashioneds.

"A pleasure indeed to see you again, Walter," Mackay greeted. He inquired after Walter's health, and Mrs. Stone's; asked if she were spending the summer again in Signal Springs, and how young Wendel Stone was getting along in Washington. To these questions Walter replied briefly. His wife was well (he said) and so was he. No, she was not at Signal Springs; she was spending the summer with friends in the San Jacinto Mountains—and he lifted his wineglass, letting his eyes brush across Chantry's face in the same movement; but Chantry who was tapping a cigarette against the side of his silver lighter, appeared not to be following the exchange of courtesies. Walter did not bother to place the corresponding inquiries. He could see that Mackay was sturdy enough by looking at him; and as for his wife, he was not even quite sure he had one, and saw no reason to pretend much anxiety as to the state of her health.

Perhaps she was in a sanitarium too, he thought. Certainly that would be appropriate if he had a wife; for Mackay, who had once been a state senator from one of the Central Valley counties, now held some post in the state liquor control apparatus. He must know where Sylvia was, Walter thought, people like this never missed such details. Richards would certainly have kept him posted in any case. Sipping his wine, Walter waited for the other to finish the preliminaries and get down to whatever business he had in mind. Clearly it was Mackay who was the initiator of the luncheon—Chantry had already told him he served merely as go-between.

The headwaiter, appearing beside them, breathed into the host's ear, "Your table is ready, sir," and they rose and followed the waiter into the dining room. But over the soup, Mackay continued the small talk; labor law was an expanding field these days, a challenging field; he himself had enjoyed many stimulating contacts with labor, both the CIO and the State Federation; both while he was in the Senate and now as a member of the control board, he always maintained excellent relations with top men in labor, fine public-spirited men they were too. "I happened to be in Sacramento last week," he informed them, "where I ran into a client and good friend of yours. I had stopped to discuss a problem with the Governor, and as I was leaving the Governor's office, I met Garnet, of the Shipbuilders' Union. He spoke very highly of you both. Oh, I've known Garnet for fifteen years, a man of courage and integrity. . . ."

Walter smiled: the other was presenting his credentials.

"Good, here's the menu. What shall we have?—How's the abalone?" he asked.

"Oh, yes, sir," the waiter agreed. "The abalone steak is very nice today, sir."

"For some time, Walter," Mackay continued, after the waiter had taken their orders and departed, "I have been hoping for an opportunity of talking to you . . ." He paused, placing his hands palm down on the table, "about your son."

Now we come to it, Walter thought. It isn't only Chantry who's the go-between. Mackay himself was a go-between. A plenipotentiary from Richards, the father-in-law.

"I have had the pleasure several times of meeting your son Wendel, while he was courting the charming Miss Richards—now, as I understand, Mrs. Stone. Mrs. Stone the younger, that is. You know him of course, Chantry?"

"I've met him only once," Chantry said.

"A very capable young man," Mackay declared; and Walter could see him warming up, expanding his larynx as if he were taking the rostrum at the state convention. People began glancing their way from near-by tables. "His record in law school, his entry into the profession, his rapid rise in the armed service—all taken together, constitute a highly impressive performance." Here he paused discreetly while the waiter set the entrées before them, whisking the covers from the serving dishes; then continued in a lowered voice: "I have always—*always*—been an admirer of Franklin Roosevelt and twice voted for him, although I may say I did not do so the last time. But age, gentlemen, is no respecter of persons or parties. I feel it incumbent upon some of us at least to cast a glance forward to the period after the war. The time may not be far off," he continued, "when the electorate will be looking about for a new set of men to represent them. For capable, ambitious, well-educated *young* men—with fine war records—to take over the reins. You see," he said, nodding first to Chantry and then to Walter, "being a creature of habit, I am impelled to view every situation with the eye of a practical politician."

"A statesman," Walter interposed.

The ex-state senator turned upon him the professional smile of his pink, large-chinned face, and beneath the smile Walter caught the glint of an intense irritation. The one word, apparently, had cut him like a knife. He had not premeditated any thrust, but realized there was an exchange between himself and men like Mackay, quite apart from any intent of his own, and they were constantly wounded precisely because they felt themselves vulnerable to him, and for some reason never understood how vulnerable he was.

"On the level of the state liquor control, I suppose the term in more common usage is politician. But as a matter of fact, I welcome that designation. A hewer of wood and drawer of water," said Mackay with exaggerated stress to make plain his sarcasm. "He labors in the vineyard so that the statesman may labor in Washington." Here he paused as if to let the remark sink in, and Walter understood that the other was expecting him to be ambitious for his son. Having dangled his lure, he was now reeling in the line, anticipating that the fish would break water. Walter laughed. He saw Mackay's face redden and saw Chantry's eye flash across his in a quick admonitory glance.

For several moments they ate in silence. *Ambitious for his son,* he thought. He had been once. But as if his son now needed anyone else's ambition, that pattern and paragon, that young man most likely to succeed! Waiting in front of the fireplace in the beautiful little wainscoted room he had occupied at Cambridge, Walter remembered him in his black gown, ready for the graduation from law school, his mortarboard standing endways on the mantel; Wendel with his neat regular features looking serious and filial. Suppose he broke out one day and shouted what was really in his mind? Shouted, "That's what I might have expected! I might have expected that from you! I've spent my whole life trying to live you down, both of you, trying to get people to take *me* for what I am. Don't you think I can hear people whispering, staring at me, whispering, Yes, Wendel is a nice boy, he certainly is, his mother's such an alcoholic, in a sanitarium, you know; his father's a damn rotten prig, a Brahmin, a whirling dervish, so primed up with himself he can't even say hello to a person on the street! Yes, I might have expected this! I might have known as soon as I was getting ahead, you'd do something to break it up! You'd have to."

But of course Wendel would not say what was in his mind. No Stone would do that. He would stand there, grave, slightly perturbed as he always appeared: Carol and I have been thinking it over and we feel this is a wonderful opportunity. . . . Yet was he not right? Had he not been making his own way from the very beginning? What else could one expect but that he would seize the chance Richards offered him?

Mackay said heavily, "It is my sincere conviction that Franklin Roosevelt will be remembered as one of the great men of our times. However, I wonder if certain excesses may not have been committed under the guise of furthering the general welfare—which might appear rather alarming to persons of liberal persuasion. One calls to mind the codes imposed under the National Recovery Act, or the manner in which the Supreme Court was whipped into obedience."

As Walter offered no reply, Mackay presently continued, "I believe there is a temptation for even the most well-intentioned administrator—and let me say at once that I consider Franklin Roosevelt to be both enlightened and well-intentioned—but a temptation, because it will always appear so much easier to govern by decree rather than by consent. Perhaps the end results may be more harmful than the original ailment. I was thinking, for example—would you prefer coffee now or afterwards? We'll take it any time," he assured the waiter. "Any time. I believe we're always ready for coffee.—Yes. Well, I couldn't help wondering as I was talking to Garnet last week, whether responsible labor leaders feel entirely easy in their minds over the government's intervention in the processes of negotiation and collective bargaining. Do you think so? Or the recent rulings of the President's Committee on Fair Employment Practices might offer another example. Do you consider these to be sound, *legally*, Walter?"

"I haven't studied them," Walter said.

"But certainly you're in accord with the general intent?"

"I am."

"Oh, certainly," Mackay agreed. "We all favor equal opportunity for every citizen—this is the cornerstone of our system." He was beaming again, he seemed to have recovered himself. "But I wonder—I wonder if this may not establish, in a manner at first inconspicuous, a dangerous precedent— from the point of view of labor—with regard to the sanctity of membership? The government says to the union: You *must* have these certain people in your membership. I understand the Fair Employment Practices Committee has found such rulings in several industries in the East. Now mind you, I'm not in the labor field, I don't know that the federal courts will uphold them, I'm merely posing the question . . ."

Walter caught Chantry's eye again, signaling an urgent warning.

"This is all very hypothetical," Chantry said. "I haven't studied the legal points involved. Walter hasn't either. We're hardly in a position to answer your question."

"Of course. Of course not," Mackay cried, delighted. "Well, I see I've wandered from my subject. It was the Congress I came to talk to you about, not the President's Committee. I wish to speak very bluntly," and setting his plate aside, he leaned forward with elbows on the table. "I came to propose to you—to propose young Wendel Stone as a congressman from San Francisco. Not by next election, of course. It would be unwise for him to leave the service so early, even if that were possible. But in the one following, perhaps. What do you think?"

"Why do you ask me?" Walter said. "Ask Wendel."

"Let me be absolutely frank with you. I've discussed this with no one except yourself. Yourself and Howard here. And with Richards. Richards as you know is a very old friend of mine."

"Yes, I know."

"Richards and I had hoped that you might be the one to make this proposal to your son."

The waiter, having cleared away the plates, was refilling their coffee cups. Walter shook his head. "I'm neither a politician nor a statesman," he said. "I have no power to put anybody into Congress. If you have, or if Richards has, then you'd better suggest it to him yourselves."

He had expected Mackay to flush and turn angry again; but instead he exclaimed cheerfully, "That's what I told Richards you would say, Walter. Well, Richards is going East next month, and he might have the opportunity to talk it over with Wendel in Washington. I take it you've no objections?"

"Why should I object? What difference would it make if I did? You're not asking me to run for Congress."

"No, you and I are too old for that. Howard here might have a stab at it. He's a young fellow yet." Laughing heartily, he picked up the check and unfolded several bills from his wallet. They walked together to the street where Mackay hailed a cab in front of the restaurant. "Can I drop you off somewhere? No?" He waved his hat to them as he climbed in, calling, "We'll discuss this again before too long. Give my warmest regards to Mrs. Stone and Mrs. Chantry. Thanks. Thank you for the pleasure . . ."

"Did you know that was coming?" Walter asked, as he and Chantry walked back toward their office.

"I did not," Chantry replied. "He asked me to bring you to lunch but I had no idea what was on his mind. I told you that already."

The denial was too vehement. "They don't even have residence out here now," Walter said.

Chantry laughed. "Mackay looks into the future. He's planning for 1946 already. If your son agrees, they'll have a congressional district all picked out for him."

"It seems to me you know more about this than you've told me, Howard."

"All I know is what a certain supply of common sense informs me."

"I see. Do you mind if I ask—suppose you were in my place, would you go along with this?"

"I certainly would not close the door on it."

"Common sense tells you that?"

"Indeed it does." And in the push-button elevator, riding up to their offices, Chantry said, "A little common sense never came amiss to anyone."

"Sarcasm becomes you ill, Howard. Why don't you say what's on your mind, if there is anything?"

"I suppose," Chantry cried angrily, "if you want to make an enemy of Mackay, that's your own business. But why you must then put a club into his hands to beat us both with, is really beyond me!"

"I haven't the slightest idea what you're talking about.'

"Oh, come off it! He asked your opinion of the Fair Em ployment Practice Committee so he could go straight to Gar net with it. And you obligingly told him."

"I did? What difference does that make? I'm quite willing to tell Garnet myself. Aren't you?"

But the elevator door, opening, let them out in front of their receptionist's window, and Chantry crossed the lobby without answering. In his own office, Walter sat down at his desk, for the moment ignoring the receptionist's signal that a client waited to see him. An unpleasant sensation gripped him, which he had felt sometimes on trips in the mountains —that he was returning to a place he had left previously under the impression of walking in a direct line away from it.

That Richards must have sent Mackay seemed unmistakable. They wanted to include him in their venture, though he was not sure why, since he was in no position to help send Wendel to Congress; and even had he been, he felt certain he would not agree to do so. If the boy won his election in his own right, that was one thing; but to arrange for it in advance through a political pawnbroker like Mackay, was something quite different. Yet Chantry, with whom he had thought himself in general agreement, seemed to regard him as utterly naïve. Was this naïveté or realism? At once he doubted himself. And the doubt opened him like a gaping wound. Perhaps the desperate, the fatal weakness of the figure which was himself, the suit of armor which others regarded as that distinguished, incisive, courageous attorney, was precisely this doubt. *Oh wa'd some power the giftie gi'e us,* he thought, but altered the following line: *To be as we mak' ithers see us.*

Others than those few who know us best, that is. For he believed that his son Wendel hated him, though never in all his life would he say so. And Sylvia hated him too and at least she had no hesitation in voicing her feeling. Not any longer. "You've tried to destroy us both!" she had screamed in her frenzy of sickness and hysteria that final night before she consented to go to the sanitarium. "And you have destroyed me, Walter. But you won't destroy Wendel." He had sat beside her, drained as an empty bottle. Now she was linking herself to their son, against him; but he remembered the passion of self-pity with which she had greeted the child's first intrusions into her life.

Oh, he had not tried to destroy them, Walter thought; he had not tried to destroy anyone, ever. Yet the doubt was inside him: it was not his trying, not his intention, they accused, but *himself*. Perhaps they were right, he did not know. It was not simply that he had given up a lucrative and respectable firm in order to go into a somewhat less lucrative and considerably less respectable one—although she fastened upon this. No, it was far more. It was that always where he had gone, and where he had established the center of his thoughts, he had been unable to take her. They had traveled separately. Her own thoughts, he knew, had remained fixed upon a time and place in the past, a distant closed circle of years tinted with the almost heartbreaking beauty which the autumn evenings of that lost city of New York in the year of their youth, assumed in retrospect. Within the circle, her expectations had seemed assured. She was so young, so talented, her friends had told her; and himself among the others vehemently pursuing her. So he had persuaded her to come with him to San Francisco where he intended opening a new firm with a college friend. Richards. Yet even had they stayed in New York, could the outcome have been different? The talents were not so great as they had then seemed. The circle she looked back upon had long since vanished. She would have grown older—even in New York.

Bitterly he wished he might have found a wife who would have increased his strength, rather than fastening like a cancer upon his weakness. Was this too much to have asked? But you chose each other freely, the doubt told him; what she was, and what you were, determined the choice, and determined what happened afterwards. But then there was no *choice,* the word itself had no meaning. The lottery of hazard threw them together, the ivory ball spinning on the wheel, the blind, senseless, inexorable fortune. Alpha and omega.

The buzzer sounded again on his desk.

Reaching out for the telephone, he said, "Yes, all right, yes, send him in now. . . ."

14

"Welder! Hey, Welder!"

Joyce was coiling her line to follow the Sergeant down into the hull when the leaderman spotted her.

"You workin' with Brooks?"

She nodded.

"Need a welder up here a few minutes. Get in there, help Kimball tack up his bulkhead. Brooks don't want you right away, do he?"

Without waiting for any answer, the leaderman took off and Joyce thought oh, no, he don't want me right away, much. But she plugged in her wire to the upper bank of machines and went into the superstructure picking her way over the tangle of hoses, pipes, wires and cables. A man with a tin hat crammed sideways over his bristly white face stuck his head out of a doorway, saw her and beckoned as if he expected her to come running. Most likely she would have run too, she thought, when she first came to work, and would have tripped and spilled her rods all over the deck and then picked herself up while everybody laughed at her. She could see the man had his mouth open shouting, but she heard not a word through the crash of chipping hammers in the narrow passageway. He shoved a bunch of angle irons into her hands and pointed up to a row of chalk marks along the ceiling.

Joyce hauled herself on to the scaffold.

She adjusted her goggles, pulled down her helmet with its smoked-glass panel. Then selecting a rod, she set it in the clamp, held the angle against the plate above her and touched the rod to the steel. Blue spark and flash. The captive star, the fragment of sun itself blazed before her eyes; the shining bead of molten metal crept down the joint and a moment later the two pieces of steel, melting and fusing, had become one. The miracle she never quite believed had happened again, and she crawled along the scaffold, welding the angles at the chalk marks.

When she finished, a chipper with a pneumatic hammer took her place. He was cutting the wall of the passageway free from the plates above. Somebody must have made a mistake, Joyce supposed, and that was why the leaderman and shipfitter were in such a hurry. She stood waiting for one of them to tell her what to do next. But they seemed to have forgotten her. They were whaling away at the bulkhead now, driving wedges between the bulkhead and the angles she had welded to the ceiling plates. From the way they went at it, she thought she might have to wait around most of the rest of the shift. The noise in the compartment was ear-splitting; the air had grown thick with welding fumes. She tugged at the leaderman's arm, pointing to the end of the passage.

He waved her off and she made her way out to the deck again. It had begun to rain outside. The main deck stretched shiny and wet in front of her with raindrops coming down in silver streaks through the glare of floodlights, striking the deck and splashing in tiny fountains. The biggest part of working in the shipyard was learning to wait, she thought. That was what the Sergeant said, but he wasn't so good at waiting himself, and he'd be mad now. Mad at her. She often wished she had been assigned to anyone else except the Sergeant; the foreman had put them together, she supposed, as sort of a joke, since she had been the first colored woman welder to come on the shift—and everybody knew how the Sergeant had quarreled with the business agent over her clearance. He was a grim, silent man, the Sergeant; sometimes they would work together for an entire half shift without exchanging a word. Yet she knew she could not have learned as much from any other shipfitter about how to take care of herself. If the Sergeant had been on deck when the leaderman sent her off to help Kimball, he would certainly have told that leaderman to tend to his own affairs. He would have marched right off with her and let the leaderman go hunt for another welder. "When you goin' to get a little bit tough, Miss Allen?" he would ask. He was tough enough for two.

She thought of climbing down into the hold to tell him what had happened. But what was the use, he would know that well enough without her telling him. And if she went down, that would be exactly the time they would need her up here. You might wait around for a couple of hours, but just run off to the rest-room for five minutes, they'd be shouting all over the ship for you.

Joyce shrugged her shoulders. If you worried about all the things there were here to worry about, as the Sergeant had told her, you'd be dead before morning. Stepping from the superstructure, she skirted the gaping hole of the main hatch and leaned against the rail looking out over the yard. She took off her helmet and goggles, let the salty-tasting rain blow against her face. She liked the yard best at night. In the daytime it seemed harsh and ugly but at night she thought it was like a city in a fairy story. There were the bright windows, the palace of the pattern loft; and in the darkness beyond, the smoky glow from the open end of the plate shop; and then the countless lights of the buildings and storage racks and roadways, and all the lights glimmering, blurring in the rain.

Now as she looked straight down the vessel's side, she saw the gleam of rails far below where the tracks came in along the shipway; and she saw a couple of small figures in their tin helmets hurrying out from under the ways and vanishing into the darkness. How high the ship was! Like looking out from the top of a tower. Charlie had told her that waves sometimes broke over the main deck when a ship was loaded heavy. But how could this whole structure float *under* the water? It seemed as if it must certainly go straight to the bottom if the waves should ever come up so high. And the people, all of them in the galleys and the engine room and the cabins and passageways, like bees in a honeycomb. With a shudder, she imagined the ship sliding down and down into the black water.

Charlie had written that his own ship was in port again. She hoped they might have taken an extra long time unloading so they would still be in port on this particular night. Then she need not worry about him. Not tonight. On the other hand, if the ship had quickly unloaded, maybe they had left already, they were headed home, out of the war zone, home-bound. For a moment she allowed herself to think, maybe it's rolling in towards the Golden Gate Bridge —*now*. Maybe when I get home I'll find a note from Sally that he called. . . .

Then she checked herself, forcing the thought from her mind. This only made it harder. Another month or six weeks. She could wait.

"Hey, welder! *Where in hell did she go?*"

The shipfitter had come looking for her. "Why the hell don't you stick with the work?" he yelled.

"I told the leaderman where I was going," Joyce said. She saw him open his mouth to shout at her again, and she cried,

"Don't you shout at me or you can go find yourself another welder. It wasn't me made the mistake on that bulkhead." The man shut his mouth with a snap, turned and stamped into the superstructure; and Joyce, thinking, *Now I must be learning a little bit anyhow,* followed after him.

She climbed the scaffold again. She saw that the bulkhead had been wedged over about an inch from its former position. Starting at the corner, she moved along tacking a spot every few feet, working on hands and knees with her head knocking against the ceiling. Below her, two men welders were joining the seams of the deck plates. The fumes had become thicker than ever. She was sweating and choking and under her helmet; sweat dripped from the end of her nose, making her nose itch unbearably. The bulkhead seemed to have stretched out till it was several miles long: when she reached the end at last and swung down to the deck, she found herself face to face with the Sergeant.

"*Here* you are," he said.

"Leaderman told me to stay up here, Mr. Brooks."

"So me and two pipefitters and an electrician are all standin' around with our thumbs in our mouths. Come *on* now. You got your line?"

"But I don't think they done with me yet."

"They're done with you, Miss Allen. I just had a talk with the leaderman."

Joyce laughed. Neither the leaderman nor the shipfitter now were anywhere to be seen, and she coiled her wire, followed it back to the bank of generators, where she unplugged it. The Sergeant took the coil on his shoulder and they swung down through the main hatch.

Far below, Joyce could see the glare of cluster lights on the curved bottom of the hold, the sparkle of welding torches, and people crawling back and forth like beetles. She and the Sergeant lowered themselves from one platform to the next. As they descended into the immense clanging belly of the vessel, the staging platforms hanging by cables from the main deck above, swayed under their movements. Joyce remembered she had felt certain she was going to die of terror the first time she had followed the Sergeant into the hold. Now it didn't bother her so much—not quite.

Oh, she was learning all right, she thought.

It was one o'clock in the morning when Joyce stepped down from the shipyard bus in San Martin Village. The rain was falling harder than ever. She turned up the collar of her coat and hurried across the flats, past the shopping center of the project, up the hill between the rows of little houses. As always she began thinking about a letter from Charlie, and she felt into the mailbox beside the front door although she knew Sally O'Regan would already have fetched in any mail that might have come.

The box was empty. In the drip of rain Joyce stood groping for the keys in her handbag. The cat popped from under the house where it had been taking shelter out of the wet, yowled and rubbed against her leg, scratching angrily at the door. Inside, as Joyce turned on the light, she saw a letter on the kitchen table and jumped for it. But the letter was from her mother, not from Charlie, and she dropped it back on the table again to read in the morning. She hung up her wet raincoat, lighted the gas ring under a pan of water and went into the bathroom for a shower. When she had bathed, she sliced some bread and made tea, and sat down at the table reading a few pages from a book to comb the knots out of her thoughts.

Afterwards she set the table for Sally O'Regan's breakfast. The cat had curled into its usual spot under the water heater, and Joyce leaned down to tickle its ears, laughing at its loud purr, then turned off the light and went to bed herself.

She lay hugging the blankets around her.

The wind creaked against the sides of the house, the rain pattered over the roof. Alone now, and in the dark, in the few moments her tired body needed to drift toward sleep, Joyce allowed her thoughts, which all day she had held in check, to move where they wished. If only she had married him, she thought, and if only they had had that last week to-gether—*together*, as husband and wife. Had she really been wrong? No, no, when he came back and they saw each other again, then they would be sure, both of them, absolutely sure. And it would not be long to wait now. She had counted the nights he had been gone; she had asked other seamen's wives how long these trips were likely to last, and she was certain they had passed the halfway mark, he would be com-ing back, coming any day.

She heard a rattle of dishes from the kitchen. The cat must be on the table, she thought, but was too sleepy to get up. She was in the booth in the Chinese restaurant . . . the half-empty teacups . . . and leaning, leaning towards him. . . .

Charlie's art teacher, Joe Baratia, had given her the name of a piano instructor and she made arrangements for contin-uing her lessons. These turned out to be altogether differ-ent from the lessons she had taken in Signal Springs. Her new teacher, a woman about thirty-five, was a former concert pianist and strict taskmaster. *First of all your fingering is sloppy,* the teacher informed her, and set her a schedule of exercises to limber up her hands. Since Joyce had no piano at home, this practice was a slow process in the beginning. But when the Beezelys moved to San Martin, and Reverend Beezely opened his church in a warehouse by the railroad on the far side of town, she promised him to play for Sunday service and help rehearse the choir—in return for which he gave her a key to the building so that she could use the piano whenever she wished.

On the mornings Joyce went to San Francisco for her lesson, Sally O'Regan, who worked the midnight shift at the yard, would usually wait for her to get up instead of going to bed when she came in at nine o'clock. Then they ate breakfast together, comparing experiences on the easiest ways to make one kind of weld or another, discussing the personalities of the various foremen, leadermen, shipfitters, they had to work with. This was always enjoyable for both. Joyce talked about her piano, Sally reported developments at the last union meeting. More and more, Joyce looked forward to these mornings. She found herself thinking of Sally O'Regan rather as a friend than simply a person with whom she accidentally shared an apartment. She had moved in with Sally after she left the Hendersons', intending to stay only till she could find a place of her own. But once there, it seemed foolish to rent another apartment when both were living alone. Sally had urged her to stay and share the rent, and Joyce finally agreed, although she had felt strange living in the same house with a white woman. But this, like all the other new things that were happening to her, she presently came to accept as normal. The part of the project they lived in was a mixed area, there were Negro and white families on both sides, all seeming to get along easily enough.

The Beezelys were not far off. The Reverend was working the midnight shift like Sally O'Regan; and his wife Janet had found part-time work running the steam press in a tailorshop. Joyce, from the time she had first met the Reverend's wife, had thought of her as hardly more than her own age, despite the fact that she had a girl in high school. But she saw that Janet regarded her as if she were a third daughter. She always inquired after the latest news from Charlie; and if she were going shopping, or out to a movie with her own two girls, would send one over to ask if Joyce wanted to come. She took Joyce's dresses, and Sally O'Regan's too, along with her when she went to work, and brought them home cleaned and pressed.

Reverend Beezely had become more deeply involved than ever in the work of the Improvement League. He explained to Joyce that President Roosevelt's Fair Employment Practice Committee had at last scheduled a hearing on discrimination in West Coast shipyards, which was to be held in Portland; and the League was trying to set up a conference of people from all shipyards around the Bay to gather material for submission to the hearing. He wished to discuss this with the Sergeant, he told her; and one night came around to where she and the Sergeant were working just before the change of shift.

Joyce was busy picking up the tools and coiling her wires. She heard the Sergeant loudly announce that he held a poor opinion of the Negro Improvement League: it all had been started by white people to *improve* things a little for colored, he wouldn't want his name used as sponsor for anything they were putting on.

"Somebody has got to start things," the Reverend told him. "I hope you'll come yourself, anyway?"

"Says here it's eight o'clock in the evening. I be working then." Joyce carried her coil of wire up to the main deck to leave by the bank of generators for the next welder. When she returned, the Sergeant was saying, ". . . I don't go along with anything aimed to break up the Auxiliary, you know that. I'm trying to get our people into the Auxiliary. You seem to be tryin' to do just the contrary."

"I'm not sure yet what I should try to do, Mr. Brooks."

"But you're busy tellin' me what to do. I been around some. I can count up to five myself. All these ministers and lawyers, you bring 'em in some kind of a committee, they won't do us any good. They're not in the shipyard. They talk, that's all. But we ever just get ourselves together, *right here,* they want to call it an Auxiliary, they can call it anything they like, what difference it make—"

"There's never even been a meeting of this Auxiliary yet, Mr. Brooks."

"We'll have one. We got the date set now. First Tuesday in December. I hope *you'll* come to that?"

"I certainly will."

The Sergeant was putting on his jacket.

"I'm not trying to tell you what to do, Mr. Brooks. I'm trying to find out what *I* should try to do. Our people come into the yard, they have no job training and no promotion. No colored leadermen, no colored foremen. Colored welders stay their whole life on tacking. White welders they set right up as production welders. The union is supposed to protect us but it does not. President Roosevelt says we cannot be discriminated against, Mr. Brooks. Not in war industry. I ask, don't we have the right to membership in the union? No, not in the Auxiliary, in the *union,* I mean? Don't we? Like the others?"

"We'd never have a majority. They'd outvote us every time."

"But this way we have no vote at all. We pay money, but we have no voice at all. If we were under the same hiring and the same seniority—"

"*Oh, Hell!*" the Sergeant shouted. "They'd push us around and cut our necks off every time they felt like it! Let them have their organization and we'll have ours! That's the only way we'll get things any better. Then we go right up to the big boss. *You talk turkey with the white union,* we say, *but you got to talk turkey with us now too—*"

The whistle blew. The Sergeant, picking up his lunch pail, turned toward the gangway that led across to the staging surrounding the hull.

"I think you like being president of the Auxiliary," Reverend Beezely said.

The Sergeant stopped. He set down the lunch pail and straightened up and then stood perfectly still with his hands hanging loose in front of him. Joyce froze silent in fear; yet neither man moved till the Sergeant said at last, "You wouldn't say that to me if you weren't a minister."

The Reverend's voice came back scarcely a whisper. "You put me in the wrong, Brooks. I apologize for what I said to you."

Taking his lunch pail again, the Sergeant walked off across the gangway. Reverend Beezely dropped his hand on her shoulder and as he leaned down towards her, she saw that the smile had gone from his face. "Yes, I let my temper run away with my tongue," he told her. And after a moment, added, "He's like a wolf, Mr. Brooks, he trusts no one. Our people are so driven and so pressed, Joyce, sometimes they only have hate to live on and they trust no one."

He turned away, shaking his head.

Joyce hurried down the flights of stairs till she fell in with the stream that poured along the walkways from under the huge curve of the ship's bow. She was shivering inside from her fear at this clash: for somehow *she* was between these two, and each one expecting her to take their side. But she was not certain of their dispute. To her it seemed inevitable that the union, run by white people, would set restrictions against Negroes. Everything she ever had learned told her this. As for the Auxiliary, she had paid her initiation, she carried her membership card, she forced herself down to the union hall in San Francisco once a month to pay her dues because the foreman warned her she would be fired if she did not.

And all she wanted from the Auxiliary was to be left alone. Suddenly she thought, all she wanted from any of them was to be left alone. There were only two things in the whole world for her—if only they would leave her alone; there was Charlie and there was the progress she was making at the piano. These and nothing else. And somehow these two were not different at all, they were the same, each leading her to the other, and they *were* the same. When she played, sitting at the piano in the little store-front church—she was playing for Charlie, and to him, and with him. And at night, riding the bus home from work, or climbing up from the flats of San Martin Village, when she thought of Charlie at night, always she found a fragment of that silver pattern when they had sat together in the gallery of the symphony, the solitary web of the horns, oh, Charlie, Charlie, singing like a star in the darkness . . .

Around her, the bawling, shouting, chewing faces of the white shipfitters, the white foremen, leadermen, business agents, and the fierce dispatcher who took her money at the union office: these were her enemies. She wanted only to be unseen by them. If only they would take her three dollars a month and never touch her, if only demanding no more than that. . . .

But she dreaded meeting the Sergeant again in the morning.

15

From the armed guard pool in New York, Tom was sent down to Norfolk, Virginia, where he rode out to the docks on a streetcar crowded with shipyard workers and longshoremen, soldiers, and sailors. The streetcar had a woman motorman who left the car at a main intersection halting traffic while she scurried over to a sidewalk stand for a carton of milk and a hot dog. Apparently unperturbed by the blare of horns from four directions and the laughter and shouts of passengers aboard the streetcar, she returned munching her sandwich, started up the car and they set off again.

That was the single thing Tom saw to remember in all of Norfolk. Afterwards, whenever he thought back over his acquaintance with the *Andrew Rogers,* which he joined that day, he would picture the stalled streetcar and the motorwoman with her hot dog. For there always seemed something half ridiculous about the ship itself which fitted this beginning. It sailed the night of the same day, out through the mouth of the Chesapeake and rolled in with a huge convoy eastwardbound.

At daybreak, the horizon bristled full circle with the masts and funnels of ships nosing into the quiet swell. From his signalman's station on the bridge, Tom studied the convoy through the glasses. They were slow ships all of them, liberties, hog-islanders, tramps of various nationalities. They probably wouldn't hit better than seven knots all the way across which would mean an eighteen-day crossing at least. He glanced forward occasionally at the flagship, an ancient British rustbucket, wallowing ahead of them in the same column. Every ten or fifteen minutes, the flagship blossomed with a new Christmas tree of flags alongside her stack, and the other ships in the convoy would begin to reproduce the same pattern.

"Baker-Tare-X-ray-Three."

Tom sang out the names and his side-kick plucked the flags from the locker, strung them to the line and hauled them up, while the navy lieutenant anxiously thumbed through his code book. Then he read the message to the merchant Skipper. But it was obvious the Skipper took a dim view of the navy, flags and all.

"As if I didn't know that already," the Skipper growled and stalked away, puffing his pipe. The Lieutenant repeated the message to the Second Mate who listened with an expression of keen interest.

"Thank you, Lieutenant," the mate said; and looked across at Tom, laughing silently, and showing Tom his tobacco-yellow teeth. Tom thought all this was quite funny, but he knew better than to laugh himself—not on the bridge. The night before, down in the navy mess before they sailed, he had asked who Andrew Rogers might have been to have a ship named after him, but nobody knew. Or cared apparently. And when he inquired what kind of a ship she was, everybody began to laugh. *Well, Flags,* they told him, *she hasn't rid an even keel since she came off the ways.* Laughing. *She runs into a head wind, Flags, they got to throw out the anchors to keep her from traveling ass-backwards. Almost broke in two off Cape Hatteras*—laughing—*and now got brace plates riveted all the way around, Flags, fantail to cut water, both sides.* Tom, who was looking into the bread box for his night lunch, found half a dozen king-size cockroaches taking their lunch too. He shook them out, and when he inquired how long since the *Andrew Rogers* had been fumigated, there were new howls of laughter from the men at the table.

"She fumigate two times last three months," the Chinese mess boy told him. "Kill cats and dogs but not kill cockroaches." This brought the house down, and the messboy, grinning enormously at his success, went on to explain how the cockroaches had come aboard in Cuba along with a cargo of sugar. The sugar was long since gone, but the cockroaches seemed set to stay forever.

So as it turned daybreak that first morning, Tom from the wing of the bridge peered down, looking for the braces they had told him about. And there they were, heaving up dripping and burying lazily into the bubbling swell. Seeing them, he began to laugh, not quite sure whether he was laughing about the woman motorman and her hot dog, or the king-size cockroaches in the bread box, or the idea of crossing the ocean on top of eight thousand tons of ammunition, in a ship that was tacked together with a rupture truss.

The coast line had slipped over the horizon. As the convoy formed up, the *Andrew Rogers* moved to her permanent position in column. From the flagship ahead the signals came sprouting with monotonous regularity repeating routine instructions out of the procedure manual. The Skipper had gone below, but the navy lieutenant (who told Tom he had been principal of a grade school in Wheeling, West Virginia only the year before) remained on the bridge, patiently thumbing the code book as he tried to keep pace with the flagship. The Second Mate, stripped to his T-shirt, squatted on the starboard gun tub, glancing over at Tom occasionally with his silent laugh. Up forward, most of the navy gunners were keeping themselves busy taking the three-inch gun apart and putting it together again; and below, the engine pulsed at half speed like a retarded heart.

The engine ticked off the hours. Day followed day into the long rotation of the watches, and every watch was like the one before it; and every day like the day before and the day after.

Tom waked each morning with his side-kick violently shaking him. *"Four* A.M., *Flags. Come on, come on now, you got to roll out. GOT TO!"*

He crawled into his jeans, doused his face with cold water. In the alleyway he snatched a mug of the vicious black coffee that had stood all night in the coffee urn, then headed up towards the bridge. If it were a bright night with the moon riding over the stack, the decks would be brighter than the inside of the ship. But if it were dark, as it often was, then pushing under the blackout curtain at the end of the alleyway was like knocking suddenly against a blank wall. He would halt, paralyzed, waiting for his eyes to adjust, for the familiar outlines of the lifeboats and ventilators to take shape against the slightly lighter blackness of the ocean beyond.

On the bridge, he called to the mate that he was there and the mate said, "Okay, Flags"; and he and the starboard gunner checked the other stations on the intercom and then sat with their feet hooked under the rail listening to the creak of the wheel as the helmsman nudged the ship back to her course, and the hum of wind in the rigging, and the footsteps of the mate pacing past in his endless circle, and the throb of the engine. The minutes of the watch moved past as slow as the stars until at last the sky brightened in the southeast, fencing the horizon again with the masts and funnels of the convoy.

The ordinary brought up fresh coffee at daybreak; and sometimes the junior radio operator stepped out for a breath of air after his long night in the shack. And all of them, Tom saw, even the mate, who was a silent, sarcastic type at other times, were drawn together during these few moments of the early morning. He remembered how daybreak had come to the construction gangs on graveyard shift, how the men would liven up and begin to talk. So at sea too, even at sea daybreak had a life of its own—the lightening sky, the sudden freshness of the air. From the complete silence of a few moments earlier, they would all begin jabbering at once about the latest news the Junior Sparks had brought up from his short wave—how the Yanks and Bums were making out, and there was a heat wave in the Middle West and a drought in Texas, and the U.S. Air Force had blasted Berlin and Stuttgart again, and the Germans had captured some new city in Russia. Or they would move on to that favorite of all topics—*after the war*—and the Junior Sparks would begin telling them about his girl in Liverpool, how they were all set to get married, and the job he had waiting for him— *after the war*—in a broadcast station in Bangor, Maine. The Second Mate meanwhile winked at Tom and pretended to be gnawing his fingernails.

The breakfast bell clanged down below.

Tom went down for a plate of scrambled eggs fried hard as rubber. Then he crawled into his bunk, hoping the Lieutenant would forget to rout him out before noon. And while he rolled back and forth trying to fall asleep, the morning routine of the ship would be getting under way. The steward would be having a wrangle with the mess boy in the alleyway outside his door; the deck gang overhead would be making a noise like a boiler factory with their hammers and wire brushes as they prepared the boat deck for a new coat of paint. He dozed at last: and immediately the bell rang for dinner. He got up, ate, returned to the sack; or else lounged in the navy mess waiting for four o'clock and the start of his own afternoon watch to roll around.

He was often glad to get back on watch.

From the pile of armed-service paperbacks heaped together in the closet in the alleyway, he read westerns and mystery stories until he got so bored he couldn't bring himself to look at another. Then, searching through the book closet, he discovered an old *Beginners' Spanish* under the heaps of westerns, and took to studying Spanish. At least that could be useful, he thought, he might go to Mexico after the war or get a construction job in South America. And it helped pass the time while he was on watch. He would copy words on slips of paper which he could hide in the palm of his hand, and learn the words while he pretended to be tinkering with the intercom phone or straightening the flag locker.

But there was a limit to how much Spanish grammar he could take in one day. Sometimes he joined the Junior Sparks in the radio shack to practice copying code. In radio a man could look forward to a bright future, the Sparks assured him, and the code would be easy for him to pick up, since it was the same he used on the blinker signal, only by ear instead of eye. But it did not take Tom long to decide that radio operating was not his line. The chattering of the earphones made him feel as if he had bugs crawling over him. After copying out a few code groups, to prove to himself he *could* learn it if he wanted, he would pull off the phones and wait for the Junior Sparks to reach a stopping place. Then they sat talking while the various receivers cracked and sputtered and the Sparks kept one ear cocked for the call letters of their convoy.

The Junior Sparks, Tom learned, was interested in two subjects: his girl friend in Liverpool, and radio. These were the only things he was ever willing to discuss. In the middle of a serious conversation on whether he ought to get married right away or wait till after the war, the Sparks would suddenly pull a card from his pocket and shove it at Tom. "Here's one of the best contacts I ever made, Flags. Like I was telling you yesterday, two hams make a contact, they got to mail each other their station cards . . ."

Capetown, South Africa, Tom read. *Abbie and Hal Slotz;* and then neatly written in pencil below: *contact 14:35 GMT 7-12-38. Best wishes old top.*

". . . just happened to catch Capetown on a skip distance," the Junior Sparks was saying. "Held contact about five minutes. That was after I stepped up my rig to three kilowatts with RCA power grids—"

"Oh, bullshit," Tom told him, and flipped the card back at him. "Is your girl friend a ham?"

"Not yet."

"She'll have to be taking it up, won't she, or else get a divorce?"

He never could provoke even a grin from the Junior Sparks. The other only shook his head, dead serious all the time. He was a skinny fellow with glasses and a pimply face; obviously smart, and he probably would make a good thing for himself in radio, Tom thought. He liked him well enough. He even envied him for being so set and sure of what he wanted. But after he had copied all the code he could stand, and taken his earful of ham operating and the girl in Liverpool, he slacked off going much to the radio shack.

More and more, he found himself just sitting in the mess hall. He would leaf through a magazine now and then, but most of the time sat talking, gossiping with the other men about the ship, or about home, or about nothing at all, joking and nagging and riding each other. Tom was the only rating and the oldest man in the gun crew outside the Lieutenant. The others called him Uncle O'Regan, but he took this as a sign of respect; and he made an effort to be always tossing out something for a laugh when he came into the mess hall.

"All right, Jack Benny," they would greet him, "what's the good word today?"

"Chief Engineer's cat got into the Skipper's cabin this morning. Took a crap right on the Skipper's bed."

"Aw, cut it out, Flags!"

"Skipper mistook it for one of his cigars in the dark."

"Aw, no, Flags!"

"Drop dead, you son of a bitch."

Howls of laughter. Good old Uncle O'Regan, he thought. Always a kick.

On the bridge one morning the Second Mate called over to him, "What the hell are you up to, Flags?" The mate was beside him, leaning over his shoulder before Tom had a chance to slip his Spanish vocabulary cards out of sight. "Are you still boning up on those signals, Flags, like that bone-headed Lieutenant of yours?"

"I'm learning Spanish," Tom said. "I got to do something or I'd go nuts."

"Spanish?"

"Sure. What's wrong with that?"

"Aha," the Second Mate said. "Youthful vigor. Ambition. I like to see that. What do you want to know Spanish for?"

"We might make a trip to South America."

"You don't need to speak Spanish to get your nooky in South America, Flags."

"Don't need to speak any language for that, Second."

"No. You're right." The Second crossed the bridge to check the distance of the next ship to port and returned. "What did you do before the war, Flags?" he asked.

"I was a carpenter. What did you do, Second?"

"Jack-of-all-trades," the other told him. And then suggested, "Want me to join you in learning Spanish? Always have been a great believer in self-education. They laughed when I sat down to play. But oh, how they howled afterwards."

When his relief came that morning, Tom fetched up the Spanish book and passed it along to the Second Mate. After that, they spent fifteen or twenty minutes each morning firing Spanish vocabulary at each other, to the great amusement of the AB on wheel watch who spoke Spanish fluently—and the disgust of the Junior Sparks.

Tom was uncertain whether he liked the Second Mate or not. He could see that most people regarded him as an odd one. Sometimes, in the mornings, he would be pleasant and friendly, and at other times drank his coffee without joining the conversation at all, standing there with his fists shoved into his trouser pockets; and once suddenly slung his coffee mug over the side, turned and went down the ladder without a word to any of them.

When he felt like talking, he had a sharp tongue and a gift for putting his finger on whatever was mean or ridiculous about other people. Tom had an uneasy feeling listening to him, yet enjoyed his remarks nonetheless. During the long watches he stood on the bridge, he had come to know the ship's officers quite thoroughly, and he could see that the Second's comments about them were nearly always accurate.

Tom noticed that the other officers took care to keep a distance from the Second; but the Second stayed pretty much to himself too. He seldom sat in the officers' saloon except for meals, and never hung around the bridge during the day like the other officers. Tom would see him sometimes in the crew's mess playing chess with one of the AB's; outside of that he stayed mostly in his own cabin. There he kept a shelf of books which Tom had seen through the doorway, and spent part of his spare time at least studying to go up for his chief's papers. He told Tom he had first sailed as an ordinary and worked his way up; and that he had the best job now he ever had held in his life, and he intended to stay with it after the war.

At first glance the Second seemed not much over twenty-five, a good-looking man with a big angular face and brown hair that started far back on his forehead. But when you looked more closely you could tell he was older—thirty-five or better, Tom guessed. He was always blinking his eyes as if he had sawdust in them, and the skin under the eyes and under his chin seemed red and pouchy, and there were heavy lines slanting past each side of his mouth. He looked better from a distance than close up.

They continued the exchange of Spanish words for almost a month, and then the Second exploded one morning, "For Christ's sake, Flags. Don't be so damn methodical! Let's take up yoga for a while." Tom did not know what yoga was, but he did not ask.

Most of his letters from Sally he found too cheerful to be entirely reassuring. He could see that the shipyard suited her perfectly. She sent him a snapshot taken in her welder's outfit—boots, jeans, leather apron, gauntlets and helmet—which he passed around the mess hall for a laugh. But in the same envelope she had enclosed a picture of herself with her new roommate which he did not pass around because the other girl was obviously a Negro—a fact she had not mentioned earlier; but he supposed it was a good thing she had let him know, at least, in case he happened to come home unexpectedly and found a colored boy friend in the house. For God's sake, weren't there any white women around the shipyard she could have asked? He carried the photograph in his wallet for two or three days, not caring to leave it in his locker, then tore it up and threw it over the side. Yet he was always looking forward to her next letter. There would be half a dozen waiting when they tied up in Norfolk or Boston, and sometimes a letter or two followed him over to Cardiff or London or Liverpool.

They crossed the North Atlantic five times in that summer and fall. Summer brought the fog down from the north, and the ship would glide along within its closed circle, the gray curtain always at arm's length from the rail, for days and nights at a stretch sometimes without ever seeing the next ship in convoy. Then the ships would keep position by blowing their numbers at five-minute intervals. Four shorts and a long. Pause. One long and four shorts. Fourth column, sixth in line. *Andrew Rogers* still here. Over and over and over. Sleeping or waking, they lived in gasps between the thundering blasts of the whistle.

He waked sometimes with a sudden sense of freedom as if an abscessed tooth had stopped hurting; and realized the whistle was silent, the fog must have lifted. Yet even the fog held certain advantages. For once it was gone, he knew the silhouettes of the convoy would be moving in slow procession across the horizon. The destroyers now and the corvettes would be zigzagging at full speed. Presently he would start up, wrenched tight and cold as an icicle at the distant crunch of depth charges. Blump, blump, blump, sharper and closer till they banged like a hammer against the hull of the ship.

He lay waiting. Maybe they had chased it away. Maybe it was just somebody's imagination on one of the escorts. Maybe. Sometimes it was. Sometimes the bombing would dwindle into the distance and Tom would stretch down, relaxing slowly. And sometimes—not very often—the frantic clamor of the battle stations tore the fo'c's'les open throwing them into the alleyways, bumping and shoving, struggling into their life jackets as they raced for the bridge and the gun tubs.

And always beneath everything else the slow thud of the engine, the wrack and twist of the turning screw as the *Andrew Rogers* slogged its way onward and onward.

16

Joyce tried to close her ears and her thoughts to the sharpening intensity of conflict. But this assailed her wherever she turned; it was in the lunch-hour talk of the workers; it was in a hundred conversations around her—in the overcrowded bus that ran between San Martin Village and the shipyard; in the shopping center; in the laundry room where they went down to run their wash through the plug-in-a-quarter washing machines.

One morning, waking, fumbling her way to the kitchen for the coffee which Sally usually left on the stove, Joyce found the morning newspaper spread out on the kitchen table. A half-page headline announced:

FAIR PRACTICE BOARD HOLDS
UNIONS, SHIPYARDS GUILTY OF BIAS

As she leaned down to read the story, she heard a knock at the door, and one of the Beezely girls thrust her head in. "You wake yet, Joyce? Daddy says to ask you come over. Says he's got coffee ready and he fix some biscuits." At this, the girl broke into giggles, withdrew her head, and Joyce saw her through the window bounding up the steps to the road where the school bus passed by. She dressed, pulled on her raincoat and went out into the gray morning. Following the path that angled across the hillside, she cut through the eucalyptus grove to the other wing of the project. Here the flat roofs mounted the slope like a flight of stairs, the forest of thin stovepipes smoked softly into the mist above them.

The Beezelys' kitchen was crowded with men and women in jeans and overalls, back from night shift at the yard. Reverend Beezely, pulling a batch of quick-mix biscuits from the oven, was explaining that he was not quite as handy at this type of business as he used to be—and his wife Janet was off to work already. Meanwhile one of the women served coffee around. Everyone kept talking at once, handing back and forth copies of the newspaper. The Reverend then rose to his feet and stood beside the table till the noise subsided. He began speaking, using the same tone Joyce had heard him use for his sermons in the church, a rolling, almost singing voice.

The Improvement League had sent over a message this morning, he told them, asking him to hurry out to other shipyards and visit the people there too. So he would have to leave them in a few moments. The news was very important. Time was short. Tomorrow in the afternoon they would go down in a delegation—all those who were willing to come with them—to call upon the union and ask the union to open its doors to colored workers in accordance with the spirit of the President's Board. This message he urged them to pass along to their friends: *Come tomorrow in the afternoon.* "The decision is something to thank God for," he declared. "Yes. Let us hope they will be moved to abide by its word and spirit."

One man said "Amen," to this; and one shouted, "That's right!" as he finished speaking. Others began to ask questions concerning the effect of the decision. Not being himself a lawyer, the Reverend said, he could not tell the exact legal significance; but this much they could be certain of: the Board had declared that there *was* discrimination in the yards—of course we all knew, but now *they've* had to find it out too—and charged the companies and the unions with having joined together in this practice. The Board had ordered the companies to cease from discrimination in hiring, training, and promotion. And told the unions either they must give up the closed-shop contract, or grant full and equal membership to all qualified workers.

"What do they mean by an order?" someone called. "Can they make that stick?"

"This morning I talked to our chairman in San Francisco on the telephone. Even the lawyers he's consulted cannot yet say how far that order will go." The Reverend paused, searching the faces around him, and presently resumed his sermon-speaking tone: "I have confidence the President's Board will find its way in proper legal processes. We pray the parties concerned will heed moral suasion. Yes. We pray they will hear us and be moved to comply with that which is humane and just. We join together, all, *all of our people,* to appeal they be so guided."

There was a heavy, moving earnestness in his voice. Joyce, listening, recalled suddenly the comment Charlie had once made to her: Rev sounds phony as a nine-dollar bill sometimes. She looked hastily down at her feet, embarrassed and guilty to have harbored such a thought at such a time. Certainly Charlie had not meant that. And yet he *had* meant it too, she knew he had; and now, as she remembered, she understood why. For Charlie, things that were most serious of all needed to be spoken as if there were always a little joke about them. The Reverend was the opposite. Everything needed to be grave and serious for the Reverend. Serious matters called him to his sermon-speaking voice. In her own secret thoughts, Joyce knew that she always pictured herself as a musician; and she could see now that the Reverend must picture himself as a great preacher, a shepherd leading the flock. It was this that Charlie had made fun of; but wasn't it right for him? Everyone must picture themselves as something that was more than any person could be.

She raised her eyes, and as her glance met the Reverend's, she could not prevent herself from smiling. He returned the smile. But she saw with relief that he had not read her thought. His smile was for everyone in the room. He held his hands out to them, while the man who had previously cried, "Amen," now repeated even more loudly, "Amen, brother, amen."

The Reverend stepped toward the door. He must go to Oakland to visit the people from the Oakland shipyard, he informed them; but turning back as he went out, he called, "You all be sure to pass the word back to your friends: *Come tomorrow in the afternoon.*"

All that evening at work, Joyce heard the yard buzzing around her with talk of the Board's decision. But the Sergeant said not a word about it. At midnight as she went home, people were at the gates handing out mimeographed letters from the Improvement League appealing to colored workers to join the delegation to the union the following day. Joyce had been fighting back and forth in her mind whether she would go or not go. She had always felt frightened of going to the union hall, even to stop there to pay her dues; and the idea of going now with the others, to *demand,* to challenge, to defy that enormous, silent enmity, terrified her. Yet the impression the gathering in the kitchen had made upon her, and her admiration for Reverend Beezely, as well as her sense of guilt that she *still* kept remembering what Charlie had said and laughing over it, would not allow her to slide the matter aside. Most of the night, it kept her awake; and by morning she had decided she was catching cold, that she could honestly tell herself she was too sick to go.

Besides, it was raining again.

But a little after twelve, when she knew Janet would be coming home from her dry-cleaning shop, she walked over to the Beezelys', hoping Janet would tell her, no, she was not going. Janet was at the stove getting lunch ready. She turned and looked at Joyce with an odd, lopsided dubious smile and nodded her head.

"Yes, I am." And then she said, "I'm scared to death."

"So am I," Joyce told her. She sat down at the table and ate lunch with them and afterwards Reverend Beezely went out to round up the group of people who had promised to go. They walked down to the bus stop and rode into San Francisco.

The city was gray and cold.

It was the city Joyce had seen the night she first went out with Charlie—the sad houses with their high front steps and corner towers, old, dim, dreary, weeping in the mist. It was the city Charlie had told her about where hungry people waited in the rain and the clouds hung low over the roof-tops. San Francisco, so bright in the sunlight: so strange and hostile. She and Janet huddled close together and when she raised her eyes she saw other eyes staring back from the window of a grocery on the corner, from the window of the tavern beyond as they passed. She saw a policeman in a doorway in his black raincoat and rain hat, staring down at them. They were like a procession, like a funeral, she thought, heads hunched and hands in their pockets, walking, walking along a gray street under the heavy frightening sky.

Dropping her eyes, she saw only the heels of the man in front of her splashing through puddles of water.

They had reached the union hall. They bunched together looking up at the doorway, not very many of them—she knew Reverend Beezely must be disappointed—fifty or fifty-five. The doors were closed, three policemen stood guard on the steps. Reverend Beezely, and three other men from the committee of the Improvement League, mounted the steps, and for a moment Joyce saw them in Janet Beezely's face: in Janet's wide brown, frightened eyes and her half-open lips. But they were talking now, the men and the policemen, and one of the policemen went inside, the door closed sharply behind him, he was gone for a long while. Returning at last, he handed a piece of paper to Reverend Beezely. The men from the committee and the three policemen seemed to be conferring together over the paper. Then the Reverend spun around, called out to them in a loud voice,

"Friends, the officer here has just taken our message to the union. And the president of the union sends out a reply. I will read it.

" 'This is our hall,' " he read. " 'We are not going to take them into membership. We have a right to refuse their admission into the union proper since our international regulations do not permit us to accept Negroes into membership.' "

There was a long moment of silence. A man climbing on the roof of a car at the curb snapped a picture with a flashlight bulb. A few voices cried out, protesting, and Reverend Beezely held up his hands: but the police officer shouldered in front of him.

"All right now," the officer shouted. "You'll have to break it up. There's nothin' more we can do for you here. We got orders to keep the street clear. Move along. Move along."

The Reverend and the other men turned down from the steps, led their little procession back up the rain-swept block and two squad cars followed beside them, waiting and watching and herding them towards the streetcar stop at the corner.

It was only when they were in the bus at last, rolling over the bridge to San Martin, that a sense of safety returned to Joyce. Then she and Janet became very gay; they joked with each other over what had happened; and Joyce was glad she had stayed with Janet, and that she had shared even in so small a way what seemed to her the incredible courage of Reverend Beezely and the others who had stood on the steps.

When she went to work, she wanted to tell the Sergeant. She hoped he might have heard already and ask her; but she could find no way of raising the subject herself.

They were in the 'tween-decks again, still setting braces and brackets in what the Sergeant explained was going to be the ship's refrigeration compartment. Most of the time they could not have talked even if they had wished, because a gang of chippers directly over their heads were hammering with their pneumatic hammers on the steel deck. At supper hour they sat down where they were—it was raining outside —still raining—and bitter cold in the 'tween-decks; but dry here at least. Other workers hunched into corners or squatted behind bulkheads trying to hide from the drafts that poured through the openings of the hull. Shivering, Joyce wished she had walked over to the lunchroom. Getting there and back took half your free time, but she would have had a warm place to sit down.

She opened her thermos, poured out tea, and a few swigs of the hot liquid made her feel better though her teeth were still chattering.

"Thought once I wouldn't care how damn cold it ever got," the Sergeant said. "If I could just latch on to some cool weather again. But right now I could use a little of that hot kind."

She thought he must be talking about the weather of the islands wherever it was he had been; and she remembered the different stories of what was said to have happened to him. People always were speculating about the Sergeant. He had been blown up in a bombing attack. Or he had been machine-gunned. Or he had fallen out the window of a building. And another story said that a truck-load of white Marines had run over him. But all the accounts agreed he had not missed being dead by much, and the doctors had hitched his broken bones together with pieces of silver wire. Whenever he had a run-in with the leaderman or the foreman or some other shipfitter, word would pass around, *Look out for the Sergeant, all those wires are sparking like an old spark coil!* She had seen him sometimes lifting a piece of steel or twisting himself on or off a scaffold, when his face would suddenly screw up in pain. But during all the months she had worked with him, she had never heard him say a word about his injury or what had happened to him in the war. Now that he had made an opening, she thought he might go on to talk; and if only he would talk, it would not be so hard for her to talk to him.

But he chewed up his sandwiches and drank his coffee in silence.

Not till the very end of the shift, when she was picking up the tools again, did he turn to her suddenly, asking, "How many people showed up down there at the union hall?"

"I—I don't know. Fifty, they said . . ."

"Were you there?"

She nodded.

"Plenty of ministers and lawyers, I guess, wasn't there?"

"Reverend Beezely was there. I don't know what others."

"But not many from the shipyard," he cried. "Fifty people —what good is that?" And leaning towards her, he demanded, *"What did that union president say?"*

She told him as closely as she could remember; and then

after the whistle blew and they had crossed over to the stairway that led down the stagings, she heard him repeating half to himself under his breath, " . . . have a right to refuse, he says, it's our hall, we'll not admit them, he said that. . . ."

17

The Second Mate, though he appeared to have the gift of pinpointing what was meanest in others, spoke little of himself, and Tom, even after they had sailed several voyages together, still felt as if the Second were only a casual acquaintance. He had known him almost half a year before the other mentioned one day that he had been a newspaper reporter before the war and had a wife and child living in New York. Tom, recalling what he had said about his berth as mate being the best job he had ever had, did not believe him. The *Andrew Rogers* was unloading cargo in the Thames a few miles down river from London at the time, and he and the Second had gone ashore for a beer after supper. They settled down at the bar in a dark, cold, almost empty pub across the cobblestone street from the quayside, and Tom for some time worked at his sour beer in silence. Then without actually intending to do so, he turned to the other and demanded,

"How the hell could you even be thinking of shipping after the war if you got a job like that and a family ashore?"

The Second, who usually had a quick answer on his tongue, seemed caught short-handed for words. His face reddened. "The romance, Flags. The adventure."

"Don't hand me that."

"Everybody gets their kicks in their own way. Going to sea's an easy life, O'Hooligan. I do my work and I have my time to myself."

"I got too much time to myself," Tom said. "I got nothin' to do with it."

"What would you do with it if you were back home?"

"Plenty."

"I know what you'd do," the Second told him. "You'd use it up getting back and forth to work and diapering the baby and fighting with your wife. You don't understand when you're well off, that's what's wrong with you. Why don't you let me teach you how to play chess?"

"You know where you can put that chess. But what do *you* do with your time, Second? I never see you down in the saloon playing bridge with the Skipper and the Lieutenant—"

"They never invited me. What do I do? All right. I read. On shore I used to be all the time writing. Writing crap. Newspaper crap. Pure unadulterated. And why was it crap? Because that's what they wanted. That's what they paid me for. Only that isn't the real reason, Flags. It's because I never had time to do anything else. I never had time to think. I never had time to read a book. Not till I went to sea." He emptied his glass at a gulp and twisted on the bench so that he faced Tom. His eyes had a lit-up look, and Tom would have thought he was drunk already, from the wildness of his gestures—except that they had just come off the ship and he could hardly have gotten drunk on one glass of beer.

"People have made a damn mess of things, Flags. I used to live like a rat in a wall before the war. And now you get all upset because I don't want to go back. Why should I? I'm living like a king now, like a philosopher. I've got time, I can do what I want . . ." He waved his hand indicating the soot-crusted walls of the little pub. "Here we are, you go outside, everything's all knocked over into heaps of rubble. And yet I got it better'n I ever had in my life before."

He sat nodding his head, tapping his fingers on the table top; and ordered another glass of beer, poured that down and waved for a third. "They close these joints in half an hour," he said. "You better drink up fast if you want a few. Alcohol helps limber a person up, Flags. That's what it's for. Gift of the gods, along with all the other blessings they sent us. You want to ask this bartender where's the nearest whorehouse?" He was fingering the under side of his chin and held his head cocked in an attentive and questioning manner. "I think you're really very moral in spite of yourself," he accused. "That's all right, though. I wish I felt the same way about *my* wife."

Why should he be telling me this? Tom wondered.

"Do you think a man and a woman ought to split up if they don't get along?"

Tom waited suspiciously, holding his glass between his hands. "I suppose so," he said at last. "Unless they got kids."

"That's very moral too. I imagine that's why my wife wanted our kid. But it's no damn good for the kid either if the parents can't stand each other. Well, I can hold out just so long, then I begin to get the urge, Flags."

"Now you're boasting."

"No, I'm not that old yet. You ever go with a woman that wasn't sexy at all but tried to pretend she was in heat all the time?"

Tom shook his head.

"That's a miserable thing. The war's broken up a lot of marriages, Flags."

"I guess it's made a lot too."

"Leave us look on the bright side of things, by all means. Did it make yours?"

"No," Tom answered; and thought, of course it did.

"I've been married seven years and if it wasn't for the war I'd be unmarried again right now. I would have walked out if I hadn't gone to sea. It won't last long after the war."

"You just said you were going to keep on shipping."

"Did I say so? Well, if a man could live like an oyster, that would be the way to do it. But man does not live by bread alone, Flags. You know where that comes from?"

"Sure, the Bible."

"I thought Catholics didn't read the Bible very much. But I guess they always serve up a few smatterings of the Gospels at Mass, don't they?"

"So who said I was a Catholic?"

"No? Aren't all the O'Regan boys Catholics?"

Tom felt an impulse to hit him over the head with his beer glass, but found himself laughing instead. "My mother's a Methodist," he told him. "I guess my father was a Catholic sometime or other but that was before I knew him."

"So what are *you?*"

"Nothing particular."

"An agnostic. You know what that means?"

"Oh, shove it, Second."

"Now don't get mad. I just want to find out if you know what I'm talking about. That's what I am—it means you don't know: maybe so, but you got to show me. I think most people really feel that way even if they go to church three times a week." He stared Tom in the eye with a drunken intensity and tried to capture his wrist as if to guarantee his attention. "Flags," he said, "I'm going to live in Paris after the war. Filet mignon and good red Burgundy every night for dinner. Going to write third-rate murder mysteries and live in Paris. You and your wife can come visit me, but leave the kids in the States."

"I haven't got any yet."

"Oh, you will have. So why shouldn't I write a book,

Flags? That's what every newspaper man kids himself about. The Jonathan Swift of the twentieth century. Oh, I'm ambitious too. What the hell would you care," he lamented. "You probably never read anything tougher than a comic book in your life. A fellow with smart brains like you, O'Hoolihan, ought to be reading books instead of studying those damn Spanish vocabulary cards all the time. Books are the only decent things people ever made, did you know that? Look at this rustbucket of ours. Took two hundred years to figure out how to put together the engine inside it. Maybe it is the bummest marine engine afloat nowadays. But it's a wonderful machine, isn't it? And what do we do? Go charging back and forth carrying blockbusters!

"So they'll use one of those, Flags, to blow up the cathedral in Cologne, St. Peter's, the Acropolis. If we could tell what was the most beautiful thing man ever created, they'd figure exactly the right dose—they'd work it out on a slide rule so as not to waste one little grain of powder—that's science—and blow it all to hell. I love people, Flags! They're the most wonderful thing in the world. Come on, let's get out of here."

But as they left the pub, the Second burst out laughing again and slapped Tom on the back. "All right, I'll write a book someday, O'Flannagan. You'll be proud you shipped on the same bucket with me. That'll be *something* to remember anyhow."

It was bitter cold outside, a gusty raw night, and high overhead, Tom could see a few cold stars gleaming through gaps of the clouds. Along the dark street that followed the quayside they stumbled back towards the ship, tripping over the curbs and the uneven cobblestones. They had almost reached their pierhead when they heard the moan of the air-raid siren, then the sharp distant barking of anti-aircraft. He and the Second jumped under the shelter of a doorway.

"No use lookin' for a better one," Tom yelled into his ear.

"They ever hit one of these ships we'll be off to the races anyhow."

They flattened against the closed doors and stared at the sky. The sky now crisscrossed with searchlights and the round circles of the lights darted back and forth against the underside of the ragged clouds, probing for the openings; and through these openings they saw here a star and there the sparkle of a bursting shell against the black sky beyond.

As they watched, three stars detached themselves, blossomed, and came floating downwards. From the doorway where they had taken shelter they commanded a sweep of the city—the warehouses opposite had been blasted down in some previous raid; and there beyond were the houses stepping off over the low hills, the smoky skyline, all suddenly aglow in the radiance of the drifting stars. The doors jolted behind them, the earth rumbled, the air contracted against their ears. A long way off, Tom thought.

After the noise of the bombing, they heard the hum of engines overhead. For an instant between the streaming tatters of cloud, they caught the high flight of geese, the silver arrows flashing as the finger of a searchlight brushed them. The Second cupped his hands.

"Let her go, God damn you," he shouted. "Right down the stack of the *Andrew Rogers.*"

Around them, on the cobblestones and across the roofs of the warehouses, they heard the shrapnel fragments from the anti-aircraft shells ticking down like a small hailstorm. The firing faded into the distance, the floating stars had burned out or been shot down. The searchlights died, the city retired into its darkness—except for a single spot on the horizon, a pulsing red glow.

The wind from Iceland brought flurries of snow. The North Atlantic came marching to meet them in a waste of foam-crested smoking rollers. The mast swept like a pendulum across the clouds. Tom, clinging to his gun tub, stared into the ocean that boiled up toward the wing of the bridge, till the *Andrew Rogers* would shake loose and go sweeping back through her arc in the opposite direction. High in the air, he would see the mast and funnel outthrust under his feet while the thwartships deck slanted like a cliff into the seas on the farther side. He remembered the rupture truss, then, and the crotchety engine below; and began to laugh, momentarily elated, yelling and singing at the top of his lungs since no one could hear him—as he had once bellowed into the grinding motor of his old pickup at night on the highway.

A fever of impatience seized him. The people around him had grown so familiar he could hardly bear the sight of them; not only the Lieutenant and Skipper and the Purser whom he had disliked from the beginning, but others whom he considered his friends—the Second Mate and Junior Sparks, the young kids in the navy crew, the cook, the bosun, Yee the Chinese mess boy. He knew them all so well, knew what each would say, what expression would come over each face whenever he saw the face in whatever part of the ship. He found himself wishing for anything to break the monotony, an attack, a collision, an air raid.

At night he went sometimes to the fantail where he could look down to see the screw in the black water and its ponderous movement illuminated by swarms of bubbles. This seemed to him very beautiful. He was amazed the ocean held so much light in it; and wondered if the water he saw uncoiling from the turn of the propeller might not be the same water that had come swishing up to his feet—up to their feet—a year ago on the beach at Bodensee. And how deep did it go down? And how little there was between himself and this, he thought. Half an inch of steel plate. One movement, if he gave the word. On the bridge in the mornings, the Second Mate had several times spoken of the same thing, and Tom felt certain others sensed this too, just as a person was not satisfied till he had crawled to the very edge of a cliff, or dared himself to dive into the surf when it was running heavy.

It must be a bad sign, he told himself, to be thinking such thoughts. But who could help thinking them if he thought at all? Whole convoys of Liberties exactly like the *Andrew Rogers* even to the tilt of the ventilators and the stale coffee in the coffee urn, had gone thumping under with their stewards and messboys, their second mates and signalmen. Or the night in London, he thought, how many people had winked out between the warning and the all-clear that night? Yet why blame that on the war? The same people would be dead anyway sooner or later. What are you, O'Hoolihan, the Second had kept asking, what *are* you?—actually it must have been this he was speaking of; and he did not know. Even his mother with her prayer meetings and church socials and Sunday suppers—did he really know what she thought? And that minister of hers, he wondered, what would he say if he stood here looking down over the fantail? Would he clap his hands and yell, that's it, that's just what I've been waiting for? Or say that he saw a house down there, and a door, beyond the bubbles?

It seemed strange to Tom that in all his life he remembered seeing only one person die. People died in hospitals, or in somebody else's family, or on a ship that was sinking, three or four miles away. But he had seen only one, he thought: the Swede. That was enough to go around. They used to tease him about his accent, he remembered, kidding him at lunch time to make him swear, because he always said *Yeesus* instead of *Jesus;* and everybody in the mill began calling John Keefe the foreman, "Foreman Yohn" in imitation of the old Swede. So his final word had been, "Yohn, cut the power, Yohn!" while the conveyor moved slow and steady up the incline carrying its load of scraps and bark strips and the Swede riding it like a cowboy, butting his head against the stanchions as he went up. Then the power shut off, the mill was silent, some of the men climbed up to fetch him— what was left.

Afterwards Tom had walked out on the sawdust bank beside the log pond where he lay down, sick to his stomach, aching and shaking in every bone. There Kallela had found him. Kallela sat beside him on the bank; and for once the big bawling voice that had something to say about almost everything, said not a word. They stayed in silence until the machines started rattling in the mill again, and Kallela got him on his feet and sent him off home for the rest of the day.

That was the story he should have told Walter Stone on the witness stand—two years later, how long was it?—instead of repeating the same things all the others had said about whether they ever voted by secret ballot for a strike. Not that it had anything to do with the strike. Or did it? What difference could a few nickels make? Still, it wouldn't have amounted to much. He was an old man and he shouldn't have been wearing an overcoat around the moving machinery. He must have caught his sleeve in the chain. The foreman had told him too, Yohn the foreman. Some things it would be much better to forget and those of course the ones that stayed with you: the eyeless, noseless, mouthless face peering down from the trestle of the conveyor.

Poor old bastard, he thought; and he remembered Walter Stone stepping into his car in front of the courthouse, waving his hand like somebody in the movies, while Kallela and all the others Stone had just gotten off the hook after the strike were giving him the big send-off. It was late afternoon then, and as he watched Stone's car move away, he thought, he'll be stopping at the hotel in Ukiah, and by midnight or one o'clock in the morning he'll drive into San Francisco, maybe buying himself a drink if he gets thirsty. He's finished. He doesn't have to come back to Saw Creek in a hundred years if he don't feel like it. There would be the life to lead.

Oh, yes indeed, Stone led a good life, Tom thought, that was very easy to see. People stepped out of his way; they respected him. But had he meant what he said that night he talked with Kallela, or was it only something to be saying? Or maybe the old man had dreamed the whole business up by himself? He kept busy as a cat with nine kittens, the old man, thinking up plans nowadays, which he'd drop quick enough if he and Sally were to split up. Still, he'd have to light on something or go back to pounding nails, Tom thought. Mainly it was a matter of time. Whatever he went into would certainly take time. To go into law might not be much slower than anything else. Suppose he went contracting, he'd need a year or two to study up for the license, God knows how long after that to get his feet under him. Or if he worked into position to snag one of the business-agent jobs in the union, that would take two or three years at least, and he might not make it then, there'd be plenty of takers after the war. And a damn poor job once you got it, too. Look at Kallela, as fine an organizer as they were ever likely to have, and they chopped him off at the ankles. You wouldn't see them handle Stone that way. Oh, no. Stone had been riding high there in the union hall with his fat brief case and his topcoat slung over his shoulder.

The best thing might be not to wait, Tom thought, but write a letter to him right away. That would find out quick enough if he meant what he said.

Or might that be pushing things too fast? How could you tell?

He sat down at the table in the empty mess hall. As he tried to make up his mind one way or the other, he scribbled out a letter to see what it would look like. The tone had to be exactly right. Interested but not eager, he told himself. Glad to accept advice, but not looking for any favors. His sloppy handwriting worried him too, and he considered asking the Junior Sparks to type it for him, but decided against that. He recopied the letter. Then he made a few changes, copied it over again; and by the time he was due on the bridge for his morning watch, he was already finishing the fifth rewriting. His fingers had begun to ache. What the hell have I got to lose? he demanded, and folded the page inside a note to Sally in which he asked her to look up Stone's address and mail the letter.

The reaching of this decision carried Tom up to the bridge again in renewed good humor. To the Second Mate he gave word that Sparks had received orders altering course for Bermuda; and while the AB on the wheel was laughing over this one, Tom called the forward gun tub to say the Lieutenant was on his way down for inspection. But afterwards the impatience fixed its grip more harshly than ever. What he had done, he saw, was nothing, not even a beginning. And there was nothing he could do. He was trapped, handcuffed, helpless, tied down tight as if he had been thrown into the tank of the Saw Creek jail. The great screw went cranking out its spiral of bubbles. The white foam streamed away into the dark. The engine pumped its heart out and yet they hung there motionless.

All his life he had been going somewhere, he thought, fighting to get around the next corner; and always there was another next corner ahead. Five years, six years, what did it matter? He'd be an old man—beat, punch-drunk, a rummy like the Second Mate over there. That was a case to be going over the side one of these days. But the momentary flush of contempt only sparked his anger at himself. You go over too, he shouted. Why would any woman want to be hooked to you for the rest of her life? So you can drag her around in that pickup truck to one construction job after another? That's what you'll end up doing! Do you think she'll wait, you crazy fool? Did you ever give her anything to count on waiting for? Where is she now? Who's she sleeping with tonight? *No, no, she's not!*—yet only half believing this, for what would he himself be doing if he was out there in the shipyard with a bunch of women welders? So you reach out and grab some as it goes by. She knew that, she knew, otherwise she never would have gone with him on that weekend . . .

Tom felt certain the Second Mate, blinking his eyes and laughing his silent laugh, knew exactly what he was going through and he half hated him for this. But in spite of himself, he was driven to the Second. He came begging him for his books. Books, he found, offered some slight escape from the enclosure of the ship. Several times already, he had culled over the westerns and hand-me-downs in the mess-hall cupboard; and now he worked through the Second's small collection of biographies, novels, books of travel. Each piece of information must be of some use afterwards, he promised himself; the parts must finally fit together. He read a life of Napoleon, a life of Lincoln in which he was pleased to discover that Lincoln had taught himself law by studying at night after he finished his day's work; and he struggled halfway through a biography of Edgar Allan Poe. All this, he saw, provided a source of considerable amusement for the Second.

"Reading's really a poison," the Second expounded. "That's the true meaning of the story of Adam and Eve. It wasn't an apple the serpent gave them, it was the book of knowledge, sort of an encyclopedia. The priests slipped the apple into the story afterwards as a sexual symbol. Only it wasn't really a book either, Flags, it was a jigger of morphine. You'll curse me for this sometime." He had removed all his own books from his shelf as soon as Tom began to show interest in them, and he parceled them out one at a time. "You got to have the right charge in each needle, Flags. Got to handle this stuff with rubber gloves."

Tom carefully chewed down his anger before he replied. "Some people don't know enough to find their ass with both hands," he said to the Second. "And they never learn it by reading about it either."

But the one book which roused Tom more than anything he had read or learned before, he discovered without the Second's help; and he was glad of that. It was while the *Andrew Rogers* was docked in Boston that some ladies drove up in a station wagon which carried a sign saying, *Seamen's Aid Institute.* The ladies trotted back and forth delivering bundles of old books and magazines to the various ships along the dock, and Tom who was on gangway watch, received the bundle for the *Andrew Rogers.* Thus having first pick, he took out several books he thought he might want to read. Among these was one titled, *Science Made Easy Series: Chats on Astronomy.*

He knew as soon as he turned the cover that this was over his head. Yet he read all the way through and when he finished felt certain he understood a good deal more than he had expected. Fragments half forgotten from high school came back to him. The book drew them together into new discoveries. Standing on deck, he looked at the stars in the wintry sky, high over the glow of the city. He could not tell the name of a single star; yet now understood that many of these pinpoints were suns greater than the sun itself, burning at a heat never known on earth. Light from stars he saw tonight must have begun its journey before the beginning of history; and he himself, the steel deck plates he stood on, the dock below, and the black waters of Boston harbor, were composed on the same plan as the sky above him—pinpoints of something traversing stretches of empty space. He was center between two endless distances, one to infinite smallness, the other to infinite greatness; as also he stood halfway in time between a time before and a time afterwards, and it was impossible to imagine either an end or a beginning.

Tom was exultant at these ideas. That he could understand them and partially state them seemed to make the ideas belong to him. He realized how much there was to know that was known already—to some people—and might be known by anyone who took the trouble; and how much more there was to know that no one knew yet, but people would know someday. Here too must be an endless distance, there could be no limit to it. How would anyone grow tired of living in such a universe? If only a person lived long enough to *know* everything and do everything! and he at once selected this thought as it moved past, bringing it back, repeating the words several times over with satisfaction. Here was something about himself. Not everyone, certainly, would feel the same way. The Second, for example, he supposed must feel quite differently. That was why the Second always talked in his sarcastic tone, and why he got drunk whenever he went ashore, and why he was intending to keep on shipping after the war. He *wanted* to be cooped up. Tom felt sorry for the Second. Compared to a man like Walter Stone who could make a whole courtroom jump without raising his voice, or even to a man like Kallela that couldn't be pushed down with a pile driver, there was not much to the Second, he thought. People like the Second would be afraid to look very far, they were half dead already. And himself? he wondered, *himself?*

18

To the reception which the Richards undertook in honor of their daughter Carol's return to San Francisco, Walter and his wife were invited both by written invitation and by telephone direct from Mrs. Richards to Mrs. Stone. Clearly this was the official reconciliation, the bringing together of the Montagues and the Capulets, now no longer postponable as Juliet with her year-old son took up residence in the house her father had given the young couple for a wedding present. Wendel however was not on hand. He was (as Walter learned from a letter he had received a few days earlier) en route to points unspecified in the Pacific, having been (at his own request, he wrote) reassigned to more active duty.

But the summons was perhaps the more binding for his absence: herein fail not. So at the appointed hour they presented themselves, in dinner jacket and evening gown, while the November fog weaved under the cypress trees along Saint Christopher Woods Drive, and the Richards greeted them at the door as if never any but friendly words had passed between them. It had been almost five years since Walter had seen the inside of the Richards' house. The young wife Carol, whose strapless gown set off a display of back and shoulders still sun-browned in November, stood to one side of the fireplace receiving best wishes of the guests. He offered his own, planting a kiss on her forehead. All these niceties properly being observed, Walter saw, with Mrs. Richards—herself a proper and precise lady—in full command of the field. Richards, however, seemed to be hovering, or fluttering. But he was not ordinarily a fluttery type, Walter thought, recalling that he had been an excellent tennis player in college with a forehand drive and a steady backhand that had carried him into—what?—the semifinals? As well as a shrewd, rather cold-blooded attorney. Yet now he was fluttering. He circled his daughter at a distance; he herded the guests up to her one after another; he kept interrupting her conversations to ask if she didn't wish to sit down. Obviously the man was consumed by his delight and pride in this offspring; and here, Walter realized, lay the motive force which had brought Mackay, the ex-state senator, to discuss with himself and Chantry the possibility of Wendel's running for Congress. Thus viewed, the project took on a somewhat different aspect. For a moment he felt envious of Richards. He hoped his wife Sylvia would hold up through the ceremony.

They ought not to stay longer than was necessary to be civil, he thought. It would be an unbearable mortification for the girl if Sylvia let go halfway through; and an unbearable source of satisfaction for Mrs. Richards, too. But that in itself would probably sustain her. He saw her across the room, talking with Carol by the fireplace. She looked all right. She looked much better since she had come back. But she was no longer unmarked. He had wondered for many years how she could keep such tight control of herself and appear always so perfect on the surface. And then the controls had snapped and the marks appeared overnight. The faltering step, the slightly bloated cheeks, the slight thickness of speech, the vague, inconclusive, fuzzy look of the eye.

That was the worst, he thought. All the others had gone while she had been away; but the look in the eye remained telling him that the ten months had been lost and the other marks were only hiding beneath the surface. He felt certain as he watched her that she had set sail inside herself for the end, and nothing would hold her back.

Mackay was with her now—the ex-senator, pink and rococo as ever. They were laughing gaily as he guided her toward the table where drinks were served. How kind of him, Walter thought, how very kind; and turning, found Richards at his side. Richards conducted him to his library to show off his latest acquisition— (he remembered that Richards had always been a collector of Oriental bric-a-brac, a great buyer at auctions)—and this turned out to be a set of Chinese lobsters, carved from brass, perfect to the last whisker, with each claw and feeler hinged to move in the correct direction.

Richards asked, "How would you like to put two or three of these together in your spare time?"

Walter shook his head. "One not only wonders *how*, but *why?* Imagine being as devoted as that to lobsters! They're beautiful pieces."

"The Chinese are very fond of shellfish," Richards observed; and added, "I'm glad to have you here again, Walter."

"I'm very glad to be here."

"I felt it was up to me to make the opening move. But I think we both have simmered down with the passage of time."

"I think so."

The other rested one hand lightly on his arm. "I gathered from Mackay that you were not necessarily opposed to —what he discussed with you?"

"Not necessarily," Walter replied. "But I told him it didn't make much difference what I thought. The decision will have to be made by the principals, won't it? Wendel and Carol?"

"Of course." After a moment of silence, Richards proceeded. "Let's understand each other. You and I have known one another a long while. We've had our ups and downs. Two or three years ago, I don't believe I would have talked to you about this at all. I would have gone right ahead, and I was sufficiently angry so that I would not have given a damn whether you liked what I was doing or not. I thought you were a crackpot then, or that you were trying to break things up for my firm—and for our two children—out of some personal malice. I realize now that I—well, that I didn't understand what you were talking about."

"That may not have been your fault," Walter began.

"No, let me finish. You're an idealist and I respect you for that. But let me be frank to say that I respect you also for having put your ideals to successful application. I would be willing to stipulate, somewhat belatedly, that your going in with Chantry and taking the line you did, was an extremely smart move. I certainly didn't see it at the time."

Walter waved his hand to pass off these deprecations.

"If we can now resume diplomatic relations, Walter, I believe we can do a lot of good for our two children."

Or a lot of harm, Walter thought; and he asked, "Have you discussed this with them?"

"Certainly."

"Do they want it?"

"Very much."

"And do you think he has a chance of being elected?"

"Mackay thinks he has an excellent chance."

"He should know, I suppose."

"Well, Mackay is no fool, Walter. He wants a candidate in Gaventer's congressional district, and naturally he says the candidate is sure to win. I don't believe it's quite as simple as that. But Gaventer is getting along and he may not run again, particularly when he finds he'll have a young serviceman opposed to him. That's hard medicine for a tired politician. Wendel might very possibly beat him. But even if he didn't win the first time, he'd be in a better position for the second try. It's never any discredit to a young fellow to be defeated by the incumbent."

"I suppose not," Walter said; and taking up one of the brass lobsters, he examined the intricate workmanship of the joints. "May I ask if the—the wedding present from yourself and Mrs. Richards happens to be located in Gaventer's district?"

"Well, Carol was going to need a place to live, and I asked Mackay to mark out the boundaries for me on a street map." Richards smiled almost shyly. "It happened to include several quite pleasant neighborhoods. The house is an old one, but solidly built."

Walter pictured it at once. San Francisco Gothic from a year or two after the earthquake: just the thing for the rising young citizen—solid, reassuring, rooted in the community, yet nothing overly pretentious or modern. And undoubtedly a sound investment.

"I suppose I'd better get back on my job," Richards said. "But I wanted to have a word with you—after all these years."

Walter held out his hand. It occurred to him that he liked Richards better at this moment than at any other time during the several decades of their acquaintance. Even when they had been college roommates, he recalled, they had never really been friends. They now returned together into the living room where Richards was at once swept away by his duties as host; and Walter looked around for Sylvia. He saw her still with Mackay. As he caught sight of them, they were moving in his direction and he presently heard the ex-state senator booming, "Oh, yes indeed, Mrs. Stone, I know the area well . . . All right then, you'll have to tell me what your system is. My own system is simple, ha ha ha. I just go up there and get cleaned out! . . . Walter! This certainly is a happy occasion. Congratulations to you both."

"Thank you."

"Your wife and I were comparing notes on the gambling hells of Nevada. She tells me she has a system to beat the game."

"Oh, no!" Sylvia protested. "I never really beat the game."

"Well then, to keep even with it. Why, I'd be happy enough just to keep even myself. Wouldn't you, Walter? Mrs. Stone Junior looks lovely, doesn't she? If only we had the husband home too! But it won't be long. I'm sure it won't be long. . . . Walter," he said, "I've a small item of business to discuss with you one of these days. I wonder if we could get together for luncheon next week?"

"Certainly we can," Walter said.

"I'll call you. I'll call you Monday morning. It's been a great pleasure to see you again, Mrs. Stone." The ex-senator with several small bows and a hearty handshake, took his leave, while Walter thought, certainly, oh certainly. Only one thing now remains: the cash. How much will they bill me for? How much does it cost to run a campaign in a congressional district? A good many thousands, he supposed. Richards had already put up the price of the house—fifteen thousand at least—which in a way could be regarded as a campaign contribution; and since he had allowed himself now to be included, they would be justified in asking him for a substantial sum. A year ago, he thought, he could have written out a check which they would certainly have considered reasonable. But Sylvia's ten months in the sanitarium had taken care of that. Still, he was solvent, he could raise the money.

Or suppose he refused? Mackay and Richards both had wealthy friends. A few thousand dollars was no obstacle to these people. But then why had they been so anxious to deal him in, he wondered. Would it not really have afforded Richards considerable satisfaction to have gone ahead without him—to have been able to say afterwards, if Wendel were elected, that this was with small thanks to the father? He recalled Richards' remark to him a few moments earlier, that going in with Chantry and taking the line he did had been a smart move. To be a labor attorney then had become respectable in Richards' eyes. Why? Why, because it succeeded, he had said that himself; because it brought big accounts. Labor itself had become a big account, that was the thing. The congressman Gaventer had always been elected, Walter knew, with labor support. Perhaps now they were not quite sure they could beat him, old man though he was, unless they could take away his labor backing, or at least divide it. Was that why Mackay needed Wendel Stone as candidate in Gaventer's district? Was that why they needed him, Walter Stone—not his money so much as himself—the well-regarded and successful labor attorney?

He would rather have given the money than the other. But he knew at once that he would give both. He was trapped; though he hoped neither Richards nor Mackay would ever understand why they had succeeded in trapping him. But Wendel would know, he thought; yes, Wendel would know.

As Walter and his wife Sylvia drove home after the Richards' party, Walter was thinking of a summer day when he and his son, then twelve years old, had set off along one of the trails from Tuolumne Meadows toward the gray granite peaks to the south; they had a burro carrying their food and sleeping gear, and Walter had fixed his mind's eye on a pond some fifteen miles ahead by twilight when the trout would be feeding. He swung along with his springy stride; but the boy was dawdling in the rear. Walter called to him, telling him about the lake, but the boy was not much interested in the lake. He had a blister on his heel, he said; and mosquito bites. So he took off his boot and his sock, the heel showing no sign of any blister. After that, he was hungry; he wanted to stop for lunch though it was just past ten o'clock. Walter tried to joke with him. This had happened on several occasions previously, and he had promised himself that for once he would remain humorous and easy-going and find some solution; but within a few moments, a black, silent anger overcame him and he strode off with the burro, figuring the boy would catch up soon enough when he realized he was being left behind.

Of course it was himself who broke down first and he walked back a mile and a half to find the boy sitting on a rock whittling a stick. They covered eight miles that day instead of fifteen; and in the morning Walter turned the burro around, hiked down to the meadows and drove back to San Francisco, never saying a word to his son all the way.

As he now remembered the incident, it seemed to make little difference whether he had covered the fifteen miles, or eight, or any miles at all. If only he could have covered the distance between himself and the boy. If he had found out what the boy wanted, if he had established some network of human feeling between them. But that had been lacking through their whole life. Knowing from the beginning that Sylvia never wanted the child, he had attempted to ignore both the mother's demoralization and the boy's existence. He had made himself extremely busy with affairs of law, and devoted his free time to his fishing and camping trips, alone. Sylvia was never interested in such undertakings. Till suddenly waking to the fact that he had a son, he had tried to turn him into a model of himself twice perfected. So preoccupied had he been with his own need, so determined the boy must share what he wanted and desire what he desired that he scarcely had seen the boy at all. Ah, this was belated wisdom. He had made him despise the values he himself esteemed. He had turned him into a stranger, a son-in-law of Richards. Perhaps even a stranger to Richards, he thought, wondering if it never had occurred to Richards that Wendel, perceiving the father's involvement toward the daughter, might have calculated the value of that relationship.

"I think I'll go up to Signal Springs again after New Year's," his wife said.

"Is it all right for you to go there? What did they say?"

"They said to go someplace restful where I'd have interesting things to do and never get bored." Then she cried out, "I've somebody to talk to there at least, I've got something to do. Where else could I go?"

He said nothing and after a moment she asked, "Will you be coming for the weekends?"

"Yes, if you go up, I will. Whenever I can get away."

"Why don't I take the car, then, and you come on the plane? You wouldn't be driving up this time of year anyway."

"No. I'll need the car down here."

"Maybe we could buy another car, Walter. I heard there're some secondhand ones on the market you can pick up now and then."

He shook his head.

"We can't afford it?" she asked. "It cost so much for the—sanitarium?"

"I've just been dunned for a sizable piece of money," Walter told her.

"For Wendel and Carol's house?"

It seemed easier to let it go at that. He nodded, and she asked,

"Did you give it to him?"

"I promised it. What else could I do?"

"I don't know," she said.

19

Joyce woke before her alarm clock went off. She heard the shower running and knew Sally had come home, and the little bedroom was all awake with the flavors of fresh coffee and sunlight. As Joyce sat up, she saw through the window the tops of the eucalyptus trees green and gold, waving in the wind, and a square of blue sky beyond them.

She put on her slippers and went into the bathroom to brush her teeth.

"Good morning, good morning," Sally called from the shower stall; and a moment later Sally herself stepped forth dripping. She threw a towel over her head and began to dry her hair. This rapid movement of the arms set her rather full stomach and her breasts to bobbing. Joyce was always amused and startled at the whiteness and pinkness of the other girl's body when she saw all of it at once. Pink freckles clustered over the white skin and around the pink nipples, and there was the bright carrot-colored tuft at the groin which for some reason showed quite a different shade from Sally's coppery red hair.

Solid and strong, she looked as if she had been built on purpose to become a shipyard worker, Joyce thought; while she herself was more like Janet, wispy and slender. Yet how beautiful a thing a woman's body really was, so molded and balanced. She knew that she never looked at Sally O'Regan, or Janet Beezely either, without a feeling of envy, a pain of envy inside because they were married, and had made love to the men they loved and she had not. When he came back, she promised, even if he could stay only a single day ashore, she would beg him to make love to her. But would she? Yes, yes, why not? And when he had gone again she would have this to know and remember during the long months of waiting.

"Listen, Joyce," Sally cried, pulling the towel from around her head, shaking her hair back as she dried herself under the breasts. "I got something to tell you. You know what . . ."

"Well, *what?* Tell me."

"I'm going to make a *speech*. On the union floor! If I don't die of heart failure . . ."

"Don't keep me *waiting*. What kind of a speech?"

"Last night, while you were at work, some of the guys on my shift came to see me—there's a bunch of shipfitters, some welders too," she told her. "They're writing a statement, a resolution that the union would stop any kind of discrimination, for color or sex either—to comply with the Fair Employment Practice Board—and they're going to introduce it in the local and if it passes, send it to the next convention. They asked *me* to get up and talk on it."

A picture of the men she knew in the yard came to Joyce's mind, the white men, shipfitters, welders, electricians, leadermen and foremen, noisy and laughing, or grim silent men; but always frightening and to her overbearing. She knew how they talked about women workers, even about white women; and as they went into the kitchen for breakfast, she asked, "Would you—would you get a chance to, Sally?"

"Well, I guess so," the other replied a little uncertainly. "The women almost never say anything at meetings. Sometimes there's two or three hundred people, and they have microphones in the aisles. Anybody that wants to speak has to sit close to the mike and make a grab for it. The guys said last night if a woman was to come to the mike, everybody would probably be so surprised they'd let her take it first. They told me there already was a resolution like this one passed over in Garleyville."

"Oh, Sally! What would you say?" She saw the other's eyes gleaming and she was holding her lower lip pinched under her teeth.

"I'll have to think what. It's a long way off yet. I'm so wound up already, I suppose I'll be walking on the ceiling by that time. You know, it *might* go over, Joyce, if they get a chance really to speak on it—some of those guys are well known too. One's on the Executive Board and another one's a delegate to the Metal Trades Council. They take the floor all the time, people know them . . ."

Joyce, smelling the toast burning, jumped to fetch it from the oven.

"They said they wanted to make sure a woman would speak too. You see, there's a clause in the constitution that even excludes women, Joyce; they haven't enforced it, but it's there and a lot of the women that come to the union meetings are hot about it, I know. And they're mad because women get a runaround on job assignments all the time . . ."

The words came in such a rush that Joyce, trying to butter the toast, could scarcely keep up with them.

". . . if a woman was to get up and tie the two together, show how the same people that try to keep colored people out of the union are trying to keep the women out too. And that membership and jobs ought to be open equally to everybody. . . ." She had run out of breath, and stopped, laughing at her own excitement.

"And you're going to say that?"

"I'm going to try."

"Oh, you will, too, Sally. But I'd die if it was me."

"Maybe I will too."

"No you won't! You're looking forward to it. Aren't you? *Aren't* you now?"

"Well, I am sort of," Sally admitted. "Only I don't know how I'll remember the things to say, I wouldn't want to write anything down, that doesn't look good. Will you listen to me rehearse, when I get it ready?"

"Of course I will."

"I ought to have Tom here. He could teach me his Irish brogue." She laughed, but then added, "I'd better not tell him. He'd go wild."

Joyce asked, "Why, Sally?"

"He keeps writing how dull things are on his ship. I guess they are too, but he sounds as if he thought being in the ship-yard was a picnic all the time. He figures he's quite a speech-maker himself."

"Do you mean he'd be jealous?"

After a moment of reflection, Sally answered, "I guess you'd call it that. While he was cooped up on the ship any-way. It would be different if he was here."

"It must be awfully hard to be shut off so long from things they want to do," Joyce said. She wondered as she spoke whether Charlie would be jealous if she were to take up painting, for example; or if she were to have some success in music. But she did not think he would, any more than she would have been jealous of his success.

". . . maybe we really were too young to get married," Sally was saying. "We were trying to get ourselves headed some direction when he had to go away. I know he's worry-ing about that now, I can tell from the letters." She finished her coffee and lighted a cigarette. "He doesn't write very often. . . . What a waste it all is! All the lives and all the years out of people's lives. All the work going into these ships."

Joyce nodded silently.

"I didn't help much either, I suppose," Sally said. "I was trying to be so sensible—no, we shouldn't get married until we knew where we were both going and what we wanted, and made sure we both wanted the same things. But then when—well, when it hit me he really was going away, in the war, I mean . . ." Getting up, Sally began to clear the dishes from the table. "You were more sensible than me," she said.

Their eyes met, and Joyce felt her lips quivering, but could only shake her head.

"Oh, he'll be back *soon*, honey! His ship probably got stuck on one of those damn shuttle runs between Australia and New Guinea or someplace."

That was what they had told her. The shuttle runs went back and forth a whole year sometimes; but sooner or later they had to bring the ship home for supplies and dry-docking. That can't be much longer now, she thought, *can't be!*

At the shipyard, the business agent that afternoon was making the rounds checking the dues books. The news of his coming preceded him and Joyce got her book from her wallet and slipped it into the pocket of her jeans jacket to have ready. But when he reached the compartment where they were working, he did not stop at all. "Hi, Brooks," he called out, and went on by; and the Sergeant, who had been marking off for pipe brackets along the bulkhead, set down his steel tape and went after the man. The other was halfway up the ladder to the main deck, but hearing the Sergeant behind him, he stopped and the Sergeant stopped too with one foot on the lowest rung of the ladder.

"How come you're puttin' off the elections again?" the Sergeant asked.

The business agent had turned and was looking down at him. It was the same one who had given her the clearance, the man with the oval face and polished red shoes. He was wearing a topcoat now, of gray gabardine, "You know the answer to that, Brooks," he said.

"I've heard a lot of different answers."

"There's only one answer. We can't hold an election in a new lodge until we get the approval from the General Office."

"That's not what you told us at the start."

"Oh, *yes* it is."

"You better get that approval damn fast or you ain't goin' to have any lodge," the Sergeant told him.

Joyce saw the man's expressionless face flash suddenly with anger. "I don't need anybody telling me how to run my business," he shouted. Then he continued up the ladder, and for an instant Joyce thought the Sergeant was going to jump after him and pull him down. But he did not. He turned away, came back to the work he'd been doing—marking off with the steel tape, and afterwards held the brackets in position against the bulkhead while she tacked them. He said nothing about what had just happened and she did not ask; but she remembered that when she had first met the Sergeant, and the Reverend Beezely, eight months earlier, people had been talking about those elections. Surely it would not take eight months, she thought, to get approval from the national office for an election.

Taking another rod from her rod box, she clamped it into the stinger while the Sergeant was dragging over more brackets from the pile. When she began to weld again, he let out a yell, waved one hand violently up and down (still holding the bracket with the other), and jerked off his glove with his teeth. A fragment of slag from the weld had jumped inside the band of his glove and burned a round red hole in his wrist.

"Oh, I'm *sorry*," Joyce cried.

She had burned herself so many times that she now carried a tube of grease in her lunch pail. She ran to fetch this and as she applied a spot to the burn, the Sergeant said, "Little bit more of this hot stuff and you could cut slices for sandwiches."

Christmas wreaths were looped over the lampposts along the main street of San Martin, and when Joyce went into San Francisco for her piano lessons, she stayed window-shopping afterwards on Market Street, looking at the Santa Clauses and reindeer, the cotton snow and buggy-loads of dolls. On no other Christmas season that she could remember had she ever looked into the store windows knowing she had money to buy if she wished. But the very fact that she did have money, that she owned three war bonds and a small savings account, made her doubly cautious. For as much money as this—if she could keep on working for a year or two, and saving—would mean enough to live on while Charlie started painting after the war. It would mean that she could continue her piano lessons: it meant money to take care of her mother when her mother grew too old to work. You got a little money ahead, she thought half resentfully, and felt more afraid to spend it than you had before.

But she allowed herself to buy a blue quilted bathrobe to send her mother, and a corduroy jacket and pair of shoes for Charlie. For Sally O'Regan, she bought a couple of pairs of all-wool socks, since Sally had been complaining of cold feet. And on the same day she bought the socks, Joyce went from the sportswear department into the toy department one floor below, and stood for a long while studying the display of dolls. She kept wishing she knew someone who had a little girl she could give a doll to. Janet's girls were too grown-up for that, one in high school and the other in sixth grade; she would have to get them clothes—blouses or sweaters. Then she considered buying a doll to save for her own little girl when she and Charlie should have a child. But that was silly: she might not have a girl at all, she might have a boy.

And certainly there would be better dolls on the market then, for less money too. Pushing herself away from the counter, she hurried out of the store before she had time to change her mind.

During the week before Christmas the days grew steadily bleaker and colder. A ceiling of cloud drooped over the bay and hung low over the hills, and it would be almost dark when Joyce went to work at four in the afternoon. The wind set in, driving curtains of rain all day long across the roof tops of San Martin Village; and across the wide spaces of the yard, half veiling from sight the buildings and the framework of ships on the ways.

The ship she and the Sergeant had last been working on was launched and towed to the outfitting dock. The Sergeant went with it, but the foreman moved Joyce over to join the welding gang in the plate shop—only for a few weeks, he told her. However it was a stroke of luck to be inside in weather like this. Work was harder and steadier in the plate shop, she learned, since there was not so much time spent waiting for shipfitters to wedge their deck plates and bulkheads into position; but on the other hand you could stay in one place and you were under a roof—not up and down all day across the open decks of the ship, or shivering inside one of those wind tunnels in the hull. The plate shop was close to the lunch counter and the women usually went for soup and coffee to warm their sandwiches, saving their thermos bottles for the cold hours between eight and midnight.

It was not till two or three days before Christmas that Joyce saw the Sergeant again. She had been over to the lunchroom at supper period, and as she came back into the plate shop, she heard voices shouting up angrily, saw a knot of people down at the open end of the building. She thought it sounded like a fight, and frightened, turned quickly back to the door. But through the other voices came one shrill and harsh that she recognized as the Sergeant's. She stopped. A hollow, sickish apprehension spread from the pit of her stomach. Whatever was happening, she had no wish to see it or take part in it; and yet some sense of loyalty to the man, if only because she had worked with him for so many weeks, forced her slowly down the length of the building.

She heard someone shout again, the voice sounding to her like a white man's. *"Brooks, you know what he said. You were right there with us!"*

"Well what's the story, Sarge?" another called out.

"What'd the man say, Sarge?"

"I'll tell you what the man said all right." That was the Sergeant.

Then the first voice insisted, "You know what he said, Brooks. He said the election had to be postponed. *Postponed.* You heard him say that. For a month or six weeks, that's all, until we get the okay from General Office—"

"I'll tell you what the man said."

Joyce had reached the edge of the circle, and standing on tiptoe she saw the Sergeant at the center confronting a white man. It was the business agent, the same one, the gray hat and gabardine topcoat, the expressionless oval face she remembered. The Sergeant, despite the bitterness of his tone, now burst out laughing; and the people in the crowd were laughing too, and she saw that most of them were colored.

"Let us in on the joke, Sarge."

"Tell us what the man said."

"We ain't goin' to have any elections," the Sergeant called back. "That's what he said."

"That's not true, Brooks. Garnet didn't say that."

"You're callin' me a liar?"

There came a stir from the crowd, a shuffling and edging forward. "I'm not calling anybody a liar, Brooks. Only I don't think you understood what Garnet told us."

Someone sang out, "Watch that *liar* stuff." And another

called, "You want to talk kind of civil down here, Mr. Business Agent."

The white man said nothing more. In the glare and shadow of floodlights blazing down from the blackness above them, the men and women stood quiet, waiting. The Sergeant raised his hands in front of him, and Joyce, who could scarcely imagine the Sergeant being afraid of anything, saw that his hands when he held them up in the light, were shaking, and as he spoke again his voice trembled too. She stared across at him with an understanding she had not felt before and a sense of sympathy that was almost pity.

"They told us we couldn't have any elections." The Sergeant spoke slowly, feeling his words out one after the other. "They called us all down to the union hall yesterday, told us a fellow named Garnet, Joe Garnet from the General Office, wanted to talk to us. How come we can't have any election? we asked. And they said, *Ballots aren't ready*. We'll run off all the ballots we need in half an hour right here in this union office, we said. *Oh, no,* they said, *you got to have printed ballots from the General Office, only they won't be ready in time*. Where does it say we got to have printed ballots? we ask. Don't say that in your constitution. *No, it ain't in the constitution, but it's an order of the president. That's the rule. That's the way it's got to be*. So we argue and argue. We go round and round.

"Then all of a sudden this Joe Garnet—fellow they said come down from the General Office to have a talk with us— all of a sudden he jumps up. *You all shut your mouth,* he says. That's what he said to us: *SHUT YOUR MOUTH! It's just like I thought,* he says. *You colored boys ain't ready to run your own union lodge. You colored boys are lucky to be workin' in the shipfitter trade. You boys are ignorant about unions as a bunch of babies. A baby's got to crawl before he can walk*. Then he bangs his hand down on the table and he shouts, *There ain't goin' to be any elections! You colored boys ain't ready for it!* Just like that— *There ain't goin' to be any!"*

The Sergeant stopped and in the dead silence he turned back to face the Business Agent. "Was that what the man said or wasn't it?"

"I didn't hear him use those words, Brooks."

"Then you're a liar!" the Sergeant screamed. "You're a God damned liar! Your God damned union's only a racket and you know it! You asked me to be president of this auxiliary, but you don't need any president. All you need's a cash register!" He shot his hand up into the air again, and Joyce saw that he was waving his union dues book; and then the Sergeant tore the book in half and tore the pieces in half again and flung the scraps at the business agent.

"Solid Jack!" howled a voice from the crowd.

"Solid Jack. That's talkin'!"

"Tell that man, truck on out while he's still in one piece!"

But even now the business agent showed no change of expression. He slid away from the rack of steel plates against which he had been standing, the circle opened to let him through.

"Don't forget your dues while you're here, Mister!" Scraps from another dues book fluttered around the man's head. And suddenly all through the crowd, men and women began yanking out their books; and Joyce, scarcely realizing what she was doing, but caught up in the surge of laughter and shouting and defiance, had her book out too, and tore it across and across again. The business agent moved away slowly, walking through the small snowstorm of paper that danced under the glare of the floodlights, while the white scraps settled on the brim of his hat and on the shoulders of his gabardine coat.

From outside and high above them, the whistle wailed for the end of the supper hour.

PART 3

PART 3

20

As the *Andrew Rogers* was taking cargo in Boston, rumors spread aboard that she was headed next trip for the Pacific coast. The merchant crew signed coastwise articles which to some extent confirmed the rumor; and Tom rejoiced secretly and cautiously. The Junior Radio Operator, however, expressed utter disgust. This was the last straw for him, he said; he was getting off.

"I only stayed on this tub because it kept going to England, and I could run over to Liverpool for a day or two," he told Tom. "I don't have to be a junior operator anyhow. I can ship as a chief." He had been shipping two years straight, he explained, and now wanted to go home for a few days to Bangor, Maine, which was not far from Boston.

"I wish I could go home for a few days," Tom said.

"Well, she'll probably make San Francisco, Flags. That's her home port."

"I'd never hit a slice of luck like that. We'll go to Honolulu and Australia, and all the way around to Liverpool again." He dared not let himself begin thinking that it might be San Francisco. But he wrote Sally: *"Quiero mucho hablar con Usted, Senora. Y otras cosas.* You can see my Spanish is getting pretty good, can't you? Maybe I'll have a chance to give you lessons one of these days." That ought to give her a hint. It was about as much as he could sneak past his Lieutenant in any case.

He and the Second Mate took the Junior Sparks into town for dinner the day he left and saw him off at the North Station in a salty cold drizzle of rain. All through dinner and on the way to the train they kept kidding him that the *Andrew Rogers* would probably go right back to Liverpool, while the next ship the Sparks got into would wind up in South Africa.

"Give us your girl friend's address," the Second offered. "We'll take her out if you don't get there."

And Tom said, "That don't need to be worrying the Sparks. He's got friends in South Africa too. What's their names?"

"Abbie and Hal Slotz," the Sparks told him. "I ever show you that card, Second?" He pulled out his wallet, went shuffling through his pack of ham contacts. But now the conductor was bawling, "All aboard, the Bangor Express!" and the Sparks grabbed his sea bag and scrambled into one of the coaches.

Next day a new junior operator came aboard and the day after that the *Andrew Rogers* sailed. Around the tip of Cape Cod they swung south, bucking a heavy blow off Hatteras and the Carolinas that followed them all the way to Cuba. Beyond Cuba they came into summer time. They dropped anchor in the tropic bay of Colon, waiting their turn through the canal; and then late on a sunny afternoon angled out into the long lazy blue swell of the Pacific.

When the Second Mate came up from his supper, he called across to Tom, "Know where we're going yet, Flags?"

"I'm hoping, but I don't know."

"Skipper just gave us the word," he said. "San Francisco

and three weeks in the dry dock. Gonna slap a new coat of paint on the old bucket. Is that good news?"

Tom could not trust himself to say more than, "Yeah, sure it is, Second," and he was glad it was almost dark. Through the rest of the watch, he felt as if he had had a large shot of novocain: he was numb from the neck up. But when his relief came at eight o'clock, avoiding the Second, he went forward along the catwalk that led over the deck cargo of crated machinery. He crawled through the hole into the main mast, climbed the ladder inside the mast up to the crow's-nest. Below him the hull of the ship seemed small and distant, wallowing in its froth, a splash of white in the circle of ocean. He traced the circle with his eyes, noticing how the earth itself hung suspended here in this glowing bowl of sky.

Somewhere to the northeast stretched the coast of Mexico, mountain and desert marching north to California. To San Diego, Los Angeles, the line of cliff and beach and red rock. It was winter there now, he thought, farther north. The Bodensee Hotel would be in the fog and rain, San Francisco under its fog bank, and the sharp little valleys of the coastal mountains beyond, cold and wet. Saw Creek: God, how it rained there! dripping down out of the redwoods and Douglas firs, flooding the mud flats around the mill. But even Saw Creek he would have been glad to see again. He had been away a long time.

Whenever they docked, he thought, he would find a telephone, there must be a phone booth around the dock somewhere, and as soon as he knew when he could get off port watch, he would call her. San Martin 237 W. And if the old pickup were still afloat, she would drive down to meet him. There she would be in the truck, and he would throw his sea bag into the back and sit beside her. Reach out his hand, touching his hand on hers.

His heart was beating slow and heavily. But the pain in which he so often wished for her had receded; the doubts and suspicions were almost at rest. It was not much longer to wait and he *could* wait. He remembered walking over the brush hills east of Saw Creek in deer season. All day over the dry ridges under the fierce sun: and coming at last to a gully where a stream bubbled down through the rocks. Clear and green and cold. He had stood there, no longer in any hurry to drink, tasting for a moment more how thirsty he was before he knelt, and thrust in his hands, and plunged his face in the water.

So he leaned back, watching while the masthead swam across the stars. He gave up trying to understand what he was thinking. There were no real thoughts in his mind, only a pulse and throb as the ship rolled forward on the long swell. Even here at the height of the mast, he could feel the engine, and the screw cranking out its spiral of bubbles. Across the circle of ocean, the depth beneath, the depth of sky above—and himself between, feeling in one instant as if he could reach out as far as the horizon and, in the next, shaken like a puff of spray. He saw his hands hooked over the rusty, salt-caked rim of the bucket which formed the crow's-nest. Staring at them, he wondered, what can they do for me when the time comes? Or will the time come, ever? But as he rose again with the buoyant lift of the ship beneath him, he thought, they can do anything I put them to. I can make a time with my own hands. There's no end to what they can do, no end. She may not have half known me before, but she never will think she made a wrong choice, he promised himself. She'll not be sorry.

Tom threw his sea bag into the back of the truck.

She moved over to make room for him under the wheel, and he slid into place, automatically gunning the motor to keep it from stalling. Then he looked at her. Reaching out his hand, he found hers; and her face was close and her eyes watching his. They were gray-green, he had almost forgotten. The face was one he had never seen before, yet knew every mark upon it, the freckles and eyelashes, the coppery red hair drawn back. She was older. She was more beautiful than she had been before, he thought, older and he no longer remembered her. For a moment he felt a panic as if he had stepped forward to the wrong person. The lips were half open, the eyes half closed. *Strawberry.* Strawberry laughing in the lunch counter, and he pressed his mouth against hers and her arms locked around his neck.

A horn blared behind them. They were blocking the entrance to the dock. Shoving the pickup into gear, Tom stalled the engine, flooded it, sat kicking the starter, swearing and sweating till it caught again finally and they chugged away, backfiring, into the morning traffic of the Embarcadero.

"Forgotten how to drive," he said. "It's been so long."

"It's been so long," she repeated.

She let her head rest on his shoulder. He found the ramp to the bridge and they swung up over the city, over the docks, over the ships, over the bay. The tunnel of Yerba Buena island came together in a ring of darkness and was gone. Coming in on the beacon. Steady as she goes: the long line of traffic, and Oakland with its bright morning windows aglitter, tilted against the hills. The hills were green after the rain, crowned with sunlighted tufts of cottony fog.

"I've been waiting and waiting, Tom. Waiting."

So had he. For him there were no words to say. Her head was on his shoulder and he smelled the odor of her hair. He saw that one of the windshield wiper blades was gone and the thermometer on the dashboard was no longer working. Well, it was an old car now. An antique. He stopped in the flat space dug into the edge of the hill at San Martin Village, alongside all the other jalopies that were tethered there, and they walked up the steps past the rows of little brown houses with their downhill ends supported on stilts. He noticed that some of the stovepipe chimneys had blown down since he had been here last; and the windows were open to let in the sunlight.

Sally hunted for her door key while a cat which had been sleeping on the step rose and stretched and glided back and forth in a small circle.

Inside, the kitchen smelled of soap and coffee and kerosene.

"You hungry? Want some breakfast?"

He shook his head. "Ate before I left the ship."

"Want some coffee?"

"All right."

By the stove she stood watching for the water to boil. She was wearing a green skirt and a knitted sweater and silk stockings and high heels. He did not remember the skirt, it must be new, he thought; and wondered how she held up her stockings, with garters or with a belt and straps? The cat came rubbing against her ankle, kept yowling and looking up under the skirt and its tail stuck up straight as a bottle brush. She gave it a little kick with her foot. "There're some letters for you on the cabinet. I was going to forward them, but I . . . I had a hunch from what you wrote . . ."

Tom reached for the bundle of mail. From his family, he saw—his mother in San Diego, his sister in Eureka, from Sally's mother in Saw Creek. He shuffled through, searching for his answer from Walter Stone, which he found at once. He tore open the crinkly paper envelope, skimmed over the page: . . . *delighted to hear from you again . . . remember with pleasure my talk with your father-in-law when I offered the suggestion . . . looking forward to hearing from you when you get back to San Francisco.* . . . That's all right, he thought. It wasn't any brainstorm of the old man's then.

"I mailed your letter," Sally told him. "Wasn't that the

lawyer, Tom? The one who came to Saw Creek? That must be from him. Isn't it?"

He nodded.

"I wanted to open it, but I just waited. What does he say?"

"Says I should call him when I'm in town."

"Will you?"

"Of course. That's why I wrote him."

"I think you'd make a good lawyer, Tommy. Don't you?"

"How should I know?" He felt his face flush, and after a moment of silence asked, "So how's your Mom and Dad getting along?"

Sally poured the coffee and they sat down at the kitchen table. ". . . it was about five months ago they went up," she was telling him. "That was in the summer still, September I guess. They're out by the new mill now, north of town—out where Giraldi's ranch used to be, remember? Mom's working again at the Pine Tree Café. And Dad's steward already," she added, laughing. "You'll have to call them long distance, Tom. . . ."

Trust Kallela to be steward already! He'd be president of the local, or business agent again, give him another year. Tomorrow or sometime else he'd call them. She was not looking at him.

". . . and we'll just have to call *your* family too, Tommy. They wrote me they haven't had a letter from you in—"

"Oh, I've written them two or three times," he said. Never mind my family for Christ's sake. Can't we talk about anything else? Maybe she didn't know what to say either. It was like when he met her in the bus depot the weekend they went to the Bodensee—but afterwards, afterwards they would be able to talk. "Where's your roommate?" he asked. "What'd you say her name was?"

"Joyce. I wrote you about her, Tom, didn't I?"

He nodded. The colored girl: he had half expected to find her in the kitchen waiting for them when they had come into the house. "How did you happen to—to get to know her?"

"We were both in the welding class together. I needed somebody to share the house, and she needed a place to live." Her eyes fixed for a moment on his. "She went over to stay at a neighbor's when you telephoned this morning."

"Just so it's a girl you're rooming with," he said. "That's all I care."

"Oh, yes, she's a girl, I can guarantee that. A very pretty girl too. You'll like her."

Sliding his coffee cup aside, he reached out across the table, and she, taking his hand, peered back at him gravely. "What shall we do now, Tommy?" she asked. Then in an explosion of laughter, she jumped over to him, kissing him ravenously all over the face. He struggled up from his chair, seized her in his arms and heaved her up, almost dropping her because she was no lightweight and eighteen months aboard ship had made him soft as a jelly roll. Another couple of years cooped up like that, he thought, will turn me into an old man. She was shrieking to put her down. He stumbled into the hallway, she between shrieks saying,

"It's the door on the right," and he pushed open the door, dropped her on the bed, losing his balance and falling over on top of her. There they wrestled together.

"You'll tear my new sweater. Stop now," she protested, pushing him away. "Let's be serious." She pulled off the sweater, folded it into one of the bureau drawers, and then turning back to him, asked in a businesslike tone, "Would you like to have a baby, Tom?"

"*Have a baby?*"

"I don't mean *you* have it, ducky. I mean *me. Me,*" she cried with her hands linking together on her stomach. "Would you like to? Don't look so surprised!"

"You're kidding!"

"No, no. I'm not."

He could see now that she was not. This he had never thought of—or only as something for a long while off. Women thought of it sooner than men, he supposed that was natural. The idea touched him with pleasure and at the same time with alarm. Once they had a baby, they were tied all right, tied for keeps. And what would happen to his studying to be a lawyer? He remembered what the Second Mate had said: you spend all your time fighting your wife and diapering the baby. But even so, he felt glad to know she *wanted* a baby.

"Wouldn't it be better to wait awhile for that?"

Sally shook her head slowly. "You don't know how a woman feels, Tom, when she decides she wants to have a baby. I got the baby half made already just waiting for the other half. From you, Tommy."

"Seems like we ought to think it over a little bit more. Might be another year before I even get back again. This may go on God knows how long, two three years yet . . ."

"Isn't that all the more reason?" she asked.

"But I might be going to school," he said, glancing up quickly to catch her reaction.

She had begun nodding her head at once in agreement. "I know you will, Tom. You should. With the GI Bill you can do it too. That's what I'm thinking about."

She was thinking of that? She didn't want to go back to Saw Creek either; or to be spending the rest of her life with a boomer carpenter, that was clear. "It maybe won't amount to anything," he said. "I'm probably too old already."

"No you're not. Of course you're not."

"I don't know, I guess it takes years to get to be a lawyer. I might go into teaching, that wouldn't take so long."

"What do we care how long it takes," she cried, "once you're back home? And wouldn't that be good for us, too, if you were a lawyer, Tommy? You could do all your arguing on the job and when you came home, you'd be sweet as a peach. Wouldn't you? Wouldn't you?" She stepped out of the green skirt then, and he saw that she was not wearing a strap for the stockings; the stockings were rolled above the knees; and she pulled them off and drew her slip up over her head. With her eyes fixed upon his, she came to him, the coppery red hair, the laughing freckled face, and the gray-green eyes —suddenly no longer laughing at all.

They slept until evening, till the dusk came down through the eucalyptus trees. She had bought a bottle of whisky in celebration when she had driven to the dock that morning, and they sat in bed sipping from the bottle. He was telling her about the *Andrew Rogers,* about the cockroaches and the rupture truss; London and Liverpool and Immingham, the Irish Sea and the North Atlantic. He described the Junior Radio Operator with his girl in Liverpool and his plans for after the war—which brought Sally back immediately to their own plans. She had been squeezing by on the allotment he was sending her, she explained, and almost everything else she earned in the shipyard she was putting into war bonds.

"I already got enough for us to live on for about a year. Oh, Joyce and I have planned and planned how to save our money. You can start school, Tommy, and with the GI payments—"

"Every GI from here to Boston will be in school trying to learn some damn thing."

"Well, that's good isn't it? Want to know something?"

"*What?*" he demanded.

"I missed you." She removed the bottle from his fingers, drank and passed it back. "I'm getting loopy, we ought to eat some supper."

"Couldn't find a safer place to get gassed up than this."

"I don't want to get drunk, it's so nice being sober." And she said, "I'd be working too."

"You'd be working? You just told me you wanted to have a baby."

"But you didn't agree."

"What difference does that make? How could I tell? Maybe we've done it already."

"You shouldn't be so impetuous then, ducky. But I wouldn't ever do it unless you agreed. Want me to make us some supper?"

"All right."

She climbed over him to get out of bed and took her dressing gown from the hook on the closet door. "I was thinking, Tommy, if we *did* have a baby, I might ask Mom to come down and stay with us for a while. I think she would. Then I could be working while you were in school . . ."

She had it all figured out all right. She must have been thinking plenty about it. With a woman it wasn't ever enough just to make love. Nothing ever turned out quite the way you expected it, either. He could hear her moving around in the kitchen, the sound of water running, pans on the stove. Cooking his supper for him. He thought what a lucky accident it was that women and men were so perfectly suited for each other. It would have been triplets today, he thought. Getting up, he rummaged into his sea bag for his shaving kit, went to the bathroom to wash and shave.

He was rubbing off the dabs of lather that had gotten up behind his ears when he heard from the kitchen a knocking on the door. A moment later Sally's voice exclaimed,

"Oh, my God, Henry! I'd forgotten all about you coming."

Henry. He stood motionless at the basin with the washcloth dripping in his hand. From the kitchen he heard feet shuffling, the boards of the floor creaking. Then a man's voice,

"Looks like we'd waked you up."

"No, no. I was making supper. Come in. Please come in. My husband just got back this morning . . ."

"He did! Well, that's wonderful!"

"Well, I guess we came at the wrong time, Sally."

"Oh, no, it's all right."

"Well, we won't stay now." There was another man's voice: there were two of them. "We'll have time to go over it later. Shall we pick you up Thursday?" And then the voice asked anxiously, "It'll be okay for Thursday? You'll be there?"

"Of course I will," Sally cried. "Come in for a minute now you're here. You can have a cup of coffee. *Tom*," she called, "—I'd like you to meet my husband—*Tom*, can you come out?"

He had come naked into the bathroom. Taking a towel from the rack, he wrapped it around him and ducked across the hallway to the bedroom where he pulled on a shirt and pair of pants. Then he went out to the kitchen. The door was still open and in the doorway stood a man in a short leather jacket, a heavy-set, gray-haired man who looked close to sixty; and behind him on the porch out-side another man slightly younger. Sally introduced them and Tom shook hands. The one in the doorway was the one she had called Henry. He looked embarrassed and kept apologizing for having broken in on them, while Sally urged them both to sit down for coffee, but they stood shaking their heads.

"These are shipfitters from my shift," she explained to Tom; and to them: "Tom's ship just came in last night, and it's going in dry dock and he'll be home for a little while. Tom's in the navy."

The one called Henry said, "We won't stay now." And he asked again, "So everything's okay for Thursday?"

"Sure it is."

"And we'll pick you up?"

"All right."

"Your wife's got a very important job to do," he said to Tom. "She can do it too. Glad to have met you." Putting on his hat, he backed out the doorway.

"How does it look, Henry?" she called after him.

"Looks good. We got a lot of support. If we get a fair shake, I think we can pass it. . . . Good night." He and the other man were on their way down the steps, halfway into the shadows. Sally, closing the door, jumped back to the stove, where the frying pan was smoking.

"So what's that all about?" Tom asked.

"I'm boning up on my brogue too, Tom."

"You running for business agent?" he asked.

She glanced back at him with an oddly embarrassed, shy smile. "I'm supposed to make a speech in the union meeting Thursday. I had told Henry and Sanford to come tonight to talk to me about it, only when I heard from you, I forgot all about them. I should have called him. You ready to eat? There isn't very much, ducky, just scrambled eggs. You should have let me know a day ahead of time."

He laughed and sat down at the table and she began explaining to him as she served the food, "Henry's on the executive board of the local union. He's a wonderful guy, Tom. He's going to introduce a resolution in the local to abolish discrimination . . ."

She had certainly got herself deep into this business, he thought, with a colored girl for roommate, and now this resolution. From what he remembered of the Shipbuilders' and Welders' Union, it wasn't likely the big wheels would think it was such a hot idea.

"Henry wanted to be sure at least one of the women welders would speak up."

"How big is your local?" he asked.

"Fourteen hundred, about."

"How many come to meetings?"

"Henry says there may be four or five hundred people there." Henry again. She had just now been in bed with him and he stared at her trying to picture her standing up to a microphone in front of five hundred people. And on an issue like that!—he suddenly wondered if he would have had the guts himself. The biggest meeting of carpenters he had ever made a pitch to had been a hundred and fifty. A good thing that guy Henry isn't twenty years younger, I'd really have something to be thinking about. . . .

21

Returning from the day he had spent in the desert with old John, Walter found Sylvia, and to his considerable surprise, the ex-State Senator Mackay, together on the terrace of the ranch house. Mackay was wearing a straw hat and beige flannel trousers and his large stomach and rather narrow shoulders were draped with scenes from the beach at Waikiki in green and gold. His face glowed with animation and fresh sunburn; he rose from the table squeezing Walter's hand.

"I'm delighted to see you, Walter. You're looking your usual robust self."

"What brings you out here?" Walter asked.

"Oh, I'm partial to a whirl on the wheel now and then. I was visiting some friends in Carson City and I stopped over on the chance you might be here. I'm delighted to find you."

Walter did not feel delighted.

"Sit down. Join us in a drink. What have you been up to all day? Sylvia tells me you're off digging gold or something of that sort?"

"Not gold," Walter said. "Old iron. If you don't mind,

I'm going to take a dip in the pool before I sit down. It's been a hot day. You interested in a swim, Sylvia?"

"We'll watch from here, Walter."

He crossed the patio to their cottage. Inside he found a bottle of bourbon standing on the coffee table. Had she been drinking all afternoon? he wondered. Ordinarily she did not start much before dinner time. But when he lifted the bottle, he saw that no more than a couple of drinks had been taken from it. There were two empty glasses on the table, each with water from melted ice in the bottom.

He put on his swimming trunks, dove into the pool and swam; then dressed in his business suit for the trip back to San Francisco that evening, set out his brief case and his hat. Returning to the terrace, he joined the two at the table. They had cocktails together and ate an early dinner. The sun was sinking behind the Sierra, leaving the wall of snow-sheathed peaks ghostly and forbidding across the west. The full winter snows were still upon them. He could see the place, almost exactly to the spot that he and old John must have reached, there where the gray slope of the desert curved up to the snow line.

"I could offer you a ride in town in the morning," Mackay was proposing.

"Thanks," Walter told him. "I've an early appointment at the office. I'd best take the plane tonight."

"Well then, let me drop you off at the airport."

"Not necessary. The ranch sends over their station wagon."

"Why, I go right past the airport on my way back to Carson City."

Walter made a gesture of acquiescence, and the other asked after Wendel. Sylvia told him they thought he had been sent to Guam, but they did not know for sure; Mackay then discoursed briefly on Wendel's abilities and achievements, though he said nothing of their undertaking on the congressional election, for which at least Walter was grateful. He pressed Walter again for details of what he had been doing during the day. Digging, Walter said; and pointed in the direction they had been, where the mountains now were lost from sight, only the snow mantles hovering like clouds. No, not gold, that wasn't worth digging even if you could find it, with the wartime price on precious metals; but pieces of old iron.

Mackay displayed keen interest, or a facsimile thereof. Four wagon-wheel rims and a collection of pins and bolts buried several inches under the gravel. Some scraps of charred wood. In the desert of course there was practically no decay. Walter explained that old John was the curator of the county historical museum, and such a find was like winning a case in the Supreme Court.

"I can well understand that," Mackay cried.

Walter felt no desire to expand this report of his day's outing, but there was nothing else to talk about, and it was better to talk than be silent. Why was he cursed with this man? There had been some kind of record on the matter in the county museum: a family from Illinois, in 1851 apparently, who had had difficulties coming across; their oxen were dying, it was late October before they reached the mountains here. They had jettisoned their wagon and gone on afoot. Old John, who had been hunting the remains of that wagon for the past five years, finally came on one of the wheel rims up by the snow line. But he needed someone to help with the digging; John was past seventy, Walter added.

"He must be a remarkable old fellow," said Mackay. "I'd enjoy talking to him."

"Just drop in at the county museum," Sylvia suggested. "Any time. But you won't talk to *him*. He does the talking." The ex-state senator laughed heartily at this, and Sylvia, who was looking out over the valley toward the west, asked in a low voice, "What happened to them? Did they ever get across?"

"Yes, they were lucky. A scouting party came all the way from the Feather River looking for them."

"I'm glad," Sylvia said.

Why was she glad? What difference did it make a hundred years later? But he had had the same reaction: he too had been glad. He supposed no one could look out at this bowl of desert and the mountains, and hear the story, without asking, Did they get across? and feeling the same throb of relief and pleasure to learn that they had. The man and his wife had opened a dry-goods store in Honey Valley, John had told him. And probably they lived long enough to die in less enviable circumstances than the splendor of that mountainside. Yet one was glad; one always had to be.

"Yes, that's very interesting," said Mackay. "It's a stirring, colorful history, the background of this section. A historical tradition to be proud of. That's extremely interesting."

Walter, glancing at his wrist watch, saw that it was almost time to leave for the airport. Sylvia had now turned quite kittenish and coquettish, a manner which seemed sadly incongruous, he thought. When she spoke either to Mackay or to himself, she would lean forward, placing her fingers on the arm of the one she addressed. She laughed frequently and loudly and was almost skipping as they walked to the parking lot where Mackay had left his car. She kissed him good-by, full on the lips in a way she had not used with him in many years.

"I'll see you Friday, dear," she called; and to Mackay she called, "Good-by, it has been such a pleasant evening."

They drove across the salt flats to the airport at the outskirts of Reno. There the plane stood warming up on the runway. They shook hands, Mackay asking to be remembered to Chantry, and to Garnet, whenever he might see him. And then, only after the car had turned, and as he watched the two red taillights moving off toward the highway, he understood suddenly that the other was not going to Carson City: he was going back to the ranch house and Sylvia was waiting for him. The significance of the bottle and two glasses in the cottage, of her coquettishness, of the final kiss she had given him, confronted him like the signs at a road junction.

She had intended him to know. She was saying to him, this is what you have brought me to, Walter. You know what I was once, you see now what I have become. Not that unfaithfulness itself would have been much to either of us—but with this man! this roll of blubber, this pink belly walking on legs! This is the final degradation, she was saying, I welcome it, welcome it because I hate you so, Walter.

He leaned against the pipe rail fence by the gate to the runway. He felt dry, dry and desiccated as the scraps of old wood from the burned wagon, as if every drop of juice had been scorched out. Only deep inside him there was a taste of nausea, a puddle of green bile working like a footprint in a bog. He wished he were dead. He wished he were on the slope of the desert in the gravel between the clumps of sagebrush while the wind stripped from his bones the last morsel of the filth that encased them.

The loudspeaker was announcing the take-off. He could have taken a taxi back to the rancho; but he showed his ticket and went through the gate.

In the morning Walter walked to his office as usual. He did not have an early appointment as he had told Mackay, but he had foreseen during the previous week that the crisis shaping up in the firm of Stone, Chantry and Greenwood would probably come to a head this morning. He felt like a small boy who had neglected preparing his homework. He was going to be called on and he did not know what answer he would give. Month after month he had let this issue ride along, postponing the moment of making up his mind. He had intended during the weekend to think it through. He had been going to think about it while he was out in the desert with old John. And he had been going to think it over on the plane ride back—until the other had intervened. For a moment he entertained a ridiculous resentment against Mackay, not for what he had done, but for the time he had chosen. And from an Olympian height, was momentarily amused at the impervious stupidity of his own thoughts.

Yet he knew the question had never been debatable. There was only one possible answer, only one course of action. But was he willing, was he able to follow that course? —that was what he had never yet determined, and even now knew that he was still hoping somehow to be spared the choice, hoping the teacher might pass him by and call upon someone else.

He sat at his desk, going over the medical reports in the case of a man named Anton Novak who claimed to have injured his back in an iron foundry. As always in such cases the doctor for the insurance company insisted there was nothing wrong with the man at all, a temporary wrench or sprain which he was trying to make a good thing of. The man himself said he suffered acute pain when he stooped over. *Examination, complete X-ray, Dr. Huntington,* Walter wrote. Then the buzzer sounded, he switched on his office speaker and heard Chantry's voice telling him that he had to leave for Los Angeles that afternoon and wanted to see him before he left.

When Chantry came in, he set a wire basket full of manila folders on the desk and Walter saw the label, *Shipbuilders', Welders' Union* on the outside of the top folder. "I haven't asked you to come in on this business, Walter," Chantry said, "because I know how you feel about it. I feel the same way myself. But I've been doing the dirty work for you and Greenwood and now I've got to have some help."

It was clear that Chantry was excited and upset. He pulled over a straight chair, sat down on it with his legs straddling the back. "They got out a federal injunction against the union in Los Angeles yesterday——"

The teacher was looking his way with unerring direction. "Who got out an injunction?" he asked.

"The Negroes. The Negro shipyard workers. They've set up a committee, an organization, operating all along the coast. You know that. So now there's a show-cause hearing on the injunction for tomorrow morning. In Los Angeles. I think we can block it, Walter. I'm taking the plane down today. But Garnet just phoned me, they're in federal court up here too. There's two hundred people slated to be laid off over in San Martin this afternoon; you know they refused to pay dues. I suppose they're practically certain to get a temporary restraining order. If the hearing for the injunction is scheduled for tomorrow, you'll have to take it."

"Pardon me for asking," Walter said, "but wouldn't it be simpler just to comply with the injunction?"

Chantry looked up, a pained expression on his face. "It would always be simpler to file a plea of *nolo contendere*. But who needs to hire a lawyer for that?"

"One reason for hiring a lawyer," Walter said, "is to get his advice as to whether legal grounds for contention exist."

"Try telling that to Garnet."

"Well, I will."

Chantry sat silent for a few moments, and after a time he said, "Walter, you've got yourself a reputation as a crusader. That's very fine and very comfortable. But a person can get too pure to live in this world. As I said before, I've been doing the dirty work on this case for the past eighteen months; and I might add, earning ninety per cent of our retainer from the Shipbuilders and Welders; and apparently you weren't too pure to remain in the same firm with me. Now I ask you to take over one hearing in the case and you act as if I were desecrating the Sabbath. You don't like this case. I don't like it either. But as a matter of fact there are ample legal grounds, and I think preponderant ones, for opposing the injunction.

"From Garnet's point of view, he's been paying us a monthly fee and a good one, to stand ready to service his organization. If we decide we'll only service his organization when we happen to like the case, he'll go looking for other counsel. He's done it before."

"Let Greenwood handle it."

"I really don't understand how it would preserve your purity to push off on Greenwood what you're unwilling to do yourself. But Garnet won't have Greenwood. He doesn't think he's competent. He wants you."

Walter pulled the basket toward him and thumbed through the folders which contained the background material, the constitution of the union, the agreements between the union and the shipbuilding corporations, resolutions of the last union convention dealing with auxiliary locals, orders of the President's Fair Employment Practices Board, half a dozen acts of Congress, a sheaf of typed pages of references to precedent cases. This discussion with Chantry brought back to his mind the conversation he had had with Richards several years earlier, at the time of their dispute over the Saw Creek case. Oh, yes, how similar they were. Yet the situations were different, very different. There was the file on Anton Novak he had laid aside when Chantry came in. How many Anton Novaks had he helped salvage something for themselves and their families out of a catastrophe—and out of the flinty grip of the insurance companies? What was that worth? How many good cases had he argued *and won,* in the past five years—for one wrong one?

He thought of the bill he still owed the sanitarium, thought of the weekly cost of maintaining Sylvia at the rancho, thought of the amount he had yet to raise for Richards, *and Mackay.* Could he back out on the commitment he had made for Wendel? Or could he abandon his wife? Even after this, could he abandon her? Least of all after this. And in any case, he was not certain; he could never be certain—oh, it was best not to be. If only this had come a year before or a year later, when he had his hands clear. *How would he decide the issue, he thought, if all this were set apart?* Certainly the good cases would still outweigh the single bad one. What other possible logic could one live by? Yet what an incredible and malevolent prescience seemed to govern random events!

"Well," Chantry said, "what do you propose?"

"I don't know, Howard. I haven't made up my mind yet."

"I hope you succeed in making it up one way or the other," Chantry told him bitterly. "Garnet wants you to come over and see him this morning. Will you go?"

"Certainly."

"All right. I don't know what else to say to you."

After Chantry had gone out, Walter packed the folders into his brief case, put on his hat and went down to the street. At the corner, as he was waiting for a taxi, he picked up the early edition of the afternoon paper which carried the headline: S.F. JUDGE HALTS LAYOFF OF 200 SHIPYARD WORKERS—TEMPORARY RESTRAINING ORDER GRANTED.

He folded the paper under his arm without reading it. He had made up his mind he would advise Garnet not to contest the injunction.

Ten or fifteen people were waiting in the anteroom of Garnet's headquarters; but the secretary, a stern gray-haired woman with horn-rim glasses, swept Walter past them to the inner office. Garnet rose to meet him, began speaking before they had finished shaking hands. "This is a tough nut, Stone," he said. "I'm not asking what you think about it and I'm not telling you what I think about it." Chantry must have talked to him already, Walter thought. "Here's the thing," Garnet said. "I'm an elected officer of the Shipbuilders' and Welders' Union. I have my instructions from the Executive Board and I have my instructions from the General Convention. Those instructions are: *Fight this thing all the way through the courts!* That's what I'm going to do, Stone. If I didn't do that, I'd be derelict in my duties as an officer."

Garnet stopped speaking, and in the silence Walter heard the traffic below on Market Street; and he heard the rapid, slightly wheezing in-and-out of the man's breath as the huge bulk of his chest rose and fell under the blue-striped shirt and the blue suspenders. He had pulled his tie loose to make room for the bulging trunk of his neck, and now he wiped his hand over his head. Garnet, Walter realized, had done precisely what was necessary to pin the issue down. There remained no possible argument. Walter had the choice of sitting down to discuss how to handle the case, or taking his hat and walking out.

He sat down.

"I know this has been Chantry's baby up till now," Garnet said. "I haven't got much time, you can see how many people are kicking around outside there waiting to chew my ear off. I don't guess you have much time either, and you don't need me to tell you how to go after this, you're the lawyer, not me. But here's where the union stands, Stone, I want you to know this. There's three main arguments, and I want you to hit heavy on these.

"Number one,"—and he brought both his hands down flat on the desk—"a union is a private organization. The membership has the right to decide who they'll take in as members and who they won't. That's ABC. You couldn't have a union without it.

"Number two, the union has closed shop agreements with the shipbuilding companies arrived at by collective bargaining and approved by every government agency that legally has anything to do with bargaining. Don't forget that!

"Number three, Stone. This President's Fair Employment Practice Committee is strictly phony. It's got no act of Congress behind it. It's got no legal right to tell any union or anybody else what to do. It's got no power to set aside our contracts. That's the position of the union, and that's the position of the shipbuilding corporations we hold contracts with. No court has any authority to enforce its decisions, by an injunction or anything else, because it's nothing. It's got no right to make any decisions.

"Those are the arguments, Stone. Not in legal terms— you and Chantry can set 'em up the way they need to be." He waved his hand at Walter's brief case. "Any others you can dig up, so much the better.

"Now. I'm a union man, you're not. I want to tell you a couple of things. Any union man will fight to the last ditch to keep the government or the courts from telling him who he's got to take into his membership. Why? Because that's a principle. You take that away and you're finished. You got no free union left, you got a Stalin-Hitler union.

"Who's behind this whole Fair Employment Practice business, Stone? A few commies in Washington; a bunch of bedtime pinks in the CIO. That's exactly what they want to do —destroy the right of a union to determine its own membership. They're smart, Stone. They got their people yelling like lunatics, tryin' to get everybody else agitated. Here, look at this——" He yanked open a drawer of his desk, drew out a mimeographed sheet which he handed to Walter. "That's a resolution they got passed down in the Garleyville local. How'd they do it? Well, the local officers was asleep on their dead ends, that's how. They had the meeting pretty well stacked, they made a big play for the women that never been in the union before and don't know any better; they lined up some guys to hog the microphones. So they pass it, send it off to the convention—let everybody into the union, don't matter who they are. Convention will throw it out the window, but that don't mean there wasn't some damage done by it. Plenty.

"And they're goin' to bring one just like it into the San Martin local. That would be a pretty picture, wouldn't it? Goin' into court to fight for the union and you have one of your biggest locals cut your feet off! But they won't pass it, don't worry." Leaning forward over the desk then and lowering his voice, Garnet said, "I got pretty good information who's back of this move. There's some commies back of it too, you can take my word for that. We got files on 'em."

Walter sat silent. He could see the other watching, studying him through the eye-slits of the red-veined, blue-jawed slab of his face; we assume you're on our side, Stone, we assume you are but we're not quite sure; and he had just told him the alternative: if he wasn't on this side, whose side he must be on. Walter felt a violent rebellion against the overbearing power of the man. He had come intending to advise him not to contest the injunction. And certainly now was the time to say, *Look, Garnet, I've listened long enough to this harangue. Here's my advice as an attorney: the courts, all the way to the Supreme Court, have held that a man's right to earn a living comes within the due process clause. You and your union are depriving these people of the right to earn a living and sooner or later they're going to make it stick in the courts. . . .* He had come intending to convince Garnet of this position. But he knew now, he had known in fact from the beginning, that he would not be able to convince Garnet. So if he spoke, the outcome would be either that he would end by knuckling under, in which case it would be far better not to have spoken at all, or else that he would end by saying, *You'll have to find someone else to represent you in this action.* And that would be the end of the firm of Stone, Chantry and Greenwood.

He could not do it, and he said nothing.

"When you get down to the facts——" Garnet resumed in a quiet, businesslike tone, and Walter wondered whether he had followed him through each step in his own internal debate, "—when you come down to the facts, Stone, the Shipbuilders' Union has done more for the colored folk than all these professional sob sisters put together. We used to have a clause in our constitution that would not allow any of them into the trade at all. We knocked that out in 1937. We don't say they can't work, Stone. Any job they're qualified for, they can have. They've got to join the union. But so does anybody else works in the trade. We've got a closed shop and we worked like hell to get it, and we're not going to throw it away because a few black boys don't like it."

Garnet heaved himself up from behind his desk, his face flushing across with anger. "Now they're all screaming about auxiliary lodges. But most of these people don't know how to spell their own names yet. I never went much to school either, Stone. But I taught myself how to read and write, I taught myself the shipfitter trade too. And I didn't start tellin' other people how to run their business before I knew a Stillson wrench from a chipping hammer.

"I could take you down to the shipyard, Stone, and show you bunches of these black boys, ten and twelve at a time, that's supposed to be qualified welders or shipfitters. And what are they doin'? Hidin' down bottom of a deep tank, shootin' craps. I can show you steel plates worth thousands of dollars, Stone, ruined, shot to hell, because some black-ass speedball couldn't read a blueprint, couldn't even follow a chalk line, couldn't listen long enough to hear what his leaderman said to him.

"Those are the people are squawkin' about being in auxiliary lodges, Stone. Why, I had a man get up right here in my own office and threaten me with all kinds of things because I wouldn't let him hold an election with ballots they were going to run off themselves on a mimeograph machine. *Look here,* I showed him, *it says in this letter official ballots printed by the General Office. Can you read?* Why, they'd had those mimeographed ballots sailing around here like snowballs. Seven hundred votes cast when there wasn't but seventy men in the hall. I've seen it happen like that too.

"And you know what he done next? Goes out in the shipyard and gets all these people to tear up their dues books. Threatened to beat the crap out of one of my business agents. Yeah, about two hundred were goin' to gang him out there, but they didn't quite have the guts for it!

"I tell you, Stone," he shouted, "some of us have put in years, maybe our whole lives, building this union. It ain't just a hiring agency. It belongs to the men. It's fraternal, it's social. It's—it's a lot to them. And I'll be God damned if we're goin' to stand around and see a bunch of wild niggers just out of the canebrakes come up here and smash it all to hell for us."

Garnet stopped and sat down abruptly. He was still breathing hard, but after he had caught his breath, he said in a mild voice, "Hard for a man to see how it is if he never was in a union. That's why I wanted to tell you. You and Chantry are the best legal counsel we ever had out here, best the union's got anywhere in the country. You been worth every cent we paid you. We got plenty of confidence in you, Stone." Now he was reaching out, flipping over the pages of his daybook. "Well, I'll be here all afternoon if you need me. Or I'll be home tonight after eight."

"All right," Walter said.

He took his hat and his brief case and went out.

22

Down the hill through the dancing shadows of the eucalyptus branches, Joyce walked to the shopping center where she caught the little bus that ran to San Martin. She got down by the freight depot. Here the railroad tracks came curving in across a flat field; a few houses were scattered along the roadway opposite the tracks, and among them the church showed its new stucco front which seemed to have been glued to the old clapboards behind. Unlocking the door, Joyce stepped into the square, bare room. Rows of chairs faced the minister's table, emptily listening as the purple banner on the wall in gold letters demanded,

"ARE YOU PREPARED TO MEET YOUR MAKER TOMORROW?" and "WHO WILL BE BORN AGAIN IN CHRIST JESUS?"

She took her place at the piano, ran through a few finger exercises. Then jumping up, she threw open the back door and looked out into the field with its orange poppies and carcasses of abandoned automobiles over which the birds were flittering. In the distance across the flats, she saw the sparkle of the bay, the masts of ships, the high framework of the shipyard and smoke rising into the blue sky.

Here was her third spring in San Francisco. But generous though San Francisco had been to her, she thought that she always would look to the desert as her real home; and remembered running outdoors after a rain to find the tiny blossoms feathering the gravel. When Charlie came back, she thought, and after the war, they would spend a spring in the desert, someplace where there was no one else at all, and he would paint, and she would—do what? She would have to learn to play some instrument she could take along, an accordion or a guitar.

Now the spring had brought Sally her husband back, and she was glad for this. She had seen her face on the morning Sally had answered the telephone, how she closed her eyes and stood with the phone pressed up to her mouth and her ear, and all the while groping behind her with the other hand trying to find a chair. Joyce had packed her suitcase then and gone to Janet's with the envy making only a small spark inside her, thinking, I'm glad, I *am* glad; and another month, two months, will bring Charlie home and it will be our turn.

Our turn. Sitting once more at the piano, she started through the assignment the teacher had given. The twelve contredanses of Beethoven to practice, the teacher saying casually that she might wish to include several in her annual recital. *Suppose she herself were asked to play in the recital?*—and her fingers tripped and back she went to the beginning. That would be like Sally, she thought, with her speech to the union meeting: she would die of stage fright. But she laughed at her own anxiety, for the teacher had fifteen students besides herself and never included more than one or two in her recitals. Oh, she was safe enough!

Mistake. Repeat, please, repeat.

She struggled for a perfect touch to match the perfection

of the little dances—the slim legs, the sweeping skirts as she imagined them in their crystal patterns—till she came at last to the one she always waited for, the theme he had used for the final movement of the Third Symphony; and here the keys and fingering, steps, figures, brocade walls were whirled aside. A whole orchestra thundered around her, filling, engulfing the empty, creaking, echoing chamber.

She came to the end, stopped with her hands resting on the keyboard.

How could this patchwork of artificial sounds all marked with signs and numbers like parts of a ship when they came from the plate shop—make music? Yet as you drew the sounds together, they became something that had not been there before, something that once joined could never be separated. Painting was more than lines and colors, music more than notes. But what more were they? She did not know. They were like life; you lived . . . but did not know exactly what you were living.

Her fingers moved at random seeking some response from the silent keys. She was at the crossing again in the morning and her father standing beside her. The train roared past, the steam and smoke hissed out, the faces in the window and the laughing black cook in his white jacket at the door of the dining car. *San Francisco, Denver, Omaha: any place the train go.* She fell upon the bass notes and the trebles as she had so often done when she was a little girl, half expecting to hear her mother's voice call, *Joyce, Joyce, that's not practicing.* Or if someone came passing by, they would surely think she was crazy. No, of course it was not practicing, it was not anything, it was only imitating the sounds and that was nothing.

Yet somewhere must be the combination of notes that would give her the key, that would open the silence within her. I wish I could make a song for springtime, she thought, how it is to me only, to me. Or for the little church in its stucco front. Or for the shipyard, a whole symphony for the people in the shipyard. Who ever could do that? How ever could she hope to find notes that would say how beautiful she saw Janet Beezely, or gay and confident like Sally O'Regan, or sweet and strong as Charlie; or like Richard Brooks the Sergeant, burning like an ember from some dark fire?

Her hands explored and came back empty. Maybe that was all. Maybe someday she would find her own music; but did this really matter?—there was enough already to keep her playing for a thousand years. Her hands traveled over the keys and returned with only the snatches of old familiar tunes. Or a child thumping the bass notes.

What would her teacher say? Your fingering is not yet what it should be, Miss Allen. No. Back to the contredanses. Repeat, please. Repeat, repeat, Miss Allen, that's showing some improvement. . . .

She locked the doors of the church behind her. Over beyond the freight depot, the bus was coming and she ran to catch it. She had stayed too long practicing as she always did, and now when she came back to Janet Beezely's, had barely time left to get something to eat, change her clothes and hurry off to the yard.

She still was working in the plate shop.

The two-week stay for which the foreman had first sent her there had extended to several months and now that the weather was turning warmer again, she would gladly have gone back to the shipways. Here in the plate shop at the benches assembling small parts, she found none of the excitement she had felt clambering over the stagings with the Sergeant, up on the superstructure one day and deep in the bottom of the engine room the next. There was not so much a sense of *making* something, of being herself part of the building of the ship. Over and over again, she put small steel boxes together, not knowing what they were to be used for. She was like a machine; it was hard to believe any purpose in what she was doing, and the time passed slowly.

She had tried sometimes taking advantage of the routine to free her mind for thinking about other things while she worked. But this she found was hopeless. The machine could allow nothing separate from itself. The welding rods, and the generator like a cantankerous child, demanded a ceaseless attention, and she had no choice but to give in, plodding through each half of the long shift till the whistle would set her free.

At lunch hour she joined the circle where the colored women in the plate shop usually ate together, squatting on blocks of wood and on the timbers that made up the plate racks. She had not had time to fix a sandwich for herself coming home so late from the church, and instead had thrown a piece of cheese, bread and a paring knife into her lunch pail. She set to slicing the cheese, trying to touch it as little as possible because her hands still smelled oily even after she had scrubbed them under the water faucet (there was only cold water) in the washroom.

Across the smoky expanse of the building, separated as always into groups of colored and groups of white, were the other workers, each group bunched down close over their lunch pails and thermos jugs; while the flavor of coffee penetrated slightly into the harsh odors from the welding and burning of steel.

Someone nudged her from behind.

Turning, she saw one of the women she had worked with in the cleanup gang when she had first come to the yard.

"Sergeant say he want to see you," the woman said.

"The Sergeant? Where is he?"

"He just outside the door over there."

To see her outside? Why didn't he come in?—he came often enough to the plate shop. She felt her heart begin hammering with anxiety. What did he want to see her for, *outside?* The woman had started back toward the door. Gathering her food which she had just spread across her lap, into the lunch pail again, she got up and hurried after her. Outside, it was almost but not quite dark and the electric lights of the yard seemed to make scarcely any light at all; there remained a pale glow in the sky, a streak of lavender along the west where tails of fog curled over the clefts of the hills.

She saw a group of men beside the doorway and the Sergeant leaning against the wall of the building.

"Reverend Beezely got a telephone?" the Sergeant asked.

"No, he hasn't."

The group opened to let her through. As she moved closer she saw that the Sergeant's face was streaked across with blood, his eyes swollen shut. She felt a gasp of nausea in the pit of her stomach, felt the sockets behind her own eyes turn dizzyingly.

"Go with Johnny Hanks," the Sergeant said. "He drive you to Beezely's. . . . Tell him watch out not come down here alone . . . you tell him not go out alone at all, they're layin' for him maybe too. . . ."

One of the men was pulling her by the arm, but she hung back, still staring at the Sergeant.

"Go on, go on now," he said. "You go along, show Johnny Hanks where to find Beezely."

"What happened?"

"Look bad, hunh?" He spoke in a gruff, half-laughing, half-choking voice. "Went for my coffee and a couple of live ones were waitin' for me. . . ."

She reached out, touching his face with the tips of her fingers. "My face'll be all right," he told her. "They couldn't hurt me any in the head." Some of the men guffawed; and as Joyce turned to follow the man who was pulling at her arm, she heard the Sergeant add, "If my back's all right. Guess they missed the right spot . . ."

They hurried towards the gate; but the sight of his face kept coming in front of her and she took deep breaths trying to drive away the dizziness that assailed her.

23

Sally at the stove was cooking supper and Tom reading the newspaper at the kitchen table, when he heard a knock on the door and opened it to find the Second Mate standing outside. Dressed up in his high-pressure too, what the hell does he have to come here tonight for? And was on the point of saying they were busy, they were expecting company; but the Second stepped in as if he had been invited. Sally turned from the stove and Tom introduced them.

"I've been hearing a lot about you, Mrs. O'Regan," the Second told her. What a damn liar, Tom thought, I never said a word to him about her. The Second took off his coat and Sally urged him to sit down, while Tom tried to pass her a signal and a scowl, but knew she had her mind on too many other things to notice. All afternoon she had been studying her speech. "Tommy," she called over her shoulder from the stove, "there's some beer in the icebox, isn't there? Pour your friend a glass." For Christ's sake, don't ask him to supper. He found only one can left, and glumly poured that out, while the other began recounting the news from the ship since Tom had been away, as if he gave a damn. They had had her fumigated again and now were ready to come out of dry dock; and neither the Skipper nor the Lieutenant had been aboard in the last ten days. He thought the Skipper had gone to Los Angeles.

"Watch the hamburgers a minute for me, will you, Tommy?" Sally asked; and he stood poking them occasionally while she disappeared into the bathroom.

"Everybody figures we're off for a nice long cruise in the Pacific next trip," the Second was saying. "We're supposed to move over to Port Chicago after we get out of dry dock. I guess you know what that is?"

Tom shrugged his shoulders. What difference did that make? The *Andrew Rogers* had hardly ever carried anything except ammo since he'd been aboard her. How long was the son of a bitch expecting to sit there?

Sally returned, in a dress now, and her hair rolled up, looking as if she were set to go to a dance; and he could see the Second following her with his eyes. "Oh, sure, they're done now," she announced. "I'll put the coffee through. You'll stay to supper with us, won't you? It's not much of a dinner, I'm afraid . . ."

The Second rose gallantly from the table. "I hope I'm not intruding. I didn't mean to come just at your dinner time . . ."

"You carry a watch, don't you?" Tom asked.

The Second glanced his way and grinned. But Sally had already set another place—endeavoring to be the gracious hostess, though she scarcely ate a bite herself, and Tom saw her all the while with her lips moving as if she were praying under her breath, and knew she was repeating her memorized lines, frightened to death that she might forget them. The Second, still apologizing for his intrusion, at the same time kept fishing for answers. "I shouldn't have stayed, I can see you must be getting ready to go out. Please don't let me hold you up . . ."

"I have to attend a special meeting of my union," Sally

explained. "Tom doesn't have to go anywhere, I don't think."

"What union do you belong to, Mrs. O'Regan?"

"The Welders' and Shipbuilders' Union. Tonight—"

Tom kicked her under the table. She jerked and stared across at him, and then concluded: "Well, there's an important meeting that all the members are supposed to come to." But the Second, Tom felt certain, had not missed this exchange either; and they were beginning on dessert when Sally's two shipfitters arrived. Half coming in, half not coming in, they jostled each other in the open doorway, Sally urging them to sit down for coffee, and they declining the invitation. She put on her coat and hat, gave Tom a kiss on the cheek. "Ten-thirty in front of the hall, honey. Okay?"

"Will it be over by then?"

"Has to be out by ten-thirty," the older of the two shipfitters, the one called Henry, assured him. "On account of the midnight shift."

"All right, I'll be there."

"Glad to have met you."

"Good night."

"Glad to have met you."

They were on their way down the steps, the three together, and he returned to the table as the door closed behind them. I never even wished her good luck, he thought, and was on the point of opening the door again to call after her, when the sight of the grinning face of the Second Mate restrained him. As they finished their coffee, the Second asked if some special business were coming up at the meeting, and he said he didn't know if there was anything special, maybe electing officers or something.

The Second then insisted on cleaning up the dishes.

"Leave them," Tom told him. "We'll do them in the morning."

"Oh, hell, no, that wouldn't be right, O'Hoolihan. Your wife's working, isn't she? Midnight shift, didn't you tell me? She comes home from a long union meeting, rushes right off to a hard night in the shipyard. You don't want her to get back in the morning and find these dishes all over the place, do you? What kind of a guest would she think I was?" Removing his brass-buttoned coat, he rummaged in the closet till he found one of Sally's aprons, which he tied across his middle, then stoppered the sink and ran it full of water. "What do you do all day, Tom?" he asked.

"Same thing I do on the ship," Tom told him. "I sleep."

"Sleep all the time waiting for the wife to get home from work? Good God, man, I don't see how that poor girl gets any rest at all!"

Tom began to laugh in spite of his irritation; he took a dish towel and dried while the Second washed. "You can see I know my way around a kitchen sink, can't you, O'Hoolihan? That's what *my* wife thinks a husband is meant for—somebody to wash the dishes and purify the diapers. You ever scrub out a diaper?"

Tom shook his head.

"Well, you've a new experience waiting for you. You'll get used to it, though, kind of begin to like it, there's something satisfying about a diaper. Most normal kids learn to discharge cargo exactly when you sit down to a meal. They usually feed kids mashed prune and stuff. Has a little bit of a sweet smell. Oh, I'm an old hand at this." When he had emptied the sink of dishes, he lighted a cigarette and asked, "So what's next?"

"You might scrub the floor in the bathroom if you feel like it," Tom suggested.

"I do hope I haven't been intruding."

To this Tom offered no reply, and the Second, after a moment of silence, proposed, "If you'll come downtown with me, I'll buy you a drink. Guess I owe you one in return for the dinner. I have to be back on the ship by ten o'clock anyway, I promised the Chief I'd relieve him." At least that would get him out of the house, Tom thought. He went to fetch his pea jacket from the bedroom and returned to find the other looking through a batch of newspaper clippings which apparently he had picked up from the top of the radio. Sally had been sitting there before dinner, Tom remembered, working on her speech.

"You don't mind, do you? These were lying right out here." And as he pulled on his overcoat, the Second said, "I can see your wife is on the right side of the fence, Flags. Tell her I'm glad she's going to that meeting. I hope she votes twice."

"Thanks," Tom said. "Thanks, I'll tell her."

They climbed the flight of steps to the parking lot, and he let the pickup coast downhill, bouncing and shimmying over the rough spots; then along the flats by the bayside, past the shipyard glittering with lights, while he remembered the hours he had put in there. Ahead of them stretched the marshes and mud flats, drearily illuminated by distant lines of intersecting roadways. The Second seemed to have nothing more to say and they rode in silence all the way to the Oakland city limits. But once settled at the bar in a gin mill on San Pablo Avenue, he opened up again.

"How did a guy like you get hold of a girl like that?" he demanded.

"Some girls are pretty lucky."

"The one that hooked on to you, Flags, was born under a dark star. Do you serve navy personnel in here?" he asked the bartender, and answered himself: "No, sir, we serve drinks." The bartender giggled politely, and the Second told him, "A couple of whiskies, I guess. Want a beer chaser, Tom?"

"If you think you can afford it, Second."

When the drinks were in front of them, the Second suggested, "Let's quit kidding. I know you've been mad ever since I stuck my head in the door. I guess I should apologize for coming, I just looked you up in the phone book and found my way over. But I was—kind of lonely. Why the hell didn't you ever invite me?"

Tom, touched in spite of himself, grumbled, "Oh, I was going to, Second. Only I was so glad to be shut of the *Andrew Rogers* for a few days . . ." He mixed the bar whisky with his beer, trying to ease it off a little. The place smelt of wet cigarette butts and stale beer; and an odor of urine puffed past them whenever anyone pulled open the door that led to the toilets.

"Well then, here's to the Mrs.," the Second proposed. "I'm glad I met her anyhow. I can see she's a girl with *joie de vivre*—joy in living, that means," he translated. "Enthusiasm. The divine fire. Just to see a girl like that restores a certain gusto to an old cynic like me. You're a lucky man. My own wife, to tell you the truth, is kind of a bag. Oh, not the loose kind, I don't mean, she's very tight, rather prim—maybe I picked the wrong metaphor . . . But if I were home, she'd be crawling all over me, trying to arouse the sagging libido. Not because she wanted to, but because . . . oh, well, what the hell, skip it. If we were in New York," he said, "I wouldn't invite you either."

And I sure wouldn't invite myself, Tom thought.

"What shall we talk about, Flags?" asked the Second. "Cabbages and kings? The state of the world?" Leaning sideways, he hissed into Tom's ear, "Want me to tell you what's wrong with this old globe of ours? All right, I will, whether you want me to or not. It can be abbreviated into one letter of the alphabet. One letter repeated three times. CCC: capitalism, Communism and Catholicism. Do hope I'm not offending you?"

"Think nothing of it."

"Didn't you tell me once you weren't a Catholic?" Without waiting for an answer, the Second continued, "I can see you're not a capitalist by looking at you. And I'm damn sure you're not a Communist because you don't talk like one."

"So how does a Communist talk?" Tom asked him.

"You don't know? That's all the more reason you might be one. Second Mate is full of *bons mots* tonight. But since you're not an adherent of any of the three C's, I assume it's safe to proceed. Damn the torpedoes," he cried. "These are the evils of the world today, Flags. Take away any one of the three, and you and I could stay home growing our petunias and cucumbers. If there hadn't been Communism, Hitler would never have come to power. If Hitler hadn't come to power, there wouldn't be any war. If there wasn't any war, capitalism would collapse—you can take that from an old newspaper man. And if capitalism collapsed, the Catholic Church would go down along with it. But now we come to the tricky part. Watch this, Flags!—and then Communism would collapse too, because the Communists wouldn't have anything to talk about. Do you follow me?"

"I follow some of it," Tom conceded, as he looked behind him for the clock.

"Imagine a world with none of those three in it! What a paradise! Then we'd start building all three all over again; that's human nature. . . . Funny thing, Flags, all three C's are fighting each other like crazy; but they're all exactly alike. Ever think of that? They all tell you the same thing. Leave your brains outside and follow the leader. Trust to Authority. Set 'em up the same," he called to the bartender. "Now those two gents who came to escort your wife, O'Hoolihan," he asked, "did you know them before?"

"Sure, I'd met them. Why?"

"Just wondering."

"Wondering *what?* They're a couple of shipfitters. In the same union she is."

"I'd be willing to bet you my scrambled egg hat they're a couple of red-hots."

Tom swung around on his stool. "What the hell do you mean?"

"Well, you know what I mean. Uncle Joe's boys. Woikers from the party."

"Oh," Tom said. Then after a moment he asked, "I suppose you could tell that by looking at them for a minute and a half?"

The Second lifted his glass in one hand, blinking, and with the other hand rubbed his eyes. "You're absolutely right," he agreed. "I had no business to say a thing like that. No business whatever. Strike it from the record. The fact is, it's the cynic in me coming out. I find it hard to imagine anybody going out of their way to take somebody else's wife to a union meeting . . ."

They had good enough reason, Tom told himself, with Sally primed to hit the mike for them. Then he remembered that people always had been accusing Kallela of being a Communist, along with everything else they had blamed him for. Not to his face though. Why, this son of a bitch! He cleared his feet from the rungs of the stool, thinking, about one more word out of you, friend, and I'll be ready to knock you onto your keester. But the other sat there rubbing his eyes. Despite his anger, he felt half sorry for him again.

"Funny thing, Flags," said the Second. "I used to be a Communist myself for a while." And as Tom stared at him, he continued, "Oh, I had my fling at saving the world too. I discovered Authority. And then I undiscovered it. I'll tell you the story of my life sometime, O'Regan—if you ever break your leg and can't get away. It's quite interesting. *Quaite.* My father was a teacher in a boys' school. I had

233

things pretty soft when I was a kid, softer than you did, I guess. Then we hit some hard luck when I was about fifteen and I figured God had really done us wrong. Decided I ought to lend a hand in overturning the system. Establishing Authority. Ending injustice on earth. I was very sincere about it. Most Communists really are well-meaning, sincere, ordinary people. They don't intend any harm. Just like most Catholics. Or most capitalists. I suppose we could say *we* don't mean any harm either. Couple friendly Joes, that's all. We'll tote our wagon-load of dynamite wherever they tell us, but we don't mean anything by it. . . . Well, Flags, I don't wish to be keeping you too late."

"You aren't," Tom told him.

He got up and went to the toilet. The guy must have been half gassed before he ever came to the house, he thought, leaning over the galvanized trough that ran out through a hole in the back wall. Should have slammed the door in his face. But as he buttoned his trousers, it struck him that the Second might just be right at that. The suspicion and resentment flared inside him. This wasn't anything for a woman to get into anyway. She ought to stay the hell out of a business like this. Let the damn shipfitter go paddle his own canoe! If that Henry was any younger, Tom thought; and then told himself, come off it, come off it, he must be pushing sixty!

Outside, he found the Second Mate standing gloomy and silent, ready to leave. They walked several blocks up San Pablo Avenue to another tavern, then on to a third. What few remarks the Second now offered were again along the line of shipboard gossip, repeating mostly what he had told already, while Tom spoke hardly a word. The hour and a half dragged to a conclusion. He dropped the Second off at the Key station, drove back through the empty streets of Oakland, and over the flats till he reached the main intersection of San Martin.

The movie theater was letting out. He noticed two or three pairs of soldiers on the prowl for girls; and beyond, across the railroad sidings, he spotted the old Elks' Hall from a block away by the crowd in front of it. The meeting appeared to have ended and he pulled slowly by, looking for Sally, but saw no women on the sidewalk at all. There was a swirl and commotion, the beginnings of a fight shaping up near the entranceway. As he came abreast, he could see one man dodging and ducking while three others circled, punching at him. Tom rounded the next corner, stopped and dug out the jack handle from under the accumulated litter of shopping bags and old inner tubes in the truck bed. Then he drove back around the block, pulled up directly in front of the entrance. The fight was over, the crowd appeared to be thinning. A few women were coming out of the building. He caught sight of Sally with the older of the two shipfitters, the one named Henry, and was about to call to them when the shipfitter suddenly staggered forward, half falling, and spun up onto his feet, while Sally jumped down the steps after him. She saw the truck at the same instant and tried to pull the other towards it.

A voice yelled, "Hey, sister, you like layin' that black meat?"

The shipfitter retreated, backing up slowly, facing the men behind him and Tom yanked Sally into the cab. The motor was still running. "Take the wheel," he said, "and be ready to move." Then sliding out on the driver's side, he circled the truck. A knot of men had closed around the shipfitter, knocked him down to his knees as he tried to crawl through the door and threw him over against the hood of the engine. Tom whipped the jack handle from under his tunic. He heard the sing of it in the air knowing the steel would snap a head like a watermelon. But a voice shrieked, "Look out, Mac! Behind!" and the one he aimed at must have caught him from the corner of his eye and half turned, taking the blow on the elbow. Letting out a series of yipes like a dog, he stumbled off holding his arm with his other hand. Tom swung once at a back that went dodging away from him, and swung again but there was nothing within reach. He groped behind him with his left hand feeling for the door and shoved in backwards. The pickup, jolting away from the curb, threw him into the lap of the shipfitter.

Sally turned the first corner, and another, and another after that, while Tom stared through the rear window to make certain no one was following them.

"You get hurt much?" he asked the shipfitter.

"No, I'm okay. Soaked up a few bruises, that's all."

"You won't be the only one," Tom told him. "What happened to the fellow that was with you?"

"He left already. Got a ride home with some guys live near him in Oakland. Here it is, Sally. The chevy beyond the fire hydrant." The shipfitter climbed over Tom's knees, and from outside, thrust his head back through the window. "You did mighty fine, Sally. We give it the best we could, anyhow." And pressing Tom's arm, he said simply, "Thanks." Then he got into his own car and they followed him out to the main street, where he waved and swung north toward Oakland.

At the intersection of San Martin Boulevard, the traffic light turned against them, and Sally, as she brought the pickup to a stop, said, "You drive, Tom." He squeezed forward, letting her slide underneath him. He felt no particular reaction yet to what had happened. When the light changed again, he gunned ahead of the other traffic, thinking that his own nerves were pretty solid and picturing himself wading in with the jack handle and how he must have looked to that gang on the sidewalk. As if he had meant murder—and he had, too.

Beside him, Sally asked, "Was . . . anybody hurt, do you think . . . very bad?"

"They got out of the way too damn fast." The first one must have a broken arm for himself, he thought, but he did not tell her that. They were passing the shipyard and he saw that she was leaning back with her eyes closed and her mouth open slightly, and her hands pressed against the seat on each side of her. She looked sick. He wondered suddenly if anybody had roughed her up on the way out. "You feel all right, Sally? You want me to stop?"

"Go on," she whispered. "I'm a little bit dizzy. I'm all right."

"Did you get hurt?" he demanded.

"No, no, it isn't that, Tom."

Just nerves, he told himself with relief. He never had asked her how the meeting came out, though there was hardly any need to ask. She had been a fool to get mixed in with a deal like this. God damn shipfitter, he thought, he better go peddle his fish someplace else. I should have thrown him right out of the house when I first saw him, told her to keep clear of the whole mess. Only she wouldn't have done it. Remembering the night behind the lunch counter when she had punched him in the face, he knew there was no better way to make sure she would do something than for him to tell her not to. Yet she wasn't so tough when you came right down to it. She looked about ready to pass out and he wondered how she'd get along swinging down the lines into a lifeboat from a torpedoed ship. She'd be all right, he told himself. Nerves never hit you much anyway till after a thing was all over. Somebody else put in a couple sleepless nights too, remember? And suddenly he felt sorry for her, angry and sorry at the same time, he wanted to stop the car and put his arms around her. But they were almost home.

"Didn't go so good, hunh, Sally?"

"No it didn't."

She said nothing more; but she held on to his arm all

the rest of the way except where he had to shift gears up the steep hill to the parking lot, and when they came down the steps to the house, she asked, "Call the yard for me, Tom, tell them I'm sick tonight." That's no lie, either, he thought. As he was making the telephone call, he saw her sit at the table, and then get up to put on water for coffee. The cat scratched at the door, and she let the cat in and fed it, all the while looking half a dozen times or more to see if the water were boiling.

"You don't need any coffee," he told her. "You're jittery enough as it is. Why don't we go to bed?"

"I wouldn't be able to sleep anyway. Coffee usually calms me down."

"I should have bought you a couple of shots on the way home."

"You don't have to stay up for me, Tom."

"I don't mind," he said. "I got nothin' else to do but sleep."

She began to laugh. He had finished with the telephone and she came to him, pressed her face against his shoulder and he put his arms around her. "I'm so ashamed," she whispered. "I forgot all the things I wanted to say, Tom. I—I froze on the mike."

"The hell you did!"

"Oh, no," she wailed. "I did! There was so much noise," she told him. "There was everybody shouting. I started off all right, I guess, and then—I couldn't think of a single word. There was some man near me kept shouting, *Spill it, sister, spill it!* and the guys waiting for the mike kept trying to grab it away from me. Finally I just yelled into it, something, I don't know, I'm for the resolution, something . . ."

He led her to a chair at the table and poured a cup of coffee for her. "But a lot of people clapped even so. I heard them. And there was a woman in the row behind when I sat down leaned over and said, 'You did good, kid!' and I knew I hadn't, but I was so grateful I wanted to cry."

Tom brought the bread and margarine from the cabinet.

"Henry never even got a chance to talk, there was such a mob around the mike, the ones on our side hardly got in at all, just two or three. He's a good speaker," she told him, "Henry is, everybody knows him, but he almost had a fight right there on the floor trying to take his turn, and he said about three words when the loudspeaker went out of whack. I don't know, somebody fell over the wire or something . . ."

"They sure had it rigged on you."

"I guess so. I guess they did."

"You should have had your old man there. He wouldn't needed any mike."

"Oh, how could I, how could I, Tom! I was one of the first ones up and when they tried to push in front of me, people began to yell, 'Give the sister a chance,' and they had to let me have it. And then I forgot."

"It could happen to anybody."

"Maybe it would have swung the other way, the whole thing, I was one of the first speakers . . ."

"Will you listen to me, Sally? They had it rigged. It wouldn't have made any difference what you said."

"I knew it by heart. I knew—I knew every word." She was up again, hurrying about the room, to the stove, the window, back to the stove.

"Sally, for Christ's sake calm down!" She did not even hear him. He pulled her into her chair and held her there. For a moment she remained quiet, subsiding as if she had drawn into herself, and then hesitantly she began over again at the beginning, going through each instant, each detail; and how afterwards the chairman declared the resolution lost on a voice vote no one could hear scarcely

239

through the shouting. Henry had jumped up, and others, trying to call for a division. And they were drowned out, the noise, the banging gavel.

He said again, "Sally, it was rigged. There's no use knocking yourself out over it. The union's got a bunch of locals down south, down along the Gulf, and they swing plenty of weight in the national office—No, sit down, listen to *me* for a change.—I don't know what exactly happened, but I been around enough to make a good guess. The orders came from upstairs they better not let any resolutions get by out here; and they were scared a big meeting like this might run away from them. So they called in a bunch of their stooges and they rigged it."

For the first time she seemed to be hearing him.

"You've seen the same thing happen to your Dad," he told her. "You know what went on in Saw Creek as well as I do. They sent down word not to let Kallela run a successful strike, and they moved in and busted it. And busted him too. Or tried to."

"I know," she said.

"Of course they got a tough customer in Kallela. There're not many around like him. But even so, he's never going to do anything much except knock his head against a stone wall. I've heard you tell him that yourself."

"I know."

"It's like me tryin' to wise up my Lieutenant. He don't know as much about the ship as the mess boy, and man to man I could kick the crap out of him. But I don't stand a chance. The muscle's all on his side. It's the same way with a union, they're run from on top, kid."

She looked at him as if she were about to laugh. "Oh, how could I, how could I have done that, Tom, I knew every word!" She drank down what was left of the coffee in her cup; and Tom, taking her by the hand, led her into the bedroom. When they were lying in bed together, she was cold and distant. He wanted to shake her and shout at her; but was so sleepy himself that he had scarcely lain down before he dozed off.

When he waked, it was beginning daylight, the window misty gray and the room still almost dark. She was sitting up in bed looking at the window. Had she ever been asleep? he wondered. Hearing him move, she turned, leaned over him with her fingers touching his cheeks.

"You awake, Tom?"

"Sort of."

"All the way?"

"I guess so."

"Make me have a baby, Tom. Will you?"

She must have been waiting for him. He lay still looking up at her, at the shape of her head and her throat, and her shoulders, and her arms and her breasts in the gray light. Why not, if she really wanted? The half-assent silently to himself lighted his own hunger; and reached for her and pulled her down beside him, while she came to him, yielding, silent, supple, and the knowledge of what they were doing united them in an intensity that was almost pain. He wanted to cry out as if they were a thousand miles apart although her face was close beneath his own, and the teeth set and the eyes fixed and hard.

Yes, afterwards he thought they were slick as a couple of cats purring together in a chair; and two first things he had done in the same night, he thought, he had hit out with the intent of killing and made love with the intent of having a child. As the lawyers said, the intent made all the difference. And strange the two came together, what was there left, he wondered. But for her it was only a beginning and he half envied her, though if she did have a child, it would be his child. He could easily check back, finding for certain it was, and felt proud, rejoicing inside himself that he knew what being in love really was, *really* being—this was a first thing too; he had never known before. While I'm on the next trip, if it takes, that is, he thought, if I haven't been shooting blanks—while I'm gone she'll be pregnant, the baby start growing while I'm away; how many months till you can tell by how she looks?—four maybe, five? Better than leaving a ring to wear around, she might just slip the ring off her finger some night, anybody might. Be no more speeches at union meetings either, not for a while. . . .

Hey, put your arms around me, he said, pressing her tightly again. There was no answering movement and he realized she had fallen asleep finally, exhausted after the day and the night. But he was glad she slept and glad to feel the softness of her beside him and the soft stir of her breathing.

24

The Beezelys' two girls were running out to catch the school bus when their father came back from work. The older one who was in high school paused long enough to give him a sedate kiss, while the younger climbed him like a tree and hung squealing around his neck. Janet had already gone off to her cleaning and pressing shop. Closing the door after the two girls, the Reverend set down the morning newspaper on the table and washed his hands at the kitchen sink.

"Bad news, Joyce," he said.

She turned from the stove where she had started the eggs for their breakfast.

"We lost in federal court," he said. "It's bad news."

She did not know what to say except, "O-oh," trying to let it sound the way she felt. His face wore a surprised and hurt expression. *"What will they do?"* she asked.

"I don't know. They can go on with the layoffs. There's nothing to stop them now."

She set the plates on the table and sat down opposite him.

"In the federal court I never thought it would go that way. President's Fair Employment Practice Board says one thing, the federal court says, no you don't have any authority to do that." He spoke as if some personal friend had betrayed him, shaking him to the heart. "You going in the city today, or over to the church?" he asked.

"I don't have my lesson till tomorrow. I was going to practice at the church."

"I have to go in the city," he said. "Soon as I change my clothes. I have to go to the committee."

"You ought to get some sleep."

That was what Janet would have told him. He nodded and smiled at her. "I'll catch a little nap this afternoon when I come back. Did Mr. Brooks come to work yesterday, Joyce?"

"I didn't see him at all."

"Stopped to call on him yesterday morning," the Reverend told her.

"How is he?"

"I think he felt mighty bad yesterday. But he had a doctor in to look at his back. Said the doctor thought it was all right, but still wanted him to keep to his bed a couple of days to make sure."

"Oh, I'm glad of that!"

"Told me they'd had him under the knife five times out there in the islands, patching his back up for him. That's what he was worried about. I better stop, see him today. Can't tell what he's liable to do when he finds out about this—" He tapped his finger on the newspaper. "Mr. Brooks never did think much of going into the court."

"But is it all over in the court?" she asked. "Can they just drop it like that? Isn't there . . . anything else . . . ?"

"We still can make the appeal. That takes so long everything is likely to be all finished by the time we get our answer. Or the lawyers might take it into the state court too. They're hunting for some state law they can bring an action under. They thought the best chance was in the federal court, but they might try it in the state court now. Nothing else they can do." He had finished eating and pushed his chair back. "Better get dressed and get started. Thank you for making my breakfast, Joyce."

He never had failed to thank her for cooking his eggs for him in the morning—even though they were the hosts and she the guest.

From the cooler she took out some apples and oranges and some cookies from the cookie jar and wrapped them. When the Reverend came through again in his dark suit, with his white shirt and his minister's black tie, she handed him the package of fruit and cookies to take to the Sergeant.

"Why, all right," he said. "I'll give Mr. Brooks a get-well message from you, Joyce."

"And from Janet," she insisted. "Janet made the cookies."

"That's right," the Reverend agreed. "From Janet too."

From her practicing in the church, Joyce returned that afternoon, stopping first at her own house to fetch herself a clean set of work clothes. Sally and her husband, she thought, would probably be out, since Sally had taken the week off from the shipyard to be with him; but she listened outside the door for a moment making certain the house was empty before she went in. She had met Sally's husband only once. He had seemed pleasant and friendly, but she had felt the strain and knew at once that the less she saw of them while he was home, the easier it would be for Sally.

They must have gone out early. The milk was still on the doorstep. She put the bottles in the icebox and brought in the mail—a handful of advertising circulars and end-of-the-month bills. The cat had come in too, pretending to be starved, and she thought, poor kitty maybe Sally forgot to feed you this morning, she's got other things to think about than you, kitty; and she opened a can of cat food and spooned some of the mash into the cat's plate. After that, she fetched a clean pair of jeans, underwear, and a work shirt from her closet.

The cat, who was not fond of canned cat food, came rubbing her ankles again, marching in a circle, tail erect, gazing at her first from its fiercely whiskered face and then from its ever-smiling rear end. Joyce watched with amusement. She thought of the cat in "Peter and the Wolf": that cat had a melody too if she could only remember it, on the clarinet—how did it go? She hummed the cat's melody while the cat paced around its circle, till the tune fitted so perfectly that she laughed aloud. But at this the cat appeared humiliated. She had noticed that cats often seemed to take offense from being laughed at; it stalked off and lay down under the water heater.

Joyce glanced through the circulars and looked over the bills. One was from her music teacher, one from the dentist, one from the meat market. There was another envelope which she had thought must also be a bill or an advertisement. Now she saw that the address was in capital letters like a telegram, but it was not a telegram either, it did not come in a yellow envelope. She opened it; the letter inside was typewritten in capitals too, the whole letter half a page long, and at the bottom a name she had never seen before.

DEAR MISS ALLEN,

I AM WRITING YOU ON BEHALF OF THE CREW. CHARLIE GAMMON WAS RESPECTED AND HIGHLY REGARDED BY EVERYONE ON OUR SHIP. WE KNOW YOU WILL HAVE LEARNED THE FACTS FROM THE OFFICIAL NOTICE . . .

No, she said.

Oh, no. No. There was no notice. What did they mean, notice? With her hands flat on the table in front of her, she remained perfectly still. She raised her head and looked through the window at the tops of the row of eucalyptus trees. The branches were bright with sunlight. They were bending in the wind exactly as they had done before. They had made a mistake then. Or the letter had come to the wrong address. There was no notice. But if anything had happened, they would have sent a notice; of course they would: they had to. And she thought, *they would have sent it to his father in Texas, not to me.* Her hands folded the page and replaced it in the envelope.

Then she took it out again and opened it.

. . . . SOME OF US WENT TO THE HOSPITAL AND HE WAS VERY COMFORTABLE WHEN WE SAW HIM. HE SAID HE WAS NOT IN ANY PAIN AT ALL. HE ASKED US TO TELL YOU THAT AND SEND YOU SOME THINGS IF HE DID NOT GET WELL AND WE WILL DO THAT WHEN WE COME BACK TO THE STATES. I WISH TO EXPRESS THE DEEPEST SYMPATHY OF THE OFFICERS AND CREW.

YOURS VERY SINCERELY,
John Gibson,
RADIO OPERATOR

Joyce rose from the table. She walked to the front door and back to the stove, and then turned towards the table again. Now the cat was sitting in front of her, the cat with its tail curled around its forepaws, staring up out of round green eyes. She knelt and pressed her hands on each side of its head which felt small and furry and soft between her fingers. The little tune of the cat came into her mind again and she remembered how she had thought of learning to play the guitar or the banjo so she would have something to take with them. Why did she think of that? Why could she not feel what had happened to her? Why did she keep repeating over again the melody from "Peter and the Wolf"?

It was as if she were frozen inside, as if her heart had turned to wood and her mind to sand and sawdust. There was nothing. There was no thought, there was no feeling.

She picked up her bundle of clothes and went to Janet's house. Janet had not yet come home and she was glad. She packed the thermos jug and a sandwich into her lunch pail as she had done every day for more than a year. Then she put on her clean jeans, her boots, and her jacket and tied a scarf over her head, took the lunch pail and walked down the hill through the afternoon sunlight.

She had not even a picture of him. Her mind and her heart were empty and dry as sawdust. If they felt what had happened to her, she thought she would die.

All during the afternoon she went about her work in the plate shop. She was a figure on a stage, she was someone else playing her own part. She spoke to the people she had to speak to, she listened to the foreman, understood what he said, followed his instructions welding the angles to the chalked marks down the long lines and back again and down and back. When lunch hour came, she sat with the others, poured out tea, opened her sandwich as if she were intending to eat. But she ate nothing.

Then, coming towards her from the far end of the plate shop, she saw Sally O'Regan. Sally was picking her way between the benches and the machines and the piles of steel, vanishing into the shadows and appearing again through the bright cones of the floodlights. Sally had come looking for her, Joyce knew, and she was afraid for Sally to find her. She got to her feet and moved away, hurried towards the open end of the building. The darkness outside received her. She turned and her knees buckled, she dropped down with her forehead pressed against the corrugated iron wall.

Sally O'Regan found her there and led her away.

At the gate of the shipyard, Reverend Beezely was waiting

with the taxi that worked from the bus station in San Martin Village. "I saw the letter on the table," Sally told her. "I didn't mean to read it, but I saw the last line, and then we were afraid . . ."

Afraid of what? And Joyce heard herself saying, "It's all right, thank you for coming."

When they reached the Beezelys' house, she went to the bedroom and lay down. Sally pulled a blanket over her, and Joyce, turning her face to the wall, lay still. She knew that sometimes Sally O'Regan and sometimes Janet were sitting beside her. Sometimes she heard voices from the room beyond. And later she heard a familiar voice that was neither Janet's nor Sally's, a man's voice, and the door opened, and in the light from the doorway she saw the Sergeant. She wished he had not come. She did not want to have to listen to him, or even to look at him, and she thought of closing her eyes and pretending to be asleep.

"I heard you got taken sick, Miss Allen," the Sergeant said.

He must have come back to work today, she thought. Something in his face and in the sound of his voice penetrated her own grief, and she knew that something had happened to the Sergeant too. Then she thought they must have told him about the letter; and she thought they should never have told him; she had not spoken to him about Charlie before.

"I . . . I know you got some terrible bad news, Miss Allen," he said.

She was sorry for him. Looking at him, she felt tears of sympathy rise in her own eyes. She reached out her hand which he held for a moment, then turned and left. Afterwards when Sally came back, Joyce sat up holding the blanket wrapped around her, and she rested her head on Sally O'Regan's shoulder and wept.

25

Sally was waiting at the corner of Mission by the bridge terminal. The street itself and the people around her wavered and half dissolved in a puzzling though agreeable manner. But Sally remained in bright focus, cool in her summer dress with her red hair brushed back over her head. Tom made the introductions. He was proud to present so pretty a girl for his wife; and the impressive, successful-looking Walter Stone as an old friend. This is it, he kept wanting to tell her, this is very much it, we're in, kid; but also restrained himself with an effort.

"All right, let's all have some dinner," Stone proposed. He signaled a taxicab, they got in with Sally between them and the street wheeled in a wide circle—Market Street behind, and narrower streets, faces, dresses, uniforms, lights streaming past across the sidewalks. They were going into the restaurant. Dark and crowded inside, Stone leading the way; a waiter in starched shirt front hurrying alongside while Tom with Sally on his arm brought up the rear. The waiter pulled a small table from the row of tables along the wall. Sally went in first and he behind her catching his foot on the leg of the table next and saying in a loud voice,

"Excuse me, please."

He saw the waiter rapidly mopping up water from a glass that had overturned, wondered if that were a result of his bumping the table. So close you were crawling into somebody's lap, how the hell could you help it? The woman was giving him a cold look which Tom returned, accompanied by a wink. Walter Stone seated himself opposite them. The menu, very long . . . Should he look at the prices? Was Stone picking up the check? Certainly he would, he'd invited them, he could afford it anyhow. Never mind fish, you can get fish any time. How about that steak? Two and a half —that might be too fancy a price, he thought. Let him order first.

But Stone had ordered a round of cocktails.

"We're a few jumps ahead of you, Mrs. O'Regan," he was saying to Sally. "Your husband and I have been having a serious discussion. In a bar naturally. But it wouldn't be fair to deny you a drink before dinner."

Sally said she would like one very much; and Tom, noting the lilt of her voice, was sure that she too was considerably impressed by Walter Stone. Wait till she hears the rest of it, he thought. Stone was making inquiries about the Kallelas; they were both well, Sally told him, she had had a letter from her mother only yesterday. And Stone, when the drinks arrived, explained how he had been discussing with her husband the legal profession, following up a remark he had made once to her father a year and a half earlier. There ought to be some way of encouraging young men with a background in industry to step into the law and become spokesmen for their various unions. Oh, not easy, of course, Stone said, he felt this keenly. But of greatest importance, and he had no doubt Tom could be a lawyer and a successful one if he set his mind to it. What was her feeling on the matter?

She told him she was sure Tom could too.

Never mind the crack about the Irish brogue, he thought;

while Stone leaned towards Sally raising his glass. "I said to your husband, Mrs. O'Regan, that I would be delighted to lend a hand if I'm still in business in these parts. And I mean that." Tom felt her fingers touch his under the table, she turned to smile at him, her eyes saying, *Congratulations*. He was glad Stone had told her himself, she might have thought he was laying it on too heavy otherwise. The menus again. As he hesitated, Stone suggested, "Why don't you try the steak, Tom? I don't imagine they have much of that at sea."

Guy must be reading my mind. Lawyer have to learn how to do that too? Jesus, what a price. "All right," he said. "That looks good to me." Sally settled for chicken. Stone ordered Sierra brook trout and Tom, taking a last stare at the menu before the waiter flicked it out of his fingers, saw that trout was worth three dollars and seventy-five cents. And he'd been worrying over the price!

"I get so hungry for a mountain trout I can't resist," Walter Stone explained, "though I ought to know better. Trout doesn't belong in a restaurant. You pull it out of the stream and plop it into the frying pan. That's the way trout should be eaten. Well, I don't need to tell *you* that, do I, Mrs. O'Regan? You come from upcountry too."

"I'm not much of a fisherman," Sally admitted. "I never had the patience."

Stone then began telling her about a fishing trip he had made, somewhere, before the war sometime, when you still could get gasoline—how he lost his footing and fell in the river just after he hooked a big one, oh, yes, *the* big one of course—saw it jump once, measuring it with his hands larger and larger while Sally seemed to be laughing uproariously. When he got a grip on his rod again the fish was gone. Still up there most likely. . . . Tom realized he was scarcely listening. The drinks had removed him to a distance, an uncertainness in which he had to concentrate all his attention on the rapid blurring and intermingling of faces, objects, movements across his eyes. Why the hell had he taken that last cocktail? It wouldn't do to get drunk in front of Stone. Not now. But it was Stone who had kept buying the drinks— maybe wanting to see how he could carry it. Well, he could carry it all right. The steak appeared before him, bleeding through the crisscross marks of the grill. Wonderful to look at yet when he chewed up a bite there was no taste at all. Was that him or the steak, he wondered. But he set to packing it away along with the potatoes and large slabs of French bread. If he could get some food into his stomach it would help ballast him down.

What were they talking about? Sally saying she never had been outside the state of California. Stone saying California was not like any place else in the country, unusual geography, combination of seacoast high mountains desert and forest. ". . . never wise to carry too much gear," he was saying, "people get so weighted down with gadgets they can hardly move. . . . Fishing with me," he was explaining to her, "is really a side line, only an excuse for going places nobody except a fisherman would have any reason to go."

Tom, having finished his steak, salad, potatoes, and consumed all the bread to be found on the table, felt the dizziness gradually receding. But it left him half asleep and he wished now the waiter would bring on the coffee. *Mount Whitney.* Stone was climbing the mountain, going in with a pack train, golden trout in the High Sierra lakes. He looked across at Tom again, shaking his head regretfully. "Been a good many years since I've been up into that country. Getting old, I suppose. Oh, it's partly the war, trouble with gasoline, all that. My wife never liked camping much either, she's the hotel type. Then I just seem to be busier than I ever was before. Oddly enough as I look back on it, Tom, I seem to have had a good deal more free time when I was a corporation lawyer than I do nowadays. You may want to take that into consideration when you select your branch of the profession. The forty-hour week has not yet penetrated to those of us in the legal trade who serve the labor movement. . . . Are we ready for coffee? All around? Bring us the menu again, please."

"Tom tells me you're very famous as a labor lawyer, Mr. Stone," Sally said. Watch him take to that one, Tom thought; she wasn't doing so bad herself when it came to the buttering up.

"Famous?" Stone laughed, shaking his head.

"I know I must have read the name recently. Haven't I? *Stone.* Stone and Gentry, something like that? Didn't I see that somewhere? Is that . . . ?"

Tom felt her stiffen beside him, and he jerked sharply out of his own drowsiness. Across the table, Stone had taken the menu from the waiter, but he was not looking at it. He was looking over the top of the menu, at Sally and then at him. Was he laughing or what? What the hell was the joke?

"That's a reasonable approximation," Stone told her. "The name of my firm is Stone, Chantry and Greenwood. I didn't suppose we were so well known. That *is* an honor." And to Tom he said, "Shall we throw caution to the winds and have a French pastry? Will you keep me company? Eat, drink, and be merry—tomorrow we may be eating beans? Yes, bring us your pastry tray, please. How do they feed you in the navy, Tom?"

"It all depends. Usually starts off pretty good at the beginning of a trip."

"I was once in the army," Stone recalled. "But that was a long time ago. And the food as I remember was unbelievable. Unbelievably bad, I mean."

Sally asked, "Will you excuse me for a minute?" and she rose from the table. After she had left, the waiter arrived with the tray of pastry.

"Do you know your wife's taste well enough to pick for her, Tom? Oh, that wouldn't be quite fair. Let's let her make her own decision. Half the fun of French pastry is the paralysis which overcomes us all when we confront the choice. Bring us the tray again when the young lady comes back, do you mind?"

They sat silent, both of them. Walter Stone had turned his chair sideways from the table and was holding his coffee cup between his two hands. After a time he raised his eyes, met Tom's, and said as if with an effort to bring himself back, "I suppose on a long run the food does get awfully monotonous."

"It sure does. They run out of fruit and vegetables first, then eggs and meat. Before long you're down to beans and canned Spam . . ." Was he even listening? Tom stopped; Stone said nothing and they were silent again. The head waiter, the one who had first shown them to their places, was leaning over the table. He must be bringing the bill. But then Tom realized both were looking at him, the waiter and Stone both, and the waiter saying, "The young lady, sir, she asked if you would step out for a moment into the lobby—"

"*Me?*"

"Yes, sir."

"What's the matter?"

The waiter made a wordless gesture of not knowing what was the matter, and Tom stared from him to Walter Stone who was sitting with his eyes half shut and the coffee cup still held in the palms of his hands. Climbing out from behind the table, Tom hurried across the restaurant. She was standing in the corner by the telephone booth and when he came up to her she caught his arm and said into his ear,

"*That's the lawyer for the union.*"

"What do you mean? What are you talking about?"

"The injunction, Tom. The court order. I told you—"

"What injunction? What's wrong with you?"

"You *know,* Tom! What Reverend Beezely was telling us

about." Her fingernails dug into his wrist. "I can't go back to the table with him. *I can't!* They'd think I was a traitor."

"Don't be a damn fool!" Then he saw the expression of her face and he stopped, took both her hands in his. "Listen to me now. We're almost finished. Nobody's going to see you here. Calm down, come back and finish and we'll go home."

"No," she said. "No, I won't."

"For Christ's sake, Sally, the guy's offered me a loan to get me through college, that's what we were talking about before you came. Do you understand what that means? It means he's willing to try me out in his firm if I can make the grade through school. He said that. He said it . . ."

"Oh, Tom!"

"We can't walk out on him now. Are you crazy?"

"Tell him I'm sick," she whispered. "Tell him anything. I'll go home by myself if you want . . ."

Go on, go ahead then, he was on the point of saying; but thought, how could he tell Stone that his wife had gone home sick while he himself stayed to finish dinner? Taking a grip on her arm, he started back into the restaurant; but she wrenched away.

"I won't go in, Tom."

He noticed the worn spots of the red plush carpet and the little light glowing over the telephone book by the phone booth, and the crowd lined up three deep at the bar; and wanted to throw her against the wall, pounding her with his fists until she gave in. They faced each other silently.

"All right," he said at last. "All right, I'll tell him."

But I won't forget this, he thought, I won't forget it for a long long time. As he returned to the table, he saw Walter Stone rising and coming to meet him. "She must have got sick, Mr. Stone. Sick to her stomach, I guess. I better take her on home."

Stone put his hand on Tom's arm. "I'm awfully sorry. I'll get you a taxi."

"No, no, don't." But the other already had gone. When Tom and Sally came out to the sidewalk, he had flagged a cab from the corner, and as the cab drew up to the entrance of the restaurant, he was leaning down speaking to the driver. Then he straightened up, opened the door for them. "Good night, Mrs. O'Regan," he said. "I certainly hope you'll feel better tomorrow." She made no answer and Tom avoided his eyes. "Will I be likely to hear from you again before you go?" he asked.

"Well, I expect I may be out in two or three more days . . ."

"I plan to be away over the weekend," Stone told him. "You might call me on Monday if you're still in town."

"Sure. I'll certainly do that, Mr. Stone. Thanks a lot. Thanks for everything."

He got in. As the cab pulled away from the curb, he remembered you had to tell a taxi driver where you were going. "Take us to the bridge terminal."

But the driver called over his shoulder, "Guy just paid me the fare to take you folks out to San Martin Village."

"We're not going there," Sally cried. "He made a mistake. We're going to the bridge terminal."

Tom could see the driver staring at them in his rear-view mirror. Then he shrugged his shoulders. "Suit yourself," he said.

From the terminal, they rode the bus over the bridge, sitting side by side without speaking, and beyond all the way to San Martin in silence. There, as they climbed the hill from the flats, Tom walked rapidly ahead leaving her to follow or not follow as she chose. Banging open the front door, he stood waiting for her in the kitchen. When she came in however, she went straight through without a glance in his direction. He forced himself to sit down, lighted a cig-arette, watching the alarm clock over the stove, thinking I'll give her just fifteen minutes. But before five minutes had passed, he stamped into the bedroom. There she was hunched on the bed, she had not even taken off her coat.

"What a God damn fool thing to do!" he shouted.

She did not look up.

"What difference does it make to those people whether we eat dinner with him or not? Does it do them any harm? Will you answer me?"

Still she said nothing.

"You'd sooner insult a man who wants to help us. It doesn't make any God damn difference to you whether I go to law school after the war or not. Only thing matters is what these colored people think about it!"

"Don't talk to me like that, Tom."

"I'll talk any way I feel like."

Getting up from the bed, she stood, not facing him, but looking into the shiny black darkness of the windowpane, in which he could see her distorted reflection; and suddenly she spun about catching at him with her hands. "Don't you *understand,* Tom? They're telling people they aren't fit to live. It's like killing them."

"Well, *he's* not doing it, Sally. He probably had to take the case. He's the attorney for the union."

"He doesn't have to be, does he? He's got plenty of money, hasn't he? We don't need his charity, Tom. You don't need *him* to go to law school . . ."

"I guess you don't have much idea how tough it's going to be. Six years. And with a kid maybe, too. Who the hell did you think I was doing it for anyway?"

She tugged at him until he sat beside her on the bed. "We can make it, Tom. If we stick together we can do it all right. I'll keep on working and Mom'll come down and help us—"

"Oh, sure," he said. "Your Mom! Then we'll have four

people to support!" He shouldn't have sat down, now she had him on the defensive, here he was arguing with her as if it was him that owed *her* the apology. Oh, yes, let's discuss it back and forth for a couple of hours! But there in the restaurant she hadn't discussed anything. She had him over a barrel and she gave it to him all right, what did she care about law school?

"I should have grabbed you by the hair and dragged you back in there," he shouted at her.

For a long time she sat silent, twisting her fingers together on her knees. "I feel sometimes like I don't know you at all, Tom," she said at last. "What makes you do things? The other night, why did you jump into that fight . . . ?"

"Well, for God's sake!" he exclaimed. To keep that pal of hers the poor son of a bitch from getting his block knocked off, what the hell did she think?

"You didn't care what happened, Tom. It doesn't make any difference to you, it *couldn't,* or you wouldn't feel like this. I know why my Dad does things," she cried. "Maybe he is crazy, maybe he's knocking his head against a stone wall like you said. But I know why he does it. But *you,* Tom, I don't know why you do anything, I'm scared of you sometimes, sometimes I think it's just so people will say what a great guy you are." And she added in a low voice, "Maybe that's all you want me for."

How much of this you figure to sit here and take, he asked himself; and said nothing, sat quiet, fetched out his cigarettes, offered her one, lighted one for himself. He noted with pleasure how steady his hand was when he struck the match. No matter how mad he got it never shook him up any. You got a long long way to back down, sister, he said to himself, and he puffed on the cigarette, then suggested, "Why don't we quit chewing each other's ears off, Sally? I don't want to fight with you."

"I don't either."

"Well, let's knock it off then. Let's forget about it. Call the guy tomorrow at his office, tell him you're real sorry you were taken sick, and all that . . ."

"Call who?"

"Call Stone, who do you think?"

"I won't either call him, Tom."

He felt almost glad she had said this, a sense of relief and satisfaction that he had something to take hold of. "I guess you can call him or get along without me." Bringing out his sea bag from the closet, he began to pack his clothes. Not much difference, he thought, liberty would be terminated the next couple of days. She'd climb down before he ever got out the door. He tied up the bag, threw it over his shoulder with a glance back at her as he stepped into the hallway. She was lying on the bed, her face shoved against the pillow. In the kitchen, Tom put on his jacket and his hat. He waited for a moment expecting her to call to him. But she did not call. Closing the door behind him, he walked down the hill to the bus depot. There wasn't enough gas in the pickup to take him as far as the docks anyway.

26

From the restaurant, Walter Stone walked back to his apartment, laughing at himself. He had tried to woo them, to beguile them with the grand manner. *Delighted if I can lend a hand along the way;* and, *Wouldn't it be unfair to deny you a drink before dinner, Mrs. O'Regan? Shall we throw caution to the winds and have a French pastry?* He had been acting a part. Yet also he had been himself. You've been acting a part all your life, he insisted. To be yourself is to act a part. But tonight he had acted only part of the part, that was what left the taste of falseness. He had wanted them to see only the kindly man of affairs, sufficient unto himself, charming, successful, understanding—the Dr. Jekyll to that strange Mr. Hyde who had humbled himself so readily before Garnet. And he had not wished them to know that he came begging a share in their lives.

Why had he been so eager to receive O'Regan in his office this afternoon? Why so beforehanded with his offers and promises? Why had he leaped forward in his own mind to the notion of bringing this young fellow into a law practice with himself at some future date, with or without the approval of Chantry and Greenwood? Had he not sensed in

261

Tom O'Regan a spark, a rebelliousness that seemed lacking in his own son? If I were to give this young man, he had imagined, something of the knowledge and direction and subtlety I have myself acquired, might he not go riding like a champion over the Mackays and Garnets and Richards of this world? And the girl! He only wished she had been born twenty years earlier. Yet he supposed that if he had met such a girl, he would probably have passed her by. And so too if he had had Tom O'Regan for a son—perhaps he never would have found a time or an occasion for him either. All this comes afterward, he thought. You are what you are. You have been acting a part. It was not merely the wish to be generous; you were begging a place in their lives.

He saw that his thoughts moved in a circle and he had swung around again to the beginning. Oh, she had caught him, dead to rights! "You're famous as a labor lawyer, Mr. Stone? Haven't I heard the name?" He remembered having half convinced himself that what had happened in court had been a routine matter, a formality, move and counter-move by the attorneys as the courts ground toward final determination. Beyond that, in so far as he still disapproved his own part, he had weighed it against other benefits, the case of Anton Novak and all the others. Credits and debits, like an accountant's report. The mind is like an oyster, he thought. Around the intruding grain of sand, it forms a protective pearl to render the sharp edges round and comfortable. Now as the pearl disintegrates, the edges set to work. He shuddered. The thing he had done then, under the pressure of Garnet and his own circumstances—was it so shocking, so horrible, that these two would get up and walk out rather than go on sitting at the same table with him?

Perhaps it was only coincidence. The girl really had been taken ill? Certainly she had appeared so as the two were getting into the cab. The cocktail? The rich food? But why had she not answered him then? Was she too ill to speak? Or too embarrassed to face him? He could neither accept nor dismiss the alternatives. They presented themselves to him, replacing each other in constant variations as he walked. So he laughed—what other reaction could there be to such an event? His agitation was ridiculous. What difference did it make why they had left the restaurant? Could that change what his own action had been, or the reasons for it? If the reasons, to him, justified the action, then that was the end of it, what did he care what this girl, or Tom O'Regan, or anyone else, thought about it? Ah, what an infallible formula! To thine own self be true, and it shall follow as the night the day . . .

He stepped into his apartment, snapped on the light. The familiar room, empty, neat, powdered with a slight fuzz of dust. What next? Too early to go to bed. Should he sit down and read? He wished he were by himself, in the open. Or that he were with old John, not for the sake of talking to him, but only to listen, or be silent. He tried to remember what was on his calendar for the next day. Since it was Friday he had kept the afternoon clear, to be able to take the early plane to Signal Springs. The Gunderson hearing that was scheduled for the morning had been postponed. A brief case full of notes, most of which he could take along with him. What if they got out their restraining order in the state court tomorrow? No, it would be the following week; even if they did get the order, they could not possibly set the show-cause hearing before Tuesday or Wednesday. It had been so long since he had taken the car and gone somewhere, out of the city, by himself. The thought of driving into the mountains on this spring night fixed and held him. He would have to see his wife next day in any case, whether he drove tonight or took the plane in the afternoon. And though he felt no desire to see her, he felt no particular aversion either, which surprised him. Sitting down at his desk, he opened the drawer where he kept the gas-ration stamps.

He had enough to make it, though that would leave him short for the coming month. Let the month take care of itself! He'd borrow from Greenwood.

Walter fetched out his sleeping roll and knapsack and went down to his car.

Sometime past midnight, he stopped for coffee in Honey Valley, then went on, driving over the crest, and bedded down finally on a shoulder of the desert against the eastern slope. The wind moved past and he lay on his back, his hands joined behind his head; the mountains, the night sky, had lent him a certain detachment. This was their most valuable service to man; they reminded how minuscule he was; how unimportant were a man's hopes—even one's own. Yet what value could there be in that reminder? Was it not hope alone that made life worth the effort?—hope, or the ability to believe in hope? It could not be more than a few miles at most, he thought, to the spot he and old John had reached that Sunday, where the family from Illinois had left their wagon. Left it and everything they owned inside it and, with mother and child riding the remaining ox, had plodded toward the glittering peaks in the western sky, racing the labored steps of the ox against the first flakes of snow. He was deeply moved by this incident now, as he had been before. They were the ones who believed in hope! And what had they found across the mountains? A dry-goods store on the main street in the town of Honey Valley. That was all the record told and so bid them adieu, but the iron rims of their wheels were still resting on the mountainside a hundred years later. . . .

Walter said nothing to his wife, nor she to him, beyond what they had spoken on many previous weekends at the rancho. They lay beside the pool in the sunshine, swam, ate dinner; afterwards gambled a little and drank a little as they waited for midnight. On Sunday old John arrived with his truck for which Walter borrowed a tankful of gas from the proprietor. With two other couples from among the rancho's guests, they drove up for a picnic to the hot springs. Here they hard-boiled their eggs at the first outlet, while John bathed his arthritic knees in one of the cooler pools below. John rattled along with his cackling laugh, his stories merging one into another, peopling the leafy silence under the aspen trees with the fantastic characters out of his own recollection. Indians, miners, curators from museums in the East, tourists, cattlemen, gamblers—they all trooped past, and John massaged his knobby legs and chewed up the remaining sandwiches from the picnic basket.

Late in the afternoon, they bumped down out of the canyon, through the clay hills, across the flats to the highway. The guests disembarked by the gate of the rancho, and as old John waved them good-by, Walter called after him,

"How's the arthritis?"

"Feels mighty good now. Tomorrow morning, won't be a skidgeon of it left. Thanks for the gas, Walter."

The truck sailed off towards town; and Sylvia, as they watched it out of sight, said, "He's the nicest old man I know. He isn't depressed by being old. Even the arthritis, it's like a game. He outwits it."

So she had seen this too. "Yes, it's a game," he agreed, "that all of us play." They stood for a moment looking at one another. After the two couples had gone in, he said to her, "She walks in beauty like the night,"—not knowing why he said this, though he remembered that he had spoken the line to her once a long while ago. He saw her wince and she turned to follow the others through the gate.

She had decided to go back with him to the city. They packed their suitcases and he paid the reckoning at the desk. When he came out to the car, Sylvia was warming the motor. "Shall I drive first?" she offered. "When I get sleepy, you can take it the rest of the way." And as he hesitated, she added, "I'm sober, Walter." Yes, she was; they had had nothing to drink all day except a little wine with the picnic lunch. And he himself felt suddenly unbelievably tired— the cumulative effect of the week behind him, he supposed. So he sat beside her; they rolled into the valley and through town, and up the first slopes of the mountain which reared purple and blue, high against the sunset. He wondered what Tom O'Regan and his young wife had said to each other. He wondered if the state court would grant another restraining order to the shipyard workers. He wondered if Chantry would be back yet from Los Angeles. And now that he and Chantry had, temporarliy at least, cleared the legal obstacles from the road, he wondered if the San Martin Shipbuilding Corporation was proceeding with the layoffs which the union had demanded.

It was turning dark when they crossed over the ridge of the Sierras.

"I'll drive down to Honey Valley," Sylvia said. They had nearly always stopped for coffee in Honey Valley. "We can swap off there."

"All right," he agreed.

The highway flowed into the beam of headlights. Closing his eyes, he let his head drop back, drowsing, his body rocking with the swing of the car.

He heard her cry out and jerked awake.

What he saw first was her face in the glow of the dash-light, the graying hair blown back, the wide eyes, the lips parted, the teeth set edge to edge. Then he saw the guard rail pivot towards them and he grabbed for the wheel. A crash and screech of metal, the car hesitated, staggered sideways and plunged forward again. He saw the hood drop. For a moment the finger of the headlights reached down into empty darkness. The car struck, twisted, throwing them together and apart.

27

For Joyce the days and nights were a blank wheel, waking, sleeping, eating, a repetition of movements without meaning. The whistle blew. The women hurried to their benches, the leadermen came by setting up the work. The welder helper pushed his hand truck loaded with pieces of steel. Parts for pipe brackets. How could they ever use so many? Boxes, scuppers, ventilator hoods. And pipe brackets. Laying the square of steel on the bench, she set the triangle against it, ran a bead down one side of the joint, turned, ran a bead down the other side. One bracket every three minutes, she had timed herself. The work was a machine and she was part of a machine, shafts and levers that brought the arc to the steel and moved it and brought it back. Reach down, set, weld, turn, weld again. Before, she had been building a ship with her own hands that would sail over the ocean, carrying men and carrying something from within herself. She was only making brackets now. On her right hand the brackets accumulated, rising like a wall beside her till the helper returned with his hand truck to take them away. Before, she remembered that she had tried to set her thoughts free, but now she was eager to surrender them. The machine-like motions, the blue flare of the arc, these commanded every part of her and she was grateful.

After midnight when she returned to the house, Janet was sleeping and the two girls were asleep and Reverend Beezely had gone. In the quiet house she lay in her bed looking into the darkness. If she had never met Charlie, she would never have felt the pain. His dying would not have touched her. Would it have been better then if she had not known him? No, those weeks were worth any pain that came after. Part of him must remain with her, she thought. Something which had once happened could never be changed. The time they had spent together, nothing could take that away. It would remain for always, like the mountains in the distance. Yet it was gone. Gone, yes, yes, gone! If only she had married him as he had wished, if only she were carrying his child inside her! The pain came clawing at her again, the bitter regret of waste and loss.

When she slept, she was half dreaming and waking. To places known long before, she returned. She walked up into the dry canyon that cut through the hills behind the house. Up to the old mine diggings where you could pick up pieces of blue stone called chrysacola, where once she had seen a tarantula. Oh, long ago. Yet part of herself had been waiting there to meet her and now silently acknowledged her return. The other was with her again. The other ran hopping, jumping over the rocks, watching her, watching with a silent speculative look as if to say, You came back after all, Joyce, you came back alone just as you went away. Oh, the other was with her again, cool and cold, watching from a distance.

Day was a shadow between waking and darkness. The welding torches sparkled and the huge cranes moved against the night sky. Shadows danced in the darkness around her. The Sergeant passed by, the men, the women in their helmets, coming and going. She heard the women already numbering the days; heard the men apprehensive and angry. There came a notice attached to their time cards which she read with the others saying, In pursuance of the instructions of the General Office of our Union it is our duty to inform you, under the terms of our master contract with the West Coast Conference of Shipbuilding Corporations . . . you must, she read, must be present for your initiation, must pay your dues into the auxiliary lodge having jurisdiction, or failing which will be severed . . .

"Severed from the employ!" shouted the Sergeant in the walkway outside the doors of the plate shop. *"You* can all pay up if you want. Numbers racket!" he shouted. "That Garnet might as well hold a gun to a man's head—here, boy, lemme have your change. I'll never pay in that Auxiliary again!"

With Janet, she went into San Francisco to the Improvement League and pasted stamps and stuffed envelopes which they carried in bundles down to the post office. People handed out leaflets at the gates of the shipyard. When the time came for the first meeting of the Auxiliary, no one attended. She heard that no one had gone from the plate shop or the yard, the union hall had been empty. They laughed over this next day at lunch hour, even the white shipfitters and white welders laughed at the joke—how the union summoned the Auxiliary and only two people showed up and those were the colored janitors who worked at the union hall. "You got to hand it to that Sergeant, he sure got his people organized!"

She knew that Reverend Beezely was delighted and she saw the triumph on the face of the Sergeant. But the days and nights were a blank wheel, the words to her were no more than words and she said them, she wished with them, but she could not care.

The music was all that was left her now. There had been two things and now remained only the one; but the music was a bridge and a remembrance and it was her only escape. *I quite like your handling of the contredanses,* the piano teacher had said to her. *I want you to pick out three dances,*

Joyce, to play in the recital. She? Could she? Her own fear would overpower her. Yet she knew he would be glad if he had heard of it, and the music was a bridge to him and all she had left was the music. She dared not refuse for fear of losing this. "All right, I'll try," she said, feeling the teacher's surprise at the drabness of her answer.

Several days in a row, she called the shipyard saying she was sick and had to stay home—so that she would be able to practice for the entire day. Still it was a long while off. In the public library, she looked up the origin of the contre-danses; and pored over photographs of German towns, and the Danube, and Vienna, and the countryside around the city. She studied biographies of Beethoven, half hoping to forget herself in the books. The dances were a tiny fragment, they were like a crystal, a prism, through which she peered trying to make out the shape of the vast chambers beyond, the gigantic music, the motionless figure waiting, alone—oh, God, she understood that if nothing more! And often a line from a letter she had found in one of the biographies came back to her. *We mortals of the immortal spirit,* he had written, *born only in sorrow and joy.* Oh, Charlie, she cried, buried in the sand dunes of some lonely island. He too had gone singing to his death.

Reach and turn, the captive burning star . . . the brackets accumulated like a wall beside her.

When she drew out her time card at the gate, she found a pink slip attached to the card. *You have been reported delinquent in dues to the Shipbuilders' and Welders' Union,* said the slip, and she read this through in the crowd walking with the slips in their hands, studying them, a slow stream along the walkway toward the plate shop. *It is our duty to inform you under the terms of our agreement with the Union that the Company shall be required to terminate your employment within fourteen days of the above date unless we are advised that you have restored yourself to good standing.* It was signed by the Personnel Officer of the San Martin Shipbuilding Corporation. As she passed the drinking fountain by the door of the plate shop, she heard one man demanding,

"How come they pick me and not you?"

"Guess they put the names in a hat, drawed out every other one."

The first said, "They tryin' to scare us. I guess they want to see how we all take it."

She joined the women welders bunched together by the small-parts benches. In cautious voices, the women were repeating an endless round of contradictory rumors. The day shift had already received notices, some said, and others insisted that was not true, the day shift was supposed to get notices tomorrow. One woman had heard that only the afternoon shift was getting the layoffs because that was the shift the Sergeant worked on. All the men were fixing to walk out and set up a picket line like a strike, another told them; and more voices joined in to say that the company never would dare lay all those people off. Or that the government was going to close down the shipyard anyway. Or that the men on day shift already were paying dues to the Auxiliary and maybe that was the best thing to do.

The women hurried off to their benches. The leadermen came past, the welder helpers. As the routine swallowed her up, Joyce was still repeating to herself the things she had heard. Wondering, where would the people go if they laid them off? To some other shipyard? Wondering if the same thing were not happening in the other yards too, and where would they go? Then she wondered about herself. Would she go hunting a job as a waitress or bus girl again? She thought what that would do to her music, to her playing in the recital. If she worked as bus girl, she'd have no money for the piano lessons, she'd be too tired from the work and the long hours to practice—or care. Maybe she didn't care anyway. Why wouldn't they just pay the three dollars a month to the union? If a man held a pistol to your head—the Sergeant himself had said that. If a man had a pistol you'd pay him instead of let him shoot you. . . .

The arc flared in front of her. The molten metal flowed into the joint. She reached for the parts with one hand, the brackets mounted into a wall on the other.

At the lunch hour, the Sergeant came into the plate shop. She saw him at a distance moving from one group to the next, stopping for a few minutes with each group and moving along. "Here come the Sergeant makin' the rounds," one said; and as they followed him with their eyes, someone whispered, "Old Sergeant's spark coils must be jumpin' to beat billy hell today!" The women giggled, the men guffawed, holding their sides as they passed the joke back and forth. Till he came up to them—then they were all grave and attentive.

"You honored with one of these pink slips, Sergeant?"

He shook his head. "They pass me by, I guess."

There was a long thoughtful silence at this. One of the men asked, "Most of us here got these slips now, Sergeant. What you think we ought to do?"

"I don't know. I wouldn't know what to tell you. I don't feel very good myself," he said. "Don't know if I can last out the rest of the shift . . ."

Her eyes flashed up to his face, but he did not look badly. There was still a patch of adhesive tape on the side of his head, but the swelling of the eyes and cheeks had gone down. His back then, she wondered, he had gotten up too soon . . .

Glancing around the circle of questioning faces, he asked, "How do *you* all feel?"

"Guess I don't feel very good either," the man who had first questioned him said; and she saw the others doubtfully exchanging glances, the eyes traveling from face to face and back to the Sergeant.

But the Sergeant turned to her as if to take up something

between them alone. "I want to thank you for those things you sent over to me by the Reverend."

"*Oh, that wasn't anything.*"

"You and Mrs. Beezely both. They sure tasted good."

"It wasn't anything," she insisted and studied her own feet certain everyone must be staring at her. When she looked up he had gone; and she was glad to hear the whistle blow for the end of the lunch period.

She saw him again halfway through the second part of the shift.

She had stopped for a moment, lifting her helmet to wipe the sweat from her face, and she saw him on the far side of the plate shop, clear and sharp for an instant under the flood lamps, walking with his jerky gait, and he was gone into the shadows and vanished through the doorway. Had it begun already? Why had he come from the outfitting dock? Had they fired him? She saw that a group of Negroes had drawn together; the foreman went hurrying towards the group; and she could see the foreman shouting and the men shouting back, though she heard no sound at all of their voices through the roar of machinery. Suddenly several of the Negroes walked out the same door the Sergeant had gone through and others followed after them. Now the leaderman was coming along the aisle; she tugged her helmet down and set to her welding. But as soon as the leaderman had passed, the colored woman from the next bench came over to her.

"Welder helper just tell me the men are taking early quit slips," the woman said. "What you think we ought to do, Joyce?"

What we ought to do?

And she cried out inside herself, wasn't it enough she had lost Charlie, wasn't that enough?—but now they came to drag away the one thing she had left of him, the one thing to remember him by, the piano, the concert? She wanted to sink back into the safety and routine of the machine that welded steel parts. She wished the night had remained the way it had been before and night before that. But it was not; nothing she could do would make it the same, nothing was ever, ever the same. When she peered about her the plate shop appeared suddenly half empty. Of the many Negroes who had been there before lunch hour, she saw only half a dozen or so remaining. *What would Charlie do?* Well, what would Janet or Reverend Beezely or old Mr. Henderson do? What would her own father do?

"We better go too," Joyce said.

The woman nodded. They put away their tools, walked out of the building into the darkness spotted with lights and headed toward the main gate. Here they found a long line moving through the turnstile past the wicket where the guard checked the badge numbers. As Joyce came closer to the window she heard the people in front of her saying,

"Ain't feeling very good tonight. Guess I better check out, Mister."

Or saying, "Just got a terrible dizzy spell. Come near fallin' off the scaffold. Give me early quit slip, please."

As she came to the window herself, and as the guard time-clocked her slip, she caught a glimpse of the flabbergasted expression on his face.

Joyce saw Reverend Beezely climb out of a car at the edge of the highway and she hurried to meet him. The crowd had thinned considerably since the first rush through the gate, but there were still a good many people scattered about the open space between the highway and the fence; and now that it was nearing time for change of shift, the crowd was building up again. The buses, rolling to the stop one after another, let off their loads.

"Where's Brooks?" he cried out to her. With the Reverend were three other men, dressed in business suits and wearing neckties, colored men all three, and one she remembered seeing in the office of the Improvement League. "What happened, Joyce? We heard our people had walked out here."

She showed them her termination notice, told how the colored workers had taken early quit slips. The Reverend was introducing her to the others, but she lost the names except that the one she had seen before was the president of the League in San Francisco. He kept shaking his head, pulling his mouth up into an expression that was not quite a smile. "Oh, man," he said. "Now we're really into it. Where's this Sergeant keep himself?"

"Where can we find Mr. Brooks, Joyce?"

"There, over by the fence, I saw him there a few minutes ago."

The Reverend squeezed her arm. "Hold on now. We got to catch the Sergeant quick." He stepped past her with the others at his heels and she turned, following uncertainly behind them. They skirted the fence toward the gate till they came upon the Sergeant.

"Mr. Brooks," the Reverend called. "Can we talk to you, Mr. Brooks?" She saw him draw the Sergeant aside, speaking close to him; and then other people came shoving between herself and them. A moment later the Sergeant's voice burst out,

"I be God damned if I see that, Beezely!"

"You can't go on a strike, Brooks! You've gone out of your mind! You'll turn the whole country against us! There's a war on, Mr. Brooks. If our people walk out of the yard—"

"How they goin' to run this shipyard without us? You tell me that?"

There was a clash of angry voices, people elbowing and shoving.

She caught a glimpse of the man who was the president with his hand on the Sergeant's shoulder. ". . . we still have legal remedy, Mr. Brooks. I tell you we anticipated losing in federal court. Our best case is in the state court where we're taking it now. Can I make you understand, we destroy our complaint if our people give up their jobs voluntarily—"

And then a voice shouted, "Hell no, they can't build no ships without us!"

"Let some of them lard-ass business agents come around, try weldin' the double bottoms—"

And the Sergeant's voice cut shrilly across the others: "Don't you talk to me about this war! It's a white man's war. I've seen it! We walk right out of this shipyard and we make our own union, then we talk turkey—"

"But we've no right to make a decision like this without seeking the advice of our people in the other shipyards—"

A voice bellowed, "I got a mind to give you a punch in the nose. You act like you're workin' for Garnet!"

And then, "Go it! Go it! Give it to him!"

Over the shoulders in front of her, Joyce saw the president spun sideways; and Reverend Beezely covering his face with his arms while a great barrel-chested man she had sometimes seen in the plate shop cocked and weaved getting set for another punch. Suddenly she heard herself screaming in a voice she could not have believed was her own.

She kicked, scratched, clawed past the people blocking her way. The Sergeant had come back with his face all bloody and now they had to do the same to the Reverend? She thought of Janet getting up in the morning to go off to the dry cleaning shop, and she screamed,

"No, no, no, you can't!" throwing herself in front of the barrel-chested man. He brushed her aside. She caught his shirt and clung to him, hitched one arm around his neck. Then the Sergeant and some of the others had come between the man and Reverend Beezely. She heard the barrel-chested one pleading,

"Come on, come on, come on now, woman, turn me loose,

we ain't going to fight no more. God damn, let loose of me, will you?" But she would not let go until their hands had pried open her fingers. For a moment she saw the man's face, laughing, sweating, harassed. "All right, all right, all right now, sister, all right, what you actin' so crazy for?"

Someone held her by the arm and was leading her out of the crowd. She stumbled across the uneven ground of the parking lot. It was the Sergeant walking beside her and they sat down together on the running board of a car. He was breathing hard and she could see that his face, his whole body, was trembling as if he were half frozen with cold.

Over by the bus stop, a long distance away from them now it seemed, people were packed close together, shoulder and shoulder and heads under the lamplight, and the jackets and scarves and shiny tin hats and the blue crisscross of overall straps. Someone was up higher than the others, must be standing on the bus-stop bench, she thought, making a speech.

"Aren't you going over?" she asked.

"I can hear good enough right here."

She recognized the voice. It was the Reverend, the round, rolling, sermon-speaking voice of the Reverend: ". . . this has been a wonderful demonstration, brothers and sisters, believe me. An action to make known to everyone this shameful situation. But we cannot allow this action to be misconstrued. This cannot, must not, become an interference, a *stoppage* of work. In this time of national emergency, friends, however shamefully we have been treated, we could not find it in our conscience to speak of strike or *stoppage* . . ."

His words were drowned for a moment by the hum and screech of a bus pulling in to the stop.

". . . and all my colleagues, all our counselors in the field of law, they say to us, legal means will prove *worthless* unless the men and women are working in the yards. Believe me, brothers and sisters, this is the best *course*. Go back to building the ships while we seek redress through the medium of law . . ." She sensed the appeal of his voice, earnest, perturbed, and yet reassuring. When he stopped speaking, it was obvious from the clapping that most of the crowd agreed with him, and she felt a surge of relief.

"I hope he's right," the Sergeant said. "I hope he is."

The dead flat tone of the words shattered her own preoccupation. Why wasn't he with them, it was *his* crowd, he had brought them out. "Why—why don't you talk to them?" she whispered.

"I expect it would tear things all apart if I went over there." In the glow from the highway, she saw his face working, the jaw bulging and stretching out again as if he were chewing, or as if he were biting the skin inside his lips. "I thought I knew good enough, but they shook me all up. Beezely, when he talk like that, he's like a bugle, all wind. They listen for the sound, not what he say. But he was right about the Auxiliary. Maybe he's right now, I don't know. . . ." His voice faded off, and began again, "I saw these pink slips, just passed the word around on my own. Seemed to me the right thing to do. They thought I was all wrong. Beezely likes that black suit and tie he wear. He wouldn't want in on anything that might strike those white ministers a little bit rough, or those lawyers he goes with . . ."

He turned to her suddenly with a look in his eyes like asking for help, she thought; but she did not know what it was nor how to answer it.

"Maybe I was thinking like that because I come back mad, wanted to fight. Rest don't really feel that way. They want to stay in, I guess, they got their families to support. A man's got to fight sooner or later, family or no family, or he don't amount to much. Cost a man too sometimes. Cost me a year and a half in the jailhouse . . ."

He had started talking. Never had she heard him say so many words together, only that once in the plate shop when they had torn up the dues books.

"I always been kind of a lone wolf, Miss Allen. I used to think it don't matter much if a man eats his peck of dirt, so he advance himself a little bit for it. Then I got shot up over there. I thought I was gone. Everybody else thought so too. Doctors and all give me up. Three, four months layin' in the hospital, and then it seem to me a man don't walk a very wide path, he don't have much of a lease on his house. It seem to me it don't make so much difference if he goes today or he goes tomorrow. And he hasn't got much to take with him except he have the satisfaction he's been a man when he had the chance."

The whistle wailed high and shrill from the yard.

"I guess I don't much give a damn any more. I'd as soon they chase me clean out. Took the heart out of me when Beezely and all the rest come down. Now they all agree with 'em. They goin' to eat their peck of dirt."

"*I don't think they're eating a peck of dirt,*" Joyce said, frightened as she spoke for fear he might be angry at her. "I don't think they're giving up."

"No?" There was an anxiousness and doubt in his voice, but not anger. "Maybe not. Maybe you're right. But they'll have to pay into the Auxiliary now they gone back in. I'll never pay in. *Legal remedies,* that fellow says. He won't catch Garnet with his legal remedies. They have us all into the Auxiliary, break us down one by one, throw us out on the ash heap while that man still arguing in the court. *Legal remedies. . . .*"

Out in front of them the crowd was breaking up.

They watched the line of people moving through the gates into the yard, the long line stretching out. What a strange thing to see, Joyce thought, rising to her feet. Where were they going, where were they all going—not just through the gate—but where were they going? She saw the lights of the traveling cranes in the distance and the dark structure of the shipways; and now the welding arcs began to sparkle and die through the darkness like falling stars. An andante for one more bitter defeat. A prelude of some finale that yet awaited them.

She turned to look at the Sergeant. He too was staring at the line. His mouth opened and his face had broken and tears were running down out of his eyes.

She could not bear to see him. "Don't," she cried. "Oh, don't!"

He made no movement nor seemed to hear.

"No, *don't,*" she begged; and seizing him, pulled him violently against her. His arms went around her and his face pressed down against her throat.

PART 4

28

During the autumn of 1944, the *Andrew Rogers* had carried a load of aerial bombs to Australia. There she filled her holds with Australian wheat, picked up a deck cargo of slightly used graders and bulldozers consigned to the American army in North Africa, and set forth westward across the furnace of the Indian Ocean. November found her in the Red Sea. She passed through Suez, convoyed across the Mediterranean, and one bleak winter morning picked up a pilot at the outer breakwater of Port Mayence and churned through the canal into the salt lake that formed the inner harbor. A ring of gray hills encircled the harbor; Tom saw houses tumbled together climbing from the water's edge, and larger buildings in ruins along the shore. Here they set off the road-building machinery on the quay; and received aboard the first sack of mail which had reached them since Australia. Along with the half-dozen letters from his family in San Diego, Tom found a single note from Sally, scarcely a full page, saying that she thought she was pregnant and she had not heard from him. He thrust the letter into the pocket of his jeans.

In the morning, the ship nosed out through the canal

again, dropping anchor under the shelter of the breakwater. Several merchant ships were lying there already,
mostly British, but a few American. A launch came out from
shore to take off the Skipper and Navy Lieutenant for their
instructions on whatever they were supposed to do next,
while aboard ship the men lined up along the rail, watching
the launch as it made the rounds of the other vessels, and
speculating what the orders might be. Naples, some suggested, or Bari in the Adriatic, where a lot of grain ship-
ments had been going. After four months at sea, Tom knew
that everyone was trying to dream up the best possibility
for getting rid of their cargo and taking themselves back
to the States. For himself, he thought, it hardly made much
difference.

He did not know what to write Sally, nor even if he
wished to write her at all. One earlier letter had caught
up with him in Australia, in which she seemed only to be
repeating what she had said the night they had left Stone
in the restaurant; and he had been too angry to answer it.
He no longer felt any particular anger. But she probably
was wrong about being pregnant, he thought. That was a
way to get a hook into him again; and what was the sense,
if she cared so little about what he was trying to do—for her
benefit too—as to want to kick a hole in it? The war had
made plenty of marriages, and broken plenty; and he had
half expected this from the beginning. A man was a fool to
tie himself down before he had his feet all the way under
him. She would be sorry afterwards, he thought. She would
be very very sorry after it was too late. But he ought to write
Stone again, he told himself, though even after these many
months he had not done so.

To get away from the gossip session along the rail, Tom
went up to the wing of the bridge and sat by himself on the
gun tub. A couple of other ships, both American Liberties,

were holding a conversation by blinker, the signalmen chatting back and forth with each other.

"How's chow with u?" one blinked.

"Lousy."

"Same hr. Anybody Milwaukee aboard?"

"N."

"U got softball team?"

"Roger. Play u?"

Then another ship cut across the conversation, blinking its light rapidly for attention and flashing, "Anybody from Cleveland Ohio?"

A ship beyond the *Andrew Rogers* answered, "Hank Ritter Cleveland." And the other blinked, "Johnson to Ritter. Howdy pal."

So the conversation continued, exactly like people talking in a bar, Tom thought, all the usual questions and answers, but drawn out endlessly as the blinkers formed the words letter by letter:

"U g-o W-e-s-t C-l-c-v-e-l-a-n-d H-i?

"Y-e-s. C-l-a-s-s 4-2."

"U n-o H-e-r-b S-i-m-o-n-s?"

He saw that a fourth ship which had not taken part in the small talk was flashing directly at the *Andrew Rogers*. Tom acknowledged and waited for the message.

"H-l-l-o F-l-a-g-s."

"H-i," he blinked back.

"H-o-w r t-h-e c-o-c-k-r-o-a-c-h-e-s?"

"B-i-g a-s e-v-e-r," Tom answered. "W-h-o r u?"

"J-r S-p-r-k-s."

The Junior Sparks! He must have picked out the *Andrew Rogers* from the other Liberties; and that wouldn't be hard to do either with its homemade wheelhouse sticking up here on the flying bridge. "H-o-w-s t-h-i-n-g-s?" he signaled.

"O K."

"C y-r g-r-l f-r-n-d?"

"N-o-t y-e-t."

"T-f-f l-u-c-k," Tom replied. "T-l-d u s-o."

Throughout most of the rest of the day, Tom continued the conversation at intervals with the Junior Sparks, who said he was no longer a junior now but a chief. Tom could see that he had come up in the world in other respects too, for his ship was a brand-new tanker, sleek and dark gray, lying low in the water. That must be an eighteen-knotter, Tom thought, the kind that usually ran special convoys and crossed the Atlantic in five days. Trust the Junior Sparks to find one like that! Others came up to the bridge, and Tom relayed their greetings and sent messages from the Second Mate and the old Chief Operator. Tom and the Second kept laughing over the fact that their conversation with the Sparks was the same as it had been every morning when he used to come up for coffee—the girl friend in Liverpool; and yes, the broadcast station in Bangor was still holding his job for him; and he was working his code speed up to forty words a minute. When they had last seen him, it had been thirty-five he was shooting for.

"Things are always getting better with the Sparks," the Second said. "He's a success in life."

The launch returned at sundown, the Skipper and Lieutenant scrambled aboard with their brief cases, obviously in a mellow mood and spreading a delicate odor of Scotch whisky. The ship, after having been half asleep all day, sprang into a hubbub of activity. The Bosun made the rounds of the fo'c's'les checking blackout screens. And up in the chart room, the Second Mate and the Chief Operator were sweating over the electric fathometer. This had been out of commission since the Red Sea, Tom knew, but the Skipper swore he had to have it by God, and they could work all night if they needed to. Tom tried to help them for a while as they yanked off panels and replaced tubes and fuses and argued over the instruction manual. But seeing he was only getting in their way, he sat on the chart-room bench and laughed at them, offering to run fetch a crowbar or a top maul from the engine room. The Chief finally walked out in a huff and the Second turned on Tom, "Well, I got rid of *him*. Now will you get the hell out of here so I can concentrate on this thing?"

"Sure," Tom said. "Good luck, pal," and went down to supper.

The ships moved out after dark. Once clear of the African coast they swung west, instead of north or east, which ruled out both Naples and Bari. This raised spirits generally; there seemed no doubt they were bound for England again; and by the time the little convoy had shoved through Gibraltar the next day, picking up a pair of British corvettes and three more British merchant ships, the mess-hall navigators were already arguing whether they were more likely to put in for New York or Boston after discharging their cargo of wheat in England.

When Tom came on watch at four in the morning, they were standing a course two points north of west. The sea was running medium heavy, not half bad for Christmas holidays in the Atlantic, he thought; and the *Andrew Rogers* was rolling but holding her screw steady under water and driving along with a rapid purposeful thumping of the heart inside her. The sky was overcast, the moon was up; and occasionally when the moon swept across a rift of the clouds the ocean would turn black and silver and the crests of the south-running seas would shine like snow. Tom, perched on the gun tub with the intercom phones hooked over his neck, could see the dark shapes of the other ships stretching out ahead and behind—tramp, Liberty, rustbucket, and the new tanker, one down from the end of the column. They must have plenty of good chow on that wagon, he thought.

At five, they altered course to the north and the waves began smacking up over the bows.

"You wet down there?" Tom asked into the intercom.

The voice of the forward gunner came back, "It's always wet here, you bastard."

Another winter night. It was almost a year since he had last been in the North Atlantic, and he felt as if he had waited out half his life fighting nights like this on the bridge of the *Andrew Rogers*. But it couldn't go on much longer. How long could they hold out with Italy and most of France gone, and the beating they were taking in Russia, and the Allies getting set now, as they certainly must be, to hop across the Rhine? Never mind, he thought, when they finish here, you'll be off to the Pacific for five years. He whistled the first notes of "Pistol-Packin' Mamma" into the intercom, and heard the forward gunner and the after gunner join in, and they all whistled together, harmonizing. Out of the corner of his eye, Tom caught a glimpse of the Lieutenant sliding up behind him.

"Knock that off, Flags," the Lieutenant said.

"Yes, sir. Just a way of checking stations."

"Do it some other way."

"Yes, sir." He waited till the Lieutenant had moved back towards the wheelhouse, then covering his mouth with his hand, said, "Cracker's up here tonight. He says knock it off."

"What got him out of bed?" the rear gun tub asked; and the forward gun tub said, "He been up all night playin' gin rummy with the Skipper."

"Tell him to ram it."

"You tell him," Tom said.

"I will. Don't worry. Pretty soon now."

"How long?" Tom asked.

"Pretty damn soon. Don't worry. I'll tell *you* to ram it too, Flags, you rawhidin' son of a bitch."

"Better tell me by mail," Tom said.

The moon was dropping down into a solid wall of cloud that lay along the horizon. Wind and spray drove in gusts against the bridge. And as the moon sank Tom noticed that it seemed to gather speed, vanishing second by second —a half, a quarter, a squinting orange eye, growing longer and narrower until it winked out altogether. Almost daylight, he thought. The moon had been setting late. Maybe there'd be space enough near where they docked for a softball game, they could get a team together and take on that other liberty—

"Hard Right!"

He saw the helmsman swing down. The *Andrew Rogers* burrowed into the sea and sluffed sideways. And with the suddenness of an explosion a ship swept across the bow, a corvette, Tom saw, heeled over, decks awash; and they jumped to the rail staring after it as the darkness swallowed it. Far behind them a spark lighted like the flare of a match, they heard a sharp dry crack; and suddenly there was the tanker bright as day, silhouetted by its own spouting torch. There it was, he saw it clear and precise, the sleek lines, the raking masts and stack. And then it was gone. The fire wrapped it from end to end, the fire leaped high as a twenty-story building, a roar and a wall of noise picked Tom up and flattened him against the side of the gun tub.

He heard the battle-stations bell clamor through the ship and feet pounding over the decks and ladders. Groping for the intercom phone on his neck, he called the fore and aft gunners. They were still there. As Tom scrambled to his feet he saw the Skipper and the Lieutenant staring back at the burning sea behind them. The fire lighted a vast circle of ocean, showed the racing corvettes half buried in foam, and the line of the convoy itself, the Liberties, tramps, rustbuckets, with the black smoke pouring frantically out of their stacks. He felt the *Andrew Rogers* shuddering and lunging, the heart hammering wildly, the whole ship wracking, straining its guts while the smoke came boiling out of their own stack too in a black oily mass.

He had pulled on his life jacket and he checked the gun stations a second time, and now he unhooded the signal lamp in case they should need it. Once he looked back through the glasses. The fire had simmered down from its monstrous height, and on the water there was nothing, no wreckage, no lifeboat, only the flames and smoke skittering over the waves.

Turning, he stared straight ahead.

They returned to the same port he had come to before, the little North Sea port of Immingham. He remembered the evenings he had spent here at the end of his first voyage, the common and the bombed-out blocks beyond, and the quiet town in the spring twilight. When the Second came looking for him to go ashore, Tom said he was too tired and thought he would hit the sack instead. He waited till after the Second had left, then put on his blues and his pea jacket and rode the tramcar into town. He had no particular place to go, no desire to see the town again; but he had wanted to get away from the ship and the people on it.

He walked about the back streets, past the railroad station, through the blocks of ruins and across the common. There was no spring twilight this time. The darkness had fallen long since—a cold November night with stars glittering in a frozen stream across the sky. His hands remained numb even after he thrust them into the pockets of his jacket. It occurred to him suddenly that the sky might seem as luminous as the ocean; that the streams of stars were like bubbles uncoiling behind the ship. So he was looking over the rail then. He stopped still searching into the sky above him. Below him. It was all the same: the pinpoints of light spiraling into the darkness. And as he clapped his cold hands together, he at once remembered the Swede in the mill who had suffered from cold too, and so was wearing his overcoat on the last day. The face sheared of features, staring down out of the holes of its eye sockets. Was this what the Second Mate had been telling him from the beginning? All right, he was like the Second Mate, he thought, he only wanted to go and hide somewhere. He went into a pub for a couple of beers and could not finish the second glass.

Outside, the movie theater on the main street was letting out its audience. Tom waited at the corner watching the crowd move past. They were young people most of them, soldiers and sailors and girls from town, and girls from the anti-aircraft batteries in their black, tin-buttoned uniforms, chattering, laughing, singing, as they tripped along the street. He saw an American sailor go by with a girl on each arm and one of the girls glanced his way. Tom followed.

"Can you use a fourth?" he asked as he caught up.

The sailor turned and a look of relief came over his face. "Sure can, Sailor," he said. He released his hold on one of the girls and Tom took her arm and they fell in behind the other two, walked along with the thinning crowd and then over the grass of the common. The first couple went on by themselves, while Tom and the girl sat down on a bench under a high leafless tree whose branches stirred and crackled in the wind.

She was very young, Tom saw, a straight, drab-looking girl with brownish hair and a hat pulled down over her ears. The Junior Spark's girl friend, he thought, the one in Liverpool, must look like this girl, and he felt sorry for her and could think of nothing to say. He lighted cigarettes and they sat and smoked. The girl was shivering. When he put his arm around her, she giggled while her teeth chattered.

"I guess it's too cold to stay here," he said.

"I'm very cold," the girl agreed.

"Shall we go have a beer and get warm?"

"The pubs are closed now," she told him.

"I keep forgetting about those pubs."

"Don't the pubs close in America?"

"Oh, they're supposed to. But there was always a bunch of places that stayed open all night."

"Were you ever in Chicago?" she asked.

"I worked there two or three months."

"That's where all the gangsters are and all that—in Chicago?"

Tom laughed. "The gangsters are all in uniform nowadays. Strictly legal. Chicago's safer than Immingham."

She tittered uncertainly and Tom said, "I guess I better walk you home."

"It is terrible cold, isn't it?"

They walked back across the silent town and past the station again, beyond the tracks into a section where there were unpaved roads crossing stretches of open field, and rows of brick houses pressed together, all just alike, with slate roofs and high front stoops. It was a long way. As they walked the moon came up on their right hand casting a network of shadows around them and lighting the narrow fronts of the houses. The same moon. The late moon that would set just before daybreak.

"Here's where I live," the girl said.

He had seen a thousand prettier girls than this one. Why couldn't it have been one of those? She was just a kid anyway. He put his arms around her and kissed her, thinking she would probably be frightened and run off into the house shutting the door behind her. But as soon as they kissed he realized she was not so young as she had seemed; and he thought, what's the use then? and asked, "Can I come up with you?"

She twisted coyly, unlocked the door and let them into a black pit of a hallway. Then she pressed her hand on his arm and whispered, "Now please be *quiet*."

They tiptoed up the stairs together.

At the top was another hallway faintly lighted by the glow from a half-open door at the far end. Tom could hear the sound of someone snoring. The girl pulled him into a room near the head of the stairs, closed and bolted the door behind them. It was a small room with a white iron bed and a bureau and a curtainless, soot-streaked window through which poured the moonlight touching the bed and floor and walls with the crisscross shadows and watery squares of the windowpanes.

The girl had stopped in the middle of the room. Holding out her hand, she said, "Give me some money."

Her voice was whining and sharp. He half expected her to ask for a lollipop or a piece of chewing gum. He squinted into his wallet and gave her a pound note.

"Give me another," she said.

He shrugged his shoulders, peeled off a second bill, and the girl put the money into a coin purse which she dropped behind the bed. She pulled off her clothes and Tom crawled in beside her. At first she giggled, and later breathed deep and hard; and seemed not at all disturbed by the creaking of the bedsprings. When they had finished, Tom lay beside her for a few moments, then got up and began to dress.

"Why don't you stay?" she asked.

"I have to get back to my ship."

"The tram's not running any more. You'll have to wait till morning."

"I'll walk," he told her.

At this the girl began to whimper. "What if I was to call out to my Dad. How would you like that?"

"Go ahead," Tom said. "Call your uncle and your grand-dad too. What the hell do I care?"

He tied his shoes and put on his jacket and when he looked at her again, she was lying with her face pressed into the pillow whimpering like a dog. She had taken his two pound notes all right, he thought, but now she wanted him to stay for nothing. She was lonely too. Leaning down, he stroked her hair; and she reached out sideways trying to hold him back, but without lifting her face from the pillow.

Tom let himself out. He returned through the deserted streets of Immingham, more empty than he had felt in his life before, and down the country road beside the tracks of the tramway. If there were nothing more than this, if you thought this and found it out, if there were nothing but this to look forward to . . . I'm scared of you sometimes, he remembered she had said; Tom, I don't know why you do anything. Why? Why did *she* do anything? The speech she had been going to make—why did she try so hard? Her wanting to have the baby. They all wanted something. Kallela knocking his head against a stone wall, the girl crying there on the bed, the Junior Sparks. A sense of rebellion fired him. She would know well enough why he did any-thing. She might be surprised what he could do, with Stone's help or without it. Nobody will be stopping me, he shouted.

Then he saw himself climbing the stairs in the rain with his sea bag on his shoulder, past the parking lot where the old pickup was standing, under the eucalyptus trees. What if she was not there? What good would it all be to him if she were not there? Where would he be looking if it was too late? Wait for me, he begged, wait for me. Long before he had covered the six or seven miles to the docks, the moon dropped behind the hedgerows, and later, in the first gray daylight, he saw the masts of ships as if they were growing among the fields.

29

Walter had lived virtually alone for so long that the death of his wife made little apparent difference in the routine of his daily life. His leg healed; he bought himself another car, which he could easily afford now that he no longer had to carry the expense of the Signal Springs rancho and her trips to the sanatarium.

He processed through the case of Anton Novak and won a reasonable settlement; and handled successfully a number of similar cases. The automobile accident saved him from having to go into court when the Negro shipyard workers appealed a second time for an injunction, and the state circuit judge, to the surprise of almost everyone concerned, granted their plea. The argument before the State Supreme Court, many months later, Chantry handled and lost. The court then declared that auxiliary locals were in violation of the public policy of the state of California, and the union quietly dispensed with them, in California at least. Walter had hoped that Garnet might take this defeat hard. But he did not. He simply dropped back to his second line of defense, which was to hold to a minimum the number of Negroes who would gain admission to the regular lodges. And this he was able to do quite effectively since the war was now almost over and the shipyards were tapering off.

Coming into their office one day, Garnet jovially told Chantry and Walter: "We held 'em off just long enough, fellows. If we'd had to take in a couple million of those wild men while things were popping, we'd have been in tough shape. But now, ninety per cent of 'em will be out of the industry inside a few months."

Walter, with a certain spiteful satisfaction, thought that Garnet had probably lost more than he had realized, or was willing to admit. The famous three-hour strike of the Negro workers in the San Martin yard had flashed across the headlines of almost every newspaper in the country. That action had stated the issue more precisely than two or three years of legal arguments could have done. The episode, Walter felt certain, must have played its part in inclining the mind of the state circuit judge toward granting a plea under the vague auspices of "common law and public policy," which no specific statute in the California code could be found to authorize. And after the State Supreme Court adopted this same view of the situation, then the federal government at last moved in to ban any auxiliary lodge as hiring agent for shipyards under government contract. So the besiegers had taken one of the ramparts by storm. Doing *themselves* little enough good in the process, he supposed, as must always be the case with those who had the courage, or the bad luck, to be first over the top when the bugle sounded. Nevertheless they had knocked a breach in the fortifications through which others in other industries and other unions would be able to force a passage. And Garnet, or some of his innumerable counterparts, would feel the weight of the loss.

But Garnet thanked them both; and he told them again, as he had told them so many times before, that the union did not mind paying a good price for good service.

Walter's wife Sylvia had been buried in the Honey Valley cemetery while Walter was still in the hospital; and it was more than half a year before he could bring himself to visit her grave. One morning in late autumn, he drove across the valley to the mountains, ate his lunch in the café where they had used to stop for coffee, and went out to the cemetery. The sky, which had been overcast before noon, now showed a few patches of blue through the clouds and there was a scattering of sunlight across the hill slopes and the wind came blowing down cold and steady out of the north. A burial was in progress at the cemetery when Walter arrived.

Leaving his car behind the cars of the funeral party, he went through the gate and followed the wheel tracks up the hill, limping slightly as he walked. He passed the hearse with its gaping back doors, took off his hat and stopped to watch, a few steps distant from the small group of mourners. The priest in black gown with smooth blue jaw and bone-rimmed spectacles was saying the words of the Lord's Prayer while the mourners joined and followed him: *hallowed be thy name, thy kingdom come, thy will be done on earth as it is in heaven* . . . The prayer ended, the priest stood silent, his head bowed, while with a ticking of well-oiled cogs the coffin, suspended by straps over the grave, sank slowly into the earth. When it had settled to the bottom, six pallbearers stepped forward, removed their suede gloves, plucked the white carnations from their lapels and let the gloves and the blossoms fall fluttering into the pit.

They were husky young fellows, the pallbearers. Their identical dark suits and the fumbling precision with which they carried out this routine, gave them a grotesque resemblance to a male chorus in some amateur theatrical. Walter half expected them to burst into song and dance away, kicking and bending in unison among the headstones. Instead, they retired sedately behind the hearse, and there stood waiting while the ceremony came to an end. The priest circled the grave, paused to shake the hand of each of the mourners.

Having thus vicariously assisted in her burial, Walter went on to keep his appointment with his wife. The cemetery at this height was sparsely settled and he had no difficulty finding the place. He crossed to the Protestant side of the wheel tracks and came presently to a new marker of plain granite bearing the name and dates:

SYLVIA ALLISON STONE
1895 — 1944

Over the mounds the grass had been scythed down to stubble and when he looked about him at the other mounds, he saw that these too had been scythed and trimmed. But in the aisles between, the grass grew tall and unsheared, stiff and dry-stemmed now in the autumn, matted with half-withered blossoms of the morning-glory vines.

His leg pained him and he sat down, holding his homburg hat on his knees. Below him the mourners straggled across the hillside. The empty hearse sailed off in the direction of town, while the cars backed and turned and followed after it in a dusty procession around the shoulder of the hill.

He was alone in the cemetery.

What had he come for, he wondered. To make his apologies? Or was there some paleolithic conviction in the marrow of man that grave-side ceremonies could ease the burden of the dead? Had he come to drop his gloves and carnation? More likely the intent was to ease the burden of the living, he thought. For he understood that within himself he had foretold what would happen when she had offered to drive the car that night. Perhaps he had hoped they would both die. In any case that was the final act: the beginning had been long before.

Had he destroyed her then? How many times had he asked himself the question? Or had she destroyed herself? Always when he thought of his wife, he thought of *illusions*, of her having deceived herself with illusions. Yet he knew that somehow he was wronging her, he was underrating and misjudging her.

That she was dead now, and the six months which intervened since he had seen her last alive, veiled the memories of her, all except the first. The weary, overpainted figure waiting on the terrace of the rancho with Mackay, faded into unreality. He remembered her as she had been when she was twenty-three years old. She had wished her life to be a dance, a *pas de ballet*, a figure whirling and gliding. The desire and pleasure and delight of her had glowed like moonlight; she had wanted everything about her to be beautiful. In beauty like the night: but if the night came, the morning was not far behind, and the day that followed for her was a bleak and dreary one. *Whose fault was that?*

She had lacked the strength. And he might have reached out to help her a long while ago, but he had not. He had lacked the strength too. Both had needed help and neither one could give it. Both had sought their private escapes—she in drinking; he in the solitary camping and fishing trips, in the pursuit of some quality of his own mind, in the illusion—yes, *illusion*—that goodness and truth were to be found in nature, but were defiled by man. The only real difference between their escapes, he thought, was that hers had destroyed her physically, and his had not, not physically. Perhaps it had destroyed him in every other way. Turning his new brown hat between his hands, he thought of the bank account he had opened in fulfillment of his promise to Richards and Mackay; and of the case he had argued for exclusion of Negro workers from a voice in the shipyard union. Yet he had believed, when he broke with Richards over the Saw Creek case, that he was opening a new door in his life. Well, there were so many doors, and every decision remained to be made again, and only the wrong decisions were utterly irrevocable. Even now he clung to the recollection of the settlement he had won for Anton Novak; and to the scores of similar cases he could claim credit for.

This was the foundation of his plea for leniency.

He put on his hat, pushed himself up from the ground, and walked back, limping, down the wheel tracks toward the road.

At the bottom he paused for a moment to look at the oldest stones, close to the gate. A sense of amazement gripped him at what had befallen the occupants beneath them. These too had lived, worked, loved, hoped, feared; and now had come to dwell with the others in the California hillside. Here the dates went back to the fifties and sixties of the last century; yet the story was essentially the same as the story on the marker above that bore his wife's epitaph—the long road from East to West. Some of these even were inscribed with names of faraway cities—Toledo, Ohio; St. Louis, Missouri; Albany, New York. Only fifty miles from Poughkeepsie where she had been born: she would have company, neighbors from home.

He supposed that the family from Illinois who had left their wagon on the Sierra slope must be here somewhere too, but he did not know the name; and he remembered the distances he himself had crossed, although not afoot or by wagon as these had come, and the mountains on the horizon, the cold gray twilight dropping over the wastes of empty land. Mile after mile, each deliberate footstep, each creaking turn of the wheels through the sand and gravel bringing them closer to the final mountains, closer to Honey Valley to lie down here under the bending yellow grass of the California hillside.

Oh, America, he thought, a paragraph in a schoolbook, a history carved on the headstones of country graveyards. And what remained of all this? The glow of neon signs where the highway dipped down from the darkness? The hopeless lost promise, the memory of an ecstatic smile? The arrogance of Richards and Mackay, the grim fierce power of the man Garnet? Were these the purpose, the outcome of such abundance of hope and labor and death?

He walked on towards the gate. Now this particular thread of the web had reached its end. Sylvia Stone had taken up residence with her permanent companions; and her husband, filled with wonder, turned away from the grave.

A belated jaybird squawked in the thicket behind him. The sun slanted towards late afternoon.

30

Among the brocaded chairs, Joyce waited. The room had walls of green and gold, a red carpet, two ash-tray stands, a lamp with a tasseled shade. The air smelled of dust and cigarette ashes, and brass polish. She kept searching about her trying to discover some object on which anyone might possibly have used brass polish. But the doorknobs were glass, the lamp of wood, the ash-tray stands made of some substance like marble or onyx.

From beyond the door that led to the stage, she could hear faintly the notes of the grand piano. Now and again came bursts of applause. Four numbers till the intermission. Then it would be her turn. She had wanted to listen to her teacher's playing to hear if she made any mistake under the stress of the performance. She hoped she would not make any; but knew at the same time that she rather hoped she would. It would seem easier for *her* if the teacher would make even one. But she did not really listen; she could no longer focus her attention. The stage fright which had been so intense earlier in the day had parted from her now. She felt numb. This was what she had feared so often in the past—the dividing in two, the watching herself from a distance. It had always been with her, returning always in moments of crisis. She remembered when she had forced herself to the decision of leaving Signal Springs; and remembered when she had taken the welding test; and when Charlie had asked her to marry him; and the first time she had climbed down the swinging ladders into the hold of a ship. And when the letter had come.

It was like an anaesthetic. It separated one from pain, which must be why she had acquired the habit—she supposed it was a habit, like taking drugs. How otherwise could she recall her childhood as not having been really painful at all, but only slow and lonely and uneventful? In the very moments of her life when there would be most to know and remember, it was as if she had only half been there. As if she were a stranger or passer-by, one to whom no moment could hold anything of great importance. Better to have lived the moments entirely, even if living them were pain. Could *he* have made his music, or could Charlie have struggled from the shadows of his own past, striving to become an artist, in any but sorrow, or agony, or joy? Or Sally O'Regan, she thought, weeping at the kitchen table of the house in San Martin Village; or Sally as she had seen her on another morning, six months pregnant, having just heard from her husband for the first time in half a year, and her face gleaming like a child's? *Oh, I'll manage to hold out long enough to come hear you play in the recital,* she had promised.

A sense of familiarness touched Joyce as if she had returned to a situation, or to a place she had once known well but forgotten. The carpet, the green walls, the brocade chairs, the smell, the taste, the sound. A moment she had dreamed of all her life, yet sat here dull as a mouse and puzzled over the smell of brass polish.

This set her laughing.

It reminded her at once of the high-school graduation and how she had thought she might as well be wearing mittens for all the audience would have known the difference. *That* audience. But this audience would know.

And she was still laughing when she heard a prolonged burst of applause from beyond the door, the door opened and her teacher came in, arms loaded with flowers. The first half of the program had ended.

"Tell me, how did it sound, Joyce?"

"I don't really know," Joyce admitted. "I tried to listen, but I just couldn't. . . ."

Dropping down on one of the stiff little chairs, the teacher asked, "Are you nervous?"

"I guess so. I was hoping I'd hear you make a mistake so *I* wouldn't feel so bad."

"Oh, Joyce! You should have listened then. I made three in the first number."

"I guess I wouldn't have known if I had heard them."

"After you play a few concerts, Joyce, you'll find out nobody ever does quite as well in a performance as in practice. But if the practice has been good, the performance will be good too." The teacher stretched her legs, lighted a cigarette, eased the straps of her evening gown over her slightly puffy shoulders. "I often think of a line from Emily Dickinson," she said,

> *"What fortitude the human soul*
> *That it can thus endure*
> *The accent of a coming foot,*
> *The opening of a door . . .*

Worst part is the waiting. Every performer needs an audience. You'll love it when you get out there."

Joyce hoped she would. She still smelled the brass polish. They sat silent while the teacher watched her with a half-smile. From outside they heard the buzzer calling the audience back to their seats after the intermission. She thought of her mother with her white hair and flashing little bird's eyes behind the pinch-on glasses—out there; and Richard Brooks escorting her mother. Probably he would be telling her now about the house he was going to rent for them on the other side of San Martin which had a workshop he could use in the basement and plenty of room for a piano upstairs (would they really rent to colored, she wondered) and about the truck he had bought and the repair business he was going into. He had been laid off at the shipyard during the summer. After the failure of the first injunction, while waiting for the court decision on the second, the Improvement League finally had advised that everyone pay dues into the Auxiliary again, under protest. They had to pay, to stay at their jobs. Many had done so, but not the Sergeant.

"Guess I don't much care if they do chase me out," he had said to her. "I won't pay into that outfit."

The night before he left the shipyard, he came to her at dusk under the track of the traveling crane. "How you think you can play the piano with your hands like that?"—and turning her hand over, he touched the calluses of her palms and the hard pads of her finger tips. She remembered she had felt very angry with him. It seemed as if he were offering a bribe. But then it came to her mind that she never had told him about playing the piano. Yet he had understood how important this was, most important of everything to her. Before, she would not have imagined he really would understand. Charlie had understood because he was an artist. But Richard Brooks—no, it was not like promising a bribe; it seemed to her he had been trying to tell her that even though he might not talk quite as easily, might not understand as well as someone else might, still he had learned about her, and he knew what she was, and what she wished for most. He was saying to her, let me wish for this too. She remembered how much she had let escape her once because she had been afraid. And her answer had been made already, months before, on that night when they had watched the colored workers returning into the yard. So they had stood together with her hand palm up and his hand enclosing hers, and she said, *All right, Richard.*

She had told Sally in the morning, and was delighted at the pleasure and enthusiasm of Sally's congratulations. But it was several days before she could bring herself to go to see Janet and Reverend Beezely, for she did not think the Reverend felt very friendly toward the Sergeant since their dispute in the shipyard. Janet came around the kitchen table to her at once; and after a moment of silence, the Reverend said, "He found someone he trusts, in you, Joyce." Then he had added, "Maybe we should have listened a little more to Mr. Brooks that night. There don't seem to be much rhyme or reason to court decisions. They're like the weather —good one day, bad the next. If a person really wishes to go somewhere, I suppose he makes up his mind to take a walk in the rain sometimes. I often thought we might have done better for our people," he said, "if we'd known how to listen a little bit."

That had been while they were still waiting for the decision from the State Supreme Court. When the news came that they had won their case, the Improvement League put on a celebration in the community building at San Martin Village, with a loudspeaker and dance orchestra from the city, and the lawyers and the president of the League and Reverend Beezley all making speeches. Richard was not going to come. She remembered half regretfully how she had nagged at him till he lost his temper, but he came with her finally. Then the Reverend up on the platform said had it not been for what the swing shift in San Martin yard had done, they might never have won in court. Everyone began shouting for the Sergeant and people sitting beside them pushed him to his feet while the crowd whistled for him and clapped till he walked up to the front and joined the others on the platform. She did not think anyone who ever had worked in the San Martin yard would be likely to forget the Sergeant.

"All right, Joyce, it's almost time for you."

Are you ready, she wondered. Was anyone ever ready when the time came for them? Outside, the audience, and the people from the shipyard among them, were taking their places after the intermission—the Sergeant with her mother, and Janet and Sally and the Reverend, and so many others who had told her they were coming, though not many had ever been to a piano recital before, any more than she had herself. She had wanted all her life to be part of them, yet never had quite felt herself part; and now they had come to listen to *her*. Some she knew had already been discharged from the yards, and like the Sergeant were struggling to find their living in what was for all of them a strange city, far from homes they would not likely return to. Yet they had spent the money to sit in the ballroom of a fancy hotel where few colored people ever had set foot before, to hear her play.

As Joyce rose to her feet, she knew that she would never forget how she had seen them go through the gate that night, and Richard Brooks' face, watching them—back into the yard, toward the dark structure of the shipways where the welding arcs sparkled like falling stars. She was playing for them—*if only she could;* for the victory they had, and the defeat and the loss, for the shining bright web of hope in the darkness.

The teacher straightened the yellow roses on Joyce's shoulder and smoothed the gown of yellow Chinese silk that Janet had made for her.

A coming foot. The opening of a door. The teacher stood in the half-open doorway peering out to see when the audience would be ready. Now she beckoned, she gave Joyce a kiss on the cheek, she pushed her onto the stage. There was a blur of faces below her—*don't look at them*—the grand piano enormous and black hanging unbelievably in its circle of blue smoky light. They were clapping. Her heart died, fluttered, died. She felt that she was carrying an unbearable burden as she moved the long distance toward the piano bench. . . .

AFTERWORD

Yes, a long journey to the concert hall for Joyce from that tiny Nevada railroad town which had been her entire world, hers' the lone Black family; carrying with her only the heritage of them, a lone suitcase, and her dreams, fears, longings, aspirations to San Francisco, her "magic city"; to the shipyards with all that happened there; and now to this night of her recital; she who had never even been to a piano concert before.

Yes, and a long journey, too, for those who came to hear her, this girl old for her years, unknown to them even a year before, they, who like her had nearly all come from distant places to be plunged into the New: various human beings, unaccustomed situations, encounters; a less and less completely ghettoized life—and the shared Baptism of the Shipyard experiences and struggles; now to sit in the ballroom of a fancy hotel "where few of them had ever sat before," to listen to Joyce "playing for them, *if only she could*, for the victory they had, and the defeat and the loss, and the shining bright web of hope in the darkness."

Yes, and a long journey for Saxton, who through a dark time created them all so livingly on the pages of this book, ten long years in the writing, 1948–1958.

And each and everyone so marked, changed, deepened, in the course of their journeying.

~

In those World War II years, the ever increasing succession of newly launched Liberty Ships, crowded with their loads of men, arms, materials desperately needed on the War Front, became the symbol of the proud and dedicated productivity of which the Home Front was capable. Rosie the Riveter ("We Can Do It"), upraised arm bent at the elbow, sleeve rolled up to display her muscle, became the Poster Girl representing millions of women working in the war industries. And yet, astonishingly, even these more than fifty years later, nowhere else in literature except on the pages of this book are they central.

But Bright Web is far more than Rosies, Shipyards, and the struggles, the journeyings of Joyce and the others from where they were in the beginning.

Bright Web is a micro/macrocosm of what was taking place not only in war industry after industry, but in human life after human life. Here in this one book—as in a microcosm —is encompassed the journeyings, the valorous three-shift round-the-clock work, the immense changes in, for, and because of millions of human beings in that time.

Here is the omnipresence of the war effort; the young men leaving for the war front; the marriages, so hasty; the death of a loved one and the haunting sense of the vulnerability, the preciousness of life; the newfound camaraderie, independence, joy, knowledge of competence, skill, experienced by the women at work; and "the common mind, common heart, that moves people when they move in unison." "These ships are for freedom in Germany, France, China." The response of the young black man Charlie, who would be killed in the war: "I'm for freedom in Texas, too."

But *Bright Web* is a micro/macrocosm most because the struggles there in the Yards for upgrading, for fair employment practices, for access to the kinds of work, pay, skills, unions* from which women and men of color, indeed *all* women, had been historically excluded; occurred in workplace after workplace— became a common national struggle against what we now call racism and sexism to bring our country closer to the ideal of "one Nation indivisible, with liberty and justice for all."

A successful struggle then, but presage: "A shining bright web of hope in the darkness."

♂

World War II was a period of change like none other before, and in some respects since, for women: social, economic, cultural, "consciousness" changes, and the changes which more blossoming circumstances breed. Women (many of whom, contrary to myth, had worked before) were now one-third of the work force. Previously, the work available for women was domestic; stoop labor; standing on one's feet jobs—the lowest paid "shit-work" (what W. E. B. DuBois called "the manure theory of social organization"). Joyce and Sally, proud welders, exemplify this. Joyce's work in the shipyards had been picking up scraps of wood, sweeping sawdust, other cleaning. Sally worked as a waitress behind the lunch counter. Sexism.

Although Joyce and Sally become roommates, closest friends, comrades in battle, it is through them both that in the beginning we see the contrast in different treatment, circumstances, because of the different colors of their skin. They meet in the welding class. Joyce is urged to go by the Sergeant; Sally—flouting Tom's disparagements—assumes it is her natural right. Joyce, like Sally, earns her welding certificate,—but is the one given a bad time; told there just are no more jobs, learns from Sally how

---

*I refer only to the old AFL craft unions. Wherever trained skill, previous apprenticeship, was essential, as in the shipyards, they held absolute power. The majority of CIO and all of the west coast ILWU unions gave full union membership to all who worked on the job.

immediately and easily Sally is hired, has to battle with the entrenched union leadership to be hired, has to fight to be upgraded. Racism.

Yes, for Joyce, a qualitative difference from Sally's on the job. As was true for all African-Americans in World War II. Their advances and experiences did not equal those of white women. Traditionally "last hired, first fired,"excluded from most factory work, let alone skilled jobs and their craft unions—only in the 1930s, as a result of active recruiting by largely left-led CIO unions in various occupations, mostly in the North—did some experience full union membership and participation. Jobs were still too scarce; it was still the Depression time.

The change came when the need for "manpower" in the expanding war industries, and the passage of the Fair Employment Practices Act (FEPC), opened up hundreds of thousands of fair-paying jobs in the North; irresistible magnet for "the great migrations" to the North away from Southern racism and starvation wages (the latter the reason why many Southern white workers also came North).

Bright Web alone details how the changes were experienced not only in the shipyards, but in other war industries as well.

In order to work in the yards, colored people (the term in use then) must get a card from the union, but are not entitled to full membership rights—an edict protested by Henry, Sally, and other white rank-and-file union members. They must pay dues, but can only belong to a specially set-up auxiliary. Which is not allowed to meet.

"Our people come into the yard, they have no job training and no promotion. No colored leadermen, no colored foremen. Colored welders stay their whole life on tacking. White welders are set right up as production welders...." So Reverend Beezely states the case to the Sergeant; "The union is supposed to protect us but it does not.... Don't we have the right to membership in the union? No, not in the Auxiliary, in the *union*, I mean? Don't we? Like the others?" The question of the Auxiliary is a divisive one for them both—with a long foreground—and a very current afterground among African-Americans. Integration without equal power? or stay apart? ("What we ought to do?")

"We'd never have a majority. They'd outvote us every time," the Sergeant answers.

"But this way we have no vote at all. We pay money, but we don't have a voice at all. If we were under the same rules and the same seniority . . ."

"Oh hell! They'd push us around and cut our necks off every time they felt like it! Let them have their organization and we'll have ours. That's the only way we'll get things any better. Then we go right up to the big boss. You talk turkey with the white union, but you've got to talk turkey with us now too . . ."

"They can't build ships without us," is the rock of truth "The Sergeant," Brooks, clings to. And it is his strategy which is supported at the time: to demand their rights, "to challenge, to defy." The Auxiliary *will* meet, have an election, officers. Which only happens "illegally" *after* they have defied Garnet, the official representative sent by the union to deal with the situation. "Illegally" they print their own ballots; refuse to pay their dues; are issued discharge slips—because they no longer have the required union cards.

Again the "what we ought to do?" to be decided. It is wartime, a war they believe in; strikes are a betrayal; and they "go back to building the ships," seemingly giving in while "seeking redress through the medium of the law."

How brilliant, the swing-shift's walkout demonstration led by Brooks. "The long, long line of people stretching out through the gate into the night" after him; in solidarity making their point: how many and how strong we are; "you can't build ships without us"; we defied your power, did not yield to rules that were unjust, to inequalities of treatment that were humiliating. We acted. Together. As Joyce and they all would never forget:

this long procession "turning back into the yard toward the dark structure of the shipways where the welding arcs sparkled like falling stars."

"Mortals of the immortal spirit"— those in the never ending procession of humanity who, throughout human history have evidenced the will, the capacity, the courage to act against the wrongs, indignities, harms of their time, their place, their circumstances. The Changers, the Advancers. The truth of the past, the present. And Presage. Joyce's (and this book's) vision of their beings, their actions: "the bright web of hope in the darkness."

—Not the vision of Walter Stone, that ever more solitary, complex figure of such promise and hope in the beginning, when he had acted on the side of the sawmill workers in their strike. "The smartest springer in the league, the man who got me out of the pokey," Kallela called him. Walter's reply: "All you did was organize a union." Walter's explanation, proud of his "decency." "There was every reason to defend you." "The apex of one of the turning points in his life," he reflects then.

A starkly different turning point. There is the new law firm he helps form; his specialty: labor law. There are Chantry and Mackay and Garnet: they, the successes, the possessors of material comfort, the men of power, acting on the side of power, with whom Walter allies himself. And compromise after compromise.

There is the gathering struggle in the yards, organized and fired most by the Sergeant, by the Reverend, by those whites in the Boilermaker Union who also want the black auxiliary done away with, full membership in the union with all its rights for everyone, regardless of color, who does the same work.

There is Walter's final betrayal, when (for all his self-questioning, ambivalence, better instincts), the successful attorney for the union now, he must meet with Garnet to advise what to do in the shipyard situation. Prepared to tell him that "the courts all the way to the Supreme Court have held that a man's right to earn a living comes within . . . due process of the law. You and your union are depriving these people of the right to earn a living and sooner or later, they're going to make it stick in the courts." As if gagged by Garnet's "overbearing power," his stream of invective, Walter is unable to say anything of this; nor add what is in his heart to say: "*and if you refuse my advice, you'll have to find someone else to represent you.*"

And says nothing of this, and says nothing of this, and swallows the gag, for—among other reasons—that would be the end of Stone, Chantry and Greenwood and the future political career planned for his son. And—with all his resources—he fights the cause for the union as Garnet wishes.

At the closing, his vision of the past, the present, the future, so different from Joyce's. Standing in utter aloneness and despair, by the grave of Sylvia, his neglected, alcoholic wife; thinking not only of the ruin of her—and his—life, both of which had begun with such expectancy and promise; wandering the century-old, crowded graveyard, reading the inscriptions—all the work, hopes, beliefs, desires, buried there,—"The arrogance of Richards and Mackay, the grim fierce power of the man Garnet? Were these the purpose, the outcomes of [what had been] such abundance of hope and labor?"

"Oh, the hopeless lost promise of America. . . . This particular thread of the web had reached its end . . . "

Not for him, alas, Joyce's belongingness, hope, beliefs—based on her journeyings, experiencings of, with, her sister, fellow human beings. Out of his experiencings, Chantry, Mackay, Garnet, "Goodness, truth, were in nature only—not in man."

Two disparate visions, two webs: Joyce's "bright web of hope in the darkness"; Walter's "hopeless lost promise."

℘

How they remain with me, Saxton's created people. Yes, Walter too. Garnet, the almost stereotypical official of the old entrenched craft unions at the time. The Union as is, a "fraternal, social" closed men's club, as he describes it to Walter, is his life. Proud and jealous of their long apprenticeship-honed skills, their victories: "we worked like hell to get a closed shop, and we're not going to throw it away because a few black boys don't like it." His open, unself-conscious foul-mouthed racism: "I'll be goddamned if we're going to stand around and see a bunch of wild niggers just out of the canebreaks come up here and smash [all we are] . . . to hell for us" And yet: "I never went to sixth grade." The sense of what shaped him and the actions of those craft unions.

Brooks, "the Sergeant," Reverend Beezely: those complex, passionate men, so dedicated to their people, so knowledgeable of the changes necessary in the yards—access, upgrading, solidarity—the development of the human beings without whom changes would not be possible; their sense of the forces arrayed against them—so differing as to approach, the best strategies to be adopted.

The Reverend is a family man, longtime resident, at home in the black community, part of the network of established organizations—social, political—raising and acting on current issues, working for social change.

The Sergeant's territory is at work; there is his life. He seems to be everywhere, walking with his jerky gait, making his rounds, observing, intervening when necessary, telling off the leadermen, stiffening backs, instilling courage in the handling of situations when one is wrongly treated.

In the beginning Beezely does not understand Brooks. "He's like a wolf, he trusts no one," he tells Sally. "Our people are so driven and so pressed, Joyce, sometimes they only have hate to live on and they trust no one." The Reverend does not see the every day evidence in Brooks' actions, his profound love for, knowledge of, belief in and trust in his people—in their historic capacity, will to resist. Brooks' hatred—and it is an active hatred—is for the system and those who have exploited, demeaned them, denied their rights and capacities.

His body has been broken, almost destroyed, as a front-line soldier in the war to make the world safe for democracy. Always he is in pain, and the pain and anger of the travesty of his return to what has not changed, still needs to be changed.

Sally Kallela is already the presage of the feminists who would come into being thirty-five years later. She is proud of her independence, skill, competence; demands equality, respect, in her relationships. When Tom, angry because she has gone out bowling with someone else, insults her: "I won't be standing in line like the last dog in the pack," she knocks him "half off his pins," bloodies his mouth.

But hers is a class-conscious feminism. Class for her predominates; working people of either sex, any human hue, are her people. So it is, that so naturally she becomes Joyce's roommate, ally, closest friend; takes on the battle for full admission of all her co-workers into the union as her own battle. And agrees, braves herself to speak at the stormy meeting in her union where no woman had ever spoken before. Prepares endless hours to do so; cannot be comforted for what she feels was her failure.

Loving, almost typically the war bride in her letters, her worries for his safety, her lovingness, her happiness when he is back with her while on leave, but the chasm between her and Tom opens when he fails to respect and understand how much her resolve to speak entailed. So too when he cannot understand, resents, and is angered by her refusing to stay at dinner with Walter Stone—so important, Tom feels, to his future.

The fact that "He's the lawyer for the union" for the *union*, is what matters—not that their personal fortunes might be advanced.

Tom O'Regan is Sally's love and trial. Passionately in love with her, but from the beginning jealous, possessive. When they marry, very much a male of his time, he takes it for granted that he will "wear the pants in the family,"—and that she will be a model wife, putting his interests and needs first. Theirs is a stormy relationship, much to be worked out. "Don't think you own me," she warns him.

He wants more in life than the jobs he's had, he tells Sally, or what happened in his parents' generation: "they all knocked around, trucking, sawmilling, railroading, not because they wanted to, but they had to." He intends to have choices, perhaps even become a lawyer like the Walter Stone of the lumber strike time.

"I hope you get almost everything you wish for," Sally encourages him. "Almost? Almost? That's not enough. *Everything*."

How much he wants or is capable of, he did not know then. Drafted into the merchant marine, "enclosed" in the ship at sea, there is freed time. There is the Second Mate, the first college-educated person he has ever known, who furthermore spends time with Tom, likes to argue, has a library of books he is willing to lend. Tom becomes a hungry reader; discovers his love—and capacity—for enlarging his knowledge, widens his horizons.

I imagine him in that time when—after the war—the G.I. Bill fully financed, made it possible for tens of thousands of Toms from families like his in which no one had gotten through high school—to become full time college students, superb ones, the pride of their campuses. Many had never thought of themselves—or been thought of—as college material.

We have forgotten that lesson in the rich yields, not only for the Toms, but for our country; their contributions in field after field of human endeavor, when we enabled the circumstances for full development of human capacities, invested in wide educational opportunity.*

---

*The G.I. Bill also began the proliferation of free or low-cost community, city, and state colleges.

Joyce Allen is for me one of the rarest, most beautiful creations in literature—and unprecedented. I fell in love with her, her depth and openness, her response to people and the responses which she evokes: her eagerness for life from the beginning (what some would call innocence); her sense of other horizons, possibilities. Her precept: "Everyone must picture themselves as something that is more."

"Small-town girl," her excitement that there are other classes than welding in the city, her "magic city," "full of schools." Her plans for college through evening classes—and dearest of all, to take up music, her piano lessons again.

Yes, Joyce is a fledgling musician. Joyce's first symphony (Saxton's descriptions of music are masterly), sitting with Charlie high, high up in the balcony, the only seats they can afford:

> . . . Each note anticipated, and her eyes now clos-
> ing. . . . becoming the shape and substance of the
> music. . . . the bright web in the darkness, the heart
> singing like a violin string.

Joyce's patient practicing; becoming a scholar on her own, too: looking up the origin of contra dances, for instance; and no matter how exhausted from work, never missing a lesson.

But Joyce must get a living. In the yards, cleaning work—until thanks to the upgrading strategies of the Sergeant, she becomes a welder, working on the great ships, proud, respected, well-paying work.

It is through Joyce, that sensor, that we are given the sounds, the weathers ("the fog was full of an immense clanging and hammering, roaring, hooting), the hurrying and waiting, the smells, the various tasks, the stupendous number and variety of people required "like bees in a honeycomb," the immense clanging belly, the huge height and bulk of the ships they were building:

> Far below . . . the glare of cluster lights, the sparkle of

welding torches, and people crawling back and forth like beetles ... Small figures in tin helmets hurrying out from under the ways ...

As Saxton observes: "Work, subjectively, even aesthetically experienced, has seldom entered the mainstream of American fiction."* Indeed, work—the everyday job and maintenance of life work which consumes so much of most human beings' lives—takes up less space in the sum of all fiction than any other human activity. Work's presence, the experiencings, descriptions of it here, are one of the consummate distinctions of this book:

Joyce, goggled and helmeted, hauling herself onto the high, high scaffold. "Reach down, set, weld, reach, set, weld again. One bracket every three minutes ... The work was a machine and she was part of a machine, shafts and levers that brought the arc to the steel, moved it and brought it back. Reach down, set, weld, set, weld, set again. ... The shining bead of molten metal crept down the joint and a moment later the two pieces of steel, melting and fusing, had become one. The miracle she never quite believed had happened again."

Joyce, "working on hands and knees with her head knocking against the ceiling, the fumes ... thicker than ever, ... sweating and choking under her helmet, the bulkhead seeming to have stretched out till it was several miles long."

Upgraded now, Joyce is the first (and only) "colored woman" welder. The foreman on her shift is not about to allow her teammate to be a white male. So it is, that the shipfitter transferred to work on her team is—Brooks. Observing, intervening when necessary.

"He is a grim, silent man, the Sergeant," Joyce thinks. "Some-

---

*Only recently has this begun to change, with the emergence of a number of writers, mostly of color, who are the first generation in their families who have had the education, the circumstances, to become so.

times they would work together for an entire half shift without exchanging a word. Yet she knew she could not have learned as much from any other shipfitter about how to take care of herself."

"When you goin' to get a bit tough, Miss Allen?" he asks her in their first weeks working together. "I'm learning *something*," she says to herself proudly as she begins to refuse out-of-place or demeaning orders; sticks to doing her own work better and better.

But still so much to learn:

At first, she cannot understand all the goings-on about having to be members of an Auxiliary, instead of the union. "To her, it seemed inevitable that the union would be run by white people who would set restrictions." Only gradually does she come to realize that these restrictions are responsible for the unequal treatment on the job for her people, for her sex; the higher dues; their exclusion from the powerful grievance committee's prosecutions for on-the-job mistreatment, substandard working conditions, violation of union contract stipulations. And that her heritage is one of resistance, acting to change what is not right.

The Sergeant is her teacher, clarifier.

The example of how he conducts, involves himself on the job—as he had encouraged and acted for her too. His leadership in effecting the walk-out; how, caring so much, "he, who she never could have imagined would be afraid," stood before them all at the Auxiliary meeting trembling, his voice and hands shaking, as he presented the reasons why they should take such an action.

Yes, and the forces against them he knew, (as now she did) were so powerful; and he would be beaten up, too. His courage. Yet—and it haunts her—why he refuses to speak at the next crucial meeting when the decision must be made whether to continue to stay out, or—as so eloquently presented by the Reverend—honor the "no strike during the war" pledge, "seek redress through the medium of the law."

"I expect it would tear things all apart," he tells her. And then the flood of words. "Never had she heard him say so many words together"; revelation after revelation. "I came back [from the war] mad. . . . They got their families to support [but] a man's got to fight sooner or later, family or no family, or he don't amount to much. Cost a man too sometimes. Cost me a year and a half in the jailhouse . . . "

"I always been kind of a lone wolf, Miss Allen."

(Lone wolf? He who cared so much? acted for, with, them? No, it was only that in his life he had had to develop a wolf's wariness, cunning, armor—let no one near him.)

Heartbrokenly: "took the heart out of me when Beezely and all the rest come down. Now . . . they goin' to eat their peck of dirt."

"I don't think they're eating a peck of dirt," Joyce brings herself to say. "I don't think they're giving up."

Even before what will happen, the later demonstration walk-out and return (the Bright Web of Hope) which he will be leading—Joyce knows, ineradicably, that never will she, as never he has, as her people never have, or will, —"give up." Her music, her place, is in their age-old procession: "mortals of the immortal spirit."

"She had wanted all her life to be part of them." Now she is.

It is when she sees the tears running down out of his eyes, his broken face, as they watch the defeat of the turning back into the gate that she seizes Brooks, begging, "Don't,"—and his arms go round her.

She has pierced his armor—as this book pierces mine. In this gallery of created human beings, it is the Sergeant and Joyce whom I found most moving, revelatory, true. But so are they all.

Remember, there were real people like this; there were real

such struggles all over our country in those World War II industries. And loss, and defeat—and many, many victories.

♧

Rare, rare, is there a portrayal in fiction of how such a struggle develops, what it brings out in and between human beings, and the moral testing—"which side are you on?"—which takes place.

Brooks (the Sergeant), Reverend Beezely, Joyce, Sally, the other Kallelas, Walter and Sylvia Stone, Garnet, Henry the shipfitter, Mackay had a multiplicity of "real life" counterparts throughout the nation. It is through Saxton's created beings that life, visibility, actuality is given to what transpired in that time, and the human beings who lived and acted then: their motivations, relationships, hopes, dreams, struggles. Visibility creates reality.

I know of no other work of fiction which, set in the workplace and concerning itself with an actual labor struggle, so superbly illuminates the workings of those intertwined three —racism, sexism, class—in relationships and in society—and has this beauty, depth, scope, and power.

♧

How is it that such a book vanished almost at once after publication, slept in the forgotten, the never-heard-of-it, for almost forty years?—as did the remembrance of an actual Richmond Kaiser Shipyard event which inspired it?

Why did Alexander Saxton, that distinguished and much loved UCLA professor emeritus of history, "one of the foremost interpreters of the United States' past in scholarly books,"* write no more fiction after *Bright Web*?

---

*David R. Roediger, *Towards the Abolition of Whiteness: Essays on Race Politics, and Working Class History* (1994)

If there are flaws, unevennesses, in this book—and there are—what impeded?

The answer is eloquent of erased truth, and the consequences of the Cold War in personal lives and lessened creative productivity.

Born into privilege, educated at Exeter and Harvard, Saxton came into his youthhood (as did I) in the 1930s, that time of "burgeoning solidarity in the nation, bridging differences in color, background, creed, walk of life," of "millions in motion, acting together for freedom from want, from fear";* assembling, petitioning, speaking out, organizing to remedy hunger, misery, joblessness, despair.

Deeply affected, stirred to participate, Saxton left his advantaged life and moved to industrial Chicago, where, he writes in his introduction to the fall, 1997 reissue of *The Great Midland*,** he was "stunned by its beauty and horror.... In 1941 or 1942, I joined the Communist Party, which in those days attracted young people across class lines....

"I remained in the party while I wrote *The Great Midland* and for a great many years afterward.... I never held the American party, or myself as a member of it, responsible for Stalinism. ... Membership cost me dearly in some ways; it also was a privilege I would not wish to have missed."

During World War II he shipped out as a merchant seaman—that most dangerous of all the services, suffering the highest casualty rate of them all. One of the lucky ones to return, the war over, he and his wife Trudy moved to California, where he went back to his beloved writing—the interrupted *Great Midland*.

It was 1945. Hopes were high that the war's end would usher

---

*From my article in *Newsweek*, "The 30's: A Vision of Fear and Hope," January 3, 1944

**University of Illinois Press

in the next great advance for humanity—beyond the "right to life, liberty and the pursuit of happiness"; to specific "equal and unalienable rights of all members of the human family, which are the essential foundation for freedom and peace in the world." These are detailed in the last section of the Universal Declaration of Human Rights—argued over, mediated by Eleanor Roosevelt, finally agreed upon and adopted by every member state of the newly founded United Nations. As revolutionary for its time as the 1776, 1781, 1787 great proclamations, the Declaration specified economic, social, cultural, educational rights. Among these are rights to "just and favorable remuneration ensuring an existence worthy of human dignity; a standard of living adequate for health and well-being, medical care, necessary social services; the right to security in the event of unemployment, sickness, disability, widowhood, old age; special provisions for motherhood and childhood; the right to a free education, . . . directed to the full development of the human personality and the strengthening of respect for human rights and fundamental freedoms . . . friendship among all nations, racial or religious groups, and the maintenance of peace." A threat indeed to the prevailing power structure with its privileges, its ownership of resources, industry, wealth; its influence in government, and the resulting inequalities.

Within a year, Winston Churchill gave his Fulton, Missouri, Iron Curtain speech. The Cold War had begun. By the time *The Great Midland* was published in December of 1948, right after Truman's reelection to the presidency, as Saxton writes, "the Cold War had shifted into high gear. The fact that some Communists were portrayed in a favorable light doomed the book." With little, then no income to continue as a full time writer and support his family, "I learned the trade of construction carpenter at which I worked over the next fourteen years, trying to write . . . over the weekends or on rainy days when construction work closes down."

"In 1951, the House Un-American Activities Committee summoned me to Washington. All I told them was my date of birth and home address, which they already knew . . . I was not a very important bird. I declined to sing for them, and it was just before Christmas recess; and the courts were now beginning to uphold the Fifth Amendment." He was not cited. But previous job offers—script writer for Paramount, creative writing teacher at San Francisco State College—suddenly evaporated. "The FBI went to the trouble of hounding my wife as if she occupied a post in high-tech defense; actually she was a consultant to diagnostic clinics for crippled or birth-damaged children." Party membership had indeed begun to cost him and his family dearly.

Saxton continued to be active, part of the stubborn resistance working to retain the economic and social gains won in the 1930s and the World War II times. It was some years later that Saxton, having only a B.A., began to explore going to graduate school so that he could qualify for teaching. Working part time, he earned his doctorate in five years, 1962-67, and began to work on his scholarly books, all of which remain in use and in print.

Two sections in the personal narrative parts of his *Great Midlands* preface, and a portion of a letter to me replying to my asking him his response to the reissue of *Bright Web*, illuminate the singular background of passion and comprehension which Saxton brought to all this published work—history, fiction. They have special pertinence for the creation of *Bright Web*. They are combined here:

> Almost everything I have written as a novelist and subsequently as a historian has focused on racial exploitation and 'white racism' in the United States. Yet when I was a college student during the 1930s majoring in American history at Harvard and the University of Chicago, I learned absolutely nothing about either of these problems. Although I was born

in the same small New England town as W. E. B. DuBois (Great Barrington, Massachusetts), I never heard of him as a child; and although DuBois was, one would suppose, memorable as the first African American to complete a doctorate at Harvard, I never heard of him at Harvard either. What I learned about DuBois, and most of what I learned about racial discrimination in United States history, I learned in the Communist Party. On race, as on the condition of women, the American Communist Party stood fifty years ahead of most of the rest of this country including its government, its organized labor movement and its mainstream churches. Had American Communism done nothing else but to push forward these two issues, that would have been enough to have earned an honorable place in political and intellectual history.

On the origin of *Bright Web* and the problems of writing it:

I hoped to construct perhaps a trilogy of the maritime industry in which I could intertwine the lives of men and women of different race and class backgrounds and divergent political outlooks. *Bright Web* was to have been a step in that direction. Several people from whom I heard accounts on which the novel is based were Communist Party members deeply involved in the shipyard fight against racial discrimination. But—after *The Great Midland*—neither I nor my literary agent thought there was any chance of finding a publisher if I portrayed leading characters as Communists. So I compromised reportorial accuracy: in the interest of telling the story of black shipyard workers (which had never been told), I sacrificed the story of black and white Communists in the shipyard.

In reality—and I mean in *reality*—Reverend Beezely and some of his close associates would have been *in*, or in close contact with, the Communist Party; the white shipfitter who takes Sally to the union meeting would have been an active Communist; Sally would have joined the party. To that extent I falsified history, and to that extent contributed to the monstrosities of the Cold War. I remain bitterly ashamed of the compromise, although when I think it through again as often I have done, I don't know how I could have done it differently. In any case, the novel ten years in process brought home less than a few months at carpenter's wages . . . and in the effort to hit on some mode of expression that might be saleable yet not shameful to me I found myself increasingly distanced from what I really wanted to write . . . and I had given up so much of what I'd first hoped the book might contain that I regarded it as a loss, a cop-out, and a failure.

ᑐ

No, dear Alexander Saxton, no cop-out, no loss, no failure. To no extent did you falsify history and contribute to the monstrosities of the Cold War.

And yes, the problem of self-censorship remains. But who and how many self-censored? Why? Why was there no chance of finding a publisher if you portrayed leading (or any decent) characters as Communists? What had happened in our land of the free and home of the brave?

There was an inescapable reality reason why "self-censorship" became so prevalent—self-censorship, and (no, not from you, by others) self-betrayals, false witnessings, and lessening of creative productivity, sometimes creative integrity as well.

It was the fourteen-year era of "The Great Fear," "The American Inquisition," "The Time of the Toad." The time (loosely termed) of McCarthy and the Un-American Activities committees, national, state, local; —and without the un-American title, of individuals and purge groups (also without troubling with due process of law, the right to examine witnesses, trial by jury, or other protections guaranteed by the Constitution, Bill of Rights, and historic Supreme Court decisions) who took it upon themselves to define who was un-American, seditious, a threat to security and all-we-hold-dear, a spy, apologist or agent for the Soviet Union, that is, a Communist or fellow traveler or guilty by association or belonging or contributing to an organization on the Attorney General's list, or being active in a trade union, recommending the "wrong" books, etc., etc., etc. Therefore, with their family members, to be condemned to firings, joblessness, deportations, blacklisting, shaming, disgrace, ostracism, possible physical attack and prison terms.

It was the time of alien and sedition laws: the McCarran Act, the Subversive Activities Control Act, Taft-Hartley (against unions); the time of informers, paid informers and perjurers mantled now as super patriots, heroes, heroines; the time of loyalty oaths, guilt by association, the infamous World War II Japanese-American internment camps being readied as concentration camps for suspects and their families; a time of expulsions, anti-communism as proof of patriotism, and Fear, Fear, Fear.

The heavy body of the Cold War lay over the land. That singular post-war vision of what the next great step for humanity must be, and those who tried to make that vision a reality, as the truth about those who betrayed it, lay smothered, gagged, choking. Melodramatic words; I cannot write without anger of that time.

Dear fellow writer: yes there was a reality reason why no publisher would publish *Bright Web* if you wrote the truth about blacks and whites, let alone Communists of any human hue organizing, working together to right a wrong. A based fear.

With every reason to do so, you did not compromise. In the

midst of that terrible time (1948) you began to write *Bright Web*, set in a different time of *honorable* national struggle. You clung to the truth that the "real life" Joyces, Beezelys, Sergeants, Sallys, Henrys (as always they have and will) keep existing. Historian that you were even then, you recorded an incident in 1945 when, in the Richmond Kaiser Shipyards, there had once again been evidenced "the human will, capacity, courage to act"; Black workers segregated into an auxiliary of the Boilermakers Union, marching in the heavy rain with their white Brothers and Sisters in solidarity through Oakland streets to union headquarters, to make their protest visible. Because of you, the actualities are there; the working conditions and the nature of the work, the defiance of the union leadership and injunctions; the torment over whether to strike or "seek redress through the medium of the law."—But you created the people, made them unforgettably real and present for us; yes, the Toms and Hendersons;—the Walters too, their yielding to the pressures of their times; the Garnets. You made it possible for us to *live* the process of that workplace struggle, made visible the testing, the changes, the growth; gifted us with comprehension. Again: visibility creates reality.

Instead of contributing to the monstrosities of the Cold War and falsifying history, you remind us of that part of the truth and hope in it seldom given visibility: that "consciously willed human actions reshape human history," that as a species from the beginning we have been resisters, changers, standing upright, leaving the cave, inventing agriculture, clothing, shelter, doing away with ancient slavery, war lords, Pharaohs, the feudal caste system, the divine right of kings; came to the "rights of man"; now in visionary, not-yet-realized documents, to the Universal Declaration of (Universal) Human Rights and the Beijing Declaration ("the rights of women are human rights"). Yet still no end in the world to the class system/sexism/racism—to the denial of these circumstances in which human potentialities can truly blossom.

It is not only my voice that speaks in those last words, it is Constance Coiner's who, with her twelve-year-old daughter Ana, the world lost in the crash of TWA 800 last July. Constance was one of the great enabling, inspiring teachers (as is Alexander Saxton, her teacher and dissertation advisor in her UCLA days)—bringers to all who come within their range perspicacity, hope, strength, joy, courage, defiance.

She was to have written this afterword. Inadequate as it is, it is dedicated as am I to the beauty and memory of her.

And honor to you, Alexander Saxton, true patriotic American, for this book and for your others; for your vision, steadfastness, integrity, beauty, and the contribution which your life and work have made.

Tillie Olsen
San Francisco
July, 1997

Alexander Saxton served as a merchant seaman during the
Second World War and worked as a construction carpenter in
the San Francisco area during the 1950s. He has published
three novels: *Grand Crossing* (1943), *The Great Midland* (1948,
1997), and *Bright Web in the Darkness* (1959, 1997). After com-
pleting a doctorate at the University of California, Berkeley in
1967, he taught United States history at UCLA until his retire-
ment in 1990. Among his writings in history are *The Indispensable Enemy: Labor and the Anti-Chinese Movement in California*
(University of California Press, 1971, 1995) and *The Rise and
Fall of the White Republic: Class Politics and Mass Culture in Nineteenth Century America* (1990). His wife, a social worker, also
taught at UCLA. They now live near Santa Rosa.

California Fiction titles are selected for their literary merit and for their illumination of California history and culture.